The Lover

A Sufi Mystery

Laury Silvers

Published by Laury Silvers, Kindle Direct Publishing,
Copyright © Laury Silvers, 2019 All Rights Reserved

Cover calligraphy and art by Abdulhussein Alrekabi,
copyright © Laury Silvers, 2019 All Rights Reserved

This is a work of fiction based on historical places, circumstances, and, in some cases, historical persons as read through primary sources of the period and secondary scholarship concerning it. All historical places, persons, and interpretations are ultimately the product of the author's imagination.
Limited selected quotes adapted from secondary and primary sources fall under "Fair Use." Alexander Knysh kindly gave his permission for the use of quotations adapted from his translation of al-Qushayri's *Epistle on Sufism*.

ISBN 978-1-9991228-4-3 (paperback)
ISBN 978-1-9991228-3-6 (electronic book)

For Michael, my champion

and

In memory of the women,
some named, but mostly unnamed,
some remembered, but mostly forgotten,
who lived their love of God, despite everything.

Acknowledgements

I did not write this book alone. Sure, it was me who sat with the computer in my lap tapping away. But it was my partner, Michael Quinsey, who listened to me everyday when he got home from work as I told him about what trouble Zaytuna had got herself into now. It was he who read every single word, correcting and engaging me, but, most importantly, pressing me to grasp where I had not quite got down what was in my head, including, athlete that he is, helping me to describe all the physical action in the book. He walked through every moment of this process with me. He is a true companion.

The following scholars have my admiration and appreciation for giving me their valuable time and expertise: Michael Mumisa, most of all, answered all my questions along the way, guiding my research, especially concerning Muslims of African descent and daily life in Baghdad at the time and read the book in a nearly completed draft for historical accuracy. He is a true mentor. I could not have written this book without him. Amina Wadud read chapters concerning Zaytuna and Tein's mother and gave me crucial feedback. Alan Godlas answered queries at the drop of a hat about early Sufism when I was unsure of myself. Scott Lucas read a draft to check my representation of hadith scholars and scholarship and gave me helpful story feedback. Mathieu Tillier helped me sort out how my characters in this book and the next would navigate the by-ways of the complicated judicial system in Abbasid Baghdad. Sherwan Hindreen Ali, a native of Baghdad himself, corrected me on Baghdadi linguistic and cultural cues as well as offered detailed comments on characterization that led to several important changes. Aun Hasan Ali, who named Ammar, shared his unpublished scholarship with me on Shi'ism in Baghdad at the time and kept me from making several uninformed narrative choices. Peter Gray found critical documentary evidence for me on Islamic legal debates as well as guided me on book design. Kristian Petersen helped me create YingYue, the Chinese Muslim spiritual prodigy and answered every question I threw his way about Chinese Sufism. Thank you to the Department for the Study of Religion at the University of Toronto for providing me with a research fellowship allowing me to do the research that brought this story to life.

To my dear friends and family, Kathleen Self sat with me at the beginning to help me sort out who had died and why, thinking through the major characters and basic story arc. Noor Naga read a very early, very rough half-draft, offered me needed insights, and most importantly, encouraged me to keep going when I was not sure whether or not I could write fiction. Joud Alkorani talked over characters with me one day, exploring with me the spiritual crises they would face. Greg Recco gave so much of his time to the book, ultimately sending me nine single-spaced pages of notes. Mishi Prokop, Nancey Silvers, and Susan Peters all guided me to find literary gaps that I couldn't for the life of me find myself. Nasrin Mahdavieh helped me create Yulduz, Zaytuna's Turkmen neighbour and provided me with her song. Nasrin and Sarah Shah gave me detailed resources on Shia prayer and shared how they, as Shia, would respond to Ammar's circumstances. Ahsan Moghul kindly shared many sources and bits of fascinating historical data with me. Saad Wadi and Hamed Murad helped with Baghdadi slang. Katrina Daly Thompson and Sara Abdel-Latif helped me find the Old Nubian word for "my babies." Nakia Jackson, Almas Zakiuddin, and Shaheen Ali provided careful editing under critical time constraints. I cannot thank you all enough.

And thank you to all those unnamed who read bits and pieces for input, those who piped up when I asked questions via social media, and those who pointed out errors on my website. Anyone I've forgotten to mention, I ask you to forgive me for the lapse.

I also want to acknowledge the scholars whose works played a major role in the writing of this book: Judith Ahola, whose dissertation, *The Community of Scholars*, on *Tarikh Baghdad* got this book started; Mohammad Mansir Ahsan for his *Social Life under the Abbasids*; the editors and authors of *Continuity and Crisis at the Abbasid Court*, especially Judith Ahola and Letizia Osti for their work on the topography of Baghdad and Hugh Kennedy's work on caliphal administration and the police; Mathieu Tillier's social histories on judicial systems; Herbert Mason's translation of Massignon's *The Passion of al-Hallaj*; Alexander Knysh's translation of al-Qushayri's *Epistle on Sufism*; and most of all, Abu Uthman Amr b. Bahr al-Kinani, otherwise known as, al-Jahiz, for his delightful and detailed commentary on the life and times of Abbasid Iraq.

Any errors in this book are mine.

My love to my family, Michael, Kaya and Ryan, Mishi and Ben, Eleonore, Evelyn, Tracey, Nancey, Catherine, and Candace and all the Quinseys for their unwavering support in the writing of this book. My thanks to my neighbours Bev, JoAnn, Claire, Cathal and the kids for cheering me on, and Billie Girl for long walks that cleared my head. My sincerest gratitude goes to my teacher, Murat Coskun, for his guidance, and our community for their constant support and companionship. Finally, this book could not have been written without my mother, Evelyn Silvers, who pored over every little bit of this book, sending me corrections and questions, but most of all, as always, giving me strength through her belief in my ability to do anything.

On History and Fiction

While the background, some storylines, and even some of the dialogue are adapted from historical and literary accounts of Abbasid Baghdad and its inhabitants, this is a work of fiction. The book takes up some of the uncomfortable realities of life at that time. Social norms such as slavery, racism, shadism, gender divisions, marriage, drinking habits, mosque attendance, and class divisions are all grounded in historical sources. Interested readers may want to read al-Jahiz's delightful satire *The Book of Misers*, which accurately depicts the social life and material details of the Abbasid period.

If your interest in reading my novels is to understand Iraq and the experience of the Iraqi people, please close this book and turn to the work of Iraqi writers such as those found in Hassan Blasim's *Iraq + 100* collections, Shakir Mustafa's anthology, or *Baghdad Noir* collections of short stories, and the works of Shahad Al Rawi, Sinan Antoon, Dunya Mikhail, Leilah Nadir, and Ahmed Saadawi. Also see the online journal, "Arab Lit Quarterly." My novels do not assume to speak for or about the Iraqi people nor the nation of Iraq, they are an exploration of an Abbasid past and, ultimately, the way that past is remembered in the Muslim present.

If you want to know more about the characters, how I drew my narrative from history, and what's history and what's not, I have posted historical resources, a teaching guide, and book club questions on my website: www.llsilvers.com. Follow me on twitter @waraqamusa.

The Ninety-Nine Names of God

Allah
The Lover
The Merciful The Compassionate
The Holy The Peace The Guardian of Faith The Protector
The Firm The Compeller The Dominating The Creator The Crusher
The Praiseworthy The Forgiver The Evolver The Bestower The Provider
The Dishonouring The Knower The Constrictor The Expander The Abaser
The King The Forbearing The Exalter The Honouring The Hearing The Seeing
The Everlasting Refuge The Opener The Subtle The Aware The Great The One
The Trustee The Grateful The Most High The Most Great The Preserver The Wise
The Restorer The Embracing The Glorious The Resurrector The LightThe Responsive
The Patient The Nourisher The One Who Forms The Revered The Generous The Watchful
The Strong The Mighty The Friend The Reckoner The Accounter The Originator The Able
The Unique The Life Giver The Slayer The Alive The Equitable The Finder The Noble
The Avenger The Powerful The Expediter The Delayer The Most Exalted The First
The Last The Outward The Inward The Governor The Accepter The Pardoner
The Clement The Gatherer The Distresser The Possessor of the Sovereignty
The Lord of Majesty and Bounty The Self-Subsisting The Sufficient
The Enricher The Witholder The Incomparable The Everlasting
The Open-Handed The Right Guide The Supreme Inheritor
The Wise The Good The Truth The Judge The Just
The Witness The All Forgiving

Baghdad, 295 Hijri (907 CE)

The First Day

Chapter One

The little one tucked in through Zaytuna's open door, standing breathlessly with her back against the wall, eyes moving with worry that someone saw her come in. Zaytuna looked up, then went back to the task of sorting the grit from her lentils, saying, "Sweet one, close the curtain behind you, come sit here, and help me with this."

The girl stayed flat against the wall, her eyes still worried, but her breathing began to slow. Zaytuna leaned over slightly on the handwoven fishskin mat where she was seated to get a hold of the red earthenware jug that was cooling water by the far wall. She took the cup placed over the top of the jug and filled it. Zaytuna held the cup out to her, "Have a sip. You can't come for a visit and not have a sip to drink. Show some manners, come now."

At this, the girl recovered herself well enough to sit down beside her. She took a long drink followed by a deep breath, and as she settled in she moved a bit nearer to Zaytuna, as if to find her way into Zaytuna's lap, but knowing, even in her state, that would not do with this woman. She gave the cup back to Zaytuna instead.

Zaytuna took the cup from her and held her face with a matter of fact look, asking, "Would you like some more? The water is sweet, isn't it? I collected the clay to make the jug myself. It's from the dried-up canal bed by the tomb of Maruf al-Karkhi, may God preserve his sanctity. My cousin, Mustafa, is a hadith scholar and a potter. He shaped and fired the clay himself. He's pure of heart. This jug, this cup, is free of any human ugliness. The water from this jug mixes with that clay and gives God's ease with every sip. It unravels every tangled knot." She poured the girl another cup, "Now, tell me what knot needs unraveling."

"Zayd is dead."

Zaytuna's face fell. She put the cup down on the mat, letting out a breath and a prayer, "We belong to God and we return to Him."

Zaytuna held back for a moment, then leaned in toward the little one, placing her long, thin arm around her, but not touching her, to let her know she could come closer if she needed to. The girl bent over, falling into comfort somehow in Zaytuna's bony lap and began to cry. They were child's tears, full and free, her body shuddering and releasing her sorrow. Why is this girl here? Did she have no one else to weep with over the loss of this boy?

Zaytuna put her hand lightly on the girl's back and wished she could remember her name. More than that, she wished she could remember which of the servant children who scramble around her alley every day was called Zayd.

She kept one hand on the back of the girl, her other hand finding its way to the lentils laid out for sorting on the faded red muslin scarf folded over into a large square before her. She looked at her hand. Long-fingered like her mother's, but not beautiful like hers. They were old, cracked and calloused hands on a young woman's body. She'd dried herself up with fasting and barely eating, long nights standing in prayer, and days washing other people's laundry. She pressed her index finger down onto one lentil lying with the others in grit and bits of dried grasses and pushed it slowly towards the pile of those she had sorted clean.

Zaytuna stopped midway and picked it up, eyeing it, and silently gave it her heart's sincere counsel. Look at you thinking you are being brought out of hardship and into ease. Not so, little one. You can't run from being crushed by this world. You'll rest in my bowl for a while, then you'll be boiled in the heat of the pot. After that, you'll be pounded by my teeth. Then you'll be destroyed in my stomach. It's life, little one. None of us escapes getting to know each of God's names, and intimately so. It's the truth. God may be The Lover, but He is also The Crusher. So do not complain. But you'll end up feeding me. God is The Life Giver and The Nourisher, too. Take some solace in that.

She placed the lentil carefully back onto the cloth with the rest. Then sorted the last of them, scooping them with her free hand into a red clay bowl. The girl seemed to be calming now. Her body spent. Zaytuna took her hand from the girl's back and folded the red cloth over so the grit would not fall out. She covered the bowl with a rag and tied it in place below the rim so mice and insects would not get into it. Then stretched her arm up to place the bowl of cleaned lentils on a shelf above her jug and cup.

The girl finally pulled herself up and wiped her eyes, blowing her nose on a length of the torn wrap she used to cover her head and body. Zaytuna sighed at this, thinking, Who is she dressing up to be with that ratty piece of shawl wound around herself so? Lord, all that thing does is get in the way of her work. Just wrap it under your arms and then throw the long end over your head in the street like the rest of us. Now look at it, soaked with your tears and smeared with your snot.

Zaytuna carefully took up the rough cloth on which she'd been sorting the lentils so the grit wouldn't fall out of it and stood, "Come with me down to the canal, if you've got the time. *Insha'Allah*, God willing, we can rinse out that wrap of yours."

She stepped outside into the courtyard and shook out the bits of grit from the cloth, letting the wide strip unfold completely to fall to its full length. As she came back in, she laid the cloth over the top of her own head, making sure it covered her pitch-black hair, then pulled its ends around from the front to back, tying it under and around, cupping her long, thick braid, with its one matted strand threading three round stone beads, into a cloth covered bun at the nape of her neck.

She bent down and lightly touched the girl on the shoulder, holding her hand out for the girl's wrap. The girl was unwilling to give it to Zaytuna at first, but Zaytuna kept her hand outstretched. So the girl did as she was told, pulling it off her shoulders and head. Zaytuna could see it had been fine once. The green muslin had been block printed in a design of repeating vines and roses with red and yellow thread woven through it and even had a band of densely embroidered linen sewn onto its edge, but it was now deeply stained and worn through. She could see how dear it was to her all the same.

Despite Zaytuna's prompting to come with her, the girl refused to get up, "They'll see me."

Zaytuna wanted to tell her that no one gives a whit about the modesty of a girl like her. Only wealthy girls were wrapped up and stored away like little treasures, protected in the streets from ugly words and casual attacks. How she covered her head, the length of her *qamis*, or even whether or not she even had *sirwal* to wear underneath it, would always be limited to what she could pay for and what was practical, not propriety.

She asked herself again, Why is this girl here?

She could listen, give the girl an ear to unravel her woes. But there's nothing she could do for her beyond that. Nothing she could do for anyone. The way the girl cried, she hadn't settled into the nature of this world yet. She'd expect a girl of ten, give or take, a girl like this, would be used to hardship already. Be done with sorrowful weeping. God knows she came to know it at a much younger age. Better this little one toughen herself up to not expect more from her life. But it wasn't for her to say. So she did not say out loud to the girl, Everyone dies. Everything will be taken from you, little one.

Then Zaytuna understood what the girl had meant by "They'll see me." Zaytuna said to herself, scolding, How slow you are, foolish woman, this isn't about someone seeing her hair, her face, the shape of her body through her *qamis*. That girl is afraid *someone* saw her come in, will see her on the street.

Zaytuna asked her, "Who are you worried will see you?"

"Imam Ibrahim."

"Ibrahim *as-Silafi?*"

"Yes, him."

"Ah." This little one was one of Imam Ibrahim's household servants. Salman, that fat grandson of a traitor, was always boasting that one of Imam Ibrahim's boys came to him to learn about the Prophet rather than from the "illustrious" hadith scholar himself. Then she recalled the boy, remembering this odd, wrapped-up girl running in and out of the neighbourhood with a loud little boy. That must be Zayd. He was a regular in the main alleyway outside the cluster of homes where she lived, and where he would sit and listen to Salman's stories.

She remembered the boy plainly now. Sorrow came and pulled her spirit down, dropping it into her gut, making her want to sit. But she stood. He was one of those ugly children made beautiful by their charm. He was nothing but trouble, always mugging, turning things upside down to make people laugh. She had remarked to Saliha about him once, "There's a survivor." And now he's dead. She asked herself, Zaytuna, woman, why didn't you ever ask his name?

She looked down at this little girl who seemed to know her well, well enough to come to her with a problem this heavy, and yet she never bothered to ask the girl her name either.

She said, "Sweet one, Imam Ibrahim is not in this alleyway. He doesn't come here."

She turned around and bent over to open a wooden box sitting next to long drum nestled in the corner and pulled out her spare wrap and handed it to the girl, "Here, get up, use this."

The girl rose and wound the wrap around her like one of the rich girls, loosely covering her whole body and head, trying to hide her face with one edge. She was only short a *niqab* to complete the costume. Zaytuna thought the little girl looked ridiculous. But at least she was willing to head out dressed this way, warily following Zaytuna out into the courtyard through the twisting, narrow passageway that led around and past the houses that fronted the alley.

Without speaking, they walked past the one-story houses not far from the Shuniziyya cemetery in Tutha. They were made of sun-dried yellow mud blocks with roofs of thick reeds packed with mud and dried to fill the gaps. Some were even dug down into the cool earth a bit, but none offered more than one room for each family on a small central courtyard, like hers, or sometimes not even that. Mainly, they were just rooms built onto rooms like a sprawling house of cards, with narrow passageways turning corner upon corner leading in between the houses from only slightly wider main alleyways. Everyone living up against each other. Everyone in each other's business. But better here than inside the walls of the cemetery itself where the poorer of the poor did the best they could against the elements, even if it meant burrowing a den into its thick walls to sleep.

Zaytuna knew this girl came from someplace like this. She spoke like a Baghdadi street urchin, with a mix of sounds culled from the immigrants who kept pouring into the city from every corner of the caliphate. Muslims, Jews, Christians, Arabs, Persians, Abyssinians, Nubians, and Zanjis, Turkic peoples, even from as far east as China and south as Sind. Most free, some enslaved. Despite an inquisition, the civil wars, the sieges, the floods, and even the caliph moving the capital to Samarra, people kept coming. Labourers, artisans, scribes, hopeful young religious scholars. They thought the opportunities were here. Plenty had made good, it's true. Some made their wealth here. Others lived well enough and the enslaved lived as well as their masters permitted. But as sure as God is the Withholder, not just the Open-Handed, many never found a way and ended up sleeping rough, picking through road sweepings, begging, or cutting reeds and collecting dung to sell for fuel, if they were lucky.

Here in Baghdad, this girl's parents probably found themselves in worse poverty than wherever they came from. And here is where they likely indentured their daughter to work so she'd at least eat and have a safe place to sleep. If she were lucky. More likely she'd be beaten by the women and ready to hand for the boys and men of the household. Zaytuna looked down at the girl, hand in hers, orphaned whether her parents are dead or alive and wondered if she had anyone to love her.

The street narrowed quickly into a pathway where they could no longer walk side by side and the girl fell behind her and grabbed onto a bit of Zaytuna's long *qamis*, tugging at it as they walked the last few steps to the small, busy square. The square led out onto four small streets, like Zaytuna's, and one, directly ahead of them, leading down to the canal. Small stalls were set up in front of one or two room homes open to the square, this one selling stews and bread to take home, that one dry goods, another tinder and fuel for cooking, dung cakes, reeds, thorn bush, and dried bones stacked in neat piles. While some people rushed through the square getting to where they were going, others lingered at the stalls, haggling, chatting with friends. A couple of men sat on stools outside one stall, a tavern barely masquerading as a shop selling fruited drinks and mild cider, one of them openly drunk. Beggars lined the footpath on the far side, winding down towards the banks of the Isa canal past the lean-tos and shanty shacks. People kept building there even though floods had washed them away before. Zaytuna hated that they returned to build in the same place time and time again, but where else did they have? The little girl reached up to take her hand again and they began to weave their way through the square, heading toward the canal.

Zaytuna heard deep laughter coming across the square and felt the girl flinch at the sound of it. It was Salman, but Zaytuna didn't want to give him the satisfaction of noticing and having to greet him. Then she heard him call out, "*Assalamu alaykum*, Zaytuna! Ya Layla, sweet one! Where is your friend Zayd? He missed his lesson yesterday!"

The girl nearly jumped hearing him calling her name and pulled at Zaytuna's hand to hurry. Zaytuna looked down at her pleading face. So, her name was Layla. She said to her, "Don't worry, I don't like him, either."

Zaytuna looked over at him now. Salman, like always, was sitting on his stool in front of his drinks stall with one of his cronies. He was smiling at them, smiling like always. She thought, What are you smiling about? One of your boys is dead and I'm not going to be the one who tells you.

Without stopping, she kept walking with Layla down to the canal to gently wash her shawl and let her unravel her tale.

Chapter Two

Ammar told the night watchman to stand behind him as he waited outside the gate to Imam Ibrahim's home. A young man opened the small door inset into the large arched double gate only partway. He looked at Ammar without expression and asked without a hint of propriety, "Police?" Ammar nodded. The young man stepped back to hold the door open completely, saying, "The boy, Zayd, is in the inner courtyard."

Ammar took in the young man who opened the gated door. The cursed instincts that got him forcibly transferred into the Baghdad police from the Infantry were awake and informing him on everything he saw. The young man was obviously not a servant. Ammar pegged him as one of Imam Ibrahim's students, likely nineteen or twenty years old. A very wealthy student at that, going by his attire. What's that, *washa* silk he's wearing? Imam Ibrahim did not have that kind of coin, although he'd been told, the scholar was aspiring to it. The young man's casual display of wealth, his alabaster skin and nearly blond, red curls tumbling out from underneath his snow-white turban, suggested that this boy's mother was or had been a high-priced slave. He thought, she was probably enslaved by the Muslims right out of Byzantine slavery—maybe to a governor, had to be someone who could afford her— taken by them first from somewhere much farther West. No doubt skilled in poetry and music, too. She would be as good as a wife to her master with her child born a free Muslim. Now look at this rich, free boy. No doubt thinks himself quite the thing. Ammar wouldn't call him a man; all that flash only made him look like a mother's son. And those long curls. The scholars liked to have a close-cropped head; he wondered what they made of him. At least Imam Ibrahim made him answer the door, as he should.

The student ushered Ammar through the gate opening set to one side of the property. There was a narrow garden fronting the house with fruit trees set out in a line. An apricot tree was heavy with ripe fruit on his right, near to the gate door, and two apples and pomegranate were just filling out on the other side. He saw a wide passageway just around the corner of the house beyond the apple trees where the second floor was built over to a shared wall with the neighbours. He could make out a narrow well at the opening of the passageway. No water carriers needed here to fill a house cistern. The kitchen door is likely back there too. The young man walked ahead of him and opened the door to the house itself. A wide, low couch was set out by it. Maybe the Imam held classes outside in cooler weather. It had the morning shade now, but not for long. He stepped down two steps into the dim light and cool of the house, grateful to be out of the morning heat.

Ammar had deliberately left the local night watchman standing in the street. The watchman had reported that a boy as big as a man had run up to him as he was patrolling that night to say that one of the servants of his household had died in an accident. The boy was crying such that the watchman could barely make out what he was saying. Ammar was given the case when he arrived for work first thing. He had to go searching for the watchman, and found him snoring in an alcove while waiting for him. Ammar gave the man a kick and he pulled himself up heavily to take Ammar back to the house. The child's dead body would have to have been there for at least part of the night and now the sun was rising rapidly. This would have to be done quickly before the body started to stink. He would have felt bad for the watchman, as tired as he was, but the man still found energy to stand at the gate posturing, tossing his stave between his hands. He looked as belligerent as any hung-over mean drinker of wine.

Despite his irritation with the watchman's bluster, even in his exhaustion, Ammar understood this type. He had to admit he was one. He'd prefer to let his sword do all the talking like the old days. And, no doubt about it, his sword had turned out to be a fine communicator in many of the cases he'd had to solve so far. Mainly he dealt with street crime that ended in fatal stabbings and beatings. But these jobs dealing with the rich were about close observations, talk, and, most importantly, social negotiation.

Observe he could do. It was his observations about a murder in his garrison that had got him transferred against his will from the Frontier

Infantry to The Grave Crimes Section with the Baghdadi Police for a fraction of the pay. He wished he'd kept his mouth shut.

Talk he could also do. For a short and wiry man with a bull of a face, he could charm even a careful woman into a compromising flirtation.

Social negotiations with the wealthy were harder. He hated them all with their open greed or worse, dressed up greed as piety, whether they be Sunni scholars like this one or—and his mother would slap him hard across the face to hear him say it—Shia administrators and viziers sucking at the tit of the caliphate. He hadn't fought against the Byzantines on the Frontier for the Caliph al-Muktafi or any of the other pretenders to the throne; he fought for Islam. He fought for the Prophet, his blessed family, and the Shia Imams, the rightful inheritors of the Prophetic line. To him, they were the true rulers of the people.

He'd objected to being told he could not wear his cuirass on these jobs. His sergeant had explained to him that when the police showed up in battlewear at the estates of the wealthy, it only meant one thing: they had displeased the Caliph and they were going to rot in the dungeons. All the more reason to wear it, he thought, but did not say. Objecting instead, "It's just a leather cuirass, not chain mail."

His sergeant, tired of him already, replied, "Just the black turban. No armour."

There was no mention of his sword, thank God. It fought for him as if it were a part of his own body. He felt the hilt in his hand, straightened its strap crossing his chest, and readied himself to deal with the likes of Imam Ibrahim.

The Mother's Son left him in the reception hall and went through a wide doorway into a room to Ammar's right. Ammar couldn't see into the room from where he was standing, but he could see straight through to the courtyard from there. The watchman told him the dead boy was out there, but he could not yet see the boy from where he stood. He could hear that fop of a student say, "Excuse me, Imam, The police are here and would like to speak to you." He could hear Imam Ibrahim reply, but not the words despite the quiet of the house.

Ammar examined the high ceiling and the stuccoed niche with its carved designs. Stylized vines and flowers were interlaced, framing the words, *There Is No God But God and Muhammad is God's Messenger*. He saw it was delicate work, expensive and understandably confined to just a niche in the wall. It was a tasteful choice. He could have paid less to have pre-moulded and carved blocks of calligraphy inset into the wall surrounding the room, but it would have looked exactly like what he paid for it. This hadith scholar with only a few paying students and a middling patron at court was indeed hoping to move up.

How ironic that the Imam spent his life devoted to the study of accounts of what Muhammad had said or done since Muhammad and his blessed family had lived and ruled from a state of extreme poverty. Ammar's sergeant had told him no Hanbali mosque would allow Imam Ibrahim a pillar to teach from because of the way he sucked up at court. He could only imagine that this man's beloved Ahmed ibn Hanbal, would not be pleased knowing how he and his like clambered for caliphal influence and money after he and so many others had been persecuted by them during the inquisition some sixty years earlier. No wonder Imam Ibrahim chose to live around the caliphal taxmen and secretaries rather than one of the neighbourhoods known for its hadith scholars.

White Turban returned and led Ammar through the main reception hall out into the central courtyard. Ammar held his hand up to cover his eyes as he stepped out of the dark hall into the morning light hitting the courtyard and saw the small body lying face down on the far side, uncovered. He felt the boy lying there like a punch in the gut. Dead bodies were daily business for him now, and he'd buried his unfortunate share on the battlefield. But he'd never gotten used to the bodies of women and children. Not then, when the Byzantine troops would slaughter the families of soldiers in the camp towns or in the villages on the borderlands, and not now, policing in Baghdad. Every body of theirs was a tragedy to him. He felt a hollow loneliness that no one would ever know these unimaginable losses but the ones who were closest to the dead and those who leant their mourning to the families' grief.

All he could think was how few feel for a loss of life that does not touch their own. These kinds of thoughts always wove their way through him to the spectre of Karbala. His love for the Prophet's family, and the bitterness he felt over the theft of their lives and noble rule in those years of civil war after Muhammad's death, overtook him in these moments. Although the sun was not yet on this boy and the dirt in the courtyard was packed as hard as rock, to him it was as if that day at Karbala were before him and this boy were Qasim, the son of Hasan, slaughtered and trampled by horses. He felt the thick of that day's blistering heat bearing down on the gentle child and imagined the dry plain's dust rising around the boy's body like a halo radiating the expansive tragedy of his lost life. Ammar tried to pull himself back in from the panoramic scope of the massacre of the Prophet's own family at the hands of other Muslims, greedy for power, religious and political, as if he were dragging a wailing woman from the body, so he could attend to the boy sensibly. He wanted to fall to his knees in grief, but he remained standing, his face impassive, breathing, saying inwardly, Boy, may you meet Husayn, son of Ali, and Qasim, son of Hasan, and may you take your place near them in the next world.

He forced himself to look around the area where the boy's body lay, to note everything around him. Keeping to the details calmed him. From here it seemed like they hadn't touched anything. He observed his surroundings. There were two stories, but the courtyard was not large enough to allow for the second floor to be cantilevered over it. Low couches were laid out along the walls and small tables set here and there. They'd have shade along one wall or another except midday here. But it'd still get cursedly hot. At least the courtyard was pounded earth, not brick radiating heat. At the centre of the courtyard, there was an ornamental basin of water that a servant would have to fill from the hand pumped well. The basin was surrounded by pots filled with vining and flowering plants with delicate red and white blossoms, and a twisting jasmine, rooted into the earth floor of the courtyard itself, vining up an arbor made of reeds bending under its weight. There was a wide door in fine wood, carved with flowers and painted light blue, and two large shuttered windows on the east wall, nearest to the body. On the north side of the courtyard, he could see a small window cut out of the thick wall and a narrow door carved and painted like the grander door on the far wall, leading to what must be the kitchen and servants quarters. Yes, the Imam paid dearly for this house. He wondered how far the man was in debt.

As he walked further into the courtyard, he glanced into the room where the Imam led his classes. No one was there. He looked behind him to see if the Imam had come into the courtyard to meet him. Not yet. The room had a wide arched doorway opening onto the courtyard. The floor of the study was covered by layers of rugs with sheepskins placed before three low desks. Nothing was on the desks, but the closed inkwells and the reed pens sat waiting for the Imam to read out the hadith, and for them to copy what they had heard, then read back what they had written to double check it. A few more steps and from there, he could see the Imam's place on a low pallet, not too far off the floor but high enough to know who was who in the room. There were layers of sheepskins for him to sit on and what seemed to be a large volume sat on his desk covered with cloth. On the far side of the pallet there was an area screened off from view.

From here, inside the courtyard, he could hear whimpering upstairs. It sounded like a young girl. He was told Imam Ibrahim had a daughter and now he could hear a woman's voice comforting her. No women wailing. But why would they for a servant? No doubt this fine Sunni scholar would not permit it even if there were a woman here who wanted to wail for the boy, even just to honour his life and his passing. The woman comforting the girl could not be her mother; he was told she had died some years back, maybe five, six years ago. He imagined that the Imam had not permitted the neighbourhood women or even the women from his family to wail for his wife either. Women did it anyway, no matter what these Sunni scholars said. But in the Imam's own house? There would be none of that, he figured, not even his daughter for her mother. Where was the comfort in that? He wondered who it was with the girl now.

He turned to the body of the boy and saw that the morning sun was slanting quickly into the courtyard. The light would hit the boy's body soon. With the thought of the sun on the boy, the spectre of the bodies of the

Prophet's family burning in the hot sun on the plain of Karbala came up at him again.

"God guide me to the truth," he muttered under his breath, pushing the thought back.

They'd need to get him out of here, have the ritual washing of the body this morning, and buried by this afternoon in this heat. No one was wasting ice holding a servant boy over another day. This needed to be sorted out quickly.

He looked up. The two stories were not that far to fall. It was a blessing the boy died instead of being left with a broken leg that disabled him and turned him into a beggar or killed him later from rot.

He didn't wait for Imam Ibrahim's permission to examine the body. He didn't need it. He smelled the stench of the feces released after death.

"*Bismillah*, in the name of God the Merciful, the Compassionate," he said and crouched facing the boy's upper body. Then he said quietly, directing himself to the boy's soul, waiting within the boy's body for burial to be released to the angel of death, "I am going to take a good look at you now. I need to see what's happened to you. But I'll be gentle. There is no need to be afraid. You'll be in the arms of God before long. My sweet boy, say to yourself now, *There is no god but God and Muhammad is his Messenger.*" And he completed the *shahada*, as the Shia do, to himself, *And Ali is his Guardian.*

Zayd's head was turned to his left, his narrow face was slack, his eyes still open. No one had touched the body. Not even to shut his eyes. Good. His mouth drooped against the cool earth. His large nose was broken, hard enough of a hit that it had turned almost directly to the right of his face. He touched it gently. It felt firm. So that was an old break. He wondered who delivered that blow and when. Who refused to allow it to be set properly leaving this boy living with such an ugly face. It wasn't the sort of thing that would make begging easy. The men and women who ran the beggar children went in for broken and amputated limbs. He lifted the boy's small head and felt the looseness of his neck. It must have been broken by the fall. He looked at his face as best he could from that angle. There was a deep abrasion at the top left of his forehead, in his hairline, where his head had hit the ground, snapping his neck.

His arms were splayed at odd angles. Ammar's heart held still, imagining the boy falling, like Qasim from his horse, and him, like Abbas, finding the boy-warrior trampled by the enemies' horses, broken into pieces. He pulled himself back to a professional distance, saying to himself, The breaks are consistent with a fall forward off the roof. He tugged back the loose sleeves and examined his arms. There were no bruises on the boy's arms from anyone who might have been grabbing at him or holding him firmly. But would a bruise form so quickly? Did bruises form after death? He'd have to follow up with a doctor at the hospital about that. He should know for the future. There were some yellowed bruises here and there, healing, but probably from his work around the house or roughhousing with other boys.

His limbs weren't stiff, but that didn't mean anything in a child. In war, he'd dragged the bodies of his fellow soldiers off the battlefield where they'd died not too many hours earlier. He knew first-hand how bodies stiffened after a few hours, then loosened again. But he'd had to handle the bodies of children too, when they had been killed bringing water out to the soldiers on the field or when the Byzantines had beaten their troops back and moved in to slaughter the families of the soldiers in the forts and encampments. Those children's bodies stayed soft. He observed that children's bodies bruised like women, but they didn't stiffen as the women's did. So he couldn't tell from the body when the boy might have died, but there was no reason to doubt the account given to the watchman just yet.

Ammar turned and examined the rest of the boy's body. His long *qamis* was a man's, too large for him and hemmed up for his use; still, it would have hung low around his ankles without a waist sash. He didn't have the sash on, but he wouldn't have worn it to sleep. He could have easily tripped on the long end of the *qamis* and fallen. Would he have worn his *qamis* to sleep? More likely just his *sirwal*. Both were made of fine cloth, tightly woven and white once. They were clean but stained, mended here and there. The banded cuffs of his loose pants were dirtied and frayed from dragging on the ground. He could have tripped on those as well. They were likely the Imam's old clothes. He lifted the *qamis* to look at his back. Nothing there, either. No sign of being roughly pushed; but again, could a bruise develop after death? He was angry with himself for not knowing. He pulled up the loose cuff of the boy's *sirwal*, far too wide for his size, and saw that there was nothing there either.

He moved into a position to turn the boy over, his limbs heavy with death but still light. He had to be about nine or ten years old but like many poor children, he was small from malnutrition. He could see some fat on the boy now, though. They took good care of him here. He thought of whoever was comforting Imam Ibrahim's daughter and wondered if she was taking care of them all. He didn't turn him all the way over. There was a damp patch underneath him where urine let go after he died and had soaked into the clay. He took a look at Zayd's chest as best he could, then set him back down and lifted his legs, one at a time. Again, nothing that shouldn't be there from the fall or the wide bruising he'd seen in all the dead bodies who'd lain in one place for a long time. If he were standing near enough to the edge, looking over, someone could have pushed him easily. Or he could have tripped over his long *sirwal* or *qamis* as he approached it. He looked up and saw that he'd landed right where he should if he'd been pushed or if he had slipped. He'd seen enough.

Chapter Three

Ammar heard a sound and turned away from the boy and saw Imam Ibrahim seating himself on one of the low couches set around the walls of the courtyard. He was waiting for Ammar to finish, but Ammar thought that he was also waiting for him to cross over in deference. Ammar saw that nothing to drink or eat had been set out, not even water. Even the poorest households put out a cup of water and whatever they had. He would take one date or a husk of barley bread served with vinegar and salt, eat it slowly, as propriety required, but as little as possible to not deprive the poor of what might very well have been their next meal. The Imam's insult cut him, but he made note of the gesture. This scholar was ready for the palace politics that would come with moving up in his world.

He reminded himself that he knew how to play these social games too. He was careful to correct his speech on this job, not betraying himself as having grown up poor, or as a Shia unless provoking a Sunni suspect or cultivating intimacy with a fellow Shia would be useful in getting what he needed. He'd learned the need for dissimulation quick enough after he'd run off to fight at the Frontier. A boy filled with piss and vinegar, always getting in trouble with the police, looking for a way out of poverty. He talked and prayed like whomever he ran into on the road to Tarsus. It made getting fed and finding a safe place to sleep along the road easier. It was different once he was on the field of battle. There's no lying to a brother whose life depends on you and your life on him. There's no trust in this world like it.

He crossed to Imam Ibrahim, his booming voice carrying across the courtyard, "*Assalamu alaykum*. May God have mercy on your family during this difficult time and accept the soul of the boy with forgiveness. I am Ammar at-Tabbani, Investigator for Grave Crimes with the Baghdad Police."

Imam Ibrahim did not stand to meet him, but returned his greetings from the comfort of his couch, his voluminous robes pooling around him. "*Wa *alaykum assalam*, I'm sorry you've had to come to our home under such circumstances. The poor boy. May God forgive him and have mercy on him. Please sit."

Ammar sat sideways, facing the Imam, so he would not have to remove his scabbard. He felt his sword curving beside his leg, the hilt ready for him. He hoped the Imam could feel its presence as well. No one could mistake it for ceremonial or mere uniform.

Imam Ibrahim continued, "The housekeeper tells me the boy fell from the roof. They were sleeping up there to escape the heat. She said she heard a sound and woke up, saw him walk right off the edge of the roof, as if he were awake. He must have been walking in his sleep."

Ammar said, "Did the boy sleepwalk often?"

"How would I know? I do not keep an eye on the sleeping habits of my servants."

Ammar wished he could meet this one on the battlefield and see if he would treat him so dismissively then, but he kept his tone even, "Of course, Imam. Unfortunately, I am required to make an assessment of the situation and report back to the Chief of Police's administrator in this Quarter, Ibn Marwan, to close the inquiry. This involves a few questions."

The Imam sighed in acquiescence.

Ammar continued, "Would you tell me who lives and works here?"

"My daughter and I, the housekeeper, and two boys, Zayd being one, to help her with the heavy work."

"Does the housekeeper watch over your daughter?"

"Yes, but I cannot see how that matters here."

"Are there any other workers who come from outside, for deliveries, anything like that?"

"Again, I would not know."

"And your students?"

"They don't live or work here."

"I'm sorry, I need to know about anyone who is a regular visitor to the household."

"I have three students I meet with here in the morning. You've met Adam ibn Hamid ibn al-Abbas, he is my best student. Masud Ibn Imran al-Samarqandi, exceptional. Yacoub Abu al-Hasan al-Darimi, also brilliant. I expect him to take on a teaching position under Abu Sulayman within Muhammad al-Khaqani's household itself."

Ammar nodded. The way he said their names, it sounded like he should know them. He would have to ask if this case went any further. But one of them teaching in the household of the Banu Khaqan? He doubted it. Unless "in the household" meant Muhammad al-Khaqani's cousin eight times removed. It didn't matter even if it was true. All these associations he could grasp at within the caliphate meant nothing to the true scholars who held the hearts of the people. That had to be a sore spot for the Imam. He knew better than to say anything but the man had got his goat. He broached the sensitive matter with feigned innocence, "You don't teach in the mosques?"

"Of course I could have my place in the mosque if I liked, but I have no time given my work with the family of Abu Babak al-Daylami and my students here."

"You will have to forgive me, Imam. What is it that you do with your students here? Is it like teaching hadith at the mosque….?"

"Ah, of course," Imam Ibrahim cut him off, "You police, you've spent so much of your lives in filth and blood on the battlefields and now keep us safe from the filth of the streets of Baghdad. You can hardly be expected to know anything about the blessed study of the Prophet's words and actions."

Ammar chose to restrain himself from reminding him that the Prophet, whose words and actions he devoted his life to collecting and studying, had had to spend much of his time in the "filth and blood" of the battlefields defending the Muslims against their enemies. Why bother bringing up the example of Muhammad's cousin and son-in-law, the Lion, Ali, or the courage of his blessed grandson, Husayn? The Imam rarely thought of them, no doubt.

He wondered how the Imam squared the luxuries of his finely embroidered robe and tooled leather slippers with reports that the Prophet and his family only wore rough fabrics and gave away the gifts of luxury sent to him by those seeking their favour. He laughed under his breath at the Imam. He'd heard that scholars transmitted forged hadith extolling the virtues of dressing beautifully to excuse their habits of wearing even silk, just like that student of Very High Station. They refused to transmit hadith naming Ali as Muhammad's chosen successor, so lying about simple luxuries was certainly not above them. Not above this one, likely.

"They are copying my collection of hadith. I have travelled the breadth of Empire to collect hadith with the fewest number of transmitters between the Prophet, God bless him, and me."

Imam Ibrahim continued in a tone used to make children feel stupid, but, Ammar noted, most often made children think the adult was the stupid one. He bowed his head slightly in Ammar's direction, "You see, the fewer people in-between the blessed Prophet and myself, the more reliable the report will be about his words and actions. Further, my collection only holds hadith from transmitters of the highest character, those who have never been known to tell a lie. I have forty-three through the Golden Chain itself. And one hundred and forty-seven hadith that can be traced to Aisha, God bless her, the beloved of the Prophet and preserver of hadith, through transmitters of the highest reliability."

Ammar held himself back again at the mention of Aisha, she who had so obsessively challenged Ali's right to lead the Muslim community in favour of her own family members. He sucked at his teeth without thinking, a slight tsk escaping. If the Prophet's daughter, Ali's wife, and the mother of Hasan and Husayn, the blessed Fatima, had lived beyond her eighteen years, what would our hadith tradition look like then? There would be someone of perfected character to challenge Aisha's version of things!

He returned his attention to the Imam, who was saying, "There are no forgeries or unreliable transmissions among them. These young men are making verified copies of this exceptional collection so they may teach it to their own students someday. My reports are of such high quality, I am certain they will not only be valuable to support the faith of the average believer in understanding Muhammad's example but also in establishing ritual and civil law for legal scholars and the courts. I have no doubt my collection, small as it is, will become as desirable as that of Bukhari and Muslim."

Ammar bit his tongue, keeping him from laughing at the man for such delusion, saying with perfectly feigned deference, "I am sure your collection is going to be a contribution to the religion, may God preserve it for future generations."

He paused and took a breath to maintain an even tone, "Imam, forgive me, I only have a few more questions. That night, did your housekeeper come and get you immediately or did she come down first to check on the child?"

"Of course, she ran to the child first and saw he was dead. She was not in any hurry when she informed me of what had occurred."

"I would like to speak to her."

"I can't see how that is necessary."

It was obviously necessary and he had the right to speak to whomever he pleased and look wherever he pleased, but Ammar did not disagree openly. Despite the possibility of having been pushed, he suspected the child had fallen in an accident. He could insist by administrative right. Or he could insist by simple fear. He wanted the man to taste fear.

"I am sorry to ask, but I heard weeping. Was that your daughter? Would she have known the boy?" The question was as good as pulling his sword from its scabbard and holding it to the man's neck.

Imam Ibrahim's face blanched at the suggestion. Ammar held back a smile.

"Since my daughter's mother died, she spends a great deal of time with the housekeeper," the Imam spoke too much and too quickly in an effort to cover his fear. "Perhaps I should have brought in a woman dedicated to her care, but she was always close to the woman and I didn't want to break her heart further. All to say, you understand, it is possible my daughter would have encountered him in the company of the housekeeper when the boy had some work to do. My daughter has only recently gone into seclusion. But I can assure you they did not know each other beyond what is typical of such interactions.

"My daughter spends all her time studying hadith. She has great aptitude. Better than many male students, I should have named her after Aisha for her ability to memorize and cherish hadith. She is merely a sensitive girl. Waking up to a dead body of someone you've known, even slightly, in one's own courtyard would be disturbing to anyone with a heart, would it not?"

Ammar enjoyed the lengthy response meant to protect his daughter, and himself, from any suggestion of impropriety that could ruin them all. But it only made him wonder more about the girl and her relationship to the boy. Surely these things happened, but the housekeeper would be well aware that it wasn't simply a matter of a bad reputation for the girl. If someone accused them of having sex, they'd be subject to an investigation that might lead to flogging. There were commonly-used legal maneuvers around this sort of accusation. These cases rarely went forward, that is, unless they were handled by someone with a political or religious grudge. But the gossip alone would be the end of all of them. Not just the girl, but also Imam Ibrahim's career and reputation, and the housekeeper would be on the street for letting it happen. No, Ammar decided, it wouldn't have happened. The housekeeper would have been forced to get rid of the boy at the first suspicion.

In any case, it was far more likely that one of his students would have his eye on the girl. If there were any romantic feelings in this house, it would be there. That's exactly why he had a screened off area behind his desk; she studies with them, but out of sight behind it. If she were sitting in the same room as his male students during the lessons, even behind that screen, well, there was still much for these young men to imagine.

Ammar's sense was that the man didn't know anything else. The man would consider it beneath him to pay attention to the habits of his servants. Imam Ibrahim's concern was only for his family's reputation.

"You can see the importance, Imam, that I should clear the suspicion up quickly by simply confirming the matter with the housekeeper."

Imam Ibrahim stood and called for one of his students. It was the Mother's Son. He came so quickly he must have been sitting just inside the archway listening. He looked angry. Ah, he thought, so here is the sweetheart.

Lucky for you, boy, I'm not here to investigate the crushes of the Imam's household.

Imam Ibrahim asked the student to bring the housekeeper to the courtyard. He said to Ammar, "If there will be nothing else, I'll leave you to discuss this with Maryam. Please let her know when the body can be taken to the corpsewashers. We hoped to send him for his funeral prayer at the Shuniziyya for the afternoon prayer time, bury him there, and put all this behind us."

"You won't send him to the al-Anbariyya mosque right here? Won't the Shuniziyya be a bit far for a busy man like you to go for the prayer? And then the walk to the Shuniziyya graveyard with the bier, and then the burial?"

"It's better if he is with his people. I won't be attending. I fear I would only be a distraction to their mourning."

Ammar held himself back again. He doubted this boy had any family. The Imam meant to send him to the poor for prayer and to a pauper's grave with only strangers reciting the Qur'an over him as the earth is shovelled over his body, leaving him alone to be questioned by the angels. No women to wail for him. No wake for people to gather to remember him and comfort those who've lost him. This man would be right at home among the armies of Yazid, looting the bodies of the family of the Prophet at Karbala, leaving their noble persons for others to bury. He couldn't speak to keep from putting his hand around the man's throat.

Imam Ibrahim stood to leave, "I hope there will be nothing further and we can close this matter immediately."

Ammar stood up, straight. He wanted to do nothing more than take hold of the man, but he left his arms consciously still beside him. If only we were on the battlefield or on the street at night.

Chapter Four

Ammar sat down and tried to recover himself while waiting for the housekeeper. He heard the slap of her feet coming down the hall, not moving quickly, a tired sound, an old woman walking as one who had worked too hard her whole life. He expected to see sadness when she turned into the room. He stood for her. She deserved that much. But there she was before him, a heavy woman, old, but not as old as he imagined, with a face of such open kindness that he was filled with emotion for her. Grey hair stuck out underneath a kerchief tied around the back of her head in the way of the women from the countryside, her wrap around her waist like an apron with a length unwound to loosely pull over her shoulders and head for his sake. Her wrinkled face told of the laughter and love she found in people somehow despite this despicable world. This woman looked like she had raised many children of her own and still had love to spare for others. Her eyes were swollen and red rimmed from crying. He saw them move toward the body on the other side of the courtyard and tears welled up in them.

He said, "I'm sorry, should we move inside?"

"No, I don't mind being here with him. He shouldn't be alone. He shouldn't be lying there, but the Imam wouldn't let us move him. He said you would have to see him first. Can't we move him now, Sir? I want to bring him to the corpsewashers and give the boy the care he deserves."

"I understand, but he was right to tell you not to move him. I'm sorry, the sooner we talk, though, the sooner I can let him go."

She spoke Arabic with a heavy Persian accent and was formal in that way Persians so often were. He asked her to sit, but she remained standing so Ammar stood with her, "Can you tell me what happened?"

"Like I told the Imam, we were all sleeping on the roof and I heard a sound. It woke me. I looked up and saw poor Zayd fall right over the low wall on the roof. He never let out a sound. We wouldn't have known until morning if I'd not woken up."

"What happened after you saw him fall?"

"I came running downstairs to help him, but he was already dead. In all God's mercy, God made it quick for the boy."

"When you checked on him, what did you do?"

"I don't understand."

"Did you move him to see if he was still alive."

"I saw his face." Her face sagged recalling it, "His eyes were fading to grey like a freshly slaughtered lamb."

She looked down at the couch beside her and let herself sit. She didn't slump into it. She held herself with dignity despite the exhausted pain on her face. Ammar sat with her. He changed his question to move her mind away from the thought of the boy's face.

"Can you tell me who works here and who is a regular visitor to the household?"

"There's just me, Yusuf, and poor Zayd. I don't see how anyone else would matter, Sir. They don't come here at night."

"What do the boys do for you?"

"They help me with all the heavy labour, bringing fuel for cooking, getting deliveries, that sort of work. Yusuf is even learning to cook. I can't lift as much as I used to. There is a girl who comes in to help me with the washing. That can be backbreaking work. Then one of the boys will carry the laundry to the roof to help her hang it."

"This girl, who is she?"

"Her name is Layla. She works next door. They're kind enough to share her with us, although they are not kind about much else. I make sure she gets some fatty meat to eat and a sweet or two. That girl would crawl right into my lap, so starved for love she is."

"But she wouldn't have been spending the night?"

"For shame, no. Only Yusuf, Zayd, and me were on the roof."

"Yusuf, did he not wake up?"

"Not until I woke him. I came to get him after I'd told the Imam. He's a heavy sleeper. A heavy everything. I love him like one of my own, but that boy's like molasses, sweet and slow. Poor boy, he's heartbroken at the loss of his friend. Can't stop crying."

"You take good care of these boys…."

She interrupted, "Like my own, like my own."

"I'd like to speak to Yusuf."

"He's not here, sir. Yusuf's out bringing in deliveries for the Imam. He ordered more paper just yesterday for the copying of his important book about the Prophet, may God protect the Imam's efforts."

Ammar wanted to correct her on the Imam's efforts but didn't see the point.

"I'll need to interview Yusuf when he comes back. When do you think that will be?

Maryam said, "He'll be in and out. He has to do Zayd's work as well as his own now. I can't be sure, but I can hold him here. If you can tell me when you'll return."

"Alright. I'll let you know. For now, can you tell me anything about Zayd? Did he always walk in his sleep?"

"I saw him do it now and again, when things were troubling him. I keep an ear and an eye out for everything that goes on here. I'd find him and lead him back to bed."

Ammar asked, "If he was walking in his sleep, then something must have been on his mind."

At this, her eyes opened wide and she realized she'd said something she shouldn't have.

He pressed, "You're close to these boys. You must have some suspicion of what was wrong."

She began to weep. Here it comes, Ammar thought. He wanted to push her to say what she thought, but he felt himself wanting to comfort her instead. He wanted to show her she had a right to grieve, unlike her Yazid of a master. But there was no touching a woman outside one's family; he held back even kind words. He needed her answer. He wondered now if there was something to investigate here. This would tell him.

After a few moments, she recovered herself and said, tears still on her cheeks, "Sir, I should have known better than to let him sleep on the roof, but with the heat as it is…. I feel like I killed him myself. How will God ever forgive me?"

That's all, she just feels guilty.

Ammar tried to console her, consciously lowering his voice for her, "It could not have been your fault. It was God's will that the boy die, no one can prevent what God has commanded."

She nodded and wiped at her cheeks and nose, but he could see she still felt at fault. He couldn't see how this was anything other than an accident. There was nothing left now but to see the roof and release the boy's body for washing and burial.

The housekeeper led him back towards the entrance of the house to the stairs leading to the second floor and on up to the roof. He followed her up the narrow staircase. It was lit by small windows onto the street cut into the thick walls. The openings were cleverly cut so that they only looked out onto the solid walls of the building across the street. He knew there would be no view from the staircase onto the rooms occupied by the family, either. All the same the doorway to the second floor was covered by a fine linen curtain with bands of embroidery along its edges. The girl is in seclusion. She'd have no direct contact with unrelated males by herself, not even male servants. No man would see her face except those in her immediate family and whichever man her father gave her to in marriage. Bile raised in his gut. You'd think the women of Prophet's family never interacted with the men in the community. You'd think those women had never been on a battlefield. Never nursed the wounded or picked up a sword themselves when necessary or never demanded justice for the slaughter at Karbala before the Caliph Yazid himself! Women have their proper place, but it wasn't in seclusion. These asses! Locking their women up and calling it piety.

They reached the top step and the housekeeper opened the door from the staircase vestibule onto the terrace. The borders of the flat roof were defined by parapet walls of varying height, providing privacy and protection from the street and the neighbours' roofs. He could see from here that there was no rear garden. The walls of the house abutted the neighbours on three sides. The well, where there must be a kitchen entrance, was set into a dead-end passageway rather than leading to an alley. There were no alleys in this neighbourhood with rear entrances that you'd find in even wealthier neighbourhoods.

He looked north out over city. There was a good view from there. The Tigris glittered in the sun as it curved around the old fortified Round City; the original Baghdad, built some one hundred and fifty years earlier by the Caliph Mansur. It had been fully enclosed once, its battlements and ramparts encompassing markets and residences within; his garden palace and great mosque were located at its very centre. It now stood demolished in parts and used mainly as barracks, prisons, and administrative offices, including the police; but the green dome still stood, the statue of a mounted horseman atop it, while the mosque still called people to prayer each Friday and stood open for the education of young scholars and daily prayer. Succeeding caliphs had built their palaces along the Tigris in other parts of the city while Baghdad sprawled well beyond the Round City in every direction across the boat bridges spanning the Tigris, eating up villages, and old estates, making them home to some millions of people according to where you drew the city lines. Ammar thought, looking out over the city, that Baghdad had overtaken the caliphs, diminishing their power. This city, he said to himself, belongs to its people.

He turned back to examine the rest of the terrace. The interior parapet walls looking down onto the courtyard were much lower, no barrier to falling. Washing lines were strung across from the vestibule toward the front of the house to the rear exterior parapet. It was a working roof, for the servants. The Imam and his daughter most certainly never came up here. On the hottest nights, they would sleep in the cool of the courtyard below, although who knows if he would allow his daughter to sleep there now that she was in seclusion. The housekeeper took him across to the area where they slept. Three bedrolls were folded in the corner neatly. One, must have been Zayd's, had his robe and sash folded neatly on top of it with his scrap of turban beside them. She'd come to straighten up despite everything. Old habits, he supposed, but he wished she'd left everything as it was.

"He was right here. He walked off right there."

Ammar walked over toward the edge taking care near the low wall. He wasn't sure how the boy had made it to the edge without tripping, boxes and an old pot were in the way. There was an easy path through the boxes, but the pot was right up against the edge. Maybe the boy tripped on the pot and tumbled from there? He looked carefully over the edge and saw Zayd lying below. The sun was beginning to shine on Zayd's head. He shuddered at the injustice of it all. He'd need to let them take the body now.

"It will be alright now. If I need to interview the other boy, I'll send someone to get him. Please call the washers to come and get Zayd."

Chapter Five

Layla ran ahead of Zaytuna up the footpath up from the banks of the Isa Canal hurrying to get across the quarter and back to work before she was missed. Her wet wrap was thrown over her head and clung to her *qamis*, soaking her back and legs, and dripping water on her bare feet, caking them with dust from the road. Zaytuna watched her run out of view, her heart breaking.

Zaytuna didn't believe a word of Layla's story but she didn't let on. She let the girl talk it out. As far as Zaytuna was concerned, it was impossible that Imam Ibrahim would have killed Zayd because his daughter, Zaynab, had fallen in love with the boy. Not because fathers did not do this sort of thing. It was that Zaytuna could not imagine that a daughter of a religious scholar, and a rich one at that, had ever been given an opportunity to fall in love with a servant boy in her father's household. She'd been in enough of these houses, washing clothes for these kinds of people, to know how they guarded their girls. And if somehow the Imam's daughter had found a way to spend time with a servant boy in secret, she knew that no little girl with everything at her fingertips would have fallen in love with an ugly little boy like Zayd. The rich have no use for the poor in matters of love. They take what they want. They don't love. And there would be no draw to that poor thing with his bent nose. But for Layla, poor Layla with nothing in this world, she loved the boy so much she believed that everyone must love him the same.

She and Layla had climbed down the banks of the canal and sat at its edge, far enough away from a round reed boat with goods to unload so they would not be a distraction to the men pulling sacks off it and onto their backs to carry up into the neighbourhood. Zaytuna kneeled by the water, the girl's wrap grasped tightly in one hand, and let it rinse in the swift water of the canal. She pulled it out and stood to twist the water from it, then walked up the bank a bit to lay it out over the stubby grasses growing there. She turned back to sit near Layla, kicked her sandals off by the waters edge, and put her callused, bony feet in the cold, clear water. The girl stood watching her. Once Zaytuna was settled, Layla came close, kneeling before her, leaning forward on her hands, and begged her to look into Zayd's death, "...to set things right," she said.

Zaytuna listened, but she couldn't imagine for the life of her what this girl thought she could do about it, let alone why Layla had thought of her at all. None of this made sense to her, but she'd agreed, simply to quiet the girl's heart. The only thing that would come of this, as far as she was concerned, was the disquiet of her own heart at the tragedy of these children's lives. There was nothing to set right. The boy fell off the roof somehow. A short, brutal life ended in fear and pain. That's all. God have mercy on his soul. And poor Layla, she'd lost the only one whom she loved in this world. Zaytuna understood too well that none of this would ever be made right for this girl. How could Layla still be naïve enough, even at her age, to think it would?

Layla looked back at the wrap, nearly dry already in the hot morning sun, and told her that Zayd had given it to her as a promise that someday they would marry. Zaytuna thought he'd likely taken it from the rag pile at the Imam's home, one of the Imam's daughter's finely woven wraps discarded once stained or after she simply became bored with it. Her own clothes, Saliha's too, came from those piles from the houses where they washed clothes. But that didn't matter to Layla. Layla loved him without question. That worn piece of cloth was as good as a written contract in the girl's heart. Maybe it was for the boy, too. How could Zaytuna know?

As she walked up the footpath, and Layla disappeared around a corner far ahead of her, she grew angry thinking about why Zayd had told Layla that Zaynab had fallen in love with him. What was the need of it? Why tell her that he and the Imam's daughter talked about each other as if they were the storied couple, "Zayd and Zaynab"? In the boy's telling of it, God forgive him, the two had been forced apart because she was promised to "another." Zaytuna guessed the Imam's daughter was contracted to marry someone chosen by her father and Zayd made up this secret love between the two in order to make Layla jealous. A boy like that, maybe he thought Layla wouldn't love him unless he was desired by someone utterly out of reach? Layla had said, "Zaynab thought he loved her! But Zayd told me everything and we laughed at her. She thought she could have everything. But he loved me not her!" If this was Zayd's way of winning Layla's devotion, it was a way of cruelty.

Zaytuna looked askance at the beggars sitting along the footpath, close to the square. A woman sat, her clothes in tatters, her hand out, her eyes pleading, with her empty breast exposed, while a child with rolls of fat on its arms and legs, and so obviously not her own, tried to suckle at it. A man called out to her for some change, his arm bloated and red, likely from tying it up overnight to swell, and smearing it this morning with lizard blood to elicit sympathy from kind folk who didn't know their tricks. A boy lay wedged in against one of the shabby houses, not far from them, begging with his good hand; his other arm was bent at a sickening angle, likely crushed for this purpose alone. Maybe the man with the arm was running them all for his own take. Her heart was already thumping in her chest, her jaw setting hard at the thought of what had happened to Zayd and Layla, and now this. This man and what he'd done set her head to pulsing such that she was nearly choked of her senses by the sight of them. She knew begging like this was business, but why did these children's lives have to be destroyed? Did that man break that boy's arm so he could bring him back some coin each day? Her mind turned to Zayd's broken face. Is that what happened to him? She barely heard the man yelling out to her, "Sister! Don't you have some change so I can feed my family? I can't work with this arm the way it is."

She spun around on him, after realizing what he'd said, and could not hold back the pain she felt for the boy, the infant in the woman's arms destined to a life like this, Zayd, Layla, all these poor children, and hissed at him, "May you have no mother in this life and the next!"

The man turned on her, sitting up, "The Prophet told us 'charity is a smile,' but you've got nothing but filthy talk for the likes of us, you withered-up bitch!"

It took all she had to keep from spitting on him or giving his leg, sticking out into the path, a furious kick.

She growled, "You do this to these poor children, yet you tell me to correct my speech! Where do you find destroying a child's life so you don't have to work in the Prophet's example? You'll find nothing but your own place in hell!"

She turned away from him, not waiting to hear if he answered, but she could hear the woman cackling behind her. She strode up the path until she got far enough away then stopped cold. She was shaking and demanded under her breath, without propriety, without apology, "God, how could You do this to these children?"

As she heard herself say it, she automatically reached out and slapped her own hand to scold herself. She sucked in her breath through her nose, pulling herself up straight and calling herself to account, now silently. This is the nature of things. This is life. You've known this since you knew anything. You pray and fast and take care with every little thing, but you're no different from the avaricious swine in their fine clothes, touching everything for a lost fleck of gold, and gorging themselves on meat and complaining about the smallest discomfort. Stop wanting life to give you, give anyone, give these children, a taste of ease and tenderness.

She followed her scolding with a litany of theological prompts meant to pull back her anger at God's willing destruction of the most vulnerable. God is The Slayer and The Giver of Life. God is The Nourisher and The Withholder. God is The Tenderly Compassionate and The Terrible in Punishment. God's will is wise, God's will is wise, God's will is wise. But her anger was on the loose and needed a simpler object than God to lay into and found it in Salman.

Her thoughts ran to him. And where in the world did Zayd get that heretical telling of "Zayd and Zaynab's" story? Salman, of course!

She shook her head. *Walla*, everyone knows that Zayd and Zaynab were married, and married only a short time, when the Prophet Muhammad fell in love with her. Muhammad saw her uncovered, in a stolen moment, and he could not live without her, nor she without him. Zayd saw the fact of their love and let her go. Zayd and Zaynab weren't even in love, for God's sake!

As Zaytuna made her way into the square, these thoughts became louder and louder in her head and sharper in their certainty until they threatened to cut through and spill out her mouth until she said aloud, just under her breath, "...forced apart because she was promised to *another*. How can there be forgiveness for spreading such slander!"

And with that her anger settled in for an easy rage. She said aloud, in a full-throated voice, uncaring who could hear her, "One of Salman's tall tales! He sits there all day in his shop, serving wine, telling stories about the Prophets. Telling lies. Serving lies and wine to anyone who will pay. He's running nothing but a tavern! God preserve us from that grandson of a traitor! Leading people astray and disgracing the Prophet. Teaching this child that Zaynab would have preferred Zayd over Muhammad!"

Zaytuna leaned into her stride, her long legs stretching further and faster up the footpath towards the street connecting to the square where Salman sat throughout the day and night telling his stories while serving up *nabidh* and wine.

Salman laughed to the men sitting on stools beside him outside his establishment, "Here she comes! What will it be today?" They all turned to watch her approach.

She came up on him, "Are you drunk telling such stories? Only a filthy drunk would think that a woman would choose anyone over the Prophet of God. A man in direct conversation with God! A man of perfect character! How dare you say that Zayd and Zaynab were forced apart! God preserve us!"

As Zaytuna went on, Salman leaned his back against the wall and smiled at her, a woman of towering height whom a polite man might have called "handsome" behind her back. He sized her up, trying to gauge her age. He shook his head at the shame of it. What good is asceticism to a woman? All that fasting and then no fat when she did eat, praying all night, no sleep. It simply made her look dried up and much older than she must be. He tried to remember when he first saw her and her brother as children with their mother....less than twenty years ago, couldn't be more. He thought, She can't be thirty yet, but looks more than that.

Salman sighed. She might be attractive, to someone, if she put a great deal of weight on. That horse of a face, though. At least this one wasn't born black like her brother, what a curse from their Nubian mother. Her father must have been an Arab. Still, she's on the dark side, a bit too much of a toasted sesame for my taste. A Persian or Slavic woman, now there is the lightness of skin that speaks of beauty. No better. A Byzantine Christian, or a Frank. A Frankish woman, ah, there is luminous skin. Now if they would only wash regularly like a decent Muslim. That would be perfection.

His thoughts turned around the women of the neighbourhood, judging their characteristics, assessing his own tastes, smiling at the thought of some, wrinkling his nose at others. Satisfied with his thoughts, he turned his attention back to Zaytuna's voice.

She was still ranting at high volume, "You have turned a pure union, a love ordained by God, into scandal and filth!"

Salman burst out laughing, "Ya Zaytuna, my sister, sit down and have one of my special drinks. A cup of date wine perhaps? Or a strong *nabidh*? My hard cider is the best this side of the Tigris. I think you need one!"

She shook at him, "God preserve us from your lies and your sins!"

One of the men called out to her, his words exhausted, slurring, "God preserve us from your passion for the Prophet. It drives you to madness, woman."

Zaytuna looked at the man. A canal worker. He sat on his stool in only his dirty short *sirwal* with his legs spread, one elbow on his knee, his hand holding up his head. She could see how drunk he was already. His eyelids sagging halfway down. So early in the morning. She turned to Salman and spat on the ground in front of him.

Salman simply shook his head and said, "If only your madness were like your mother's. There was a woman, Zaytuna. Everyone who heard her words became drunk on divine love and eager to follow the example of our beloved Muhammad. Now she's gone and we sit here drunk on wine and you stand before me spitting at my feet because you say you love the Prophet, a man who would not spit on his own enemy. God preserve us indeed."

"You think my mother would not call you out for insulting our Prophet! How little you knew her!" As a child, she had held onto her mother, shaking with fear, as her mother hauled a man up with her words alone, sending him to his knees in tears begging forgiveness from God. But there was the difference. No one here was turning to God by the force of her correction. Her heart stopped at his words. Shame overtook her, rushing up from behind and covering her, cutting off her breath. God's love spilled through her mother and she poured it out to all who would drink. She drove that man to her knees, because it was love of God driving her words and he felt it. He became one of her followers, finding her wherever she was preaching, weeping at her every word. To be in her mother's presence was to vibrate with the humming of bees, to feel the flow of warm honey through you, to warm yourself in nourishing sunlight. Her love was not created, it was creative. It was not the knowing love of a mother built on intimate, worldly moments, end on end. It was unknowing, unworldly. It was a love that held nothing to itself, not even her own children.

Zaytuna had failed her. Now. Always. Truth be told, she wanted nothing to do with the love her mother offered. She didn't want God's love. She wanted the petty, possessive, scolding, protective, and interested love of a mother, a real mother. Not a saint. She had failed her mother by wanting *her* love. She and her brother, both. So the two of them had nothing from her but what they did not want. Zaytuna was not interested in God's love. She could not see God's love in any of the pain in this world. Not in any of the joy either. She knew she should and the shame of it all suffocated her. She stood stock still staring at Salman, eyes wide with all the resentment that unwillingly recognized shame can muster. She turned without a word to walk away.

Salman called after her, "Go with grace, sister, and tell that brother of yours we have not seen him in long time and he owes us a visit!"

Chapter Six

Ammar left Imam Ibrahim's house and told the night watchman he could go and get some sleep. As he walked through the streets of al-Anbariyya, he saw a familiar hulking black man ahead of him. A smile broke out on his face and he forgot all about the propriety of the neighbourhood, yelling out, "Ya Tein! Ya Tein!"

The man ahead of him turned around, squinting into the morning light. He realized who was yelling at him and he bellowed out across the quiet laneway, "Ammar, you ass! They can hear you braying all the way to the Saffarin market! You're going to wake up the Caliph's taxmen from their beauty sleep!"

They hurried to each other despite their old injuries and grasped each other in a great hug.

"Ammar, what are you doing in this godforsaken neighbourhood?"

"It's good to set eyes on you, Tein. I'm just coming from clearing up some business about an accident."

"I heard you'd been moved from the Regular Infantry to the Police."

Ammar mock bowed, hand over heart, "It's a position of great honour and massive pay cut."

Tein smiled but his words were aimed at locking horns, "Ho! And how do you square that with your longstanding devotion to the caliphs?"

Ammar pushed back, "I work for the people, Tein."

Tein bucked lightly, "Like when the police have to round up the Caliph's imagined enemies or the poor for blighting his view of the city?"

Ammar stepped forward, crowding him, "I work with Grave Crimes. That involves killings, serious assaults, Tein. I'm not the kind of police you're talking about."

Tein didn't move.

Ammar smiled at his huge friend, looming over him, disengaged, and stepped back, "Anyway, look at you, I heard you'd been kicked out of the military!"

Tein let it go, "True, this gamey leg isn't going to carry me into battle ever again."

"I heard there was more to it than a gamey leg."

Tein shook off the comment, "I've no interest in fighting the civil wars of these caliphal swine. Our days preserving the borders of the Empire for their greed dressed up as our piety finished me. They call us *ghazis* as if we were Muhammad's noble companions fighting alongside him, but we're no better than those Turks enslaved to fight the civil wars of the caliphs and their challengers. The poor are the ones that suffer most for their power struggles and rich tastes. May they eat the dirt of the dead they've put in the ground."

Ammar put his hand on Tein's arm, "It wasn't like that."

Tein looked at Ammar, his mouth was tight, remembering exactly what it was like, but shook the thought and Ammar's hand off. He forced a smile and slapped Ammar on the shoulder, "Do you have time? Let's go find something to eat. I haven't had anything substantial in a day or so. You can pay."

The friends walked arm and arm out of al-Anbariyya toward the clanging of the Saffarin market. Tein said, "I know a place. It's past that last stall there. It's loud. It's hot. But the food is excellent and cheap." Past the last of the coopers and smithies was a series of arched brick stalls set back for the workers to eat. It was early yet, but Tein and Ammar could smell the tang of meat braised in broth sweetened with date syrup and soured with vinegar. The server saw Tein ducking his head in and taunted him, "You old twat, back to beg for scraps again?"

Tein pushed the man lightly, saying, "Only if you have figs today, you old son of a donkey's asshole! My friend here is paying, so ladle out some of that *sikbaj* we smell simmering."

"The meat isn't quite tender yet, but I can make you some *tharid* with the broth. Will that do?"

"It will indeed," said Tein, settling himself heavily onto a bench.

Ammar sat down next to him laughing at the exchange, "Just an insult in return for that comment? Where is the old Tein?"

"The old Tein is even older. Those were younger and angrier days, Ammar. We all had something to prove. But being named after a fruit that looks like a vagina didn't help."

"What was your mother thinking? May God preserve her sanctity. But seriously, what was she thinking?"

Tein laughed, "You know what she was thinking," and recited the verses from the Qur'an, "*Wa at-teini wa az-zaytun wa tur is-sineen, wa hadha baladi'l-amin, la qad khalaqna al-insan fi ahsani taqwim....We swear by the fig and the olive, by Mount Sinai, by this peaceful land, we certainly created the human being on the most beautiful form.*"

"God how we tortured you with that," Ammar was trying not to laugh again with the memory of it and lost the effort, "'*I swear by Tein*, I'm going to drink this wine!'" Ammar realized what he said and his face blanched.

Tein pulled back and looked at him, "What?"

"How did God not strike us all dead, making jokes of His words! And I just did it again!"

Tein looked at him sideways, "Where did this piety come from? Are you back in the arms of your Shia imams?"

Ammar tipped his chin up at him, smiling, but taking some ground with his words, "If you were a different man, I'd slug you for that."

Tein retorted, "Relax, brother. Ali, the Lion on the battlefield, would not hit a different man for worse than that."

Ammar raised his hands, giving up, "Leave it to the godless to teach the pious a lesson! No he would not. Whatever the case, I shouldn't have joked like that even back then."

Tein smiled at his old friend, "I can't speak for God, but as for me, it's all good. How better to become such a killer on the battlefield? I had to beat the skin off of every kid who taunted me and more than a few of you fools!"

Ammar said, "God forgive me."

"Wait, I sense God speaking to me right now. He's considering forgiving you,"

Tein put his hand over his heart and pulled a pious face as if he was searching to hear something being spoken from deep within his soul, "Yes, God is willing to forgive you for the cost of a good meal now and again with your old friend, Tein the Twat."

Ammar smiled at him, "A reasonable recompense. Done. Speaking of '*wa zaytun*' how is your twin?"

"Zaytuna is the same as she ever was, starving herself for God's sake and pining away for the Prophet as if he were going to come back from the dead. Can't get a decent meal at her house. Nothing but dried bread, vinegar, and a few lentils. I love her, but you'll not get a piece of fat out of her cooking pot."

"She was always a hard nut."

Tein looked down, "Well, she didn't survive our mother's sanctity as well as she might."

Ammar raised an eyebrow, "Not like you?"

"At least I've got my feet on the ground of this world," he pointed down, "Right here."

Ammar looked down where he had pointed, "There never was a Hereafter for you."

"All this sudden worry about my soul, you have found some piety somewhere. Well, worry not old friend. God can forgive me if He likes, dip me by my little toe in *Kawthar* and wash away all my sins, then pop me into your Paradise in time to share a cup of wine and roast fowl with you for all eternity."

He gave in to Tein, as he always had, laughing, "Not without the intercession of the Shia Imams, so you are quite lost my brother."

Tein pushed at him, "We're both screwed with all the killing we've done."

Ammar turned serious again, "I understand. You've got reason to be bitter about life."

"It's not bitterness, it's plain dealing. We both ran off to fight to get away from here. Get away from our families. Now look at us, you've become the man we ran from as children and I've...," he sighed, "...I don't know what I've become."

The cook put out a couple of spoons and bowls of wheat bread soaked in the sweet and sour broth in front of them. Tein tried to approach the bowl with some control, but his hand shook slightly and gave him away. Ammar watched him closely. He moved at the food the way they did after marching for days and days against the Byzantines with only dried bread and a bit of salted meat to hold them over. They were foot soldiers and food didn't always reach them if their troop had to push out ahead of army and its supplies. Tein spooned up the sopped bread into his mouth and breathed deeply as he chewed, grabbing a cup of water to wash it down. Ammar waited for him to get a few more mouthfuls in him and asked again, "So what do you do all day, just hulk that huge, black body around scaring people in rich neighbourhoods?"

Tein looked Ammar straight in the eye, "I do odd jobs for people when I can. Even with the limp, I can carry more than most men. I hate to say it, but I'm looking to hire myself out to press men to clear their debts. That coin is good. More than enough for the likes of me to live on. I heard from one man that he only gets a few copper *fals* every time he visits a client, but several chinks of a silver *dirham* if the money gets paid back. If it's a big return, he's been thrown a *dirham* or more for his trouble."

Ammar winced at the thought of Tein, one of the few squarely honest men he'd ever met, working as muscle for petty loansharks.

"You can't be sleeping in your garrison anymore, where are you staying?"

"I sleep in Zaytuna's room. There's not much space in there for the two of us. Most nights I sleep in the courtyard or go into the cemetery to stretch out."

"Look Tein, I could use some help now and again. These watchmen I have to take around with me, they're not even worth the pittance they get paid. If they aren't looking to rough up any likely victim, they're half asleep or show up drunk. God protect us if there's trouble, these fools couldn't control a crowd or put down a fight to save their own lives. They'd only make things worse."

Tein picked up the bowl, drinking down the last of the *tharid*. He looked at Ammar from underneath raised eyebrows, "You really don't arrest the likes of us?"

"Only if they kill someone."

"Alright. But I have a hard time believing the Chief of Police is going to put me on the payroll because you want to do an old friend a favour."

"Look Tein, if I can direct payroll to snitches, I can put in a request for some muscle. No favours, you'll work for it. I can put you in for five *dirhams* a pay period.

"And what's the pay period, twenty-eight days now, ninety days later when the Caliph's mood changes, and a hundred and twenty days when he's sick of us? I've lived this story before."

"We're not paid out from the Caliph's coffers. We garnish the districts we protect directly."

"You literally do work for the people!"

"It's not quite like that. But, look, it'll be five *dirhams* for twenty-eight days, firm. I know it's not much. Certainly, not what you'd make beating people up for a living, but it would mean a regular bed and regular food. No uncertainty. Us together again, it'd be like old times."

Tein looked into his empty bowl and did not speak.

Ammar added, "I need the help."

Tein was skeptical, "Well, you let me know when they approve the request," and changed the subject. "So what about women, Ammar. Have you found time to fall in love yet?"

"I'm not a romantic like you, Tein. I'm fine on my own."

"Still contributing to the local economy, I see."

Ammar laughed, but said, "No, not anymore. Not since I found some piety somewhere."

"Ahhhh," said Tein, smiling, "I understand now," tapping Ammar's right hand and tipping his chin towards it, "you are fine on your own."

Chapter Seven

Zaytuna walked away from Salman's shop, not knowing where she was going. She wove in and out of people in the crowded streets, through the alleyways, away from the centre of the neighbourhood towards the cemetery, seeing but not seeing. Her head was thick with self-recrimination and sorrow; her muscles clenched, her jaw tightened, shoulders turned in on her, her fingers twitched with every reminder that she, unlike her mother, could not see through to God's love from the thick of all the misery of the world. She wanted to unwind the cloth from her head and wave it at God, a red flag, a scream for Him to come and get her, pull her out of this pain and confusion. Reaching the cemetery, she looked at the small camps set up by the poor who were forced to live there because they could afford nothing else. The people burrowed into its walls, their sleeping holes covered with small woven reed and palm frond lean-tos. And past them, beyond the stones, her mother's grave. How could she be her mother's daughter and not be lost in God's love herself?

She remained outside the cemetery, leaning against its wall, seeing herself within them, as a child, in her mother's lap, as her mother leaned back against one of the gravestones, sitting among the poorest of the poor, answering their questions, weeping from joy, falling into ecstasy. Tein, as always, stayed away, moving to the edges of the crowd, watching them, as they pressed in on her and her mother. Zaytuna buried her face in her mother's lap so she couldn't see them. She wrapped her arms around her mother's waist, shaking, holding on against the crush of bodies. Her mother would try to reassure her, holding Zaytuna closer to her, until the ecstasy was so overwhelming that she lost touch with Zaytuna's fear, submerged into the oceanic waters of God's presence rushing in around them. In those moments, she let go of Zaytuna, her back arched sharply, her head thrown upward, her arms outstretched as if to hold the entire world in the encompassing flood of the words that poured from her directly from God.

> This world and the hereafter have no pleasure,
> no pleasure except through my Lover,
> who has taken me at my asking.
> If you have stopped asking, then ask again,
> by contemplating His creation,
> by accepting His wisdom's desire.
> Each glance beholds a blessing of God,
> be grateful if it falls on pleasure,
> be grateful if it falls on pain.
> Your eye will reach its boundary of joy,
> but do not be held back by this body,
> wander into the orchards of love.
> Lose yourself there, erased from existence,
> gone, into the arms of your Beloved,
> returned, to gaze on the face of God.
> Keep asking, there can be no losing Him,
> His gentleness turned to desolation,
> His punishment your daily bread.

Hearing her words back then, Ahmad ibn Abu al-Husayn al-Nuri, whom she and Tein came to know as "Uncle," would call out from the edges of the crowd, "*Labayk Allah*! Here I am, God!"

When her mother finally became quiet, exhausted, soaked in sweat, a companion or two from the Baghdadi Sufi community would come forward and check on them, sometimes bringing a piece of candy to soothe her. Her mother would hold her then and look for Tein, smiling when she caught sight of him. Uncle Nuri would be playing at hunting down Tein among the gravestones, grabbing his ear when he caught him. Zaytuna didn't know then that these people who came forward to care for them were among the greatest mystics of Baghdad. To her they were the only family she'd known.

Her mother told them story upon story about her days wandering alone with God, in and out of ecstasy, through the countryside, cities, and towns, as she made her way from Nubia, east toward Mecca, then beyond. Zaytuna heard her mother's longing to bring those days back. That sound of longing was lost when the stories shifted to the days of her pregnancy then, afterwards, wandering with her babies strapped to her, one at the front and one at the back. She told them how people took mercy on them, feeding her fatty meat and milk to fill her breasts, not the rinds and husks she barely subsisted on before.

Her mother, herself, was surprised she could bear children at all. She barely bled anymore. Yet there they were. She was not pained or ashamed to tell them that the man who fathered them had raped her under an olive tree where she'd taken shelter in the middle of the day. She only asked God then, when it was clear to her that she was pregnant, what she had done to deserve children to distract her from her path. She struggled at first to accept that this was His will, that her path must be with her children. She told them it was only her lowest self that still longed to be alone with nothing to hold her down. Remembering those thoughts, she would mutter, "God forgive me," and hold them to her, thanking God for giving her what she needed, not what she wanted.

Her mother wandered with them, looking for a place to settle, sleeping in animal holds, in mosques, and sometimes in the homes of kind families. She washed clothes, mucked out animal dung, whatever work was thrown her way out of charity. But eventually, always, someone would be disturbed by her mother's ecstatic states and push them on, or worse.

Zaytuna knew there were long stretches of good days in those wandering years. She had shreds of memories that came and went: she and Tein playing *kharaj* with other children, Tein always guessing what they had hidden in their hands, bedding down out of the weather most nights, having full bellies, and old women whom they called "Auntie," fretting over the two of them as if they were their own. Those days came to mind now and again. But Zaytuna's body remembered other days. She would feel fleeting senses of fear while walking down the streets of Baghdad with an uncertain memory of running away from a house. Her gut would clench, and she would see herself, then, hitting her stomach to stop the hunger pangs. Exhaustion would overtake her when she saw mud caking her *sirwal* and feet on days walking in the rain while the memory that invoked it would not show itself. These memories only became stronger over the years, overtaking her when a seemingly innocent sound or sight resonated at the perfect frequency, holding her in place, forcing her to remember, and barring her from the bridges people cross to reach each other.

In the worst moments, with the worst memory, a curtain would come down before her, filling her vision with the light of the moon shining into a mosque, saturating her ears with the sounds of bodies struggling, and filling her nose with the stink of a fat man in a filthy black *qamis* pulled up exposing his bare legs, on top of her mother, pushing her down with his weight.

Zaytuna lay perfectly still beside her, frozen, watching. The man grabbed at the end of her mother's *qamis* with one hand, pulling it up, then pulling down her *sirwal*, while holding down one of her arms with the other. He pushed himself down onto her. Her mother finally screamed. Zaytuna saw Tein, sleeping by their feet, bolt upright, leap onto the man's back, riding him like a bull, with his hands locked together, grunting, pulling up on the man's throat and windpipe with all his strength. As big as Tein was, even then at just five, he seemed so small. A baby riding a raging bull. Her mother kicked at the bull's legs trying to push him away. She clawed at his face with her free hand, her nails gouging him. Zaytuna watched drops of blood fall from his face onto her Mother, into her mouth and eyes.

She saw the bull's turban shift on his head in the struggle. She knew it was going to fall. She observed it, wondering at the stripes, some in thin rows and others thick. The way the turban wound around his head it seemed like the stripes were in braids. Then the turban fell off without unwinding, its cap still within. It tumbled onto her, and she lay without moving, staring at it sitting upright on her stomach, hearing her own voice screaming.

Zaytuna saw the bull turn into a man and roll off her mother onto his back. Tein let go as the man rolled and scrambled out to his feet, kicking the man as hard as he could in the head as a thundering howl released from deep with him. She saw her mother turn toward Tein, away from her, and reach out to him, his cry becoming her own.

The man brought his hand to his head, rolled onto his stomach, moaning, bleeding, protesting, finally got himself up and half ran, half staggered, for the doors of the mosque, leaving his turban behind. Zaytuna watched him flee past the inner door leading to the Imam's family rooms attached to the mosque. The Imam standing in his doorway, holding a lamp, watching, doing nothing.

Her mother rolled onto her left side pulling down her *qamis* as far as she could while putting her left hand between her legs, holding herself. Zaytuna sat up and leaned over onto her, looking. Her mother brought her hand out and they saw that there was blood. She pulled up her *sirwal*, turned back to Zaytuna and brought her in close, saying, "I have fixed what is between me and God, the sheep no longer fear the wolves."

Her mother let go of her and sat up, looking to Tein, saying, "You've hurt yourself. Sit down and let me see that foot." Tein stood staring at them, trembling with rage and fear and would not move. She let him stand. Breathing deeply, consciously, her mother then took hold of the turban, saying to no one, "This will be of use." She got up and went outside, leaving them alone, to wash the blood from her at the basin outside the mosque set aside for ritual ablutions. Returning, she unwound the turban, drying herself with it, then folded it over and over, putting it back on the ground for them to use as a pillow.

She pulled Zaytuna to her again and lay down with her, holding her tightly, then looking at Tein, saying, "Now my baby, come here," holding her other arm out to him. But he stood over them, for how long, Zaytuna did not know. Zaytuna buried her face in her mother's chest and wept until she fell asleep. She found Tein in the morning, asleep at their feet, as always.

It was not long after that they made their way into Baghdad. It was Uncle Nuri who found them first. He said years later he could feel her mother, her love of God coming to him like the call to prayer resonating to its people. He had walked until he found her, then sat nearby, falling into ecstasy himself along with her. But, as he said, winking, also keeping his own ecstatic state in check well enough to keep an eye open, making sure her mother was safe and she and Tein were alright. Afterwards, he led them to Abu al-Qasim Junayd's home where the Baghdad Sufi community gathered every day and where they took them in as family.

Zaytuna tried to shake off these thoughts, turning away from the cemetery, walking towards Tutha. She watched the people rushing through the streets to their business. Children dodged the adults walking around them, getting underfoot as the little ones carried baskets of goods for delivery, or bound reeds or thorn bush on their backs, without even sandals on their feet, and her heart sunk into the memory of Zayd running past her in the alleyway, barefooted, a boy like them, now dead.

A young man in scholar's robes with a pleasant face and proper beard saw her as she nearly bumped into people, not noticing. He called out to her, "Zaytuna!" She didn't hear him. He walked to her through the streams of people and tugged lightly on the sleeve of her *qamis*, saying, "Zaytuna, are you all right?"

Zaytuna came to herself and cried out in relief at her childhood friend, like a cousin to her, more a brother, standing before her, "Thank God, it's you, Mustafa. I've been lost."

His kind eyes held her, "How could you be lost? These are your streets Zaytuna. You live here, you grew up here. This is where you found your family, where you slept at night, rested your days, and learned from your mother's lap."

He brought her back to her old self and she laughed tenderly at him, "Listen to you, with your formal talk!"

She tapped the white turban wound around and under his chin with a discernible twist, marking him as a scholar of hadith and a Hanbali, "You hold the blessed words of our Prophet for all of us."

"God forgive me, Zaytuna, you know better than to give a servant of God a compliment like that. My lower self is always hungry for fine words. All this could be lost in a moment, if God willed it."

She tsked at herself, "So serious, too, but right. God forgive me and protect you."

She looked down, and let out a deep breath.

He looked up at her, searching her face, "What's wrong?"

"I don't know where to begin."

"If something's that hard, Zaytuna, maybe you should go see the shaykh?"

"Maybe." She asked, feeling like a child, "Would he even accept me after all this time?"

"Zaytuna, you know better. He is your Uncle. He loves you. It's so strange you don't visit. Tein visits every week without fail. He stays a long time when Uncle Nuri is here."

"It's different for him."

"How?"

"He is just visiting family."

Mustafa asked, "How is your Uncle Abu al-Qasim not family?"

Zaytuna answered frustrated with his thick-headedness, "You know. It's that way for you too! Because he is also a shaykh, Mustafa, a spiritual guide. I know the rest of the aunts and uncles are too, but he pushes in a way the others do not."

Mustafa laughed, "You don't know your brother. He takes advice from them. You should too. It's all the more important you go see him now."

Zaytuna sighed, "When I've been avoiding him for so long? How?"

"I'm free now, come with me."

She asked, "You'll stay by me?"

"Of course, my Zaytuna."

She nodded and turned with him, neither of them speaking on the short walk to Uncle Abu al-Qasim al-Junayd's home.

***

Mustafa was never one for chat even when they were children. Zaytuna always enjoyed his company. She could sit and brood with him and he would not disturb her. When Nuri brought them to Junayd's home, she ran off to sit with the other children in the courtyard, and there he was, Mustafa, quiet, just off to one side, watching everyone. So intelligent, even then.

She walked right up to him and introduced herself, "I am Zaytuna."

He made space for her to sit next to him, saying, "My mother's name is Zaytuna, too. I am Mustafa. That's my mother over there."

He pointed to a sturdy woman at the rear of the courtyard, her hair covered sensibly by a long multi-hued striped scarf tied at the back of her neck, and her wrap wound around her waist like an apron, the way men wore it. She had dragged the reed mats and sheepskins out into the sun. She had one sheepskin hanging over a narrow trestle, beating it with one of the wide spatulas with the long handles that Old Bakr used for the huge cooking pots in the kitchen in order to draw the dust out of them.

"That's my mother over there," said Zaytuna pointing toward a long and slender African woman sitting at the feet of Junayd and Nuri. To Zaytuna, she was the most beautiful woman in the world. She had heard Mustafa's mother say once she was as noble and beautiful as a "Pharaoh's Queen." She did not know what that was, but such a woman must surely own the world simply by her presence in it. Her *qamis* and blanket-shawl were made of rough dark wool, stained and patched over and over out of necessity. Her bare feet and hands were cracked and calloused. Her knuckles were ashen. And her beautiful, long twisted locks, decorated with colourful thick glass and stone beads, and one cowrie shell at her forehead, were a secret, tied up with a faded red muslin cloth wound round into a bulky knot at the nape of her neck. But nothing could hide the graciousness of her movements and the openness of her luminous face, burnished by years of wandering in the sun to a deeply golden russet brown.

Mustafa replied matter of factly, and he was right, "I think our mothers will be great friends." And so it was that she, Tein, and her mother moved into a room in the house where the elder Zaytuna and Mustafa lived. She had always thought that Mustafa's mother in her generosity had taken them in, not learning until years later that Uncle Nuri had paid for everything.

Some nights, Mustafa's mother would send him out to get some chick pea stew and barley bread from a nearby shop and they would eat together in the courtyard. After they finished their meal, Mustafa's mother would get out her *daf*, and their mother would bring out a long, light brown wooden drum.

Zaytuna loved to rub her fingers along the carved triangular markings at its base and the curled edges of the skin at the wide end that had been pulled tight with rope and knotted every few inches, as if the drum would tell her the history their mother refused to divulge. Mustafa's mother had found it for sale in the market one day and brought it to their mother as a gift. The seller spoke grandly of its provenance, saying it had been found in a Pharoah's tomb in Egypt. But Zaytuna and Tein's mother, eyes wide and smiling, took the gift in her hands as if it were a newborn baby she recognized as her own and said, "Not Egypt," and no more. Those nights, they would warm the drums over the fire, tapping and thumping until the sound was just right. Then they would begin to lightly beat their drums. The drums would begin speaking to each other, drawing the women into their secret conversation until one of the women would call out in ecstasy, "Ya Mustafa, Ya Chosen One," and the women would begin improvising on long-adored songs about the Prophet's beautiful characteristics.

Mustafa leaned over to Zaytuna one night and confided, "When I was very little, I thought that song was about me."

The energy of their drumming and song would pull the neighbours from their rooms. They would move into the courtyard and join in. Tein would move away from the cluster of people, as always, sitting against the far wall, but clapping his hands in the rhythm of a drum as their mother had taught them. Sometimes Zaytuna could hear him sing when they came to *"Talaa'l-badru alayna,"* welcoming the Prophet's arrival to Medina. Still young enough while their mother was alive that his voice had not yet changed, it rose up over the others like a nightingale,

> The full moon rose over us,
>   from the valley of wada,
>   and we must be grateful,
>   for the call is to Allah

***

Walking together now to Uncle Abu al-Qasim's home, Zaytuna wanted to take Mustafa's arm and lean on it, but it wouldn't do in the street. They weren't exactly family and weren't more than that, either. Mustafa was a scholar now; there was no room for talk. Too quickly they reached the door. It was shut and locked. Mustafa took hold of the knocker and brought it down against its plate three times.

***

She'd heard the door was never locked before the trials. Some years before she and Tein were born, some of the Sufis of Baghdad had been hauled before the caliph's court, accused of heresy and other crimes. Uncle Abu al-Qasim denied he was anything other than a legal scholar and was let go. But Uncle Nuri and many of the others declared their passionate love of God openly before the court and were sentenced to death. The community was torn apart. Old resentments from that time carried forward into their day. Uncle Abu al-Qasim taught them all to hide their mystical states. They should speak so that outsiders would not understand. They should control themselves even when it was just them, especially during their remembrance ceremonies, the *sama*, when the music and poetry mystically transported them into the arms of The Beloved. But Uncle Nuri called the seekers to speak the truth whatever the consequence.

She had been told the story so many times she could see it as if it had happened before her eyes. As the accused Sufis walked single file before the executioner's block, Nuri rushed forward, begging to be killed first, if only to give the others another moment in this world to remember God. They say that the executioner felt the words more than heard them. They hit him like an ocean's wave coming full force, then somehow, suddenly, halting to softly wash through him. He looked down, marvelling at a watery light pouring around him that only he could see. His hands opened to touch the light and his weapon fell beside him. The clanging of the metal on stone raised him back into consciousness. He said, aloud, to no one, to everyone, to God, "I will not execute these men." He ordered the Sufis be brought back to their cell while he brought the case to the feet of the chief judge himself to plead their case. They say that Nuri's light still shone through the executioner and illuminated the judge's wisdom, and the judge ultimately ordered the men released into exile in nearby Raqqa, instead of to death. He declared, "If these men are heretics, then there is no one who truly worships God."

When Mustafa began his studies, one of his teachers had told him the story was not to be believed. Zaytuna was angry when Mustafa told her this. She was angry he did not speak up to his teacher. She was angry he did not tell him exactly what kind of loving man their Uncle Nuri was. Didn't he sneak in and out Baghdad to see his wife and children, and his friends, despite the risks? Wasn't it on one of these trips that he met their mother and brought them to Junayd's circle, thus saving their lives and finding them a home? And even when he returned from exile did he not keep a respectful distance from Junayd's circle, visiting only now and again, to keep them safe from reprisal? Had he not fed her and Tein out of his own bowl when he himself had not eaten? Had he not always sacrificed himself for others? She yelled at Mustafa, her face mottled with anger at his betrayal, "It's all true!"

But Mustafa kept quiet and took what knowledge was to be had. He told her that Uncle Abu al-Qasim advised him to hold his tongue. He told Mustafa that the scholars were suspicious of the Sufis and were only testing him to see where his loyalties lay. It wasn't that they were bad men. On the contrary, they only wanted to preserve their way to God's truth, just like the Sufis did. Uncle Abu al-Qasim said each has their way, and each way has its value and place. So he must learn as his Uncle had, from as many masters as he could, and let it all pass through the test of knowledge of the heart.

As they stood waiting for someone to open the door, Zaytuna watched Mustafa. So patient and at ease. How different they were. She would have slapped every one of those scholars and told them that their knowledge was nothing but shit piled on top of corpses. But this is exactly why Uncle Nuri had been exiled and Uncle Abu al-Qasim al-Junayd remained in Baghdad to hold the community together in the face of all that distrust.

Zaytuna's loyalty was with Uncle Nuri, and her mother, risking everything for the truth. But she also understood what made some scholars so angry about the Sufis. It wasn't just that women worshipped God openly among them, were counted among their numbers, and taught women and men alike. It wasn't just that some of these Sufis declared themselves to be passionately in love with God, and worse, to their pedant accusers, that God was passionately in love with them. It was not even that some declared themselves to be nothing other than God in moments of ecstatic seizure. It was their confidence that drove so many of these scholars mad, that the Sufis knew God intimately, directly, in a way that the scholars would never know through their books. The Sufis saw themselves drinking from the Wellspring of Knowledge directly, while they accused the scholars of cupping their hands to drink muddy water off the street. And oh how the people attached themselves to this confidence. What rivals they made themselves to the scholars! Zaytuna knew too well there was no reasoning with someone who drank from that Divine Source. The scholars would never be able to regulate that knowledge and what it made people do. She knew there was no way to get your mother to stop preaching and simply be with you while she was in that state of experiencing being chosen by God.

***

Some months before her mother died, Zaytuna watched a man in a tall judge's cap and hooded cloak follow her and a crowd that had been gathering around her in the street, where she had suddenly fallen into ecstasy, into a home that had opened its door to them. Zaytuna looked back for Tein, to make sure he was watching the man. Tein was already moving next to him, carefully, ready to push him over if he needed to so that they could run. But the man simply stood and watched as the crowd wept at her mother's every word. When her mother returned to herself, sitting on the floor, wiping the tears from her eyes with the sleeves of her *qamis*, the man approached them. Tein continued to shadow him, nodding to Zaytuna.

The scholar stood over her and her mother, looking down on them. Zaytuna thought he looked confused. He said, "The way you speak, it's piercing. But I'm worried. I'm afraid. I'm afraid it might be nothing but pride."

She replied, "Pride comes from within one's self. How can I be proud if my self is not the One Who Speaks?"

And she fell again into a mystical state, her eyes closing, her head turning slightly, lifting as she exhaled, saying,

There are elect who are chosen for His love,
He chose them in the beginning of time.
He chose them before the splitting of His creation,
as ones entrusted with wisdom and eloquence.

***

Finally someone came to Uncle Abu al-Qasim's door. A young man she didn't recognize opened it. Mustafa greeted him by name. As they made their way through the vestibule opening into the main reception room with its great archway leading out into the courtyard, she expected to see the halls and courtyard full of seekers sitting in clusters, reciting litanies, talking, or in quiet meditation, but it was nearly empty. Zaytuna peeked around the stairs leading up to the second floor, where Uncle Abu al-Qasim's family lived. No one was there, seated, under the stairs in silent retreat, like Uncle Abu al-Qasim had done himself when he was first on the Path. So unlike the earlier years.

When she was a child, the seekers of mystical knowledge came in waves from the farthest reaches of the Empire. Her mother never had any patience except for those who were truly gifted. She would grumble at these seekers, restraining herself from saying anything to them directly—they were not her students, after all—until one day when she finally broke her silence as a group nearby her was reciting, "There is no god but God," over and over again.

She and Tein were sitting with her, eating some wheat bread with raw onions and drinking fresh goat's milk they got from Old Bakr in the kitchen. They stayed quiet, keeping an eye on their mother as she became more and more frustrated by the group's ineptitude, her head ticking to the left, then her chin up, then ticking her head to the left again along with her every muttered word. The students only succeeded in hyperventilating, becoming more and more distracted as they tried to bring themselves into even a slightly felt state of presence with God. Finally her mother couldn't take it anymore. She yelled across the courtyard at them, "Look at you trying to shake off the robe of non-existence and pull on the robe of Existence! As if one could take off what does not exist and put on something that is All there is! There is no losing or finding when All is One!"

Her mother turned to her and Tein, grabbing Tein by the wrist and her by the chin, pinching her chin hard with her thumb and forefinger and looking into their eyes, said, "Remember that, *andudugu*, my babies!"

***

As she and Mustafa stepped from the dim light of the reception hall into the bright courtyard, she heard in her mind—clear as a falcon's call in an empty sky—the words her mother said to the man in the judge's cap who stood over her that day after having declared herself, in poetic form, to be chosen by God for His love before creation itself.

Looking away from the man and flicking her wrist, her mother said, "You can leave whenever you like." And Zaytuna heard then, and ever since then, in her memory of that day, that dismissal as if it had been delivered to her, too.

Chapter Eight

Zaytuna looked for Uncle Nuri in the courtyard, but didn't see him anywhere. Mustafa called out to those in earshot, *"Assalamu alaykum!"* His greeting was returned and they walked across the courtyard to where Uncle Abu al-Qasim al-Junayd was sitting on sheepskins with several of his closest companions. She had not visited in over four years and seeing him now, his kind face, she felt ashamed. He wore thin white linen *sirwal* and *qamis* with only a simple unembroidered robe over them, and with even less ostentation, a shorter length of cloth for his turban. Abu Muhammad al-Jurayri sat closest to him, as always, ready to serve his master when needed.

Junayd turned to her as she came in and she felt his presence move through her, enveloping her. His light was like no other. Not even her mother shone like this; it felt full across the spectrum, perfect and nourishing. With each step she and Mustafa took toward him, her heart seemed to lose its sense of itself, such that by the time she sat on the sheepskin at his feet, it was beating with his. Her muscles softened. Her fingers unclenched. Her shoulders fell back. Her heart was held open to him completely. The pain and anger she carried spilled out before him to see.

She tried to pull herself back from it; she fought with herself, and him, inwardly, knowing he could see her so plainly. She forced herself to reach out to kiss his hand, as she should, but did not give voice to the necessary greetings. As is the custom, he pulled his hand away before she could kiss it, but placed it tenderly on her head instead, saying, "My daughter. Should I give you a candy like I did when you were a child so that you will know that I will always love you as my own?"

He paused, then said, "You lost your mother in this world, it's true. But you never lost your family. You have Tein and Mustafa. You had Mustafa's mother, God rest her soul, for much of your life. You have all your family here. All of us who love you. God has told us, With every hardship there is ease. God gave you to us out of His love for us and out of His love for you."

He touched her cheek so that she would look up and take in his words, her eyes now filled with angry tears, and said to her, "God is The Guardian, so leave yourself in His care, leave yourself in His wisdom. Zaytuna, leave those children with Him, the dead and the living. And consider carefully why God brought their case before you."

She trembled before his knowing, without her saying anything, about Layla and Zayd. But this was one of his knowing ways; he typically hid what he knew, out of graciousness and humility, revealing it only when it was necessary.

He continued, "They are no more lost to love than you are. God is The Lover through Whom we all love. His love speaks through every moment and every thing even if you cannot hear it or understand it. Trust this. Trust God's love and begin to let the rest wash away."

"I cannot," she wept.

"My dear one, do you think that God does not know you are angry? Do you think you can hide anything from Him?"

She knew she sounded like a child, but she didn't care, "God should know I'm angry. He made my mother love Him so completely that she had no room in her heart for us. She left everything behind for Him. Then He killed her. Brutally. He chose her to die for His sake. But why did it have to be so horrible? What good did that do Him? What good did that do anyone? We were only children when He took her from us."

She dropped deeper into her pain, sitting with it openly, instead of coming at it obliquely, as she usually did, allowing herself to feel it only through other people's vulnerabilities and suffering, being angry for their sake, rather than her own. She nearly spit out the words, "We were abandoned. God left us with nothing, nobody."

At the word "nobody," Junayd looked at Mustafa with concern and nodded slightly to him, asking for his understanding. Mustafa understood, but there was no need to ask. He had loved her since childhood. He wanted her still despite what she had done to her body, despite her sorrow and anger. He reached out and held her hand, wanting to say to her, Here is somebody. Here is somebody who loves you like no other.

She felt his hand as it gently lay on top of hers and turned to look up at him, her eyes red, "I'm so sorry, Mustafa. Your mother became our mother. You became our brother. That is not nothing. You are not nobody. That was everything to Tein and I. It is everything, but still. What we've been through was just too much."

Abu Muhammad shifted uneasily and looked with concern at his shaykh. Junayd watched her closely. This daughter of their community had done almost everything that he required of his companions, without him asking. She had turned away from the pleasures of this world, she prayed through the night, she recited her litanies every day, she fasted often and ate little when she did eat, she was scrupulous in every little thing, but she had done it all without love. Another seeker would have been ready to dissolve into the ocean of God's oneness through all that prayer and fasting, having learned that nothing in this world, no pain, no pleasure lasts. Like the prophet Ibrahim watching the stars, deep into the night, sighing with love, as each star rose before him, saying, *This must be my Lord*, only to find that each also set in its turn. He declared as they fell, one by one, toward the horizon, *I do not love the setters*. This world is nothing if not a crusher of hearts and God calls the crushed to Him. So here she was, spurred to this moment, by a girl who begged for her help and a boy who died.

The shaykh's face became grave, his voice was still gentle on the surface, but the tone underneath had become more intense, its frequency pushing her, just so, to shift her from where she was stuck, "Zaytuna. You are no longer a child. It's been seventeen years and still you will not accept that everything other than God dies. *Everything perishes but His Face*. Not just people die. Not just the creatures of this world die. Even pain must die. I will say it again. Listen to me. Only love lives. Love lives forever because all love, wherever we find it, its source is God, The Lover's love. You know this. Your mother's love was an open stream from God to you. You lost the woman. You have not lost the love that came to you through her."

She felt him push, but reached down within herself and fought, throwing his own words back at him, "You just said it. It was God's love, not hers. What good is God's love to me? It was her love I wanted. I only wanted a mother like other children had. She never scolded me or fretted over me. When I did wrong she counselled me to turn away from my lower soul. When I was sick she gave me up to God's will. She never prayed that I live. Yes, *everything perishes but His Face*, so it was nothing to her if I died. All I have from my mother is pain and you want me to let that go."

He looked at her, eyebrows raised, saying, "Zaytuna, dear one, I let you argue with me when you were young." He laughed gently, "Well, I let you argue with me a lot longer than that. Maybe I shouldn't have. If you were one of my companions and not family to me, I would have been harder on you."

As he spoke the tonal frequency of his voice transformed as each word moved around her, at first gently, then closing in on her little by little, until the words grabbed hold of her with their teeth by the back of her neck, "Listen now, this is no longer your Uncle Abu al-Qasim speaking to you. This is Abu al-Qasim al-Junayd ibn Muhammad al-Khazzaz al-Qawariri."

She was compelled to lift her head, to look into his eyes. Fear spread out from her heart, as tightly bound as she had ever felt it, crushing her so that she wondered if she might die. Her Uncle was gone. This was exactly what she had feared in coming to see him. She had seen and heard this side of him with his companions, and on those days she had moved across the courtyard, to another room to get away from it. He had never turned it on her. All shook from the force of it and she shook now.

He released her neck. He said, "Listen! God's love is pure water that takes on the colour, shape, and volume of each cup into which it is poured. No cup is the same as another. The love that God poured into your mother's cup was your mother's love. No other. She held her cup to your lips and you drank from it."

Zaytuna felt his words crash onto her. A thick ocean wave arose that turned her over and pushed her under. She tumbled through it, her wrap twisting around and tying up her legs. She could not breathe from the pressure of it. It held her under for a boundless moment and then she was gone: her awareness, her body, her existence. She dissolved into the Ocean and only the Ocean remained. Then, somehow a thread of her self returned to her, just enough to hear her mother's voice calling out from each drop of water in the great expanse, "Smash the cup!"

Then, just as suddenly, Junayd reached down, grasping her, and pulled her back up above the ocean's surface. She felt the waves slapping around her, threatening to bring her back under, but he had her by the back of the neck again and dropped her gasping on the ground before him. Her senses sucked at the pieces of courtyard around her like desperately needed air. She felt for the cool ground underneath her. I'm still here. She examined the texture of each thread woven into her wrap. I'm still here. She tasted the salt of her tears. I'm still here. She heard the quiet around her. I'm still here. She felt around for the familiar pain she called her mother and found it slipping away from her. She scrambled, inwardly, on hands and knees, to pull it back to her. She's still here.

Then Zaytuna found her voice and said, exposing herself to herself, unable to deflect any longer, "I am not my mother's daughter. I cannot love God the way she did. Who am I if I am not my pain?"

She was a stubborn one. Junayd wondered if immersing her so, showing her a glimpse of the utter oneness of reality, had been an act of cruelty. Erased from herself, she had subsisted for one moment in God alone. Her awareness was piercing now. She could never turn away. She could never claim ignorance before God. If she would not allow this glimpse to widen into an all-encompassing view, she would be doomed. It all came to this. Before she was another human being lost in pain. Forgiven for her ignorance. But if she turned away from God's love now, she would be a *kafir*, one who knows the truth and chooses to cover it over.

He spoke quietly now, the tone of his voice gentle, soothing the shock of the experience, and said "You are our daughter. Blessed Muhammad advised us that we must worship God as if we see Him. But there is no 'as if' for you now. Let what you know now unfold and teach you."

Zaytuna sat silently, focusing on her breath, pulling herself back into herself, and he said no more. He gave her time to steady herself. She lifted her heavy head, Abu Muhammad moved slightly toward her, showing he was nearby to help if she needed it. She did not thank her Uncle as she should. She did not move to kiss his hand. She simply began to stand weakly. Abu Muhammad shifted to stand in order to steady her, but Mustafa gestured to him that it wasn't necessary. Mustafa put his hand to his heart and bowed his head to his uncle. Mustafa took her by the arm and they moved away from the Shaykh and his companion to a far wall and sat with one another without speaking for a time.

A black cat wandered in and out of the courtyard's porticos, sniffing the air, then walked directly to Zaytuna, rubbing against her legs. She felt the softness of its fur through her *sirwal*. Zaytuna gave the cat her hand to smell, it rubbed its cheek against her, acknowledging her with its scent, and moved away again to lie in the shade of a pillar. Mustafa said, "One of your great grandchildren or great, great, great?"

Zaytuna said, exhausted, "Who knows? They have so many litters."

"He knows you. They remember the one who kept their feline ancestors off the streets to be taken care of by the Lovers of God."

She dismissed it, "It was Uncle Nuri, really. Not me."

"No. It was you who fought for them after Old Bakr tried to throw them into the street. Mustafa insisted, "I remember how he yelled after finding the mother and her mewling kittens behind his flour sack."

Zaytuna sighed, "That gruff of an old man, he ran the kitchen like he was the caliph of its four walls. Poor Tein was so afraid of him."

"Was he?"

Zaytuna turned to Mustafa, "You don't remember? Tein tried to help him get rid of the kittens. They had them in a sack when I came in. He was trying to act tough in front of Old Bakr. Tein said the dogs in the street have to eat too."

Mustafa said, "I just remember seeing you standing in the doorway to the kitchen, legs apart, hands balled up into fists on your hips, your *qamis* and wrap blowing in the breeze behind you, quoting hadith after hadith about the Prophet's love of cats. Who knew you knew so many!"

The memory of it lifted her out of her state, "Only about cats!" She laughed lightly, smiling again, a little, "God forgive me. I told Old Bakr he was going to go to Hell just like the woman in the hadith who had tortured a kitten and so the Prophet said all her prayers and fasts were for nothing!"

Mustafa looked at her, "You were glorious."

Zaytuna lowered her head and without thinking she leaned closer to Mustafa who felt it, as slight as it was, and fell into silence to hold it to him. As if she had said to him, finally, that she loved him, too.

He shook his head at loving her so. He only ever wanted to do right by those God brought within his reach. He was never going to be a true seeker like the aunts and uncles and the people who came here to learn under them, yearning to pass away from themselves into God so completely. He was satisfied simply working at being good. They raised him with a simple teaching, one taught to them by al-Muhasibi, the "Accounter" himself. At the end of each day, he was to call himself to account for wherever he had gone wrong. Where had he shirked on kindness? Where had he let his anger slip out of his grasp? He wanted only to be a salve in this world, not a poison. Zaytuna was, for all her wild emotions, in her own way, the same. She wanted no one else to hurt like she hurt. It's true she came at it without thinking sometimes, well most of the time. But he loved her for that, too. He loved her headlong desire that the suffering should be heard, that something, anything, should be done.

She laughed quietly, breaking the moment, and sat up again, saying, "Uncle Nuri came running to see what was the matter, and let Old Bakr have it. Remember? He called me 'Professor Zaytuna' and told Old Bakr the kittens were a gift from the Beloved to His lovers. To throw them out would be to spit in God's Face."

"Poor Old Bakr, what could he do?"

She said, "And Tein, he was so angry. Stuck there, holding a bag of squirming, mewling kittens. He didn't know what was right. Uncle Nuri came and took the bag from him and let the kittens go. Do you remember?" She looked toward the kitchen, as if she could still see Tein standing there, "Then Uncle took Tein in his arms. He was almost as tall as Uncle even then. He held Tein and spoke to him so quietly until Tein was quiet too." She turned back to Mustafa, "But Tein was right. The dogs on the street have to eat, too."

"Zay," Mustafa said. "Why do you always see God's will in such a harsh light?"

"Who will be witness to the suffering?"

"Us, but also God."

"Exactly. God wills the suffering and is witness to it. God wills all we do and punishes us for it."

"Quoting Uncle Abu Bakr now!"

"Ha! I guess I am." She asked, "Is he still here?"

"He left last year. He was sent to find his own students to guide. Uncle Abu al-Qasim told him it was time for him to go. I don't think it would be safe for him to teach here, anyway. He takes so much after Uncle Nuri, the way he speaks to people. He'd get hauled up himself before a judge."

Zaytuna nodded, "*Insha'Allah*, he landed well."

He paused and looked around the courtyard, "We got news of him. He's in Marw. There's a girl here with her father. Uncle Abu Bakr sent them here for her to study. They found him teaching there. They had travelled all the way from Taraz to him, then here, on his word."

She interrupted, "Taraz? Who?"

He blushed and cut her off, "Oh, a student here." Then he placed his hand on the soft reed mat between them, picking at the frayed fibres, "Look," returning to his point. "There is one important difference between how you are quoting Uncle Abu Bakr and what he meant. He saw nothing but God's care in all of that. He wasn't naïve or bitter about it. He is in love with God, nothing else."

She didn't respond directly, but said instead, "Remember that time your mother wouldn't believe you had died? The schoolteacher said you had drowned, but she wouldn't believe it. Uncle Nuri tried so hard to get her to accept it. But she trusted that she would know in her heart if you had. She trusted that God would deal straight with her. And then, there you were, running up from the river, so excited to tell everyone how far you had swum out, proving her trust in God." She paused, weighing how to say it, then let it out, "Maybe I don't trust God, Mustafa."

Mustafa shifted uncomfortably next to her, "You sound like Tein."

She looked at him sharply, "That's not what I'm saying."

"What are you saying then?"

"I don't trust what God's got coming next. How can I love God, if I don't trust Him?"

"I've heard you say that God's will is wise. How can you not trust God's wisdom?"

"The dogs have to eat, too."

Mustafa sounding frustrated now, said, "That doesn't help me."

"I'm trying, Mustafa. Look, with the kittens and Old Bakr, I had to choose between letting the dogs outside go hungry and saving the kittens in front of me. I chose to let the dogs go hungry. What did the dogs do? Maybe they died. Maybe they found other kittens to eat. But I didn't see it. There's no escape. I trust that much." She paused to breathe, then said, "I trust that God has created a stone of a world for us to hone our selves on. There's wisdom in that. This world isn't about our comfort or pleasure."

Mustafa objected, "Zaytuna…"

She cut him off, "I certainly don't see how falling ecstatically into God's arms…," she felt the ocean wave coming at her again, she tried to turn and protect herself from it, but it overcame her. Instead of disappearing into it this time, pure, delirious joy surged through her. She saw it all for a slight of a moment. The pattern of existence always beyond her reach was before her. Her eyes filled with tears at its perfection, the justice done down to every atom, and she reached out to Mustafa and grasped his arm, holding on as if she were being swept away again, and tried to pull herself back. She sucked in the air around her, gasping.

She turned to Mustafa, her eyes wild, tears streaming, and said, with every shred of herself she could find, "How does wallowing in the joy of seeing that our existence is a poet's rendering…

…that we are words unwinding,

written on fragments pulled fluttering
  from the folds of The Lover's turban.
The ink-black curve of each letter,
  the open-throated voicing of each sound,
    trembling with beauty…."

She gasped for air again and shook her head to get these feelings out of her, reaching up and pushing her palms to her forehead, "How does wallowing in joy do justice to those who suffered once and suffer still. How does it do justice to me? To me, Mustafa? To what I've endured?"

Mustafa took her hand on his arm and held it, searching her eyes, saying softly, "Zaytuna, my heart, I'm here."

She turned away from him, eyes cast down, exhausted again, and said, "Yes. You're here. I'm here. We're all still here. Nothing's changed."

He sat quietly with her, holding her hand until she finally drew it back. He considered her, wondering, then asked, "Is this what the Prophet meant when he said, 'Whoever loves and is restrained, concealing that love, then dies, is a martyr'?"

She wouldn't look at him, "How would I know, Mustafa?"

"What you just said, Zay. It sounded like the poetry that used to come from your mother in her own moments of ecstasy. It sounds like you do know. It sounds like something has changed in you."

She became angry at the suggestion, "I don't know a thing. No, that's wrong. I do know a boy died. I know a girl is suffering."

Mustafa sat up, putting his hand on her shoulder, gently turning her towards him, "What do you mean a boy died?"

Angry still, she said, "What Uncle Abu al-Qasim said about those 'those children'. He wants me to leave them in God's care. I don't know what that means. Do nothing? Do something?" She laughed bitterly, "Wallow in joy and forget about them? These Sufi shaykhs, always so vague with their advice!"

Mustafa tried to push past her emotion to find out what happened, "What children, Zay?"

She sighed, harshly, trying to let her anger go, but it wouldn't so easily. Then she asked, "Do you know Imam Ibrahim al-Silafi?"

"Yes. Not personally. But I know his reputation." She knew by the care of his answer he would not say more and that was enough for her.

"One of his servants died. A boy, maybe ten years old." She turned away from herself and focused on the boy. That helped. She stood witness to the boy's existence. She gave his name its own breath. "Zayd."

Mustafa said under his breath, "We belong to God and we return to Him."

She waited a moment, breathing in his prayer, then said, quietly now, finding her footing in talking about it, "Another one of Imam Ibrahim's servants came to me, a little one named Layla, no older than the boy, scared out of her wits. She thought that Imam Ibrahim killed Zayd."

"Are you alright? This is horrible. No wonder you are so upset today. Honestly, Zaytuna, you can be emotional sometimes, but today you've been acting so strangely."

Her anger came back and she snapped at him, "Yes, that's right. I'm being emotional. It's the children, Mustafa. It's not about me."

He looked at her wide-eyed, unwilling to clarify, knowing it would get him nothing that he wanted in the end, saying instead, "I'm sorry, I shouldn't have said that."

She took a moment, then relented, as she usually did if left to herself to sort it out, "Uff, you're right. I'm being...I don't know what. I don't know what's happening."

"We don't have to talk about it." He reached out to hold her hand again.

She pulled her hand back, "No. I want to talk about it."

"Okay," he said. "Why, then, why would this girl, Layla, think that the Imam had killed him?"

"She said that the Imam's daughter, Zaynab, had fallen in love with Zayd and the Imam knew."

"I'm sorry, 'Zayd and Zaynab'?"

"I know. Those are actually their names. Layla said Zayd was teasing the girl about it. Or leading her on, cruelly, maybe. I don't know. This is Layla's story about what happened. I don't know anything else. Zayd told the Imam's daughter that they were like the Prophet's 'Zayd and Zaynab'. Layla said Zaynab fell for it and thought it was romantic. They were meant to be together, but could not because she was promised to another."

He asked, "Did she see the boy get killed herself or hear someone testify to it?"

"No."

Mustafa frowned in disagreement, his tone taking on a scholar's authority, no longer old Mustafa, "It sounds like this is nothing but Layla's fantasies and fears. Of course the Imam would not be the first man to kill to preserve his own reputation. But if this girl did not witness anything herself, why do you believe her? There must be witnesses, Zaytuna. You know that God has said, *Why did the slanderers not bring four witnesses? Without those witnesses, they are liars.*"

She pulled her head back and looked at him sharply, "I didn't say I believed her."

He took her tone, and the look, to heart, leaving the scholar's frown aside. She softened when he did, continuing, "She was so afraid. And Mustafa, this boy. His nose was bent clear across his face. It must have been broken, but never fixed. He was a rough boy. You know, one of these boys hired to do all the heaviest work. Layla obviously loves him so she can't see that a rich girl with everything would never fall in love with a boy like that."

Mustafa said, "The girl, Layla. She's probably just afraid of Imam Ibrahim. You know. I remember how you were afraid sometimes when you came back from washing clothes at those houses." His head dropped wishing he could have spared her that, but everyone had to work. He looked at her calloused hands from years of washing other people's clothes and said, "Poor thing."

Zaytuna sighed, "I know. She's just filled with loss and imagining things. She had her heart set on him. That's all. Anyway, that's what the Shaykh meant, the girl's loss and the boy's death."

Mustafa said, "May God give her ease and accept Zayd with care and compassion."

"*Amin.*"

"Mustafa, would you come with me to his funeral prayer today? I don't know where, though. They'll be done washing him and preparing him for burial by the afternoon prayer, don't you think?"

Mustafa nodded in agreement to all of it, "I know a friend of one of Imam Ibrahim's students, I'll see if I can find out. But I suspect he'll be brought to the Shuniziyya mosque. Don't all the poor from Karkh end up here no matter what mosque is nearer to them? I'm done working at the pottery for the day. Let's meet there and if we need to, we'll hurry to wherever he is going to be."

They heard the midday call to prayer. The sun was just passing overhead. Zaytuna got up, worried, not having realized what time it was, "Oh no. I'm late for work with Saliha, I've got to run. God willing, we won't lose this job over me."

He wanted to reach for her hand again and keep her there, "Thank you for asking me to come with you."

She yelled back at him as she hurried away, "I'll bring Saliha, too!"

Chapter Nine

Saliha handed Zaytuna the last of the washing to hang on lines stretching across the roof. Saliha had put the job off when Zaytuna didn't show up, so she could eat and avoid the midday sun. But the early afternoon sun was even hotter. At least it wasn't one of the days when the humidity rose out of the marshes, smothering the city. Today the clothes dried almost as fast as they could hang them. They were used to working and sweating in the sun like this, on roofs across the city, their wraps wound around their waist with the long end draped loosely over their heads and upper body to offer some shade, but was still hard on them and they worked quickly. Since the clothes were drying, they'd have time to fold them and bring them down to the housekeeper. That might ease her irritation that they had not shown up in the late morning as agreed. Zaytuna took a wind of cloth from her and apologized again.

Saliha stopped her, "Zaytuna, enough. You had a difficult morning. I don't blame you one bit. If we lose the business at this house, we'll find more business someplace else. I'm not going to bow to anyone."

"Well, you would know about that."

"Indeed, I do. Here, help me fold this," she said, holding out the ends of a long piece of sheeting. "What was it like seeing the old man again?"

"I didn't listen to him. It was too much. He put me through too much."

"Zay, I don't know why you went to see him if you won't listen to him."

"He helped raise us, all of them did. They are my family. We had nothing and they fed us, clothed us, and cared for us. It's shameful I visit them so little as it is."

"He's more than an uncle, Zay."

Zaytuna began to feel the pressure of the knowledge he had forced on her, the thickness of the ocean waves rising up around her to pull her down, and she felt her knees go out underneath her.

"Zay!" Saliha grabbed her by the arms, "Are you alright?"

"I'm fine," but tears were streaming down her face. "It's just the heat."

"Oh Zay, why do you go there?"

"You don't understand."

"I understand enough." She went to get her a cup of water from the jug the housekeeper had put in the shade near the vestibule for them and put it to Zaytuna's lips, "Drink this, you fool."

She continued, "I don't visit him for this exact reason. Look at what he's done to you. I know I won't listen to him! I don't want that on my head. God protect me from myself! It's enough I pray now and again. I say *bismillah* before I eat and I say *alhamdulilah* when I am through. What do I need to see God for?"

"It isn't 'seeing' God," said Zaytuna with the heavy clarity of what it was for the first time and not liking it one bit.

"Yes, yes. You've said. You learn to see God with the 'eye of the heart'. Whatever. The eye of my heart doesn't need to learn how to see. It sees just fine." She touched Zaytuna's cheek, "It sees you, my friend."

Zaytuna took a deep breath and forced herself to get up and change the mood, "Give me that last piece to hang. You old mother goat you, so concerned about me. I'm fine." Zaytuna took the wet cloth and wound it up and tried to smack Saliha with it. Saliha jumped back just in time and it missed.

"Ha! You know what else the eye of my heart sees, Zay? It sees your brother coming home alone late at night with that battle-scarred body of his. Is it wrong I can't look away? I've never seen a woman who did not at least steal a glance at him. Glory be to God's creation, Zaytuna, he has your mother's legendary beauty and it is as if I can see the sword he carried in his hand when he fought at the Frontier."

Zaytuna sighed, "You'd think you'd had enough of men."

"Zay, I'm not like you. I'm not waiting for the Prophet to fall from the sky and take my hand in a chaste marriage, a kind of marriage, by the way, *he never had*."

"God protect me from evil things, don't talk like that!"

Saliha laughed, teasing her further, "The Prophet, God bless him, *loved sex!*"

But Zaytuna wasn't in the mood to be teased; she shot back at Saliha, "You'd rather wait for a man to snap? You'd rather wonder every day when it's going to begin? I'm not waiting for the Prophet to fall from the sky. I'm waiting for one man to measure up to him."

Saliha said under her breath, "It's a safe bet no one ever will." Saliha paused, serious now, asking, "You think Tein would snap?"

Zaytuna didn't answer.

"And you think that of Mustafa, too?"

Zaytuna didn't have the energy to pretend, certainly not with Saliha, and not about this, not today, "I pray they wouldn't, but I don't know."

A crisp and consuming image was conjured before her. Mustafa and Tein stood over her, crowding her down onto the ground. She felt hard earth beneath her. A wall behind her, trapping her. Her nose filled with the stink of their sweat of their filthy black *qamises*. She tried to shake the image off, but couldn't. She dug her thumbnail into her forefinger and the pain brought her out of it.

She turned to Saliha, her voice tight, "The Prophet. A Messenger of God. He had to jump on the back of a man. A man who accepted him as bearing a revelation from God. A man who had God's beloved standing before him. The Prophet had to jump on the back of this man to keep him from beating his wife! That's how they all are in the end."

"Zay, Ayyub beat me within an inch of my life. You know. You defended me against Ayyub when my own family should have in your place. It was you took me in after I escaped. You became my family. But I was the one who was beaten. So I choose the men I want from here on out. No one else speaks for me, not even you. You wonder how I can still love men, I wonder that you cannot love them at all."

Zaytuna spat back at her, "I saw my mother raped. I might as well have seen my father rape her, too. What do you think that did to me? This is how men are, Saliha. *Walla*, how is it that you and I escaped such things when we were girls? How have we escaped it so long now?"

Saliha said, more harshly than she intended, "Don't make your problems my problems."

"So you find a man who doesn't hit. So your husband doesn't force you in your own bed. Then you want a man to have a say over you? Tell you when you can come and go? You want to submit to him as if he were a god? There is no god but God, Saliha! Marriage is nothing but blasphemy!"

Saliha burst out laughing at her, "Preach, sister! Don't ever say you don't have your mother in you. Well, you'll be relieved to know that I will always remain a Muslim in good standing. I'm not interested in marriage. I just want a bit of marriage bed."

"Saliha, really!"

"No one cares what a widow does, Zay."

Zaytuna objected, "As long as no one can see what a widow does."

At that, Saliha laughed so hard she barely got it out, "Or hear what a widow does!"

Zaytuna said, scolding, "Saliha, you know there's talk."

"What is talk to the likes of me? Do I have a reputation to be ruined? What can they do to me, Zay? Take the soaking laundry out of my hands? I've got to live, for God's sake."

"Yes, they could take the laundry out of your hands. Talk could mean no work. For God's sake, watch yourself." Zaytuna paused and looked away, saying, "You don't want Tein. He's been hurt so badly. The war. Our family. Come on Sal, you know this. He drinks a lot. I don't know what he'd be like. With you. Drunk, I mean."

Saliha thought of something and laughed again, pausing for a second wondering if she should say it, then seeing Zaytuna's serious face decided to say it, "As long as he can still get it up when he's drunk."

Zaytuna laughed despite herself, "Saliha, stop! He's my brother!"

"Yes, your brother. And one of these days, I'll catch his eye."

Zaytuna sucked her teeth, tsking, then said, "If you haven't caught it by now. The way you stare at him as he comes through the courtyard…."

"I am a patient woman."

"You are a crazy woman."

Saliha held her hand out to her, "If you didn't have me, Zay, where would you be?"

Zaytuna looked at her and took her hand, "Hanging wet clothes on another rooftop somewhere….alone."

Saliha laughed and pulled her hand out of Zaytuna's and slapped it, "Always the two of us up here on a roof, right sister?"

"That last bit is nearly dry already! It's so hot. Let's fold it, get out of this heat and head to the mosque." Zaytuna smiled at her friend, "You should do two extra cycles of prayer in forgiveness for the way you talk."

"I will, *insha'Allah*, for my soul and for your sake."

"Please. I need the prayers, Saliha. I really do."

Chapter Ten

As Zaytuna and Saliha turned the corner toward the Shuniziyya mosque they heard men's voices raised. There was a crowd growing in front of the mosque doors. As they got closer, they saw two men railing at a group of women who had stopped to return the favour.

"God protect us from these street preachers," said Saliha. "What new hadith have they come up with today about all the ways we're all going to hell?"

Zaytuna replied, "You should just ignore them, they're like flies looking for a carcass."

"More like wasps."

Zaytuna said, "Looks like the women are giving them hell. Must be 'women are temptresses' day."

Saliha laughed, "Oh look at that one, he's only got about three hairs for a beard but a full-grown mouth on him!"

The young man bellowed, "You women come to the mosque, put your heads down, and lift your asses into the air for us to jump on! If Umar Ibn al-Khattab were around to see you, he would beat you over the head!"

One of the women standing nearby leaned down and gathered some dirt from the road and threw it in the young man's face yelling, "Put dust in your eyes and stop looking, then!"

The dirt hit its target and the young man bent over rubbing his eyes and coughing out, "*Walla*, I can't help it!"

"You can't help it?! It's our fault that you are like a rutting dog looking to hump a rock?!"

Zaytuna leaned over to Saliha, laughing, "What made this man think he could mess with the women of Baghdad?"

Saliha was looking into the growing crowd. "Zay, Zay." She pointed, "Is that Mustafa?"

It was. As they came close to the crowd, they could see that he had moved forward to stand in front of the women. She could hear his voice now, it was not loud but it was clear, "You say you know what Umar would do, but it was his son who reported that our beloved Prophet said, 'Do not interfere with the women who serve God as they go to the mosque'. Surely he would know better what the Prophet said, and what his father, one of the Prophet's closest companions, would do."

The older of the two men spat on the ground before him, "You wrap your turban like a Hanbali yet you defend these filthy creatures?"

"And you? You call yourself a Hanbali, yet Imam Ahmad Ibn Hanbal himself would decry what you are doing here. You listen! I don't need to defend these believers, the Prophet himself defended them. You can take it up with God on the Last Day if you like. *Insha'Allah*, I will be there to testify against you. I will testify that you barred His believers from serving Him and that you called them 'filthy'."

The one who had been coughing now stood and faced Mustafa. Clearing his throat he threw back a hadith, "'…and the best place for a woman to pray is in the darkest corner of her house'!"

Mustafa countered, "Now you are going to add repeating a weak hadith, without naming it, to your list of sins. May God give me the opportunity to testify to that, too. Watch yourself! The Prophet warned us, 'Whoever lies about me makes his abode in Hell'."

Saliha, pulled at Zaytuna to move forward through the crowd. Looking behind at Zaytuna, Saliha said, "Well, it's good of him to do it, but I think the women had this one covered already."

Zaytuna looked at Mustafa through the crowd, sighing sweetly at him, saying to Saliha, "Poor Mustafa, he's so earnest."

The older man stood firm against Mustafa and forced a laugh, speaking clearly so that all those standing nearby could hear, "You call a hadith cited by Imam Ahmad himself forged! How did you get the right to tie your turban so, when you know nothing of his own collection. How very embarrassing for you. Here in front of all those who believe you, one of their own even, to be a scholar!"

The colour rose on Mustafa's face. He had not said it was forged, but weak. They were turning his words around! The crowd became quiet at his silence to the charge until an older woman stepped forward, poking him in the arm, "Answer him, you are our learned brother, not him."

Mustafa raised his voice at the woman's prodding, not thinking beyond a direct counter to the point to let her know, to let all of them know, that they should not listen to these men. Mustafa said, "Imam Ahmad himself, God rest his purified soul, said there were unreliable hadith in his own collection! And I declare that this is one!"

The crowd gasped hearing that their Imam of Imams, Imam Ahmad ibn Hanbal himself, the pious scholar who had withstood the interrogation of the Caliph's men during the inquisition, the man who had never compromised his principles, the man would not even sit in the shade of another man's tree without his permission for fear of stealing from him, could have lied about the Prophet by transmitting reports that may not be true.

They began to shift, speaking to one another, some voices rising in anger. They may trust their brother, Mustafa, but if they had to choose whom to trust, it would be the perfected memory of Imam Ahmad, not the living, breathing, clearly erring Mustafa.

The older man smiled, knowing he had the crowd now and said, "Ah, here is your brother and scholar, slandering our beloved Imam Ahmad!"

Mustafa scrambled inwardly. These men were using the people's ignorance of hadith scholarship to their own ends. How could he explain? The scholars did not include the people when they shared their doubts and debated every point from every angle. When they were asked a simple question by a simple man, they did not share with the people the generations of arguments on an issue or the careful reasoning on a matter. They did not explain how much context mattered.

How could he explain that when a woman with many children, who kept sleeping through her prayers out of sheer exhaustion, asked what to do, she was given a different answer than that given to a young man who slept through his prayers out of laziness alone. They were taught to tell the common person what they needed to know for their particular situation in that particular moment, no more. How could he explain that you cannot tell a canal worker with no education, an illiterate, that their simple question has innumerable possible answers but only one right answer for him? They were taught that the common folk needed certainty, not knowledge. Give them the answer that is right for them. Nothing more. Didn't the Prophet teach to leave that which causes one to doubt for that about which one could be certain? Now he was stuck needing to explain that, and stuck fast.

He turned to face the crowd, not knowing what to do, "I promise you, there is no slander here. Imam Ahmad's collection was not like what this man says! His son published this collection so that we scholars would know which hadith other scholars had used in the past to decide legal matters. Nothing more. He collected his father's notes and…"

A man from the crowd objected, "How is this any better! Now you say the Imams used forged hadith to tell us what to do and Imam Ahmad, God protect him from your lies, agreed to that!"

The two men did not just stand by to let the crowd finish him, they walked around the people now, whispering to men and pointing to Mustafa.

Mustafa objected, "No. No. I am not saying that at all!"

The old woman near him looked at him just as his mother had many times before when he had crossed lines he may not be permitted to come back from and said, "I think you better explain."

By now Saliha and Zaytuna had come close to the front of the growing crowd. It had turned into an outright street spectacle and maybe a riot with Mustafa being beaten and the crowd under the sway of the other scholars. As if he could feel them drawing near, he turned and caught sight of them. His face softened, pleading. Zaytuna yelled out into the crowd, "I trust you, Imam Mustafa! Help us understand!"

Saliha cheered, "Yes! We trust you!"

One of the scholars called over them, "Ah the women are sweet on him, too soft to see what is going on here!"

"Brothers, sisters! Please," Mustafa began, turning to the woman who prodded him to answer, "Auntie Hamida, when you sell us cups of soaked chick peas, ready for the pot, have you not already sorted them and cleaned them for us? You don't sell us dirty chick peas. You don't tell us your method of sorting and cleaning them. You do not share how you prepare them. You are the expert. You take care of that for us so that we only have to put your trusted chickpeas into the pot. We don't ask. We only eat from your nourishing hand."

One of the women said sighing, "Oh…. now that's not explaining brother, that's telling us why you don't think we need an explanation."

The younger man yelled, pointing, "This one has caught him out!"

Mustafa's voice grew firmer, "Hear me out. Auntie Hamida, when she sorts through the chickpeas she does not just sort them into good to eat or bad to eat. It's not so straightforward. She knows that some chickpeas may be just fine if mashed, but not proper for a stew, less so even a salad where each one has to stand out perfectly."

A man laughed at him from deep within the crowd, saying, "Brother, have you been eating in the Caliph's kitchen? We eat the brown and black ones with our weed greens!"

Mustafa laughed, afraid of showing how scared he was of losing them to these men who would use these decent folks against themselves for their own ends, "You know I eat the black and brown ones in my weed greens, too! It's only to make a point. Imam Ahmad's son included all the hadith that scholars *might* use in making a decision about what we should and should not do and he graded them, like Auntie Hamida here with her chickpeas. I was trained how to use them, just like every cook is trained to use each kind of chickpea….If we had the luxury of choosing our chickpeas, that is," he laughed. "But we are rich with hadith. We do have the luxury to choose."

A few people nodded with him, a man too, not just the women, and he continued, his voice rising with every word, feeling he was getting through, "Obviously, these men have not been trained. They think each hadith is as good as another and should be used to say whatever they like!"

The older man objected, "The sisters here may fall for that since they want to keep to their sluttish ways, but the men here know from here on out that you are nothing but a liar and arrogant. Just like one of the Caliph's men thinking he knows better than everyone else."

A woman called out, "That's right! *Walla*, what are these women doing? Pray in your homes sisters!"

Another woman yelled over to her, "Who are you kidding, you old bird! I see you in the mosque everyday, early for prayer, gossiping with your friends."

"Exactly! I would not gossip if I prayed at home!"

"You would have no time to see your friends if you prayed at home!"

Other women's voices called out against her, "What am I supposed to do when I am out shopping? Where do I rest? In the street like the men? All I have is the mosque."

The older of the two men yelled out above them all, "Aisha, the beloved of Muhammad, declared that the Prophet would never have let women pray in the mosque if he knew what kinds of whorish behaviour they would be up to these days!"

Mustafa raised his voice above them, taking his opening, "That word! How dare you insult these women again! These are our mothers, sisters, wives, and friends who care for us while you prattle on about what you're owed on account of not being able to control yourself!"

Several women in the crowd shouted in agreement.

Mustafa pressed on, "You two should leave or you'll be facing these women's fists."

Now the women laughed. More than a few of them wanted to get their hands on these men now and yelled, only half-joking, "Let us at them!" A couple of women broke through and put their hands on the men, pushing them.

The older man easily pushed back at a woman who taken fistfuls of his *qamis*, then looked at Mustafa with open disgust, saying, "You offer the Hanbalis nothing but shame!" He turned back to the woman who had hold of him and spit in her face, finally getting her hands off of him, and walked away.

Mustafa ran to the woman and unwound a portion of his turban for her to use to wipe the spit from her face. The gesture did not go unnoticed. He breathed with relief as he heard one of the women say, "That's our brother Mustafa, not so proud as to unwind his turban for the likes of us."

The crowd began to disperse, some of the women, and a few of the men, hailing their greetings and blessings at Mustafa. Saliha made her way forward to him. The woman gave back the end of his turban to him and thanked him, but Mustafa stood holding it, not wanting to wind back up the cloth with the man's spit on it, not knowing what to do. Saliha reached him, took the end of the cloth and said quietly, "You're going to have to wind it up." He tipped his head down to her instead and she wound his turban back up for him. He nodded in thanks, then turned, walking with her back to Zaytuna, who met them part way.

She smiled at him broadly, "Mustafa! It's nice to see that all that studying of yours came to some good use! But you know, you did not explain in the end."

"No, I did not understand a bit of it," agreed Saliha.

Zaytuna looked at Saliha and started to explain what she meant about "not explaining" and decided now was not the time. She turned to Mustafa, "Well, you might need to find more types of beans to explain, but people are going to need to know how you make decisions if you don't want them following those fools."

He lowered his voice, "Perhaps. But maybe it is better to say, I'm not sure I should explain. Uncle Abu al-Qasim says you only speak to people according to their capacity."

Saliha retorted, "Oh and we are short on capacity, are we?"

Mustafa defended himself, exhausted, "That's not what I mean."

Zaytuna answered, "That's not what Uncle Abu al-Qasim meant either."

He ignored them, "These men are not fools. I think they know exactly what they are doing. My guess is that they are Barbahari's men. He can't control them. I don't even know if he is trying to control them. This may be exactly what he wants."

"Barbahari? Who is that?"

"A scholar. Important. A Hanbali, too. But I don't know that Ahmad ibn Hanbal would recognize the man as one of his own were he alive today."

Saliha said, "I mind my own business. I'm too busy washing clothes for this."

Mustafa said, "Their problem is that they try to make other people's business their business. I'm afraid we'll see more of them if we cannot stop them."

Zaytuna raised an eyebrow at Saliha, "They're the kind that go into widows' houses to see what they're up to."

Saliha's eyes widened, "Oh."

Mustafa turned to Zaytuna, "Barbahari was a student of Sahl Tustari."

Saliha broke in, "Tustari? Who are you people talking about now?"

Zaytuna ignored Saliha, "How can what you say be true if these are his students?"

Mustafa answered Saliha with some exasperation, "One of the greatest Sufis, Saliha." Then he turned to Zaytuna, "Well, you know so was Ghulam Khalil. The teacher is not always responsible for what their students become. Barbahari may be sincere, but he is brutal."

Zaytuna sighed, "'Sincere', Oh Mustafa, you grant people too much."

Mustafa defeated, shook his head, "Enough of this. The funeral prayer is here. We have something more important to do. Let's go inside."

Chapter Eleven

They turned away from the dispersing crowd toward the wide-gated doorway of the Shuniziyya mosque. Its yellow brick walls were covered in stucco and carved with calligraphy and interlaced geometric designs just like the mosques in more wealthy areas of the City. It even had deep blue tiles like the others inset into its archways. But it had no other luxury except serving the people. It did not escape Zaytuna that Junayd and his companions lived in this neighbourhood among the poor, taught the poor out of this mosque that served them, and helped feed them out of their own pockets. Her mother had brought them to sleep in this mosque and eat the barley bread and onions handed out to those in need in the few days before Uncle Nuri discovered them and brought them to Junayd's home.

Mustafa moved ahead toward the front of the mosque where they could see a small bier with a body on it laid out under a green cloth off to the side. Zaytuna watched him stop and hold open his hands, palms to the heavens, to recite the opening chapter of the Qur'an for the boy before performing his two cycles of prayer in greeting to the mosque. Then Zaytuna watched him move and begin to pray, thinking he was like a quiet stream moving through smooth rocks. She turned to follow Saliha to the rear, quieted by Mustafa's gentleness, and looked for an open place in the area set aside for women.

The call to stand in prayer sounded and the women and children who had been resting against the rear walls of the mosque, put their things away and moved into lines facing *qibla* on the long stretches of soft woven reed mats. Zaytuna saw a large, older woman leading a young girl, her wrap wound loosely around the girl's head and body and a *niqab* covering her face, through the door at the last second. Instead of pushing their way into one of the lines in front, they wove their way to the very back and took a place at the end of the line. Zaytuna strained to see the girl. She thought, suddenly frantic, It must be her, Zaynab.

The imam called out, "*Allahu Akbar!*"

Saliha elbowed her to pay attention. Zaytuna turned back to face *qibla*, directed towards Mecca, and raised her hands to her ears and lowered them, folding her hands over her stomach. She struggled to keep her eyes on the spot on the floor where she would place her forehead during the prostration, wanting instead to crane her head around and see the girl.

"*Allahu Akbar!*"

She bowed, saying, "God forgive me" under her breath as she realized she had not recited the prescribed verses from the Qur'an as she should. She put her hands on her knees but couldn't remember what she was supposed to recite during the bow, saying to herself instead, What is wrong with you, woman?

"*Allahu Akbar!*"

She stood again, this time giving in, and turning her head to see if she could see the girl. She turned back quickly, but Saliha had caught it and threw her hand out, gesturing, "What are you doing?"

Zaytuna gestured back, "I know! I know!"

"*Allahu Akbar!*"

She prostrated and placed her forehead on the floor, along with everyone else. But she had, by this point, forgotten the words to every movement of prayer she had been performing since she was big enough to follow her mother on the mat beside her. Asking herself instead, Zaynab is here? This is no quick walk from her neighbourhood. Maybe Layla was right? Why would she come if Zayd was not something other than a servant to her? And the old woman, she must be the housekeeper. Why would she bring…

"*Allahu Akbar!*"

She sat back on her feet and remembered, at least, to say, "God forgive me."

"*Allahu Akbar!*"

She bowed in prostration again, this time speaking directly to God, What good are these questions? What good can I do? Why would You bring Layla to me? And now Zaynab and the housekeeper? They shouldn't even be here, yet here they are. What good could I possibly do? Her chest was beating hard and her head began to ache.

"*Allahu Akbar!*"

She stood again and tried to calm down, forcing herself to breathe evenly. She folded her hands over her stomach for the next cycle, but instead of reciting the required verses, she said to herself, So I ask questions, like Layla wants, I uncover the story. How does this do justice to their suffering? Nothing will change.

She looked out over the lines of people standing in prayer and the final verses from the first chapter of the Qur'an came to her, *It is You alone we worship, it is You alone we beg for help, guide us on the straight path, not the path of those who have demanded Your wrath, and not the path of those who have gone astray.*

"*Allahu Akbar!*"

She bowed, tears coming, saying, Asking questions…. Is this how I fit into the pattern?

"*Allahu Akbar!*"

She stood back up. God. Listen. Please. Tell me what You want from me!' She felt a warmth and comfort wash through her, quieting her heart, but not overtaking her, and she knew somehow she should trust the unfolding of these events. She shot back at herself, This is just the whisperings of your own soul. God is not calling you. And if He did, what then? What can you trust God to do with you?'

She answered herself back, I don't know.

Then turning to God, she asked, If this is the path You want from me, if You want me to find out what happened, do some justice for these children, then make the Imam make a mistake, say something wrong, recite incorrectly. I'll hear it and I'll know.

"*Allahu Akbar!*"

She prostrated, trying to keep her breath even, praying the rest of the cycles in form with everyone else, but she was silent inwardly, not saying to herself the required parts of the ritual. Rather she focused on listening to the Imam, so far ahead of her at the front of the mosque, for her answer from God.

"*Allahu Akbar!*"

As she stood for the last cycle of prayer she heard it. The Imam uttered the first word of the opening chapter of the Qur'an aloud when he should have remained silent. *Bismillah.* Words spoken out of place, and a clap here and there from the people in the congregation to correct him.

"*Assalamu alaykum wa rahmatullah,* Peace to you and God's mercy"

She turned her head to the right, then to the left, closing the ritual prayer, and remained seated back on her feet, in supplication, not speaking, but now paying attention to the calmness that had come to her. Her muscles relaxed in its warmth, her head lifted from the lightness within, and her hands opened out in supplication. She said quietly, aloud, "*Alhamdulilah,* Allah, *alhamdulilah.*"

Saliha heard the words and opened her eyes from her own supplication and saw Zaytuna's head back and her hands reaching up in prayer, now nearly above her shoulders, rather than looking down at her open hands, held low before her, as she should. She gently placed her hand on Zaytuna's arm to wake her from her state. Zaytuna looked at her and said, "I know what I have to do. I know what I am for."

Saliha was worried, "Okay, Zay, okay. Everything will be fine. Let's stand now for the funeral prayer. They are bringing Zayd's bier to the front."

They stood, but instead of staying in place, Zaytuna took hold of Saliha's hand, pulling her through the thinning prayer lines towards the back to stand near the old woman and the girl. As they moved she saw two older women with black sashes tied around the waist of their wrap and *qamis* marking them as corpsewashers. The boy was young enough that it was still permissible for women to wash him. Yes, they must be the ones who washed him! She pulled Saliha to squeeze in next to the two women.

"*Allahu Akbar!*"

Chapter Twelve

After the prayer ended, Zaytuna turned to the corpsewashers, saying "May God accept your prayer."

"And yours," and the two corpsewashers turned to walk towards the door of the mosque where the bier would be carried out by the men on their way to the graveyard.

Zaytuna touched the sleeve of the one nearest to her, "Such a small body. May God give ease to the poor child's parents. What heartbreak. I suppose that's his mother and sister over there," pointing at the girl she assumed was Zaynab and the housekeeper with her. "God heal their hearts."

Saliha watched with amazement as Zaytuna lied. Her dear friend, who would rather hurt her feelings than refrain from telling her the smallest, unnecessary truth, was lying with the best of them.

One of the corpsewashers turned, "The poor boy. We washed him, you know. No parents we know of. May God give him peace."

The other one shot her a look and motioned that they should go.

She nodded and turned to Zaytuna, "God forgive me, I shouldn't speak about it. My heart just goes out to the poor boy."

Zaytuna didn't have to tell Saliha what to do. Saliha moved forward and took the other corpsewasher's arm in her own and walked her ahead, keeping her occupied by inquiring about the work and how one trains for it.

Zaytuna kept her more talkative corpsewasher back a few steps and said quietly, "What happened?"

She turned her head conspiratorially and whispered to Zaytuna, "We heard from the housekeeper. That's her over there. We heard that he was sleepwalking and walked right off the roof in the middle of the night. His poor arms were broken in pieces. Must have tried to catch himself as he hit the ground. Imagine it! God protect us all! You know we're always gentle with bodies of the poor souls who have passed, but even more so with the broken body of this little one."

"Was something else broken?"

"God cover us from such things, His poor neck broken and his head was loose in our hands. Although I suppose that means it was a quick death. There's real mercy in that."

Zaytuna looked at her quizzically, "How strange, sleepwalking."

"No, my husband, God rest his soul, used to walk in his sleep. We had to keep the door tied up high so he couldn't get out. But…"

"Yes?"

"Well, you know what was strange," she looked ahead to see whether or not the other corpsewasher was watching her, "he had a silk drawstring holding up his ratty *sirwal*. It looked new, perfectly clean except dirty as sin where he tied and untied it. You should have seen the embroidery and beading on it! What I wouldn't give for it, but you know we have to pass everything along to the poor house if the family doesn't want it. All to say, dear… that wasn't his." She stopped and pointed towards Zaynab and the housekeeper, "It has to be the young miss's there. He worked in her father's household."

Zaytuna exclaimed in a whisper, "Just like in the romantic poems! The girl gives her lover the drawstring from her *sirwal* as a promise of their love!"

"Oh!" She scoffed, "Not likely. He'd have stolen it!" Then losing all sense of respect for solemnity of her work, she shared, "You didn't see the boy's face," and she pushed her own nose all the way to the side, "nose bent clear over to one side of his face. Poor thing was ugly as sin."

Zaytuna's face became hot at this insult to Zayd, despite it being an observation she had made herself; she held herself inwardly to keep from slapping the woman. Her anger fell back enough to keep up the act with this woman, letting her say, "Poor thing, may God accept him to Paradise where he will be made whole."

The corpsewasher held up her hands in prayer and said, "*Amin, amin.*"

They caught up with the other women standing by the door. Mustafa and three other men had taken up the bier and were walking toward the door reciting from the Qur'an, "*Ya Siin, I swear by the Wise Qur'an, Indeed you are among the Messengers, on a straight path...*" followed by the others. Zaytuna turned to keep her eye on the housekeeper and Zaynab who were standing at the outside of the crowd of women by the door. She moved in through the crowd until she was on the other side of the girl. She watched the girl as the bier drew closer. Zaynab tightened her hold onto the housekeeper's arm. As it reached them, she could see Zayd's form despite the thickness of the winding cloth and the green drape embroidered with words from the Qur'an that had been laid over him. The girl's knees buckled under her and she fainted. Zaytuna and the housekeeper caught her as she was going down and they moved her gently away from the crowd, so she could rest against the wall. The housekeeper pulled Zaynab's *niqab* back over her forehead so she could breathe more easily. Zaytuna saw the bit of cloth that had covered all but her eyes was soaked with tears and her thin pale face had lost what colour it had.

Zaytuna looked up and saw the corpsewasher looking straight at her, eyebrows shot up, with a look that said, "Well maybe she loved him after all!"

Zaytuna ran to get a cup of water from the jug at the back of the women's section. Zaynab had opened her eyes, but was not moving. Zaytuna handed the housekeeper the cup to hold to the girl's lips, asking, "How is she?"

"She'll be alright, she's just had a shock. I shouldn't have brought her, but she insisted."

"I knew the boy. Zayd. May God hold him in His care."

The girl raised her eyes to her, searching Zaytuna's face, saying with what breath she had, "How? How did you know him?"

"He visited the storyteller in our neighbourhood. He had to go past my street to get there. He was such a funny thing. He must have been wonderful to have around."

Zaynab's cheeks began to get their colour back, "Oh! He is....was...   He was so smart, too. We…".

The housekeeper brushed her cheek lightly with her fingers to quiet her, "Now hush child, you've had a fright." Zaynab understood and dropped her face, turning to hide in the woman's arms.

The housekeeper turned to Zaytuna, imploring yet speaking plainly, "They saw each other a bit when they were little. Growing up in the same house, you see. They played now and again, as is permitted at that age. But she's been in seclusion for sometime now and no longer saw the boy. Then this happened. It's been hard on her, you understand. Little ones, so innocent."

"I understand. You needn't worry," she reassured her. Zaytuna looked at the woman, the way her arm was around the girl, the tender way she cared for Zaynab. She herself had washed clothes for women like this when she was old enough to begin working. Her mother had died by then. Mustafa's mother, Zaytuna, stepped in and did the best she could for them. They were clean, clothed, and well-fed. It was a good home. More than that, she held Auntie Zaytuna's memory close to her heart because she had loved her and Tein like she did her own Mustafa. They never felt that they were a burden to her. On the contrary, Mustafa's mother called her and Tein *barakati*, "her blessings." But she was always hungry for more. A few of the housekeepers, women like this one, opened their hearts to her as soon as they saw her love-starved eyes. They would make time to sit with her when she'd finished the washing. They held her, her head resting on their breast, and told her stories or sung her lullabies.

She reached her hand out now and placed it on the housekeeper's knee, "But, Auntie, how are you doing? I started coming in to do laundry when I was little. Some of the housekeepers where I worked cared a lot for us little ones doing the heavy labour. You seem especially kind, like one of them. This must be a real strain on you."

"Bless you, *alhamdulilah*. You must have been like our little Layla." She looked around, "Where is she? I thought she'd be here." She sighed, "I guess she couldn't get out of the house." Zaytuna looked quickly at Zaynab to see how the name registered to her. The girl had lost her colour again, but she couldn't tell if it were at the mention of Layla's name or because grief had pulled her down.

The housekeeper brought her attention back, "I do love the little ones working for me like they are my own. This boy was dear to me. If it's alright to say...," she paused and searched Zaytuna's face. "Please understand. Well,

I think you do. He could charm the birds from the trees. I'm afraid I let him get away with a lot, but he always did his work like I asked. I just loved him so much," she began to weep quietly. Zaynab looked to her, held her more closely, and wept with her.

When they had quieted after a moment, Zaytuna said, "I want you to know that housekeepers like you made all the difference. Please let me thank you if I have not thanked them properly." She took the woman's hand in her own and brought it to her lips, kissing it lightly, then pressing the back of the old woman's hand to her own forehead.

She looked up as she let the woman's hand go and the housekeeper was in tears at her gesture, "*Alhamdulilah* to the Opener of our hearts to each other in this cruel world."

"I'm Zaytuna."

"I'm Maryam."

Maryam moved to help Zaynab get up, saying to the girl, "If you are alright now, we should be heading back. I saw a place nearby where we can get you some juice. That should help."

"Is it a far walk?"

"No, on the Muhasibin road in al-Anbariyya."

Zaytuna took note of the place. She wondered how she might be able to visit the house and ask them more questions. Maybe offer to wash clothes there? No, that would only make it seem that the concern she showed them was selfish, just wanting a job.

Maryam and Zaynab stood up and readied themselves to leave. Zaynab's *niqab* was lowered again and she adjusted her wrap to cover her whole body, her hand grasping a clutch of the cloth underneath it to keep it close to her.

Zaytuna felt all at once that she had been selfish. She'd lied, too. She'd lied so easily! She objected to herself that it was only to help the boy. It's alright to lie in God's service... isn't it?

Maryam stepped forward and embraced her, "God give you ease."

Zaytuna held her, "And you, Auntie."

Shame came over her then, followed by a wave of fear as she finally put to mind where this kind of questioning could lead. What if she did get to talk to them again and the questions led to Maryam or the girl getting into trouble? Zaynab loved Zayd. As sure as she had been before that nothing had happened, now she was sure Zayd did not sleepwalk off that roof. Imam Ibrahim must have found out and had the boy killed. Or even killed the boy himself. Layla was right.

Zaynab nodded her head as they turned to leave, she could see that her eyes were welling up with tears again.

Zaytuna argued with God, Maybe I should just leave this story to die. The boy is dead. How is it possible to be on the side of God's love by hurting others?

She hurried after them and took Maryam's hand again, saying, "I'll ask the friends of God at Shaykh Abu al-Qasim al-Junayd's to say the fatiha for the boy and to ease your hearts. Please give my greetings to Layla when you see her. Tell her to come see me."

"*Insha'Allah.*"

Chapter Thirteen

Tein unsteadily picked his way through the sleeping bodies in the courtyard in the small light of the moon. Most of Zaytuna's neighbours had laid their mats out in the cool night air and there wasn't much room for a misstep. "Tein!" he heard whispered nearby. He jumped but didn't answer. He recognized Saliha's voice, insistent, "Tein!" He was nearly to Zaytuna's door. He didn't turn around, but gestured, hoping she could see him, and went inside.

Zaytuna was awake. The room was nearly pitch black but he could hear her reciting Qur'an verses quietly to herself. She must be standing in prayer. He slumped down on the soft reed mats covering the dirt floor, sitting against the wall closest to the door to give her space. He just wanted to sleep. He'd finally got enough wine in him that he could sleep without dreaming of Ayzit's bloody body curled up over their tiny son, trying, and failing, to protect him from the Byzantine raid on their camp town in the middle of the night. But Zaytuna would be going up and down and up and down in here and Saliha would be trying to get next to him inch by inch outside.

He heard Zaytuna say quietly, "*Assalamu alaykum wa rahmatullah.* Peace to you and God's mercy," ending her prayer. Then, "God, I can smell the wine from over here, Tein." She kicked her brother lightly, "Can't sleep?"

He moaned, stretching his arms over his head, "I could if you would stop with that relentless praying."

"Oh my sweet, lie down. I'm done."

He said, "I don't know if I can sleep anymore. Do you have any oil for the lamp?" He laughed, "I have to tell you, Zay, your sainthood game is off. Shouldn't you be lighting up the room at night with your luminous soul already?"

Zaytuna reached for her lamp, "Mother never lit up at night. If a woman's soul was going to be a lamp, it would be hers. I complained to Uncle Nuri about these stories once, he laughed at me thinking they were talking about real light. He said, 'When dawn breaks, one no longer needs a lamp'."

"Well, she couldn't see in the dark, either."

"That's not what he meant."

"Do you think people will tell stories about her someday?"

"Sorry Tein, I've got the lamp but no oil. We're stuck in the dark. What did you say?"

"Stories. Will people tell stories of Mother? Will anyone know her name?"

As usual, she turned his question toward her own thoughts, "Why did she never tell us stories of her life before she wandered? We don't know anything about who we come from. Our family. We've got nothing other than the drum and the beads."

"If we should've known, she'd have told us. She left all that behind."

"For God."

"Maybe for a different reason."

"I wish I could've asked her."

"Listen. I meant will the Sufis tell stories about her?"

She thought about it and said, "I've always heard stories of the women from years past at Uncle Abu al-Qasim's. Mustafa said he heard an Auntie reciting mother's poetry recently. I can't imagine the Sufis forgetting about her, forgetting about the women. If they go the way of the scholars, though…. Women are no better than donkeys and dogs to the likes of them."

"Mustafa is not like that."

"True, but it seems like the ones who are like that get control of everything. There were two fools out in front of the mosque today taunting the women."

"And how did that go over," he asked, knowing exactly how the women of the neighbourhood would handle it.

"They would have been knocked out flat if Mustafa had not shown up and tried to argue them down. Poor Mustafa. The women should have just hit the swine. The men weren't listening to him. What use is there in arguing?"

"Said my sister who loves to argue," his eyes closed slightly as he slid a bit more down the wall to get comfortable.

She ignored him, her gorge rising as she thought of Imam Ibrahim. She nearly spat, "One of our boys was killed by one of these scholars."

He sat up, "What?"

"Uff, probably killed. I don't know."

"Zay, make sense now, tell me."

"A boy who worked for Imam Ibrahim's household died last night. They think it was an accident, but there's more going on. I know it."

"Who in the world is Imam Ibrahim?"

"One of those hadith scholars trying to kiss the ass of the Caliph."

"That could be a thousand men."

"I don't know, Salman boasted about having the boy studying with him instead of the glorious Imam Ibrahim as-Silafi, so he must be important."

"The boy?"

"Zayd."

"This Imam Ibrahim doesn't live in al-Anbariyya does he?"

"You know him?"

"No, I saw Ammar this morning. He offered me a job, by the way."

"Oh Tein! But how? Your leg? the military…?"

"No, no. Ammar works for the police now. He was coming back from a house in al-Anbariyya when I met up with him. He said a boy had died in an accident."

"Work for the police! Tein, how will you do it? What have the police ever done for the likes of us? Are you to begin beating women and children simply because they are hungry? Men for demanding their rightful pay? You can't!"

"Relax. Ammar is an investigator. Not that kind of police. He investigates grave crimes."

"Grave crimes? Does that cover all the grave sins including fornication and adultery? Will you be pulling people from their beds and bringing them before the courts?"

"Zaytuna, would you calm down please. It's murder and assault. I'm to help him. You know, to handle things if anything gets out of control."

"I don't trust them."

"You'll trust the coin I'll be bringing home."

Zaytuna went stiff at the suggestion that she'd be pleased with more money. For him to suggest that money mattered to her, that they needed more, *walla*! Worse, how could he say that she wasn't doing enough for them. They did alright on what she made washing. They had food, a place to sleep. It's true the place was small, but they made it work well enough.

Tein asked with a tone of official certainty, a touch of pride in himself, "So what do you know about this boy's death?"

She heard his pride, then castigated herself for not seeing it. He needed the work for himself. But he wanted the work for her, too, to care for her. She smiled, feeling tenderness toward him returning to her, and comfort that he was there for her, and said, "I'm glad for you, Tein."

And then what he said hit her. Woman! She scolded herself, You are so slow! Then, "Tein, you will be working with the very man who is investigating the crime that I've been asked to look into, that I *am* looking into..."

Tein broke in, sitting up at it and leaned forward, placing both hands on the floor, "You are looking into...? What are you talking about?"

"I have to tell Ammar what I know. He'll be able to investigate it...."

"Zay, what are you going on about?"

"Imam Ibrahim's daughter. She was in love with the boy who died. It is the strangest thing, Tein. This girl, her name is Layla, came here and told me about it. Then I talked to the corpsewasher, and even the Imam's daughter."

She reached out to him, found his hand and pulled it to her, saying, "God Himself brought them all to me. And now you work for the man who is investigating it!"

"God Himself? What is all this, Zay? And where in the world would you have met a rich scholar's daughter?"

"Will you bring me to talk to Ammar?"

"Slow down."

"There's so much suffering in this world, Tein. But what do any of us do about it?"

"Fine, tomorrow, if it will calm you down. But I'm not sleeping anymore tonight. You better tell me everything. Tell me about this boy. Then get back to your prayers."

Thinking about what she'd done in bringing up Zayd's death, probably reminding him of his son, she reached out to him again and said, "Tein, I'm sorry, I shouldn't have brought up a boy dying, at this hour especially. I wish you'd never run off with those men to the Frontier to fight."

"The Sufis have been fighting on the Frontier since the early days."

Old resentments pushed up too easily, "Don't pretend you went off to war in the pious footsteps of Ibn Mubarak."

"Don't pretend you're our mother. Standing in prayer all night and not eating doesn't make you a seeker. When did you ever take the advice of our aunts and uncles?"

Cutting him off, "Be careful what you say now."

"Look, I had to get out of here. You wanted to be like Mother. I didn't. What good did any of her piety do us, Zay?"

She said what she always said, "You abandoned me."

"I'm tired of this, Zay. You had a home with Auntie Zaytuna and Mustafa. You had the whole circle of family at Uncle Abu al-Qasim's. How could you possibly have been alone?"

Zaytuna took a long breath, exhaling, saying, "I was without you."

He shook his head, "And if I had stayed here with you? You would have it so that I never loved Ayzit and my Husayn, *your nephew*, was never born?"

"I'm not saying that."

"You are, Zay." He got up, "I'm going to the cemetery to sleep."

"Oh Tein, stay. I'm sorry. Stay here, I'll go outside and share Saliha's mat. It'll be fine. Please stay."

"Zay, stop it. I'll be back first thing. We can talk about it then. If I can make sense of this, I'll take you to see Ammar." He walked out the door, finding his way through the sleeping bodies again, past Saliha, who did not call out to him this time, but who watched him go; he left Zaytuna in the dark, alone.

The Second Day

Chapter Fourteen

Zaytuna woke to the sound of the call to prayer. She felt for her jug to perform her ablutions, but there was nothing. She felt heavy. She could not, somehow, get out of her room, pick past her sleeping neighbours, to the deep basin of common water in the courtyard. She said to God, "You know me. Accept this dry ablution for the morning prayer," and she patted the mud brick wall with both hands, raising some dust and grit, wiped her hands together, her forearms, and then her face. She then pushed herself up, somehow, and stood, feeling her heart ease once she lifted her hands and brought them down, saying, "*Allahu akbar*, Surely God is greater than this," opening her prayer. Afterwards, she sat for a while, simply breathing, being with God, until she heard bodies moving out in the courtyard. Then she raised herself and stepped out into the dawn light and looked for Tein's sleeping body, but he was not there. Saliha's eyes were open and watching her. Saliha got up to go to her, stepping around her neighbours as they shifted, slowly coming awake. She put her hand on Zaytuna's dusty face, "You alright?"

"Tein and I argued last night and he left."

"I heard."

"I'm sorry. I thought we were quiet."

"I only heard because I was awake already. You didn't wake anyone here."

As the morning light grew brighter, people in the courtyard began to stand and shake out their mats. Zaytuna nodded to old man Qambar. He was sitting against a wall of the courtyard murmuring the long supplication he made everyday after the morning prayer. Only he would get up to pray in the morning like she did. If it bothered Qambar that his wife, Yulduz, rarely performed the ritual prayer, he didn't show it. He always looked at her with such a tender gaze of love that Zaytuna would blush for having intruded on them simply by seeing it. Zaytuna and the old man prayed together sometimes in the winter, when everyone slept in their rooms to stay warm and the courtyard was empty. The closest Shia mosque was too far for him to walk this early, so he prayed there and she followed him. What did she care that he was Shia? God is The Hearing of all prayers. Sometimes she would sit with him in the dark cool of the early morning as he recited the long supplication. She whispered "*amin*" after the sections that moved her most, especially, when things were most difficult, those verses where curses were invoked against the tyrants of this world. Qambar acknowledged her greeting and placed his hand over his heart as his lips continued to move, never missing a word.

Saliha said to her, "You need to drink some water and wash that face," She stepped inside Zaytuna's room to grab her jug, leaving Zaytuna leaning against the doorway of her room.

Zaytuna mumbled, exhausted, "The jug is empty."

Saliha turned back, going outside to get her own, but remembered there wasn't much there either. She checked the shared basin. There was too little there. She squinted back at the neighbours. Saliha had been refilling this basin too often. Umm Farhad's boy was old enough to start hauling water from the fountain. It was time his mother got him started. She was still hand feeding him as if he were a baby bird and as if they weren't poor as dirt and didn't need him to help out.

She called back to Zaytuna, "Just stay there, I'll be a second," and took the leather bucket by the basin out into the street to get water from the fountain in the square.

She turned out the door of their house onto the narrow passage that ran between the houses fronting their alleyway and there was Mustafa leaning against the wall, "Mustafa! How long have you been standing out here?"

"*Assalamu alaykum*, Saliha. I'm sorry. Not long, I came after the morning prayer. Is Zaytuna ready for a visitor yet?"

"You are family Mustafa. Go on. Everyone's waking up."

Mustafa entered the courtyard and found Zaytuna standing where Saliha had left her, staring at the pounded earth floor of the courtyard. He took her hand, "I've been thinking about you."

She shifted to look at him and the exhaustion of it all hit her. The loss of the child, the pain of all these children, Tein and his troubles, especially what she'd been through with the shaykh, and not knowing what she should do, that she fell into his arms and wept. He held her, feeling her body trembling under his hands. He wanted to pull her closer, but took a small step back so there was some measurable distance between them. She had to choose it.

He felt the trembling smooth out under his hands and all that was left was the sense of her thin flesh and bones under her *qamis*. He hated what she'd done to herself over the years. He pulled himself back to hold her face, wanting to say, "My love…", and instead saying, "My sister… God knows our broken hearts."

She raised her hand to wipe the tears from her face and he dropped his hands to his side. She asked, "How was the burial?"

"*Alhamdulilah*. Everyone he passed in the street lifted their hands in prayer for him. We stayed with him at the grave until he was in the hands of the angels."

"I should have followed."

"Some women came along, it would have been alright. No one was out 'forbidding the wrong', thank God."

"No, I meant, I was too busy talking to the housekeeper where Zayd worked and the Imam's daughter. I don't know why I bothered. Mustafa, what makes me think that I can make any difference in this world? It's nothing but arrogance."

"I'm not sure what you mean, Zay. It was kind of you to speak with them. Of course you made a difference."

Saliha came around the corner into the courtyard leaning to one side to balance the weight of the bucket she was carrying. Mustafa hurried to her to take it from her. She pushed him off with her free hand, laughing, "Please, the wet laundry I lift is heavier than the books you carry."

Zaytuna went and got their jugs and they filled them part way. Mustafa took a few steps away and turned his back to them as they wet a rag to wipe their faces and necks. Saliha winked and tipped her head in Mustafa's direction, whispering to Zaytuna, "So concerned for our modesty! When I walked out, you were in his arms."

Zaytuna shushed her, "Sal, he's like my brother."

They finished washing up and Zaytuna filled the cup again, "Mustafa, come sit down."

Saliha raised her eyebrows and smiled and mouthed to Zaytuna, "...like your brother," and carried her jug of water with her to her room to ready herself for work. Zaytuna and Mustafa sat with their backs against the wall in silence as they shared the cup of water. When she put the empty cup down, she said, "I spoke to Imam Ibrahim's housekeeper and his daughter, Zaynab, about Zayd. Mustafa, the girl did love him. Layla wasn't lying about it. Zaynab was distraught."

"Maybe she's just a sensitive girl. It seems hard to believe."

"Layla's story makes more sense now." She proceeded carefully, not wanting to accuse someone in Mustafa's presence just because she knew it to be true, "Maybe Imam Ibrahim had something to do with Zayd's death."

"Well, it wouldn't be the first time." He shook his head, "God protect us all. If these men can't find another way to control their families, they should let the scholars handle it. There are ways around these things. The Prophet himself tried to shield the culprits from punishment. It's better to insist that nothing happened and let it go. Of course, everyone's reputation will be ruined no matter the case, but better than a court-ordered flogging or, God preserve us from such evil, the family killing one or both of them then being executed for the murder they thought would set things right."

Zaytuna breathed sharply at him talking so blithely of men controlling their families and calling two innocent children in love, "culprits." She closed her eyes and tried to keep her voice steady. She needed him to help and arguing as they were used to would not incline him to her cause. "Would you ask around about Imam Ibrahim for me? Is there anything people might be saying about him that would help us understand what happened?"

"Zaytuna, I understand you feel like you want to do the boy's life justice, but listen to yourself. Zayd is already dead. If what you say is true and it came out into the open, the girl would be ruined and her father executed for murder. The housekeeper, what would happen to her? This kind of questioning might make things worse for everyone. Whatever happened, it's done. It happened in private. I am not going to go into people's homes like those Hanbali imposters who try to right a wrong and ruin everyone's lives. Frankly, I'm shocked you would consider doing the same or demand that I do."

She pulled back, objecting, "I'm not demanding. I'm asking. Mustafa, my heart is telling me…"

"Your heart? Do you think that Uncle Abu al-Qasim would approve?"

"No," she admitted, "he would not. He would tell me not to get involved. Or maybe he would," feeling the waves coming upon her, "I think he would."

"No," he said, crossing his arms. "He would not."

"You can just ask in a general sense, nothing about his daughter."

"Zaytuna…," Mustafa stood.

She took hold of a bit of his robe and looked at him, "Please."

"Everyone suspects this man is corrupt for taking money from the Caliph's people. No one respects him. But that doesn't mean he is a murderer."

She stood up alongside him, "Would you ask?"

"I will not. But tell me, what would you do if you did know anything of substance, meaning not what 'your heart' is telling you?"

She winced. She had frustrated Mustafa before, but he had never derided her. She looked at him and decided to carry on, with or without him, "*Insha'Allah*, I'm going to be meeting with an investigator in the police later today."

Mustafa's voice was firm, "Zaytuna, this must stop now. This is dangerous. The police won't care whose lives are ruined if they begin investigating this matter. The police do not work with God's mercy as their guiding principle. How can you trust them? We grew up under their thumb. Many here, under their boot."

"It's not really the police, it's an old friend of Tein. We're just talking. Besides, he already determined it was an accident and closed the case."

"God help me, Zaytuna! So what do you hope to achieve?"

He spoke so loudly, Umm Farhad stuck her head out of her room. Zaytuna smiled and waved, "Good morning Umm Farhad, it's going to be a beautiful day." The woman raised her eyebrows and ducked back into her room.

Zaytuna turned to Mustafa, who now looked chastened for raising his voice, and said to him sarcastically, "I don't know, Mustafa. I'm just trying to follow 'my heart'."

Mustafa said, "Look, I've known you since you were five years old, Zay. I've seen you follow your heart before. It hasn't always turned out as you thought."

"This is different."

Saliha came across to them, interrupting, "Okay Zaytuna, it's time to get to work. We have laundry for two houses today and we need to knock on more doors."

Zaytuna objected, "But I told Tein I would meet him here, he's going to take me to see Ammar. The man he works for in the police."

"Zay, I'm leaving to work. I need to work. So do you. Tein will find you. You two always find each other."

"I'm going to stay."

"But I need you. I cannot do two houses on time by myself." She turned to Mustafa, "Talk some sense into her."

Mustafa raised both hands in resignation, as if one could tell Zaytuna anything.

She paused only for a moment, "I'm sorry, Saliha."

"What is wrong with you? First you fight with Tein, then Mustafa, now you want to fight with me?"

"No, I meant I'm sorry, I'm coming with you!"

Zaytuna turned to Mustafa, "Will you ask around for me?"

He sighed, "I have to go to work now, but I'm going to see Imam Abu Abdelrahman al-Azdi recite hadith at the Sharqiyya mosque later today. If I can, then. If it's easy. And if it can be done without hurting anyone. Remember what the Prophet said 'God conceals the faults of the Muslim who conceals the faults of others'."

She whisper yelled after him, as Saliha dragged her out of their house, "Murder is not a 'fault'!"

Chapter Fifteen

Mustafa held his robe tight around his body against the crowd as he turned off the Basra Gate High Road toward the Sharqiyya Mosque. Book and paper sellers leaned across the street-side counters of their tiny shops looking for trouble coming their way, while customers took refuge inside, watching the crowd pass, from within, where it was safe and one could breathe. Other than a protest or a riot, only a renowned preacher or public recitation of hadith by one of the greats could pull this many Baghdadis out at once.

Common menfolk along with scholars and students jostled for space in the cramped street. The men were packed in, held in by the walls, shoulder to shoulder, front to back. Mustafa worried about tripping, sometimes missing a step as the crowd lifted him, here and there, heaving forward inch by inch.

He felt someone behind him tug on the tail of his turban, nearly shifting it off his cap underneath, then a strong hand landed on his shoulder and held on tight as a man pulled himself forward against him. Mustafa stiffened under the hand, inexplicably panicking, but managed to turned around enough to see who had grabbed hold of him.

"Ho!" The man called out, laughing at the fear on his face, "It's just me! Ya Mustafa! Were you expecting to be stabbed in this crowd? You hiding gold under that cloak?"

Mustafa laughed to shake off the shudder of fear he felt, "*Walla*, Abdelmalik, don't grab a person like that."

"I love this, Mustafa! Look at this crowd. Everyone wants to hear Imam Abu Abdelrahman recite Imam Malik's eighty hadith with the Golden Chain!"

He smiled at the thought of it. He never imagined he would have the chance to hear them from such a well-respected scholar, but more so from a student of one of Imam Malik's closest followers. That made him, Mustafa ibn Zaytuna al-Jarrari, the Potter, the son of Zaytuna, a housecleaner, in the

Golden Chain himself. Not officially. He wouldn't have a certificate to teach them. But in his heart, he'd be in the Chain. He recited the new chain within himself: He, Mustafa, heard it from Abu Abdelrahman al-Azdi, who heard it from Abu Ali al-Yamani, who heard it from Imam Malik, who heard it from an-Nafi, who heard it from Ibn Umar, who heard it from the Prophet himself. He spoke over the din of the crowd to Abdelmalik, "It *is* wonderful."

Abdelmalik said, "I saw Burhan earlier today. He was boasting how he had heard them from three different scholars, each one closer to Imam Malik than the last!"

"Yes, he never tires of telling everyone that sort of thing."

"It must be nice to have family, money, and connections."

"He's on his way to becoming important, no doubt about it."

"He never tires of telling everyone that, either." Abdelmalik laughed, "With great humility, of course."

Mustafa was drawn in despite himself, his voice tight with resentment, "When your father is a famous scholar, and you marry the daughter of a famous scholar, and you are sent off to study with all the famous scholars those famous scholars know, from one end of the Empire to the other, *and* you don't have to waste any time making a living, your knowledge and authority are most humbly attained, no doubt about it."

He thought of Ahmed ibn Hanbal, who lived with the people of Baghdad, as one of them, who cared for the people of Baghdad, as one of them. His mind turned to Zayd, dead, and no one to care for him. Except Zaytuna. He turned his face back to Abdelmalik, "Do you think Imam Ibrahim will be there? You know one of his students, don't you?"

"Of course he'll be there. You've never wanted to meet him before." He teased Mustafa, "I thought you were a Hanbali purist, staying away from those who attach themselves to the caliph's people."

"It's not that...I..."

"Look!" Abdelmalik pointed toward an opening onto an alleyway, "There's Sharafuddin!"

Mustafa was surprised to see him, "Wouldn't Imam Abu Abdelrahman be with Sharafuddin's father right now? What is Sharafuddin doing out here?"

Abdelmalik shoved Mustafa through the crowd ahead of him toward Sharafuddin who was standing tucked into the side street watching the throng pass by. Sharafuddin caught sight of them and waved, "Brothers, get over here!"

They broke through the crowd into the nearly empty side street with relief, laughing. Sharafuddin said, "This is surely God's will! I was hoping to catch sight of you! Would you like to meet Imam Abu Abdelrahman before he recites? He's sitting with my father now in our apartment. Come, please!"

Mustafa's heart nearly stopped at the thought of it, then the gratitude he felt for Sharafuddin for thinking of them sent a rush of heat up to his face. They would never have been able to meet such a man on their own in such intimate circumstances. He took Sharafuddin's hand and pulled him into an embrace in thanks, "May I have the opportunity to do you such a good turn someday, my brother."

Sharafuddin blushed, his head bowed slightly, and said, "If God wills. I'm sorry I couldn't invite you earlier, Father limited the guests since the Imam will only be here a short time."

Mustafa quickly checked his robe, making sure it had not ripped in the crowd. It was not new; it bore the marks of repairs, patches and little sewn over bits here and there. But he had no other. At least his turban was freshly washed. He thought of the man's spit on it and felt sick. He adjusted his turban over his cap to make sure it was straight. They walked through the warren of alleyways that turned around the great mosque, passing corner shops, and house upon house, each two storeys, most with perforated clay screens in the windows for privacy, others with imported intricately carved screened wooden window boxes leaning out over the street.

Sharafuddin said quietly, "Thank God the Caliph is not in the city or this would be even more impossible! His people would have to make an entrance, to be sure, to impress upon us all his great piety and attachment to the Prophet's example."

Abdelmalik said, "If the Caliph were in the city, it would be in his mosque. So thank God, he's not here." He slapped Sharafuddin on the shoulder, "You'd not be sneaking us in the back way then!"

They reached the door of Sharafuddin's family's apartment. Sharafuddin opened a small door in a long wall and ducked inside. They kicked off their sandals quickly and walked through a long hallway past the kitchen where Sharafuddin's mother and sister were busily preparing trays with their housekeeper to serve to the great Imam and guests. They slowed down and stepped carefully into the large, open room lit by oil lamps with some light shining in from high smaller windows that opened onto the mosque courtyard. Richly woven and embroidered carpets covered the floor from one end of the room to the other with layers of sheepskins set out around the walls to sit on and pillows made from fine, old carpets and embroidered linen to lean against.

They bowed their heads as they entered the room, each saying "*Bismillah*," stepping first with their right foot, then their left. Sharafuddin pulled them to the left of the room where he saw the elderly scholar seated consciously away from what would have been the place of honour, his legs tucked under him, his shoulders stooped, and his robes pooled around him.

Abdelmalik nudged Mustafa, saying under his breath, "Imam Ibrahim is the one sitting between Imam Abu Abdelrahman and Sharafuddin's father."

Mustafa said, disappointed, "And there is Burhan's father, in his tall judge's cap, on the other side, and Burhan tucked in right there. Why do I wonder at these things, Abdelmalik?"

Abdelmalik replied, "You have to get used to how things are, my friend. Being well-connected, making money, it doesn't make you a bad man."

Mustafa whispered, "Making money off the Prophet's words, God protect us from evil things."

Abdelmalik laughed under his breath, "There's my Mustafa, the Purist."

Mustafa shot back, "If you were raised in Baghdad, you'd not say that."

Abdelmalik poked Mustafa in the arm, "Look, Amina is here with her father. Maybe Sharafuddin will get a chance to talk to her today. We'll be hearing about that all week!"

Sharafuddin gestured to them that they could come forward to greet Imam Abu Abdelrahman. They kneeled before him and each took his hand to kiss, in greeting and in respect. As each put their head down, the Imam pulled each one's hand toward him, turning it over so that he might kiss the back of their hands instead. Mustafa blushed deeply at the gesture and began to stand to find a place to sit in the now crowded room, when the elderly Imam spoke to him, "Are you a scholar *and* a potter, my son?"

Mustafa looked at him with shock, and then shame. "Yes."

Mustafa heard Burhan tittering at his response, taking pleasure in the meanness of his employment being pointed out by the Imam. He refused to look, instead setting his eyes to the ground before him.

"Most of the scholars I meet in Baghdad have some other work they do, but typically it is administrative work or they educate children. It is a city rich in scholars, but I hear not in opportunities to be paid to teach from your years of study."

"No, but I'm grateful to have plenty of work with my hands."

"And what do you make?"

"Cooking pots and jugs, whatever the master requires."

"What have you made that was the most important to you?"

Mustafa felt like he could see Burhan laughing at him as this scholar asked him questions that he would a child. Not the sort of conversation the Imam must have been having with Burhan and the others before he came in. The shame gripped him as he thought of how he would have to answer that question, if he answered it honestly, and sadness overcame him. His eyes pricked with tears and he felt even more embarrassed.

No. He thought of Zaytuna who would not be ashamed. He would feel no shame for himself, his family, his people. He told the Imam the truth. Whatever came of it was meant to be, "An earthenware jug and cup I made for my cousin, well, not actually a cousin, but just the same to me. She collected the clay from the banks of a dried-up canal not far from the tomb of Maruf al-Karkhi. As I threw the clay, I said 'Allah' with each breath. Then I sent them to be fired reciting God's words, *We created humankind out of ringing clay from black mud, transformed.*"

The Imam nodded and asked, "And who were your teachers?"

"Abu al-Faraj al-Ibari and Idris Muhammad al-Habashi. I attend the circles of hadith whenever I am able."

"Who else was your teacher?"

"I beg your pardon?"

"You mentioned your cousin took the clay for the pot from Maruf al-Karkhi's tomb."

Here it comes, Mustafa thought. He knew he was about to hear the criticism of his Uncle Abu al-Qasim and the Sufis. He wished he'd not have to learn about the prejudices of this scholar he so deeply admired. He answered, "Abu al-Qasim Junayd who continues to teach me the inward path of the Prophet."

The Imam nodded, "Do you know how I knew you were a potter?"

"No."

"There are bits of clay on your turban from where you wrapped it today. I surmised you wrapped it right when you came from work." Then the Imam lifted his hands to the sides of his own turban, carefully removing it, the skull cap underneath coming with it, exposing his bald head, setting it into the hands of Imam Ibrahim sitting beside him. The room grew quiet. Mustafa was paralyzed at this show of profound humility. Here he had thought so ill of the man just a moment ago, and now he was, in effect, stripping himself of his status before them all. Mustafa looked at the ground out of respect, staring into the sheepskin before him, seeing every hair, which one curled, which grew straight, breathing as best he could, not knowing what to do next when he felt his own turban lift from his head.

He looked up into the eyes of the Imam, seeing the gentleness in them, as the Imam took Mustafa's turban and handed it to Burhan's father to hold. Burhan's father took it, but visibly did not like it. The Imam then turned to Sharafuddin's father and took his own turban, removing his skull cap, and placed it over the skull cap on Mustafa's head, saying, "Please take my turban as a gesture of thanks and recognition of your devotion to the Prophet's words despite the hardships you endure. Nothing could be closer to the Prophet's own example than hard work wedded to such devotion."

The Imam put on his own cap, then turned to Burhan's father and took Mustafa's turban from him and, pulling at it slightly to loosen it, placed it on his own head. He said, "I will be honoured to wear your turban today as I recite the eighty hadith from the Golden Chain."

Mustafa felt the heaviness of the Imam's turban on his shoulders and did not know if he could stand up from the weight of the gesture and began to shake. Sharafuddin and Abdelmalik saw and each took him by an arm and led him to the other side of the room where he sat in silence, gratefully between his friends, as Sharafuddin's mother and sister came in bearing trays of sweets and fruited drinks for the Imam and the guests.

Sharafuddin leaned over and whispered to him, "Please look at Burhan. I know you are overwhelmed right now, but you cannot miss the obsequiousness on his face."

Abdelmalik leaned in, replying, "I think he's about to tell the Imam he is a canal worker…".

Sharafuddin interjected, "No…" laughing quietly, "…a garbage picker."

But Mustafa could not look. He kept his eyes down, only looking up long enough to take the sweets offered to him from Sharafuddin's sister without knocking her tray.

Abdelmalik nudged him, "Take a bite of that *faludhaj* then tell me, why are you interested in Imam Ibrahim?"

Mustafa said, "It's just, well, a friend was asking about him. A boy died in his household. A servant. There was some question about what happened and my friend, well, my friend wondered if I knew anything about it. I said I would ask."

Abdelmalik and Sharafuddin leaned in to him, Sharafuddin saying, "A servant died? Then this is a matter for the police. If anyone knows anything they should speak to the police about it. Are the police involved?"

Mustafa answered, "Yes, they've questioned everyone in the household already."

Abdelmalik said, confused, "If the police have already handled it, then this sounds like indulging in dangerous gossip, Mustafa. That's not like you. Who is this friend?"

"No one you know. You're right." He knew he had tried to dissuade Zaytuna, the same as his friends were trying to dissuade him right now. Mustafa looked around the room. He couldn't very well ask which of the students here were Imam Ibrahim's now, could he? He felt like he had to have something to tell Zaytuna. He wanted badly to give her something, some news, that would please her and make her pleased with him. He looked down again, sullen now, rather than sweetly humbled by the Imam's gesture.

After a time, they filed out and into the front of the mosque where spaces had been saved for the guests of Sharafuddin's father. Mustafa looked over the crowd taking up every inch of the mosque. Repeaters stood along the walls to make sure that everyone even at the very back could hear every word of every hadith Imam Abu Abdelrahman would recite that day. There were so many men there they had spilled into the women's section such that any women who may have risked the streets to be there would have been pushed out of the mosque. Zaytuna would have had something to say about that. He wished he could pull the women back in and push the men at the back out, but this is the way things were.

Any female scholars and students, at least, would be here with their own teachers. They would have been given a special place; he was sure of it, well he hoped. Mustafa looked around but he only saw Amina, without her teacher, sitting just inside the door to the family apartment with Sharafuddin's mother and sister. He pushed his discomfort with it away, thinking, Maybe they did not want to come, and turned to sit down with his friends.

Imam Abu Abdelrahman finally came in, Mustafa's clay-stained turban on his head, and stepped halfway up the *minbar* so he could be seen and heard across the crowd. The Imam opened with the *basmillah*, recited prayers on the Prophet, his family and companions, and began the recitation of the first hadith. He gave the chain of transmission in a clear voice that carried easily to the first repeaters, "Abu Ali al-Yamani heard it from Malik ibn Anas who heard it from an-Nafi al-Madani who heard it from Ibn Umar who heard the Prophet Muhammad, *alayhi salam*, say…" The repeaters called out the chain of transmission, each in turn, until it had reached the back of the mosque and outside to the courtyard. The Imam waited until there was silence, then recited the hadith itself, "Ibn Umar who said, 'Men and their wives used to do their ritual ablutions together when the Messenger of God was still alive.'" And the repeaters turned to the back and recited the hadith until everyone had a chance to hear it.

Afterwards, as the people filed out, Sharafuddin left them and went with his father and the Imam back into the house. Mustafa and Abdelmalik made their way to a pillar and sat down. Mustafa took the Imam's turban off his head, and pulled his cap out from underneath, putting it back on his head and placed the turban next to him. A few of their friends came forward from where they had been sitting toward the rear of the mosque to sit with them.

Abdelmalik said to them, "Sit, sit! You have to hear about this!"

Mustafa's hand clamped down on his, begging him, "Please no."

Abdelmalik rolled his eyes, whispering to him, "They'll find out anyway."

"Not now, please."

"Alright," and turned back to the others when Sharafuddin came out of the door to his family's apartment back into the mosque whisper yelling, "Mustafa, Mustafa!"

As he reached them it came tumbling out, "The Imam decided to stay here a bit longer and hold some private classes. He specifically wants you to come to visit him starting tomorrow to copy down the eighty hadith *with* an *ijaza* certificate verifying you to teach them from him!"

Abdelmalik said, "Mustafa! Subhanallah! Hey, wait, what about me?"

"Ha! You too, but he asked for Mustafa specifically. He said he hoped you would find time to make him a jug and a cup like you did for your cousin before he goes."

"Unfortunately, Imam Ibrahim's students and Burhan will be there. But you cannot have everything."

Abdelmalik teased Sharafuddin, "Will Amina be there?"

Sharafuddin blushed, "*Insha'Allah.*"

Mustafa got up. Sharafuddin said, "Where are you going?"

"To collect the clay and make the Imam his jug and cup, of course!" And, to tell Zaytuna. She'd be so happy for him. But more than that, he'd be able to tell her that Imam Ibrahim's students would surely be there tomorrow and he could talk to them for her.

Chapter Sixteen

Salman sat slumped on his stool in front of his shop, alone. His body was tilted at a strange angle, his shoulder propped awkwardly against the outside wall. As people crossed the square, noticing him, they walked as far away from his shop as they could. Red liquid had soaked into the ground around him, turning dark brown as it mixed with the dirt. His clothes were soaked through with it. Saliha and Zaytuna could just see him in the last bit of the day's light as they turned into the square on their way home. The red stains stood out, stark against his white *qamis*. Saliha grabbed Zaytuna's arm and pulled her, saying, "He's hurt." They ran to him until the smell of wine hit them.

Zaytuna stopped running at the smell of it and tried to pull Saliha back, "It's just wine."

Saliha pulled her arm free from Zaytuna and kept going, turning back to her with a look that said, "And?" She reached Salman and knelt down before him, her *qamis* dragging in the wine-soaked dirt, asking, "Salman! What happened? Have you been hurt?"

He lifted his head, partially straightening up, he answered, "They kicked me, yes. But not hurt, I think." He sighed, "The wine, though."

"Who?"

"Religious scholars. I don't know them. I just saw white turbans, they wrapped them like Hanbalis, twisted under the chin they way they do. But which of them would do this? I kept my wine out of sight and they pretended not to know I served it."

Saliha looked back at Zaytuna, who had stopped at the edge of the shop's tables, then turned to Salman, saying, "Two men, one older, one younger, not even old enough to have more than a few beard hairs?"

His eyes opened wide, "Yes!"

Saliha said, "Bar Bar something's followers. Zay, what did Mustafa call him?"

Zaytuna stepped in a bit closer. "Barbahari, I think."

Saliha said, "That's him."

"Mustafa warned something like this would happen. He said they were out of control."

Saliha asked, "Zay, what if there had been a crowd of them?"

"Just what Baghdad needs, more pious riots," Salman managed a laugh.

Saliha said, "Good, you're laughing. That's our Salman."

Zaytuna raised her eyebrows at that.

Saliha didn't see it, she was looking over Salman, but not touching him, "Where did they kick you?"

"I'm afraid in the ass," he laughed, ashamed. "As I ran out the door of the shop…leaving them in there with my inventory."

Zaytuna pulled out a stool and sat down, tired, saying, "At least your ass is ample enough to cushion the blows. I'm sure you'll be fine."

Ignoring Zaytuna, he said to Saliha, "I should have stood up to them. The customers scattered when they saw them heading towards the shop. These men were determined. They had iron rods."

"Iron rods! There is nothing you could have done to stop them, Salman."

Salman finally turned his attention to Zaytuna, "This must bring you some satisfaction to see this 'grandson of a traitor' humiliated so."

Saliha looked at Zaytuna as if to say, "You're on your own here," and got up to go inside the shop and see the damage.

Heat rushed up from her gut to her head and right over her. She *was* satisfied. Her mind grasped at justifications so she would not have to admit to herself that she was the kind of person who would take petty satisfaction in the attack on him. He sells wine, what did he think would happen to him? As for the insult, she was angry at being caught out at that as well. She scrambled inwardly, not sure how to recover the situation other than just walk away or insult him further. It occurred to her that she could admit to something. After an uncomfortable pause, she settled on admitting to the insult alone, saying, "You've heard me call you that."

"Everyone calls me that."

"God forgive me."

"I'm sure He does."

"And you? Would you forgive me?"

Saliha called out from inside the shop, "They really did destroy all the wine. Too bad, you could use a cup right now."

Salman simply stared at Zaytuna, not offering the obligatory response that he accepted her apology.

Zaytuna felt it as if the hand of God Himself had slapped her. Her breath caught in her throat for a moment, desperate for a way to correct what she'd done. She tried, "Let us help you clean this up."

He looked her in the eye, "No, leave it."

"It won't take long," Zaytuna continued, ignoring him. She got off her stool and joined Saliha inside to pick up the broken pieces of clay jars and lay them outside the shop near the street to be taken by the garbage pickers another day.

He slumped further forward on his stool, elbows on his knees propping up his head. Sore assed and useless. Now women were going to clean up the proof of his cowardice. "The boys will be here tomorrow to help. There's no need," he nearly begged them.

Saliha heard the tone in his voice from inside the shop and stopped Zaytuna, taking the pieces of clay out of her hands and putting them back on the floor. Zaytuna objected, gesturing to Saliha, "Please, let me do this." Saliha ignored her and turned her around, walking her out the shop ahead of her.

"I need to help!"

Saliha whispered over Zaytuna's shoulder into her ear, "Not like this. This isn't helping."

Saliha pushed Zaytuna out towards the tables and stools and stopped before Salman, considering him. Not at all the type of man who held her interest, but he needed some of his confidence back and she needed what she needed. She nodded to herself inwardly, decided, then said to him, "I'm sure you can take care of it. But please go change, we'll wash that *qamis* for you."

Then, winking just a little, "Put on that dark green one that you look so handsome in."

He hauled himself off his stool to go inside, and as he stood, his great frame was a little straighter, feeling a touch more himself for her words. He managed to reply to her with a bit of a rakish smile, grateful to her, knowing full well that her compliment was charity. He was willing to take it, allowing himself to believe for a moment that this beautiful woman, Saliha, this bold Arab woman, always ready to laugh, with her creamy almond skin, round hips and bottom, heavy breasts, and long black hair tied, but falling loosely from under her wrapped kerchief, had ever thought him handsome in his ratty green *qamis*.

He came back in the green *qamis* as commanded and handed over his stained one to her, "My thanks for your kindness."

She replied, "No thanks necessary. Maybe I'll bring it back to you later. Tonight?"

He shook slightly, sore ass forgotten. She was serious. He managed to say, "If it is no trouble."

Zaytuna heard the proposition made and accepted, she looked around to make sure no one had heard them. There was hardly anyone in the square now. She sighed, thwarted from setting right her wrong and watching these two arrange to satisfy their petty urges.

Saliha indicated they were leaving, giving her greetings to Salman. Zaytuna stood still, her eyes unfocused but staring at the broken pieces of clay inside the shop and the red stained earth. She sat down on a stool, saying, "Salman, you mentioned the boys. Did you hear about poor Zayd?"

"Yes. I heard," Salman sighed.

Saliha interrupted, "Zay, now is not the time. Let's go."

Zaytuna raised her eyebrow, saying, "There's plenty of time to this night yet."

Salman laughed, "God willing."

Saliha laughed with him, "Really, Zay."

Salman spoke, considering that this beautiful woman might change her mind once she got home, and he wanted to keep her there, with him, a bit longer, "God have mercy on the boy's soul and beautify him in Paradise," shaking his head, "He was an ugly child."

Saliha audibly stifled a laugh.

Zaytuna caught it and shot Saliha a look, but this only served to release Saliha from her pent up laughter, "*Walla*, if we cannot laugh when tragedy strikes, we cannot laugh ever. And the boy *was* ugly."

"You're laughing at him, Sal. You are laughing at him for being ugly."

"He was ugly, but smart and charming, too," Salman cut in, adding with a nod and a smile, "Let us not forget that about him. That makes up for a multitude of inadequacies."

Zaytuna sighed, "May I die after the two of you, so my soul does not have to hear what you really think of me after I go."

"*Amin*, dear sister," replied Salman with feigned gravity.

Saliha asked, "Salman, what was he like?"

"He was a charmer and cunning. He could draw the birds to him from the trees with his song, then once in his grasp he'd carve them up and eat them for dinner. That nose of his made him so, I suppose. Who would love that boy as he was?"

Zaytuna nearly growled, "Listen to you, Salman! Certainly he was loved by someone!"

"Oh Zaytuna, your piety is so exhausting! But as it happens, he was loved, by two girls. That Layla you had by the hand the other day and, between us," he leaned forward so as to speak quietly, "the daughter of the stupendous Imam Ibrahim. He had those girls wrapped around his finger."

Zaytuna's stopped still. She stepped into the moment presented to her, asking, "How could the Imam's daughter have come to that, falling in love with him, right under the housekeeper's nose?"

"I don't know. But knowing Zayd, he'd know how to hide it from the old woman. Or maybe he had her tied up too."

"You make him sound like a horrible child."

"No, simply lonely. Wanting to be loved."

Saliha asked, "Did he love them?"

"God knows. It wasn't the sort of thing he would boast of in front of the boys and me."

Zaytuna asked, "Did you get any sense from him that the Imam knew?"

"Ah, I see what you are getting at. No, not that I heard. The boys though have their own theories. They say the old Jew, Umm Binyamin, from the Candy Seller's market poisoned him and he walked off the roof in a fit as a result."

Saliha interjected, "What sort of ridiculous notion is that? That old woman is too bitter to be allowed to sell sweets, but why in the world?"

"It seems our beloved Zayd was also a bit of a thief. He regularly stole candies from her shop and distributed them to the boys. I myself have been the recipient of several of these purloined delights."

Zaytuna said, "And the boys think she made him a special batch for him to steal and get poisoned. And somehow the other boys he gave them to were not poisoned as well?"

"According to them, this most recent batch he did not share with them, but took home hoping to present them to the girl, Zaynab."

Zaytuna replied, "Ridiculous."

"Yes," he said, adding sarcastically, "Much more likely that he was killed by the Imam. I cannot imagine that 'man' killing anyone. He is ineffectual, at best."

Saliha looked hard at him, triggered by his remark, "You know families do that. Men do that."

"As is their right."

Saliha spat the words at him, "It's not their right. It's illegal. It's murder."

"A man's right and what is legal may be very different things, my dear."

Saliha's anger flared for just a moment, then she fell cold to him, done. Saliha sighed, "Well, that's that then."

Zaytuna looked at her and smiled, hearing the shift in her friend's voice, and knowing full well what she meant. There would be no worries about Saliha sneaking past the torches of the night watchmen for the sake of this one.

Zaytuna asked, "Do you know why Layla came to see me? I didn't know these children beyond their running around the neighbourhood."

"Layla? I don't know. But I do know the boys respected you. Your spiritual athleticism impressed them. They didn't know how a woman could eat so little and be so utterly intimidating!"

Saliha might have laughed just a few moments earlier at this sharp observation of her friend, but now she was feeling that Zaytuna had been right all along about this man. It irritated her that she had to wash his enormous *qamis* at the end of a long day and, worse, there'd be no sex now.

Zaytuna was confused, "Intimidating?"

Saliha rolled her eyes, thinking how thick Zaytuna could be, and put her hand on her arm to indicate she wanted to leave.

Zaytuna ignored it, "When Layla and I saw you in the street that morning, she pulled on my hand to get away from you. Why would she do that?"

"Ah," he said, "I wouldn't let her study with the boys. I shooed her along, perhaps a little too strongly and I frightened her."

"I don't understand. You wouldn't let her hear the stories of the Prophets? Why not?"

"No," he said, "I wouldn't teach her how to read and write with the boys."

"You teach the boys to read and write!"

His voice deepened with indignation, "It is not as if they had the money to attend classes. By my grandfather's memory, these children will be scholars someday! They are going to make something of themselves! These boys did heavy labour all day and then they stole whatever time they could from their masters to memorize the Qur'an at the mosque. That's how they all met, filthy working boys washing in the fountain outside the mosque so they could make themselves acceptable to memorize God's Word. They carry the whole of Qur'an memorized in their hearts, each of them is a *hafiz*! They sat in on the open hadith lessons, too, but no one would teach them to read and write beyond the basics without payment. So now they steal time to study hadith under me and are learning to write them down."

Salman began to get angry at the thought of it, his voice rising, "These boys are good for nothing but hard work in the eyes of the rich. To me, they are much more. Why do you think that Imam's little daughter fell in love with our Zayd? Because he could read! Because I taught him hadith! Her father taught her and I taught him."

Zaytuna said, "Salman, I thought you were only telling them stories…."

"I teach them, just like my grandfather did. I teach them from my grandfather's collection of hadith. It won't be lost just because he couldn't hold out against the Caliph's inquisitors. These boys will receive certificates for the transmission of this collection someday."

"Salman," Zaytuna asked, knowing the answer but needing it said aloud, "Why not Layla, too?"

"I need to have the highest standards, for God's sake. No one will be able to fault these boys because I compromised the ethics of their education by including girls in our humble schoolroom."

Saliha now spoke, the exhaustion of the day hitting her and her exhaustion with this man hitting her even harder. She counted her points out slowly on her fingers, "You sell wine, you drink wine, your grandfather was a coward and a traitor, but somehow an innocent girl learning to read and write is going to bring your reputation down?"

He sighed, "What you say about me could be said of others. People don't know what the scholars are like. They speak in high tones, correct the simple man's grammar, and, as the joke goes, will accept a cup of wine if they cannot determine it is not juice with absolute certainty. They are people just like anyone else. Some are better than others. And we have our greats, of course. All to say, Saliha, I have sat in that back room and discussed hadith over a cup of date wine or much more with some of these revered scholars. And I keep their secrets."

He leaned in toward Saliha, nearly taunting her, "I heard from one there is at least one great legal scholar who has reasoned some forms of alcohol are permissible! Do you want to know who it is?"

Zaytuna replied, sharply, "No need to spread lies!"

He continued without concern, "It is no lie. Of course, everyone disagrees with him, most sharply his own students and colleagues. As a scholar, I must admit its prohibition." He laughed lightly, "But as the man who runs this humble tavern, I take heart in his reasoning nonetheless."

His back straightened, and he became serious again."Now, as for my grandfather, I will tell you that no one outside of Baghdad cares that he collaborated with the inquisition and no one will care in the years to come. His collection will be quoted and he will be remembered. *Insha'Allah*, I will be remembered as his faithful transmitter and teacher to these boys. But a woman unrelated by blood or milk here? That is another matter."

Saliha said plainly, "You were willing to screw 'an unrelated woman' in that backroom classroom a few minutes ago."

Salman winced at her vulgarity, "I gather it does not make sense. I also gather that you will not be returning to me tonight, and I am sorry for it."

"You 'gather' right." Saliha shook her head as if to shake loose some understanding of all this. "But the Imam's daughter. She is allowed to study?"

He looked at Zaytuna, tired, "You can explain this to her."

Zaytuna answered Saliha, "She is his daughter. They are related. There's no scandal in him instructing her so closely."

Saliha looked at her, "You don't approve of this, him not teaching girls, do you?"

"Saliha, who do you think I am? I was taught alongside Mustafa and Tein and the other children at the Shaykh's circle!"

Salman spoke over them both, "By Zayd's account, Zaynab never leaves the home unattended and studies under her father's watchful eye, no other. It's perfectly acceptable and she will be in a long line of female hadith scholars who learned under the guard of their modesty."

Zaytuna came back at him, "Who have the luxury to guard their modesty. Where does that leave women without connections, without wealth?"

"You can sit in the mosques like everyone else and listen to the Imams teach."

"You know it's not that simple. Look at you! Even the poorest boys have a better chance of being taken on than a woman."

Saliha stood, tossed his *qamis* on the table before her, "Enough of this man. We're only good for fucking and washing his shirt. *Walla*, I won't wash his shirt either!" She stepped out onto the square and walked in the direction of the alleyway to their home.

Zaytuna picked up his *qamis*, folded it over, and handed it to him, "That's how it is." She paused not sure if she should speak, but then decided, yes, that she would. "I am sorry I took satisfaction in your situation and that I've insulted you all these years. That was wrong of me and I'll answer for that to myself and to God. To you, I apologize sincerely. I respect what you are doing here with the boys no matter why you do it. I'm grateful to you for that much. But I don't like anything else you do here."

Salman took the stained *qamis* from her and nodded, "Fairly said. Thank Saliha for me, and thank you, for looking in on me. You surely did not have to do so. No one else bothered. I won't forget that."

Zaytuna hurried to meet Saliha, who by then was nearly at the opening to their street off the square, and put her arm around her shoulders. Saliha leaned on her.

"What a pig-headed fool," Saliha said, looking up at her. "You'd think he'd be able to hold his opinions to himself for one day. I sorely needed a little nighttime marriage."

Chapter Seventeen

It had been a long day. It had been an even longer two days since Layla came in and gave Zaytuna the news that Zayd had been killed. Every nerve was frayed. Every bit of her heart spent on this, on them, on herself. Zaytuna looked forward to just lying down. Just this once, she pleaded with herself, she would not stand in prayer late into the night. She promised herself she would sleep a while then wake up to pray in the last third of the night. Prayer would help clear her mind, but now she needed sleep. She pushed aside the curtain and ducked in only to trip with her first step over Tein's body splayed out on the floor, sleeping soundly. She caught herself against the wall to keep from falling over him, but allowed herself a little kick to his side, that she could have avoided, to wake him up. She moved across him to the corner and sat down in the small space left to her. He kept sleeping.

It was too dark to see, but she knew he had been drinking. She could smell the alcohol on him, and she could smell him on him. She wondered what he'd been rolling in that night. He hadn't smelled this bad the night before. He was lying on her mat, probably her blanket too. No doubt working his stink into them. She wouldn't even be able to take them out to make a bed in the courtyard. Maybe she could crawl in with Saliha. Making a decision, she felt around on the reed mats and found her blanket under his legs. She yanked at it until it came free and finally there was a sound out of him, "Uff, what?"

"Get up you filthy man and go outside. You smell and I need to sleep."

Tein pulled himself up, leaning against the wall, no longer heavily drunk and not happy about it, "Where were you today? I came back here for you."

"I had to work, Saliha and I had two houses and…"

"I had to work, too."

"So maybe we can talk to Ammar tomorrow?"

"Ammar told me not to come back until I'm clean. He threw me some money to get to the bath, but I spent it on wine."

"I can smell that. You weren't at Salman's. His wine jars were smashed."

"What," he said, coming awake. "Poor man! A true servant to the community. Well, he can't complain to the police. He could, to me, but there'd be nothing I could do about it. Only the Caliph's wine jars being smashed would be cause to action there."

"Tein, how are you going to do this job? Are you going to turn corrupt, too?" She shook off the thought, "In any case, Salman knows who did it. Religious fanatics. Nothing to do about that."

He lifted a drunk finger to point at her, "They're everywhere," but she couldn't see it in the dark.

"It's better if I see Ammar tomorrow, anyway. Tein, I found out something important today. I have more to tell him."

"I'm sure he'll be all ears, if I'm clean."

"I got paid. I'll give you enough for the bath and wash your clothes in the morning. You'll be fine. You'll take me to meet Ammar."

"Alright, then." He began to slide down the wall to go back to sleep.

She heard him slide down and felt him push against her legs, "No you don't, brother of mine. Get out into the courtyard, you smell."

Tein rolled over onto all fours and crawled out through the curtain and fell asleep in front of the door, curled up, as their mother used to say, like the dog guarding the Seven Sleepers in the Cave. Zaytuna felt for her fishskin mat and blanket and sniffed them; they would do, she whispered, "*Alhamdulilah.*" Then she shook them out to get whatever might have been on Tein off them. Lying down on her side, she held her wool blanket against her through her legs and arms. For the first night in a long time she felt the sharpness of her bones against the hard earth underneath her and she shifted to find a comfortable spot. She heard her mother's voice, always reminding her whenever she wished aloud they had sheepskins to sleep on, "The Prophet told us that the earth said to the child of Adam, 'You put a cover between you and I? Yet tomorrow you will be inside me'," and she felt the ground soften underneath her. She fell into the softness, enveloping around her, the warm animal smell of the blanket following her down, and dreamed.

She found herself walking up an old dried river bed. She noticed a stream of water ahead, coursing through it, down toward her. She pulled up her *qamis*, but it and her *sirwal* were somehow already wet. Water pushed up against, then flowed around her calves, in thick, glossy ropes. She had never seen this stream before and wondered how she did not know it. The water was cool and clear, the stream bed of tumbled smooth, translucent gems were refracting the white light, that came, it seemed, from all directions, into sparkling, glittering multi-hued feelings that alighted on her. She looked down at the colours shining, flitting, then dissolving and soaking into her, flowing through her, then beyond her. She did not know what to do with all of them. One after another, she witnessed so many coloured feelings coursing through her, overtaking each other. One would divert the stream of another. One would mix, just so, with the jewelled light opposite it, transforming its coloured feeling to a new course. Then a different colour would come and push those back until they were transmuted into another newly discovered emotion, finding a different way through her, while still another saturated them all with its light. Feeding them all. The light behind the light. She wondered at it. It announced itself to her, saying, "I am Love."

Suddenly, rusty-blue lapis vengeance rushed up, thickly, clinging, and she saw her hands around the throat of the man who raped her mother that night. Streaming in from the deepest river, the clearest emerald water swirled knowledge around her, pushing her to turn and look into his face until the peridot green of small spring leaves brought awareness of the shape of his features to her. It was not that one, the one whom she saw rape her mother, but another man. She saw, as if through a mirror of shining, transparent ruby, her own face overlaying his own. She dropped her hands from his throat and placed them over his heart. Opalescent blue sorrow overtook her as the sapphire blue of his desire to dominate thrust through her and took form in her womb. She looked down at her growing belly and saw her mother's hands holding it as if it were her own, caressing it and cradling it like a full moon shining silvery light through everything. Rivulets of sun-bright amber acceptance found their way through her, gently saturating her, tugging her down with its glorious weight until she was sitting in the stream while the white light of joy flowed through it all. She could have laid back into the stream and breathed its waters into her lungs and died there with joy flowing through her. But she pushed herself up with her hands. Then her feet. She found her way to standing again in the stream. Walking again.

The stream's light dimmed as she walked. The city fell away behind her. The world fell away around her. The stones in the bed darkened. A pool was ahead. She could just see it. She walked to it. The water deepening. She was up to her waist in it. The water had no light. The sky had no features. Blackness embraced her. A blackness that accepted all light, rejecting nothing. The edge of the pool went to the horizon. First light arrived in the distance, only a thread of golden blackness illuminating the far, far edge of all things. It grew, the deepest brown, red and golden, slowly filled the sky with its warmth and clarity. Her eyes adjusting, taking in more, in every moment until she saw that the golden encompassing blackness was her mother. Her arms filled the horizon from East to West. Her mother's body held every direction. She saw then, slung across her, one on her front and one peeking up over her back, two children, and two more by her legs. Layla held on in the front, her hands grasping at the thick fibres of the wool of her mother's rough *qamis*. She was too big to be held this way, yet it was natural. Her mother did not stoop or hunch over, either, at the weight of Zayd laid across her back, his arms around her neck, his head on her shoulder, secure in his own sling. A boy, a large boy, held onto one of her legs. God, how he looked like Tein. She wanted to reach out to him, to hold him. A girl held onto the other. The girl hid her face, but Zaytuna saw the clothes were fine and realized it had to be Zaynab. Her mother spoke. Her words like a bell sounding, peeling through Zaytuna's every cell, "My babies. Take care of them."

The Third Day

Chapter Eighteen

Zaytuna slept beyond the dream and did not wake; she did not even hear the morning call to prayer. She would not remember her dream, but only feel its aftermath. Tein opened the curtain and found her, lightly snoring, curled over on her side, her blanket twisted around her.

Tein pushed her lightly with his foot, "Look at you, still sleeping! It's light out, Zaytuna."

Tein laughed at her, "What will God think? Did you even do your morning prayers?"

Zaytuna tried to pull herself up, but her limbs were stuck, as if her blanket were a rope tying her down. She insisted, "I'm awake."

She managed to get up and meet Tein in the courtyard. He was sitting against the wall watching Qambar recite his morning supplication. Then the old man pushed himself up off the ground, holding the wall to stay steady. He straightened himself and called into the room he shared with his wife, Yulduz, who came out and spoke with him for a moment. Tein heard her say, "I'll meet you there, *insha'Allah*." Tein wondered if they were heading out to work. They were too old for it. Although she was older than her husband, she was sturdier than he. He was surely too old to lift anything anymore. He had large hands, but he could see that the joints were swollen and his fingers bent.

He called out to the old man, "Where are you off to today?"

The old man answered, "Cut reeds," and no more.

Yulduz came out and handed him his sandals, "You'll cut your feet up to a bloody pulp on those reeds. Put these on, I'm not losing my man today. I'll be down there before long."

Tein stiffened as she said it and wished he had some coin to give them so they would not have to go to cut reeds today, or any day.

His wife raised an eyebrow at Tein, "And you? Now that you're police? What're you off to do today?"

Tein answered, "Kill children. Then we'll roast them on a spit."

Zaytuna slapped his arm and then turned to her, "Auntie Yulduz, he's not that kind of police."

Yulduz spit out at Tein, "There's no other kind of police."

She turned to Zaytuna, "What do you think's going to happen if trouble comes down. Will he be on our side?"

"Of course. What a thing to say," not admitting her own fears aloud.

Zaytuna went to the communal basin for water for her ablutions. She breathed out, "*Bismillah*," and squatted in front of it, using the cup to pour water into her right hand. She put the cup down and rubbed her hands together, washing them. She cupped more water to clean out her mouth and nose and spat it out into the small bricked pit dug beside the basin. She poured more water into her right hand, bringing it to her face, rubbing out the grit from her eyes. Then again, but this time letting the water drip down her arm and rubbing her right forearm with her left hand. Then the same over her left arm. She wet her right hand again and rubbed the top of her head and cleaned her ears. Finally, she washed her feet, propping out her right foot first on its heel to rub the water all through it. Then the left. "*Alhamdulilah.*"

Then she stood and returned to her room to pray. Her forehead and nose were pressed against her mat when the fragrance of freshly baked barley bread hit her and she felt her mouth water. She breathed in the moist scent deeply as she sat back on her haunches and said, "*Alhamdulilah*, praise God" instead of "God forgive me," and prostrated again. She finished her prayer and tried to force herself to sit through her supplication, but couldn't think to finish it. She got up and went outside saying, "God you know me. I don't know what this is about. Guide me to what is right and beautiful, *ya Rabb!*"

Saliha was chatting with Yulduz who had spread her mat out on the ground. Saliha tore the bread into pieces, putting each piece down in a pile next to a palm leaf basket of fresh cheese. Then she stuck her hand into a large sack, pulling out handfuls of soft, dark dates and placed them into a pile. Saliha took a square of cloth from Yulduz, she placed a bit of the bread and cheese into it, along with a handful of dates, "For Qambar."

Yulduz took the folded cloth from her and kissed it, then placed it to her forehead before setting it aside, "May God restore to you what you've shared with us."

Saliha said, "*Amin.*"

Looking up, nodding to Zaytuna, she said, "Breakfast."

Tein moved over and sat next to the old woman, saying, "You'll eat with police?"

She shrugged, "Cheese, yes. But you smell like you rolled in a dead animal." She shifted away from him.

Zaytuna laughed, "That's exactly what I thought!" She smiled at Yulduz. She could see why Qambar would leave his Shia family behind for this Turkmen woman. She must have been a wild mare when she was young. Zaytuna heard her stomach grumble and laughed at herself. She was hungry for the first time in a long time. She looked down at the feast before her, wondering at not being repulsed by the scent of the bread and the moist sheen on the fresh cheese.

Zaytuna ducked back into her room and opened the box where she kept her spare things. She crouched before it and pulled out a spare *qamis* and *sirwal*, folded rags for menstruation, if she ever did menstruate again, and her spare wrap. Underneath them all was a folded square of rough, patched wool fabric. She opened it revealing a strand of prayer beads, eleven delicate, amber-coloured glass cylinders loosely strung on a long leather thong. The edges of the amber cylinders were cracked and cloudy from abrasion but she thought that they were even more beautiful for it.

Her mother had made two of them, one for her and one for Tein after they were born, from her own necklaces. The thick strings of beads her mother wore around her neck and threaded through her locks were all that she took with her from her village when she headed out to be away from people, to be alone with her Lover. Over the years, she had restrung her beads into bracelets as gifts in thanks for those who had cared for them on the road and until all she had left were the stone beads and one opalescent cowrie shell she wore in her locks. But even the shell she gave away, to Mustafa's mother, stringing it on a thin braid made from colourful, discarded

fabric. The stone beads, Zaytuna wore in her own hair. She knew Mustafa
kept the shell necklace among his cherished things, put aside after his mother
died, but she wondered if Tein still had his beads. Perhaps he'd put it on his
own son's neck after he was born and buried it with him. As a child, she'd
worn her own around her neck every day. She rolled them in her fingers as if,
by some incantation, they bound her mother's love to her.

As a child, she took them off to rub them, pushing them along the leather
thong, mimicking her mother who did her own prayers on a length of
knotted string, until one day the thong wore through and the beads scattered.
She had panicked, barely able to breathe, until she and her mother had
crawled on hands and knees and found every last bead and strung them up
again. Zaytuna kissed the string of beads, laying it back into the patched wool
square, placed the folded square in the box, carefully putting her spare things
over it as protection. She stood, pushing herself up off her knees and went
to the door. She pulled the curtain aside, held the wrap out to Tein, and said,
"Get in here and change into this. We'll get you off to the bath after we eat."

He pulled himself up and came to her. She didn't move out of the way
immediately, but rather touched his face, holding his chin lightly and rubbing
her thumb across his cheek. She admired how strikingly handsome he was,
with their mother's beautiful, glowing, ruddy brown skin, her high
cheekbones and full lips. His face was so smooth despite everything he'd
been through, and always with only a bit of beard on his chin. She heard
herself say inwardly, *Alhamdulilah*, my God, thank you for him, thank you for
everything. He held her eyes for just a moment. She saw him softening to her,
his sister, before looking down. She thought she saw his eyes wet with tears.
Or maybe she mistook it. Either way, she smiled at him, tugging his face up
to meet hers again. She pulled on his bit of beard lightly, and said, "Make
sure and get that scruff under your nose trimmed."

She left him and sat down next to Saliha. She breathed in the sight of the
feast before her, then tore off a bit of bread and used it to grab a small bit of
the fresh cheese. She brought it first to her nose, awakening to its clean scent,
and said, "*Bismillah*, O Nourisher, open our hearts to the blessing of this food
and may all your creatures enjoy your open-handed generosity."

Yulduz sighed, "*Amin*," and dug in.

Saliha tensed, sitting perfectly still, as she watched Zaytuna place the food in her mouth, close her eyes, and chew slowly, the muscles on her face relaxing into the pleasure of it. Saliha imagined Zaytuna feeling the soft resistance of bits of barley that had not been fully ground mixed with the rest. She saw her mouthing the bread first for gravel so she did not break a tooth. Then she imagined Zaytuna tasting the smoke of the bread baked near the ashes in the local oven setting off and heightening the rich flavour and grassy tang of the sheep-milk cheese. Zaytuna swallowed and opened her eyes and breathed deeply. As her hand went back in for another bite, Saliha finally relaxed and took hold of a bit of bread and cheese for herself.

Tein came out of Zaytuna's room and walked toward them. Saliha looked up and held still again, moving only to put down the food in her hand. Zaytuna's worn-thin wrap was wound around Tein's waist. His chest was bare and his head was uncovered showing the shape of his skull and his tight black curls shorn close. Every scar from his years of battle showed on his muscles, the worst one snaking up the curve of his bicep, over his shoulder, nearly reaching his throat where, Zaytuna had told Saliha, the wound had nearly killed him. All of this brutal masculinity framed a face of extraordinary beauty, even delicacy, thought Saliha. Saliha had never seen his mother, but her beauty must have been a thing of legend. She stared at him openly, unashamed, thinking, If only for a bit of kohl around those eyes. She picked up her bread and cheese again, placing it in her mouth, and tasting with joy every flavour and texture as Zaytuna did, then said, looking at Tein, as he sat down with them, "Delicious."

Zaytuna looked up from the food, "Yes, *alhamdulilah*." Then she saw what Saliha meant and laughed, saying, "You know what the Prophet, *alayhi salam*, said, 'The first look is for you, and the second look is against you!'"

"Yes," Saliha replied, nodding, eyes still on Tein, "So lengthen the first look."

Tein smiled despite himself, forgetting in that one moment, that enjoying her, the way she was looking at him and the way she looked to him, was a betrayal of Ayzit and a reminder of his failure to save her and his son.

Chapter Nineteen

Mustafa sat against a pillar in the Sharqiyya mosque, waiting for Imam Abu Abdelrahman to begin his class. He had come early to spend some time remembering God, hoping to centre himself, sort out how to do what he'd promised Zaytuna. His friends' accusations picked at him: He should leave the investigation to the police. His meddling amounted to gossip. Then there were his own self-recriminations: He gave in to Zaytuna too much. She wasn't paying attention to the harm she could cause. He couldn't be involved in that. He couldn't ask. He wouldn't ask. But maybe he should ask? He put his hands out before him, looking at his palms, and prayed, "God, protect me from harming others without realizing it. Protect me from harming others with realizing it. Guide me in this matter with Zaytuna. I don't know what to do. God bless the Prophet and his family, and peace."

He wiped his hands across his face, trying to pull in the answer to the prayer held out to God. He tried to settle himself. Starting the recitation slowly, breathing easily and deeply, he began, "Allah, Allah, Allah," over and over. Each "Allah" said with a single, full breath. Breathing in on the "Ahhh….," taking it deep within him until his chest fully expanded, then exhaling, "…llaaaaah," the sound vibrating within him, grounding him and little by little releasing him from himself. Despite the cool damp of the early morning, he began to feel warm, relaxed, and thick with well-being. He could still hear murmuring in the background, not disturbing him, but somehow all of a piece, he began to hear teachers taking their places near the pillars in the mosque and their students mulling and sitting around them. His attention turned from his breath to a teacher's voice, somewhere in the mosque, asking, "What are the stipulations of inheritance if a man dies leaving only his wife and a daughter?" He brought his attention back to his breath before the student's answer came, breathing in deeply again, then exhaling, his own hearing tuned solely to his breath vibrating in his body as the student's answer somewhere in the distance dissolved into nothing.

"*Assalamu alaykum*," the words jolting him back into the room. Mustafa's eyes opened suddenly. It took him a moment to feel where he was; he put his hand on the leather folder next to him that held his paper to copy the first of the hadith, the cool metal of his inkwell, and the rib on the back of his reed pen laid out next to him. He looked up and saw Burhan staring down at him as if he, Burhan, were seeing some strange animal for the first time. Mustafa wondered how long he had been standing there watching him do his *dhikr*. He felt as if Burhan had seen him without his clothes on and was dumped from his state of well-being into humiliation.

"Is that something you Sufis do?"

Mustafa answered too quickly, defensively, missing a better response, "It is something the Prophet did which he taught to Ali and which is testified to in God's word, *Say Allah...*"

"Ho! I wasn't accusing you of heresy, my brother. That was before our time. My father remembers it quite well. He knew Ghulam Khalil, of course. By all accounts, a pedant preacher, but loved by the people. It's a bit embarrassing for you Hanbalis that he was so widely admired, I imagine. But the people do love anyone who can stir them up. Unfortunately, he had connections in court. So that was that. But everyone got out of it alright, so no harm done in the end."

Mustafa closed his eyes and tried to pull back the feeling of deep rootedness he had reciting the name of God and failed, saying with real bitterness instead, "Yes, no harm done."

Burhan agreed, "Exactly."

Mustafa took hold of his reed pen, pressing the tip of his thumb against its sharpened end.

Burhan saw him reach for the pen and said, "What a blessing we have the opportunity to write down these hadith directly from Imam Abu Abdelrahman al-Azdi."

Mustafa replied, "We are indeed fortunate," in such a way as to cut off conversation. Burhan did not reply. He wished Burhan would wait for the doors to open somewhere else, go for a stroll around the mosque. Pray. Something. The pause lingered just a moment too long.

Burhan broke the silence, "What an interesting story you told about the jug you made. Is that a typical Sufi practice?"

"If you want to learn more about our way of life, Burhan, you are welcome to come and see Shaykh Abu al-Qasim al-Junayd."

"I hear he is a formidable man."

"A great scholar as well."

"In name only."

"Excuse me?"

"I've heard Father say he only pretends to be a jurist when opportunity strikes."

"I would take care here, Burhan. Insulting those brought near to God never ends well."

"Another one of your quaint beliefs, like making jugs….," then with a questioning dip of the head, "and cups for mysterious female cousins?"

Mustafa turned his head away from him, looking to the door of the Imam's home, willing it to open. Uncle Abu al-Qasim most certainly did not need his defence although he sorely wanted to give it.

Burhan changed tack, "I wonder if you saw a most interesting case tried here last month?"

Without propriety, Mustafa pretended he did not hear him and looked around the mosque, everywhere except at Burhan standing before him. Then he closed his eyes and took a breath, asking God, Why is he on me like this? Then the image of Imam Abu Abdelrahman taking his turban off his head and replacing it with his own came to him and he understood. How could he be so stupid as to not recognize Burhan's jealousy and not expect this kind of attack. His anger and frustration ebbed into something like pity for Burhan. Mustafa opened his eyes and looked up at him, calmer now, and replied to him, "What case?"

"Sherwan Ibn al-Salah al-Kurdi filed a complaint with the court on behalf of a slave girl who had complained to him about her master, perhaps you know him, Hashim al-Qatifi? She claimed he was harming her and preventing her from worship. The harm, she said, was rape. Absurd of course, a slave cannot be raped. One cannot rape that which you have the right to do with as you please. So this girl would pray long hours into the night until her master would fall asleep. At first he did not pressure her, but after a few weeks of this, he spoke to her about it. She did not relent, so he put a stop to it. He took her whenever he liked from then on out, middle of a prayer or not. She testified that he would pull her off her rug or even pull down her *sirwal* and take her from behind when she was bent over in prayerful prostration. He himself admitted to all this before my father."

The calm that Mustafa had grasped for himself fled him. From the first sentence he knew where the story was going. He grew up around the frank talk of women. He knew what men were capable of doing and he knew how women had to bear up under it. Once, in his teens, mimicking the men in the neighbourhood, he told his mother that a woman known for her sharp tongue would do better if her husband took a stronger hand with her, and his mother had clapped him so hard aside his head he'd seen stars. Listening to Burhan now, he began to shake, spitting out in a near whisper, "He'll take his place in hell for that."

Burhan laughed, "Well, that was up to my father. If it were to be decided that the man had the legal right, then what sin was there in it?"

"Why did you raise this case with me?"

Burhan pushed him, "Don't you want to know what happened?" Burhan waited a moment, pleased with the look on Mustafa's face, mottled by anger now. He continued, "Ibn al-Salah knew better than to argue the right of the man over her. That was indisputable. He argued instead that the judge should force her master to free her due to her great piety. He said he himself would arrange the payment and promised far more than she was worth on the open market. He quoted all the relevant verses from the Qur'an and hadith on freeing slaves, especially pious slaves, quoting, of course, *If you know something good of a slave, free them....*"

Mustafa finished the verse, "*...and do not compel your enslaved women into fornication.*"

Burhan laughed, "Just so. Nevertheless, it is not fornication, nor compulsion, if a master has sexual rights over his slave. The master was a jurist himself. He knew all this and correctly argued that his sexual rights over the girl were well-established in law. He said that while pious injunctions are well-meaning, they are not legally binding, especially here, since her piety was not proven by her habit of praying at length."

Mustafa's anger broke through, "How in the world could her prayer be proof that she was not pious?" But as he said it, he knew the answer to the question. He knew what would be argued. The fact of it turned him inside out. They would argue, and he should agree, that she was rebelling against his right over her and using prayer as an excuse.

If it hadn't been for the way his mother had raised him and if he had not listened to the harrowing stories of the wandering women who came through Junayd's community, he would think just like these men. He would not say so to Zaytuna, truth be told he would be afraid to admit it to her, but he did not see any legal way around men's rights over women or their slaves. Maybe men shouldn't have such rights over women, but he was not a jurist; he did not know how to argue against it. It scared him to think about it. He did not know if he should argue against it even if he knew how.

No matter, he insisted to himself, having rights over women and slaves does not give a man permission to take as they please. Good men use their privilege with care. He shook with frustration. *Ya Rabb*! Why could these men not be good? There were good men, but too many were like Burhan and his father. He hated these scholars who relied on the evidence of their own desires and ignored the Prophet's most beautiful example. If they could find one hadith that supported their worst inclinations, they would ignore all the ones that called them to something better. If they could incline the Word of God their way, then that would become the centre-pole for the tent of their filthy hunger. He had done nothing but tie himself up in knots. What would Zaytuna think of him?

Mustafa turned towards the classes underway in the mosque. He could not look Burhan in the eye and continue speaking evenly. He looked at a pillar in the distance, letting his eyes lose focus, knowing he should not continue, but asking anyway, "And your father, how did he rule?"

"He sided with al-Qatafi, of course. He ruled that while he, as a judge, was obliged to do what he could to prevent the harm of him pulling her from her rug and entering her while she is in prostration, he must also affirm the right of the owner to have sex with his slave. But really, what did she expect? She was a fiery thing. A little Zanji demon with scars decorating her face. My father reckoned he was supposed to be terrified of her. But he was not."

Mustafa could not help it, "And Ibn Salah?"

"He had no proof of her sincerity in prayer. On the contrary, all the evidence pointed to her interest in prayer being conveniently timed to her master's desire for sex. She probably only became Muslim in the hopes of being released. For goodness sake, if she had any sense of piety she should have hidden her shame from testifying publicly in court!

"My father justly acted to prevent harm by instructing the girl to ask her master's permission before praying supplemental prayers. Further, he advised that she should pray her obligatory prayers immediately, so he would know that she was available otherwise. Should he desire sex, she must comply even if she would have to rush to bathe herself to perform the next obligatory prayer in its required time. That resolved the matter of her being pulled off her prayer rug or entered while prostrating. And he predicted to al-Qatifi that he would find his slave was much less interested in God than had been the case previously."

"There was no discussion of selling her."

"Of course," Burhan nodded. "As you know, Mustafa, that was entirely the right of the master to do so, and he declined."

Mustafa said, his voice now flat, "And what was the response of those observing? I assume there was a crowd, as usual."

"Not as many as usual. They limited the numbers of who could sit in to protect the reputation of the master and the shame of the slave. Nevertheless, there were a few people off the street and some the master's colleagues as well. News of the case spread among them. A few jurists, worse a fellow judge, criticized my father for assuming he knew what was in the heart of the slave. Endless quotations of the hadith on the inability to look into a person's heart and know their faith. They believed she should have been freed. al-Qatifi's reputation was harmed despite being in the right. Of course, who cares what the people think, but it was utter hypocrisy on the part of his colleagues. It is most properly the job of the judges in the *sharia* courts to decide on a person's faith, not the people."

Burhan looked to the side and snorted with impatience, sounding as if he were repeating something he heard from his father's mouth, "The caliph may think it is his court's purview, but it is far more our right, as the people's bearers of religious knowledge, than the religious judge in caliph's pocket or, worse, the chief vizier and his minion secretaries." He shook his head, "They only bother with the cases of grand political offence in any case. Who will correct the faith of the people if not us?" He looked back at Mustafa, "And so it was here."

Mustafa wondered if this excuse for a man were capable of reflecting on what he had just said. He doubted it, but could not help himself from asking, "Burhan, I am curious. If you were to stand before Imam Ahmad ibn Hanbal and tell him this story. What would be his reaction?"

"Of course, Imam Ahmad has ruled that a slave can be forced to have sex against her will. But you claim otherwise? I get the sense you believe you are not only the inheritor of Sufi wisdom but also the scrupulousness of an Imam Ahmad."

Mustafa retorted, "And he would say that the existence of a right does not make acting on that right obligatory or even preferable to God!" No sooner was the word "right" out of his mouth than he looked around him, somehow worried that Zaytuna were able to hear him.

Burhan sighed, "Imam Ahmad was a mountain of a man. We should be pleased to be the dirt at his foot and do the best we can, by following the Law that he himself helped establish. But I have not yet got to my point, here, Mustafa."

Mustafa closed his eyes, "Please tell me and let's be done with this conversation."

"The point is that despite Ibn al-Salah's best intentions, the woman lost her case and he found himself on the wrong end of the stick with my father. It seems that Ibn al-Salah's son was something of a gambler, in debt to the wrong people, and got himself into a bit of trouble. My father had his family investigated afterwards, you see, and the son was turned over to the police. You seem so much like Ibn al-Salah, I thought it only fair to warn you how preening, pious men such as yourself fare in this world."

Mustafa's eyes, now opened, focused on Burhan. He understood the threat clearly. Burhan wanted him to know that there would be a price to pay for standing up for what was right and good. Mustafa showed no fear. He said nothing except, "*There is no power or might except God.*"

Then Mustafa silently thanked God for His guidance. The message could not be clearer. He knew absolutely that he had to act as Zaytuna requested. Imam Ibrahim must not be allowed to get away with murdering an innocent boy. None of these animals must be allowed to escape. God is free to forgive them in the Hereafter, but in this life, they must pay. *Walla*, he would do his part.

Others began to arrive for the class. He didn't recognize the three who were walking towards them, one of whom was distinctively light-skinned. His *sirwal*, his *qamis*, and his robe, were all made of perfectly white silk and edged with elaborately embroidered vines and flowers in rich hues and words in *kufic* lettering that he could not make out. Red curls stuck out from underneath his white and gold striped turban, not wound in the manner of any school. The flagrant display of wealth sickened him, but maybe Burhan would be drawn to it and turn his attention to flattering him. Mustafa stood. He wanted to perform two cycles of prayer to clear his mind and heart of this conversation and to make a supplication to God for the sake of the enslaved woman and Ibn al-Salah and his family. He wanted every word he wrote of the Prophet's legacy today to be written with reverence for his example, not the lingering bitterness of this conversation and worry about the girl. More so, he needed calm to consider how to question Imam Ibrahim's students. He greeted the three approaching them and moved away to perform his prayer.

He heard others arrive and the doors open as he was in his second cycle. He finished his prayer quickly and left his supplication for later so he could enter well in time before the Imam. Mustafa got up to join the others for class. Despite hurrying, he was the last one in. Thank God, the Imam had not yet entered.

The room he had sat in just the day before, arranged for guests, was now set up for students. Low writing desks filled the room and sheepskins were laid out behind them. Amina was there, sitting behind a screen. Just as well, Sharafuddin wouldn't have been able to focus on the hadith otherwise. More sheepskins and pillows were placed where the Imam would sit and recite to them the hadith of the Golden Chain. There was only one open desk for students left. Unfortunately, it was just behind Burhan and his fellows. He took his place and waited quietly, but he could hear them talking. He arranged his paper and put his inkwell and reed pen into place when he heard Burhan say, "How surprising that the illustrious Imam Ibrahim let his students take a break from copying his collection." His friends tittered in acknowledgement of the cleverness of his comment.

Mustafa looked around to see who they referred to and realized it was the three students he did not know, including the rich one with the curls, sitting well behind them.

Abdelaziz leaned in towards Burhan and said, "His collection? I think you mean, al-Naysaburi's collection."

Burhan's back straightened. Nasir leaned in so far towards Abdelaziz that he was nearly in Burhan's lap, saying loud enough for the room to hear, "The hadith are forged?"

Mustafa sat up, trying to turn his attention to them without being obvious.

Burhan pushed Nasir back hissing, "Lower your voice."

Mustafa nearly said out loud, "No!"

Burhan turned to Abdelaziz, "This is a serious allegation, be clear."

Mustafa leaned forward in his desk, resting his elbows on it. He could just hear Abdelaziz who dropped his voice and conspiratorial tone at Burhan's remonstration.

He said, "No, the hadiths themselves are not forged. I have it on good authority that al-Naysaburi is the true collector of the hadith. Imam Ibrahim never heard the hadith himself. He has no true *ijaza* to teach them. He and al-Naysaburi just happen to have the same name, Ibrahim Ibn at-Tahir. Somehow Imam Ibrahim got hold of al-Naysaburi's copy with the *ijaza* written in the back after al-Naysaburi died and scraped out 'al-Naysaburi' and wrote in 'as-Silafi' in its place."

Mustafa, shocked, thought, The collection is plagiarized!

Nasir leaned in again, this time careful not to go so far, and said, "I thought no one respected his collection because he takes money from the Caliph's people. If he is willing to associate with those whose grandfathers happily tortured our grand-teachers, well, how can his transmissions be trusted in any case?"

Abdelaziz spoke back, "That's not it…," nodding to Burhan. "...as I heard, in any case."

Burhan interjected, "You shouldn't be so high on your horse. Many of our great scholars are presently in the employ of the Caliph's courtiers. Hadith scholarship itself would not survive without the stipends for teaching their incorrigible children. Further, I would insist that you recall that you repeat the hadith of the scholars who directly collaborated with the Caliph's people."

Nasir objected, "Only because their hadith are repeated by other trustworthy scholars, in their own collections. In any case, none of those collections were written by Hanbalis, by Baghdadis. The people remember. We remember that Ahmad ibn Hanbal wouldn't even pray over the souls of the men who collaborated!"

Mustafa's hand twitched, wanting to slap the desk, saying to himself, 'That's right!'

Burhan tried to get back control of the conversation, "Abdelaziz. Tell me, on whose good authority do you make this accusation of plagiarism? Bring the man to my face to testify to it if this is true."

Abdelaziz sat up so that he might look down on Burhan, "I do not have his permission to share his name."

"That is unacceptable, I won't hear another word of this. If you share this news with anyone else without evidence to back it up, you will find yourself on the wrong side of things. The man is an ass. But to steal another's work, to claim oneself in a chain of narration one has no right to, this is a grave sin before society and God. To accuse someone of such a sin without evidence? I will make it my business to see your reputation is ruined should this gossip reach me again."

Mustafa watched Abdelaziz's face drain of colour as he considered Burhan and the threat before him. True or not, he was not willing to argue the point now. Mustafa sat amazed at the lot of them. To Burhan, the rape of a slave was merely a tedious matter needing legal negotiation to be made pious, whereas this was worth his highest ethical objection. Of course, he corrected himself, the forgery was worth everyone's highest ethical objection! But *walla*, so was this mistreatment of the slave woman, the destruction of a man's family because he dared to stand up for her, and, then, Burhan's threat to his own person! What is wrong with these people? Mustafa's agitation distracted him to such a point, he could not focus. He held his pen again, rubbing his thumb over the rib to try to pull him back to where he sat and what task lay before him.

His dismay had so distracted him that he did not notice the Imam walking through an inner door to take his place. Mustafa looked up suddenly as all conversation stopped and saw the Imam taking his place. Imam Abu Abdelrahman was not wearing Mustafa's turban. He struggled to collect himself. This small thing hurting him in a way he didn't understand. He needed to see Zaytuna. He wanted to see her face. He needed to tell her about the forgery and to see her pleasure at him bringing her this news.

The Imam said prayers opening their endeavour and began to recite the chain of narration of the first hadith: "Abu Abdelrahman al-Azdi, who heard it from Abu Ali al-Yamani, who heard it from Malik ibn Anas, who heard it from an-Nafi al-Madani, who heard it from Ibn Umar, who heard the Prophet Muhammad, God bless him and peace, say...." They repeated the chain after him. The shaykh returned to the beginning and repeated it again.

They took out their pens and began to write. Then he repeated it again. Then they checked their copy.

Chapter Twenty

The sun was already hot enough that morning that Tein's freshly washed clothes were no longer soaking wet by the time he returned from the bathhouse. In the heat, the damp cloth felt good against his body. Saliha was long gone to knock on doors, looking for work. Zaytuna was taking the morning easy, waiting to go with Tein to meet Ammar. She didn't have to meet up with Saliha for washing until nearly the afternoon prayer. She felt good. She couldn't remember ever feeling like this. She had a sense all would be well and it worried her. She wondered when the feeling would pass, but it was more a worry of wanting to feel herself again.

She slipped her arm into Tein's and they made their way out of the passageway from her small courtyard house into the alley, and from there through the squares and streets of Tutha towards the Basra Gate High Road leading to the Gate itself at the Round City. They cut through the clustered neighbourhoods of the Karkh quarter to avoid the packed thoroughfares around the main marketplace, a district as large as some small cities, selling everything imaginable: brutishly thick iron gates made by Mandean blacksmiths as well as filigreed insets for windows. There were *washa* silks woven with golden thread, brightly-patterned and striped cottons and linens, felted and woven wool, from the fine to rough, and tailors to do the sewing for the rich and poor alike. Women lingered in front of the Jewish goldsmith shops, one after another. The butchers had their own section of the market, as did the grain sellers and those selling fruits and vegetables imported from the far edges of the Empire. Beggars and women selling curses and amulets sat by its gates. Pickpockets and con artists wandered through its streets looking for marks, while prostitutes tried to make eye contact with men from behind their *niqabs* and offer a discreet, but well-understood, cough.

But even the smaller market places they passed on their way through neighbourhoods and estates of the Karkh Quarter were busy and Zaytuna's eyes were on everything. She admired the intricately-patterned fine linen gowns and robes flicking out underneath the honey-coloured gossamer wraps worn by wealthy Jewish women who walked, heads together chatting, with their light-skinned slaves behind them, honey-yellow patches on the slaves' *qamises* marking them as owned by non-Muslims, carrying the women's goods. She wondered at herself, wishing out of nowhere that she could have one of those robes for herself, or one of their beautiful deep yellow wraps, although such a thing would be forbidden to her as a Muslim.

She looked at Tein, but he walked steadily ahead. She tugged at his sleeve, "Let's take the long way around so we can pass by the Birkat Zalzal. When was the last time we sat in the shade of its trees and cooled our feet in the pool?"

He looked at her tenderly, remembering, but shook his head with a small laugh, "Not a chance."

The wide Basra Gate High Road opened up before them. The road was bordered by the high walls of estates on either side, broken only here and there by arched entrance ways leading to narrower side streets and the neighbourhoods beyond. Not too far ahead she could make out the road that led toward the Sharqiyya Mosque where Mustafa so often went to study Hadith.

They walked behind a workman in a dusty *sirwal* and no shirt leading a donkey that pulled his tools in a cart, while two horse guardsman rode side by side beyond him, holding their staves high. The smell of dung hit her. She followed the scent and saw its collector napping by the roadside, in the shade of his cart, the bed already half full of dung from the morning's riders. She thought that in this heat, once he was able to lay them out, his fuel would be ready to sell by the end of the day.

Wealthy men in layers of delicate multi-hued fabrics and wearing weighty turbans firmly wound around their caps rode on elegant brown and black horses along the roadway. They were followed by their women in covered litters decorated with tassels and what looked like beading from where she was. One of the litters was carried by four dark-skinned servants or slaves, dressed more elaborately than their masters in heavily embroidered matching short cotton robes and *sirwals* with bright green and red sash belts around their waists and elaborately wound white turbans.

She stared openly at one of them, his skin was so black, that it glittered with his perspiration as if it were the deepest purple gemstone, contrasting sublimely with the white silk of his turban. As if he could feel her looking at him, he turned in her direction. She sighed at his beauty. She looked to Tein to see if he had seen the man as well. He had. Tein nodded to him, a silent communication. She looked back, the man nodded in return to Tein then returned to balancing the litter. There was no nod for her, in truth because she was a woman, and more to the point, as far as the man knew, Tein's woman. But she told herself it was because to him she would be just another Arab, or Persian maybe, not *as-sawda*, a black woman, not her mother's daughter, not a woman this black man would call sister.

As they came around the western curve of the road to head north to the Round City, the green dome of the Caliph's reception palace came into view. They had not even crossed the canal of the poultry market yet, but the walls loomed so powerfully in the distance they could have been right before her. Any pleasure she felt from the walk slipped away at the sight of them. The police, the watchmen, and the caliph's guardsman were beyond those walls, and jails and dungeons beneath them. She suddenly felt the morning heat press in on her and tasted the dust kicked up by the riders on the road. She leaned heavily onto Tein who looked at her, asking, "What's wrong?"

"What was I thinking coming here?"

He replied, "You can turn back. I have to go in to work whether or not you come along. There's no need to bring this story to him."

She nearly did turn around. She used the end of her wrap, draped loosely over her head and back, to wipe the sweat and dust from her face, looking to the sides of the road for someplace to sit where they could stop and breathe for a minute so she could reconsider. But there was nothing but estate walls and roadway at this stretch. She held her wrap out over her to offer a bit of shade and asked, "Couldn't we just turn off for a bit, there'll be an estate garden open in one of these neighbourhoods, a small market, a place to get something to drink."

"Zaytuna, I have to be there soon. You can come with me now or go."

She tried to look inward, to feel that warmth she had felt in prayer, the feeling that had led her to this act of trust in pursuing what had happened to Zayd. But all she felt was her heart clenching and the knot in her stomach. She held herself up and told herself sharply, Enough of this. Turn around in fear or live, woman!

She didn't say anything to Tein, she just kept putting one foot in front of the other. The great walls of the Round City grew before them to fill the horizon with each step. It stood in ruin in some places. But here it looked as it must have done when al-Mansur built it as a statement of his power. He was the centre of the world. She looked at Tein to see if the might of the city, the power of the caliphate, was affecting him as it was her. His face showed nothing. He looked like he could have been walking to any place.

As they neared the Gate House she could hear the waters of the moat slapping sharply against its cemented, brick lined walls as it flowed around the grand and fortified entrance. There was nothing on the banks of the moat to keep a person from falling in and being swept away in it. She felt a hot wind pick up and get such speed around the turrets and the dome of the Gate that it buffeted her this way and that, pushing her off-balance.

The bridge to the Gate House crossed the moat at its side leading into a great arched entry. The last time she had been here, years ago, Mustafa had brought her to al-Mansur's mosque to hear a hadith reciter. But men had crowded all the women out and they were forced to sit in the gardens surrounding the mosque. No repeaters were sent outside to them so that they too could hear. She fumed. They had walked home in silence that day. Today, she stepped from the bridge into the Gate House, making sure to go in right foot first, saying, "*Bismillah*" and a silent prayer this visit would only lead to the good.

They turned left in the Gate House and another grand archway opened up onto another bridge. The hot wind howled through the archways pulling at her wrap, nearly blowing the long end off her head and shoulders and drying her sweat as it came up on her. The next bridge crossed a circular roadway as wide as the Basra Gate High Road to another interior fortified wall, taller and broader than the first. Whole armies could be housed in the ramparts of the second wall and had been in the past. If an invading army had made it over the first wall, they'd find themselves trapped between it and the next with arrows raining down on them.

At the end of this bridge stood the Solomon Gates. She stopped and gaped at them. She imagined she would never fail to be humbled in fear by these great iron doors made by jinn for the Prophet Solomon himself. They stood open now, but it took over twenty men to close them. Tein tugged at her to keep going. They crossed through these gates, past another bridge, and another roadway past another smaller, but still fortified, wall.

He said, "His office is in the arcades ahead. The police are in the first rooms on the left side."

"What do we do?"

"We'll talk to that guard up there and he'll get Ammar for us. It's my first day at work here, so they don't know me. We'll have to wait."

She looked down the arcades stretching on either side of the palace gate road, the road itself leading through further gates and fortifications to the inner part of the city where the great mosque and reception palace stood surrounded by gardens.

She began to shake, asking him, "Are all the police here?"

"No, the police and watchmen for each district have their offices and barracks by the gate nearest it. And that's not the half of it."

He felt her shaking and leaned into her, pulling her closer, saying quietly, "Stop worrying, my sister. I have you."

She leaned back into him, letting out a breath she seemed to have been holding a long time. He laughed and pushed her away from him, "When has my sister ever been afraid of anything?"

She managed to laugh a little in return, saying, "Often. But less than most, I suppose."

As they approached the guard, Tein took in his aggressive posture. He stood with his legs spread and shoulders back, his hand on his mace hanging by his side. This young fellow was either looking for an opportunity to prove himself or trying to avoid one. Tein couldn't tell yet. He stopped several feet before him, giving him space, "*Assalamu alaykum*. We are here to see Ammar ibn at-Tabbani. He is expecting us. My name is Tein ibn al-Ashiqa as-Sawda al-Shuniziyya and this is my sister, Zaytuna.

The young man laughed, "Wait, your name might as well be 'Twat' and you take your mother's *laqab* instead of your father's and it's 'The Black Lover'! You should make something up!" He shook his head, "And, what? You expect me to believe this woman is your sister, you're nothing but a 'crow' and she looks like a fine Arab. She's too skinny to be a whore, so who is she to you?"

Tein listened to the young man's reaction patiently. Tein had taken on his mother's *laqab* himself when he went off on the long trek to the Frontier. He wanted to be known as his mother was known to others, and he liked how it provoked. He hadn't been looking to prove himself like this fellow. He was proven from a young age. In those days, he was just angry and looking for a fight, any fight. He found them easily enough.

Zaytuna sighed, expecting Tein to now approach the young man in such a way so as he would not know what was coming, disarm him, and have him up against a wall. She stepped to the side to get out of the way.

Tein caught the sigh and the movement and turned to her saying quietly, "Not today, dear sister, we're here for business. Soon I'll be working for this young man's boss and the look on his face when he sees that will be enough for me. But I would be happy to defend your honour if you like."

Zaytuna raised an eyebrow saying with mock gravity, "A true Muslim has no honour except in serving God."

Tein tipped his head to her, "Just so."

He turned to the young man, "I appreciate your thoughts on my name and our connection, but I assure you that Ibn at-Tabbani is expecting us."

The young man laughed at him and told him to wait. It wasn't long before Ammar came out the door followed by the guard. He looked Tein up and down, happy with the change. He turned back to the guard saying, "Get to know this black face and hulking figure, Rashid, he's working for me now. Whatever he wants, you help him."

Tein pretended to look down the arcade road to give Rashid a moment to get over any embarrassment, if he had any. What good would further humiliation do, especially if he ended up needing him in a fight. When he looked back, though, he saw Zaytuna staring at Rashid and grinning. Fair enough, he laughed to himself, the fellow did impugn her looks and mistake her profession.

Ammar's voice boomed across to Zaytuna, "Welcome! It has been a long time! I hope you've been in good health."

He gestured for Tein and Zaytuna to follow him. Once Rashid was out of earshot, Ammar leaned into his friend and took a long exaggerated sniff, "Like roses today, my brother, like roses."

Tein laughed and replied, "Is this a proposition? You know I've been lonely."

Offices were set into the arcade arches, some doors shut, others open. Zaytuna tried to look in at them as they walked quickly by. All of the rooms she could see had low couches with cushions to sit on and rugs on the floor. The rugs told her all she needed to know about who was important here. She slowed down at one room. It was double or triple the size of the others, maybe taking up three archways. It had a thick red carpet large enough to cover the entire floor area and she could just see a pattern of armed men on horses woven in around its edge. The low couches were backed by long pillows in coloured silk, deep reds, blues, and greens edged with embroidered vines. Tein looked back and pulled at her sleeve, gesturing with his head, "Let's go."

Ammar turned into a small room, still far larger than the room that she lived in, maybe four times the size. It had a rug, too, but thin, flat woven, and old. Its colours were fading and its geometric patterns were worn through here and there. His couches had pillows, too, but only covered in rough, undyed linen.

She sat on the couch, nearly falling into it, not feeling entirely comfortable with its give. It made her nervous. There was a raised writing desk set to one side near the couch on the far wall and a built-in cabinet for papers nearby it. Here it was. Zaytuna was not talking to Tein's old friend, Ammar, but an official in the Baghdad police. Mustafa was right. This man would not protect the girl. Zaynab would be ruined whether or not the case required it. She wished desperately she hadn't come. She looked out the door and wondered if she could just get up and walk through it.

Ammar prompted her, his strong voice penetrating and making her uncomfortable, "Would you like to tell me what's concerning you?"

She remained silent.

Ammar waited a moment longer, saying, "Zaytuna?" Then when there was no answer again, he turned to Tein and gestured for him to speak to his sister.

Tein saw the fear on Zaytuna's face. He started for her, "It's concerning the case you just closed. Zayd, the servant in Ibrahim as-Silafi's household. Zaytuna believes she's got evidence he was murdered."

Ammar sat up at that. "You'll need to explain."

Zaytuna's eyes widened, pleading with Tein to leave, but found she couldn't stand.

Tein prompted her, "Zaytuna? Ammar is an old friend, but let's not waste his time."

An image came to her, fleeting, of Zayd in a sling, lying across her mother's back, his head on her shoulder, sleeping, but she felt his weight herself. Her mother's back was her own. The words came out, "Layla, one of Imam Ibrahim's servants, came to me to say he'd been killed. She believed killed by the Imam himself because his daughter, Zaynab, had fallen in love with him."

Ammar spoke, "That's a serious charge. I should tell you at the outset that I interviewed everyone in the household, examined the scene, and the body. There was no evidence for that. Further, the girl you mentioned, Layla, she works next door, not for Imam Ibrahim. She wasn't there when Zayd died that night. Did she say how she knew?"

Zaytuna was hit with shame and confusion. How did she not know that Layla was not a servant at Imam Ibrahim's? She hadn't asked. She just assumed. What else had she assumed? She said quietly, "No."

Tein took Zaytuna's hand and said to Ammar, "There's more." Then, turning to Zaytuna, said, "Please just give it to him simply."

Zaytuna, held onto Tein, breathed deeply and spoke, "I'm concerned that Zaynab will come to some harm if all this comes out."

Ammar said, "Then maybe we should just end this here," and he stood.

She stood as well, grateful to end it, and Tein looking from one to the other, followed. But she felt heavy, not just the weight she felt across her back, but now a weight before her, as if a child were wrapped around her chest. Layla. She felt Layla's legs wrapped around her waist, her arms thrown around her neck, holding her and begging her, "Take care of me." Zaytuna fell back down sitting under the weight of the children bound to her.

Ammar looked at Tein. Tein shrugged and sat back down.

Ammar insisted, "You're going to have to tell me."

Zaytuna started, carefully, "I doubted it, too, when she told me. I was grieving for the boy. He was a regular in our neighbourhood. I decided to go to the mosque for his funeral prayer. The corpsewashers were there, and I spoke to them. But also, Imam Ibrahim's housekeeper came with the girl. Zaynab."

"Where was this?" He knew where it was. He doubted she was lying, but he wanted to make sure.

"At the Shuniziyya."

"And what happened?"

"Well, first it was strange for the housekeeper to be there with Zaynab."

He got Zaytuna's point, it was a long way off for the girl to be, but it could be that the housekeeper wanted to be there and took her rather than leave Zaynab home alone. Injudicious, certainly. But it didn't mean anything in and of itself.

He prompted, "You said you spoke to the corpsewashers?"

"One of them. She told me that she found a finely embroidered and beaded silk *sirwal* tie holding up his pants."

Ammar held his breath for just a moment. He had missed it. He didn't turn the body over. It was pinned under the boy's waist. But she didn't have to know that. "I can see why you would find the *sirwal* tie suggestive, but it is more likely that he stole it from her, probably out of the wash. It wasn't proof of a romantic gesture on the girl's part."

Zaytuna continued, "And the girl, Zaynab, she nearly collapsed when the bier was brought by us on the way out of the mosque."

Ammar replied, "She seemed overly emotional to me as well. But her father rightly suggested that it'd be natural for her to be upset by the loss of a servant boy who had grown up in the household. They'd known each other well in earlier years. Did you get any sense that their friendship had continued past her seclusion? Other than the *sirwal* tie...".

Zaytuna said, "Yes. I spoke to the housekeeper. But Amm..., sir, she knew I suspected something more. She begged me to keep it quiet. She knew what harm could come from the gossip. Someone could use it to attack his reputation and ruin the girl. The girl could be flogged. She herself would be ruined. I'm...," she fell silent for a moment, "I'm afraid of that as well. If it had just been a childhood love affair I wouldn't say a word. But Zayd is dead."

Ammar, "What exactly did the housekeeper say to you?"

Zaytuna, "She begged me to understand the situation. She told me that she, herself, loved Zayd like a son. She knew he could charm everyone, but he worked hard. And, well, that she let him get away with too much."

Ammar leaned in, hands on his knees, and asked, "But how do you think this implicates the Imam?"

Zaytuna said, "He might have killed the boy to protect his daughter."

Ammar replied, "Why not just send the boy back onto the streets rather than risk the ruination of his family, not to mention prosecution and execution in this world for murder, then burning in Hellfire in the next?"

Zaytuna said, "I can only think that it was because he'd heard the boy was talking about it. I spoke to a man who teaches the boys. He's teaching them how to read and study hadith. He confirmed that Zayd was talking about how the girl was in love with him. The man said that Zayd and the girl were with each other when they shouldn't have been. Zayd said it right in front of the other boys. Why would they keep quiet about that? The man even said he was boasting of it. You know how gossip spreads."

Ammar said, "And the man, who is he? What did he say?"

Zaytuna replied, "Salman ibn Asad al-Kirmani. He has a shop in Suffa Square in Tutha."

Ammar interjected, "Ah, better known as Salman the Wine Seller."

Ammar turned to Tein, winking, "Do you know him?"

Tein nodded, unashamed. "By the way, he was attacked by some of Barbahari's men last night. They smashed his wine jars, destroyed the place."

Distracted by this news, Ammar told Tein, "We'll need to tell Ibn Marwan about that. Salman will have to come in to make a report, but he'll have to lie about the goods destroyed being wine. Do you know for certain it was Barbahari's men? We need every bit of evidence we can get about them. There are too many people stirring up trouble where we don't need it. There is this other one, al-Hallaj, a Sufi preacher who is stirring people up. Do you know him?

Tein hardened hearing the name and said each word with precision, "He is not a Sufi. He's been disowned by them. I've heard it said. Clearly. Don't go looking to the Sufis on this. They haven't done anything."

Ammar continued, "What with the decree against street preachers, he's in trouble. But there's already been an effort to get al-Hallaj up on charges of heresy. It might be the scholars fighting with each other and using him as a pawn since he's put himself out in the open. I was told it was a Maliki judge who raised the issue and a Zahiri jurist who made the fatwa against him, but then a Shafi`i got involved and shut the case down."

Tein repeated, "He's not a Sufi."

Ammar heard him this time and took in the seriousness of his tone, "Noted. I'll be sure and clarify that when it comes up. But, Tein, who knows if they'll listen to me."

Zaytuna watched their conversation in fear for the Sufi community and relief at Ammar's attention having been turned away from her.

Ammar was weary at the thought of the trouble to come, "There will be difficulties surrounding this man. The poor and the rich love him. It won't end well. I can tell you that."

Tein repeated, "The attack on Salman has nothing to do with al-Hallaj. It was Barbahari's men."

Ammar didn't acknowledge him, "We've had too many reports of harassment and assaults linked to these hard-line scholars. Ibn Marwan says there have been discussions about how to crack down. Negotiation with Barbahari, certainly. That may be possible. But I cannot see what they'll do with al-Hallaj since he's protected by the Caliph's mother at the moment."

Ammar came back to the point, "Did Salman say it was Barbahari's men? Did you speak to him directly?"

"No, Zaytuna did."

Ammar turned back to Zaytuna his voice booming with hard laughter, "Ho! You are at the centre of things. Am I going to have to put you on the payroll too?"

This was all that Zaytuna feared. The violence of the city was always real. It landed on everyone's doorstep one day or another, even at the palaces. The police were often the perpetrators. She shouldn't have come. She should have listened to Mustafa.

Ammar's eyes were hard, his face stiff, "Ibn Marwan's people will have to interview you too, then. For now, tell me exactly what Salman said about Zayd."

She wasn't sure about going on now but didn't see how she couldn't avoid answering, "He only said that Zayd boasted of having both girls, Layla and Zaynab, wrapped around his finger. That Zaynab loved him."

Ammar's mind turned to that mother's son, the Imam's student, what was his name, Adam? He had reacted so keenly to his talk of impropriety on the part of the girl. That one was in love. He could have fought with Zayd over the girl and killed him. But why would the housekeeper cover up for a student? Out of loyalty to the Imam? He would have to question Adam, but returning to the house would be difficult at this point now the case was closed. He could see a complaint making its way above him.

Ammar tried to soften his voice to placate her, "I can see why you thought the boy could have been killed. I understand why you came here. The girl coming to you like that. It must have been very upsetting. I can see how upset you are even now. But the housekeeper, herself, said that he walked off the roof while sleeping. She didn't seem to me the type to lie. She said she was right there when it happened."

Zaytuna didn't speak. His tone picked at her temper, but she didn't want to give him anything of herself, not even her anger. Why men thought that being dismissed with false sympathy calmed women down was beyond her. She turned to look at Tein. She saw he heard it. He was one of the few men who knew not to try that with women.

Tein interjected, "She's here in good faith, no need to be patronizing."

Ammar snapped his head around at Tein, "I never said otherwise."

Tein said, "Your tone implies it."

Ammar said, "Tein, do I need to ask you to leave while I interview your sister?"

Tein shut his mouth but would have preferred shutting Ammar's for him.

Ammar turned back to Zaytuna, but this time self-correcting to an even tone, "Why do you suppose the housekeeper would lie to protect the Imam?"

"Because she was afraid of him."

Ammar asked, "What evidence do you have she was afraid of him?"

At this idiotic assumption, her temper broke through, "Have you ever been a servant? A woman working in one of these houses? Men can do what they like. She had good reason to be afraid."

Ammar retorted, "She didn't seem afraid to me. She was like a mother to this boy and was grieving his loss. But she was also feeling, like any good mother would, that she could have kept the boy from walking off the roof herself. She was sleeping nearby him when he got up and did it. She only awakened when she heard him trip over the edge and hit the ground."

Zaytuna winced imagining the sound and what that must have been like for her, but he didn't answer her question. He didn't know what it was like to work in these houses, but he thought he did.

He turned away from her and spoke to Tein, "I appreciate you bringing Zaytuna down here, but I don't think there's enough to go on to reopen the case. There are a few threads to follow up here, but nothing that I can see would lead me to change my conclusion."

Zaytuna wanted to grab his face and turn it towards her and make him speak to her directly. She blurted out, "There's just one last thing. The boys, Zayd's friends, thought Umm Binyamin from the Candy Sellers' Market had poisoned him. He stole from her regularly. They say she made some poisoned candies that caused him to go into a fit and walk off the roof."

Ammar burst out laughing, hitting her with all the force of his derision, "Truly?"

Zaytuna turned red, her voice becoming shrill, "Shouldn't I tell you everything? Or are you the type of police who decides ahead of time what's happened and doesn't want to know? You've decided he walked off that roof on his own and you won't even consider anything else!"

Tein's face coloured, he pushed his hands on his knees to stand. He understood her, but he put his hand on her back to indicate it was time for her to go.

Ammar stood and spoke to Tein, "I'm going to talk to one of Ibn Marwan's men about the attack on Salman and pick up a witness account about another case. They'll send a watchman down to get Salman to come in and make a report. You find him first and tell him to say it was bags of grain ruined. Not wine. Zaytuna needs to come back and do the same when they are ready. Make sure she comes in."

He turned to Zaytuna, "Thank you for sharing what you've heard. For the report on Salman, stick to what you observed, nothing else."

She threw back at him, "And what about Zayd?"

"I've heard what you said and I'll consider it. If there is anything you need to know or if I want to question you further, I'll go through your brother. For now, this is enough."

Tein took her by the arm, she shook it off glaring at him. He said, "It's time to go," and walked with her to Solomon's Gate.

He stayed back at the gate, not stepping out with her when she did. She asked, "Aren't you coming?"

"I have to work."

"Of course you do," and she turned and headed beyond the gate alone.

Chapter Twenty-One

Ammar finally returned to his office, hoping Zaytuna was long gone. Tein was there, feet up on the couch, asleep and snoring. Ammar walked over and smacked Tein's feet off of it. Tein sat up slowly, as if he'd got up on his own, not smacked away. He leaned over, elbows on his knees, rubbing his face.

"Tein, I understand saying 'No' to your sister is difficult."

"You said 'No' to her. Was it a problem?"

"You're her brother."

Tein lifted his head to look at Ammar so he could see the cold challenge in his eyes, "Come out and say what you want to say."

Ammar pretended he didn't hear it as a challenge and sat down hard on the couch near the cabinet, "Is she like this all the time? Discovering murders where there are none?"

"I'm not sure I like how you're talking right now, Ammar."

Ammar saw he would have to square against him, "I'm not your friend right now."

"I can hear it."

"She came to you in good faith."

"And I have work to do."

Tein shot back at him, "And that meeting lasted how long? How much of your day was eaten up by it?"

"It'll be more than that, Tein. I never questioned the other servant, Yusuf. She made me reconsider one of the Imam's students, too. You should have seen the money dripping off him, white silk turban with ridiculous red curls coming out underneath. That's probably high fashion up caliphate-alley. Anyway, he took special offence when I suggested that the daughter seemed unusually upset about the death of a servant. I can't see how he could have done it. He doesn't sleep there. But I should have followed up."

"You admit Zaytuna wasn't wrong."

"She wasn't right either. She doesn't know about the other servant. Maybe the two had a fight and the other boy pushed him off the roof. It didn't look that way to me at the time, but I should have followed it up. Now I have to go back and interview Yusuf and I have to question the student."Ammar slumped against the back of the couch, "But there wasn't any evidence of a fight. Maryam said Yusuf slept through the whole thing. You know how children sleep, especially children who labour."

Tein nodded, knowing full well.

Ammar pulled himself forward and looked at Tein, "To my mind, if anyone killed the boy in the house, it would have been that rich boy. He may have acted out of jealousy or to protect her honour. Not the Imam. You didn't meet this man. He is ignorant of his household. Everything is in the hands of the housekeeper. I told you, the girl's mother is dead. The housekeeper is a second mother to her, but also to the servants, even the girl who lives next door, Layla. The one who came to your sister. I can imagine the housekeeper letting things go on too long. And she confirmed as much to Zaytuna."

"Zaytuna was right about that."

"Not about the candy seller."

"She didn't take that seriously. She only mentioned it to give you everything."

"Tein, I'm satisfied with my judgment that it was an accident despite what your sister said. It's all written up and in that cabinet over there. Now I have to take those papers out and rewrite the cursed thing. Tein, look, I should have followed up immediately on Yusuf. Same with that fop of a student. Worse, I should have seen that *sirwal* tie. So not only do I have to admit to myself that I missed material evidence and my questioning was not thorough…"

Tein cut him off, "Ah, here we have it."

"…but I have to admit as much to the powers above me. And you and I have to go question Yusuf and that rich boy now. We'll need to see how Yusuf reacts to our questioning and see if that mother's son was anywhere near the house. If he was there that night, then we'll question him further. So you see, the conversation with your sister was not a short one. *Walla*, I will not let these threads go. But the end will be the same. I assure you."

"You're angry with Zaytuna because you have to do your job. You weren't like this at war, Ammar."

"This isn't war," he sighed. "Give me war over this administrative morass I have to deal with every day just to see a bit of justice done." Ammar put his hand on the hilt of his sword, "I'm just waiting for one of these infamous Baghdad uprisings so I can pull this beautiful Yemeni sword out of its scabbard and get back to work with it. I've only been able to brandish it dramatically so far. Does the trick, though."

Tein replied, disgusted, "You've forgotten what it's like to kill, I see."

Ammar looked down at him, "I remember, Tein."

Tein straightened up, "So you enjoyed killing?"

"For God's sake, Tein, can't a man bluster?"

Tein looked at him and decided to let it go. He shifted on the couch. He stretched his legs out again and lay back, his head against one of the stiff pillows, relaxing by way of forgiving him, "It doesn't answer why the housekeeper would protect the student."

Ammar smiled at the gesture, "Who knows, maybe he's another one of her adopted babies."

Tein said, "Maybe it's just all about the girl, Zaynab. Maybe the housekeeper would cover for anyone to protect her from what the revelation of the boy's murder would mean. The family would be ruined."

He pointed at Tein, "Now that makes sense. Let's go arrest the housekeeper! Put her in one of the rotting cells below and see how long she lasts before she tells us the truth."

Tein laughed, "Zaytuna wouldn't like that approach."

Ammar laughed with him, "Well, let's by all means not do what Zaytuna would not like. But I believe she would like us to go interview this student."

"Do we get horses? It's a long way."

"We were foot soldiers once. Have you no pride left in your low status?"

"It took Zaytuna and I nearly two hours to walk here."

"I walk it myself. I know."

"Don't you remember how to ride?"

"There are no horses for me. I know you think I'm important, but I'm only an investigator for Grave Crimes in the Southwest quarter. I've got a boss, who has a boss, who has a boss, who is the Chief of Police, who has a grand estate to live in."

"Question from a man with a gamey leg. Why the hell don't you have an office in Karkh, then? The watchmen have…"

"Tein, I'm not on street policing."

"…the watchmen have an office in there. It's on Qayyari Road. We could meet there."

"I know where it is Tein. You'd prefer to be where the smell of pitch soaks through the walls?"

Tein slapped the old injury on his right leg.

Ammar slapped his own leg and his left shoulder in response, "Are you done complaining?"

Tein stood, "I've never complained in my life."

"Glad to hear it." Ammar stood and picked up his scabbard, strapping it over his shoulder across his chest, "Now, help me think of a good reason along the way to explain why we are back at the Imam's house asking questions."

"I only have one question."

"What's that?"

"What's with you and the student?"

"He's a privileged little shit."

Chapter Twenty-Two

Tein looked for the guard, Rashid, as they walked out of the arcade, but he had been replaced by another. He guessed his shift was up. Ammar saw him searching and asked, "Did you and Rashid make friends?"

"The kind of friendship where one calls one's black friend a crow and one's friend's sister too skinny to be a whore? Very close."

"We'll have to invite him out one evening, then."

Tein said, "Speaking of being invited out, I'm hungry."

"I just heard testimony that you've never complained in your life."

"Merely a statement of fact about the noise my stomach is making."

"Uff, fine. We'll cut through the Dar al-Sahaba market. Just some dates to eat on the way, though. We don't have time to sit down."

They turned off the main road. The street, leading into a square and then to the market, was quickly filling with people. Ammar craned his neck to see what was going on ahead, "What's all this? Can you see anything?"

Tein looked out over the heads of those walking toward the square, "It looks like the entrance to the square is nearly blocked with people, even more further on. They're watching something." He looked down at Ammar, "Maybe a good storyteller? Should we stop for a bit? He winked, "Or in your newly pious state do you no longer wonder at the romantic trials of 'Talha and Tuhfa'?"

Ammar didn't laugh, "Enough, Tein. Look, if it's just storytelling, let's avoid the square. There's an alleyway up on the left, we can go around and get through to the market from the other end."

Tein registered his mood and nodded, walking ahead and parting the crowd, so they could make their way toward the alley. As they got closer he could hear it was street preaching, just a voice, not the words. Then he heard someone ahead say, "Mansur." He turned back to Ammar, "I've changed my mind about eating. Why deal with all these people? Let's just get to al-Anbariyya."

But Ammar had already recognized the tone as street preaching; his hand was on the hilt of his sword. "Tein, are you ready for this work or not?"

"Yes. But, Ammar, preaching is not a grave crime."

Ammar ignored him, "We need to make sure watchmen are here in case things get out of control. I have to find out what's going on, who it is, who else is involved. I'll need to make a report."

Tein rolled his eyes, "Another report. We should just bring a scribe with us everywhere."

Ammar shot Tein a look and said, "At least I'm not asking you to do the writing! Get in there. Break through the crowd."

Tein pushed people aside, carving a path for Ammar. A well-placed elbow or the sweep of his forearm caught the unwary off balance. Any complaints were silenced with a glance at the size of the black hand that had grasped their shoulder or a look at his resigned expression. They stood to the side and watched the shorter, bull-faced man walking in his wake, hand on the hilt of his sword and black turban on his head marking him as police. A few, Tein thought wise, turned to leave and were pushing back against the crowd trying to get out.

The voice called out over the crowd, "O People! When the Truth has taken hold of a heart, She empties it of all but Herself! When God attaches Himself to a man, He kills in him all else but Himself. When God loves one of His faithful, He incites the others to hate him, in order that His servant may draw near to Him so as to assent to Him!"

People in the crowd called back, "Tell it, brother Mansur! Truth!"

Ammar raised his voice so as to be heard, "Mansur? Is that al-Hallaj?"

Tein called back, resigned now to the situation, "Yes...it is."

Ammar stiffened and asked, "Do you see any watchmen?"

Tein yelled, "I do. It doesn't look good. I just saw one of them yelling '*Allahu akbar*' to what al-Hallaj just said."

Ammar pushed Tein forward faster, "Find a place where we can keep an eye on this."

Tein saw an area not far off, against a wall where some people were standing on stools and tables near the entrance to the market. He could force one of them off so Ammar could stand and see from the back, getting a full view. Tein could see al-Hallaj now, he was standing by the entrance to the small mosque at the far end of the square. He was alone, framed by its arched doorways, people standing back from him to give him room to preach and to be heard. Not like when Tein's mother taught in the graveyards and the people crushed in to lie at her feet. But it wasn't any less dangerous. Tein moved through the crowd with Ammar close behind. A shirtless young man with nothing but a filthy wrap wound around his waist and a woven skull cap barely sitting on top of his long, matted hair stood on the table. Tein yelled up at him, "Get down. Police. We need the table."

The young man looked down at him and spat at his feet, the spit and phlegm falling onto and in-between Tein's toes through his sandal straps. Tein felt it but didn't look down or move to clean his foot. He reached up and grabbed the young man's arm. He felt nothing but skin and bone, but he yanked him down off the table onto the ground all the same, saying, "Get out of here if you don't want trouble."

The young man righted himself and pushed Tein off him, yelling at him, "You think I fear the police when I no longer fear God Himself? Your hatred is only proof of God's eternal love for me! Listen to Mansur, you fool! He speaks from the Throne of God!"

Tein reached out with his left hand and took him by the throat, leaning down to speak in his face, "If frothing at the mouth proves a man speaks from the Throne of God, then that camel al-Hallaj is one!"

The man growled at him, "Zanji, fucker of dogs!"

Ammar shook his head. Now that boy's going to get a taste of the old Tein. Let's see how far this goes.

Tein could feel the people directly around him moving back, staring. He tightened his grip on the young man's throat just so. The young man's face began to turn red. He gasped for breath. His eyes filled with the terror. Tein whispered, "Do you fear the Police now?" He loosened his grip, just enough to let the young man grab at a full breath, to think that he might yet live, but only at Tein's pleasure. Tein coughed out a bitter laugh and looked around, speaking to the crowd now staring at him wide-eyed as he dangled this scrawny creature by the throat.

He gestured to the young man, incapacitated by his one hand only. "Look at this one! Calling a man who could kill him 'Zanji'!" Tein turned back to him, bringing his face into the gasping man's own, "I'm Nubian, you ass. But, I will be Zanji for you if that's how you want it."

He looked up again at the crowd, still holding the young man up by his throat, and bellowed at them, "I am Zanji! I will be counted among the proud black slaves whose ferocity nearly brought a caliph to his knees!"

He tightened his grip again on the young man's neck until his eyes began to turn back into his head, losing consciousness. Tein knew how long it took to strangle a person to death. He had time. He loosened his grip again. The man gulped in air and spasmed into coughs, sucking in breath and coughing again, regaining his consciousness into panic.

Tein moved closer to his face, saying, "This black man has killed better men than you on the battlefield. Men who didn't deserve to die. And you will live because I am tired of killing."

He lifted the young man by the throat again and threw him back into the crowd. He fell against the people standing behind him watching the scene unfold. The crowd, just beyond them, did not know what was happening and pushed him back, almost to standing again, yelling, "Watch it!"

Ammar spoke harshly in Tein's ear before getting up onto the table, "Enough. Go get those watchmen to do their job."

Tein didn't move immediately, but stared down the young man as he tried to walk backwards into the people who'd just pushed him, his eyes locked fearfully onto Tein's own, as the crowd swallowed him. Only then did Tein begin to skirt the square, passing the archway into the market, until he finally reached the two watchmen he'd seen calling out to al-Hallaj. He grabbed them by the scruff of their necks, one hand on each, pulling them back against him, hissing in their ears, "What are you doing? You need to start controlling this crowd! Get them moving out of here before there's a riot."

He pointed at Ammar standing on the table, "You see him? He's high up in the police and he's seen you here not doing a cursed thing to control this situation."

The legs of the one in Tein's left hand buckled as he raised his hands, pleading, "Brother, what can we do?"

The other one in Tein's right hand didn't budge and laughed, "Please, the Market Inspector has already been over to yell at us. Tell your boss to get in line."

The watchman pulled at his shabby *qamis*, "The police give us a bit of black cloth to wind for a turban and a chink of coin and nothing else. I'm not risking my life over this."

The first one looked up at Tein, his eyes desperate, "Listen! They say his prayers are answered! My boy can barely eat he's so twisted up inside. What he does eat comes right out of him. I'm going to ask Mansur to say a prayer for him. Maybe he would come to us? They say he works miracles! Maybe he'll put his hands on him!"

The other smiled at Tein, saying, "Relax, big man. This will be a small riot by Baghdad standards."

The first one pushed the other, "Quiet, he's speaking!"

Tein sighed, releasing the two, and stood back, "Useless! Where's the Inspector?"

The other one said, "How should we know?"

al-Hallaj's voice rang out, "But what happens to me? I no longer feel the least breeze of His Presence, nor the least reach of His glance! Alas!" Then he pointed to the back of the crowd, in the direction of Ammar, who could be clearly seen standing on the table by the market entrance, "And here are so many people who begin to hate me now!"

People turned to look at Ammar. A mass of them began to move slowly towards him. Tein saw Ammar settle his legs into a more balanced stance and pull his sword slightly out of its scabbard. Ready. Tein said under his breath, "Here's your riot, Ammar. I hope you're happy."

Tein started pushing his way as quickly as he could back toward Ammar, hoping to get there before the crowd broke out against him. Ammar could handle himself. But there were too many people.

As he moved back through the crowd, people pushed aside more easily. He began to hear whimpering. Then he noticed many were weeping. One man had both hands on his bare head, whatever turban he'd had lost, tears streaming down his face. A woman wailed behind him. He looked back at al-Hallaj who now stood silent by the great doors of the mosque, his hand to his forehead, looking down, his body in a stance signaling his dejection. The cries were rising around him. Tein felt himself back at the edges of the graveyards when his mother was preaching and weeping and the crowd paced her every emotion. He scanned them as he did then, eyes searching for the one who would break loose to attack his mother or Zaytuna, huddled in his mother's lap; only this time he couldn't have cared less for the preacher. He was watching out for Ammar. The crowd. But the ones who looked like they were moving on Ammar had begun to weep, too, their bodies softening, hanging on each other's shoulders.

He kept close watch. Weeping didn't mean it was over. Not at all. It was the start of something. As he reached the marketplace archway, he felt a hand on him. Tein turned, his left arm pulling back, hand curling into a fist, relaxing into the movement, ready to throw a punch.

He saw a man who could only be the marketplace inspector, gesturing toward the watchmen, "Those imbeciles over there should be executed. Who is controlling this?"

"No one!" Tein pointed to Ammar, "My boss is there. We just happened to be nearby. We'll do what we can. But can you go get more watchmen? Guards?"

"I've sent someone to tell them. We're close enough to the Basra Gate. We might get help in time."

"I have to keep moving, I don't want my boss over there alone."

The inspector nodded, "Go."

Tein finally made his way over to Ammar and stood in front of the table, Ammar above him. He caught sight of al-Hallaj. He was smiling wildly now, tear-stained, seemingly about to burst into laughter, until a cry of anguish arose from his throat. The crowd jolted up and straightened, a few wailing in chorus, shocked by the cry shooting through them. Each of them staring at him, silent and focused.

al-Hallaj spoke clearly, his voice piercing the air, "O people of the marketplace! Save me from God! Save me from God! Save me from God! He has robbed me from myself. He has left me deserted, forsaken, outlawed. God has made spilling my blood lawful to you. So kill me! Make me a martyr for God!"

The crowded gasped, and the mood shifted instantly. Tein could feel them turning on him. Where there was adoration before, now there was anger brewing. They didn't understand what he was saying and were beginning to feel they'd been had. It wasn't settling well in them. A few called out from different parts of the crowd, "What's this now!? Save you from God?! Liar!" Another yelled out, "Martyr you!? That makes us God's enemies in this fight!"

al-Hallaj cried out again, his hand slapping his chest, begging, "Will someone kill this cursed one?!"

Tein watched as two men moved out of the crowd at the front. He recognized one, saying under his breath, "Ibn Ata!" The other one he didn't know. One of al-Hallaj's followers, probably. The one he didn't recognize pulled al-Hallaj with both hands toward the doors of the mosque, pushing the door open with his body and dragging al-Hallaj in with him.

Ibn Ata backed toward the mosque door after al-Hallaj, yelling into the crowd, "He's gone mad with God's love! He doesn't know what he's saying!"

Ammar yelled, "Who is that?"

He yelled back, "I don't know the younger one. The other is an old friend of al-Hallaj. A Sufi. He'd protect al-Hallaj from a pack of rabid dogs."

"I thought you said al-Hallaj wasn't a Sufi?"

"He's not! But that's his friend. His friend is one of the Sufis."

"It doesn't look good, Tein."

"No, it does not."

Ammar yelled down to him, "Well, he's lucky he's got a friend because this crowd is about to explode."

A short man with broad muscular shoulders and arms broke out and rushed at the door after al-Hallaj and Ibn Ata. Ibn Ata closed the mosque door behind them just in time. The crowd broke open behind the first man and fell toward the door, it didn't move. Ibn Ata must have been able to bolt it. The first man pounded on it yelling, "Give him to us! Liar!" until the second wave of the crowd flowed in behind, pinning him and the others against the door. His yelling of, "Liar," quickly turned to, "Get off me!"

A man behind him, recognized him, and reached out to pull him away, "Zahrun! Take my hand!" But Zahrun's face was jammed against the door, his thick arms uselessly stuck above his head, his body pinned in on either side. Cries of anger toward al-Hallaj became mixed with cries of pain and terror as more people moved in against the door crushing those ahead of them. They fell and slipped against each other, a few falling underfoot, those near them trying and failing to lift them up. Zahrun kicked back hard against whoever happened to be behind him. He heard a woman scream from within the crowd. Struggling to breathe, he managed to lower his arms so he could push himself up against the shoulders of the two people on either side of him and turn around. He climbed up on top of the crowd, crawling over their heads and arms away from the mosque. He fought to stay afloat in the angry ocean as fists and fingers were punching and grabbing at him to pull him down. Zahrun made it to the middle of the mob when sea turned and the crowd began to move in a wave away from the mosque. He felt the mob open underneath him and he fell backwards to the ground as several people tumbled on top of him. He thought he heard the crack of a bone.

Zahrun pushed the others off and tried to get up but his right leg would not let him. Grabbing hold of one of them now standing near him, he pulled himself up and tried to make his way with the people moving in a crush to get out of the square. Then screams intensified where the square opened up onto the main road. He couldn't see the soldiers but he saw their staffs pushing and swinging into the crowd. He yelled, "Those sons of whores! Where do the soldiers think these people would go, back up against the mosque doors?" Propping himself onto anyone he could, he started to push sideways through the crowd to the far wall of the square to see if he could get up onto it and into the estate on the other side.

Ammar jumped down off the table and got behind the soldiers, pulling at them, yelling, "Get back! Give the people a way out of the square!"

Tein grabbed a staff from one of the soldiers and used it to herd those near him out through the marketplace, pushing them through the market gates, yelling "Move!"

He pulled his staff around, pushing now against the soldiers who were only making things worse. He could see from here that people were being crushed, "Get back! Give them room to get out!"

Tein moved again to direct more people out of the marketplace gate. There'd be havoc as they pushed through it in such numbers but there was no other way. Over and again, he drew groups from the mob out towards the market place and away from the soldiers. People started to make sense of the movement streaming through to the market and the huge knot of people began to loosen, moving in that direction.

Ammar started to get control of the soldiers nearest to him, moving them to the side, creating a gap out of the square to the main road, and people began to stream past them, soldiers still swinging their staffs, while Ammar yelled at them, arms waving, "Stand down!"

Slowly the square began to empty. Some of the soldiers walked behind the stragglers, taunting them with their staffs, hitting their ankles or pushing their backs to keep a move on. Others broke into small groups, talking frantically, while the injured lay where they had fallen. Ammar yelled commands at the guards to get back.

One of them turned on him, "Who are you to tell us!"

Ammar screamed, "Police!"

The soldier moved up against Ammar, still hot from the fight, "What is the police to the Caliph's guard? We outrank you, you cheap piece of scum!"

Ammar looked at the man, aghast at his stupidity, unwilling to fight him, "Fine, then clean this up if you are in charge! I'm done!"

The soldier, realizing what he'd got himself into out of the argument, started to object, but Ammar had already walked away.

The crowd was gone but more than a dozen people lay in the square injured, but at least no one died. Ammar said out loud, "Thank you, God."

Ammar looked for Tein and saw him walking toward a man seated against the estate wall. Ammar left him to deal with that and entered the dim light and cool air of the covered market to survey the damage and find the inspector to see what could be done.

Tein made his way to a man sitting against the estate wall holding his leg gingerly, pulling up one leg of his *sirwal*. His shin just above the ankle was swollen and discoloured but worse had an awkward bend to it. At least no bone had broken through. Tein could see the man was a blacksmith from his shoulder muscles rounding up to the base of his skull, his huge arms, and stained hands. He leaned over the man, saying, "You've broken your leg even though you can't see it. Good thing it didn't pierce the skin. The bonesetters can likely save your leg."

The man looked up at him. He was blanched from pain, shaking from cold despite the heat of the sun beating down on him, finally feeling the injury now that the panic had passed, but he managed with the last of his energy to sneer at Tein, "I can see that, you miserable dog, get out of my face!"

The staff he had taken off of one of the soldiers was still in his hand. He handed it to him, saying, "Take this to help you get out of here, then. There's a bonesetter not too far from here."

The man took the staff and started to pull himself up on it. Tein leaned over to help him. But he pulled back, falling back to the ground, screaming in pain, then, "Back off, crow!"

Tein looked at the man and then inward at himself. He was exhausted. He turned and walked toward the entrance of the square. The tavern owner was putting the tables and stools back into order and pulling at the cloth awning that had been partially torn down. Tein looked at him, asking if business was open again. The man gestured for him to sit down. Tein sat on the stool and said, "*nabidh*." The owner went inside and returned with a clay cup filled with drink and placed it before Tein.

"Clay? No glass in this neighbourhood?"

"No glass during a riot."

"The riot's over."

"This is Baghdad, you don't know that yet."

Tein laughed and lifted his cup toward the shopkeeper, "Well, how much do I owe you?"

"You are police? Nothing."

Tein raised his eyebrows and took a copper *fals* out of his sleeve pocket and placed it in the hand of the shopkeeper, "I'm not police, then."

Tein leaned back against the wall watching Ammar talk to the soldiers in front of the mosque and drank his *nabidh* in three gulps and put the cup down. He could imagine what his uncles would say about all of this because it was what they had been telling him since he was a boy filled with fury at this world, "Wrestle your anger to the ground, Tein, pin it and do not let it up until it has submitted to you." He told himself, It isn't much of a trick to kill. The trick is letting go before you kill. And you did. He knew how narrowly he had avoided doing something that he couldn't walk back from, but was unwilling in that moment to ask himself how he got there in the first place. Uncle Nuri would have walked him through it. But Uncle Nuri was not there. The shopkeeper came and took his cup and filled it again. Tein reached into his sleeve to pay and the shopkeeper said, "This one is on the house. Not because you are police, but because you paid even though you are police."

Chapter Twenty-Three

Ammar emerged from the market entrance, his hand shading his eyes as they adjusted to the bright sun on the square. Tein was sitting at one of the tables in the shade of what was left of the awning with a clay cup in his hand. Ammar thought it'd better not be wine. He needed Tein to get inside the mosque and speak to these Sufis. If they couldn't get out through the Imam's household door, they'd still be in there. He needs to talk to them. Get this al-Hallaj to stop. Tein seemed to know one of them, maybe he'd listen to him.

He yelled across the square, "Tein!" But Tein didn't respond. Tein sat, slumped back against the wall, legs out, looking at the sky. Ammar stalked across the square toward him, "Tein!" Still nothing. Ammar was nearly to him when he saw Imam Ibrahim's student, Adam, red curls and all, leaning against a wall by the marketplace gate, watching the scene wrap up.

Ammar changed the direction he was walking, moving towards the gate, but kept his eyes off the privileged little shit. He didn't want to scare him and then have to chase him through the marketplace. Well, he didn't want to scare him yet. He continued walking toward Adam, keeping him in his peripheral vision until he got close enough to him that he could jump forward and hold him there if he needed to. He got close enough and then looked at him directly, saying, "Adam, wasn't it?"

Adam jumped slightly and backed up against the wall, "*Assalamu alaykum.*"

Ammar returned his greetings then said, "I was just on my way to the Imam's house. The will of God has brought us together, no doubt. I was writing my report and had a few loose ends. It occurs to me you could answer these questions just as well as the Imam. You would be doing him a great service. No need to bother him, if so."

Ammar took another step closer to him, penning him in slightly. Adam looked stuck. He wanted to look to his side, to walk away, but couldn't, "Of course, if I can."

"I have to ask, though, what are you doing here? I wouldn't think a serious hadith scholar would be interested in wild talk and inciting crowds."

"I'd heard about him through my mother's friends. He has many followers in court, you know."

"I know."

"Some hadith scholars, too."

Ammar looked at him, "Apparently. Who else?"

Adam voice tightened, realizing what he'd said, "You'd have to ask for yourself. This is my first time hearing him speak. Not my style."

"You don't look like you got hurt in the fight. Not a hair out of place."

Adam tucked back his head at the comment, not sure what he meant by it, saying, "I watched from inside the marketplace. I wasn't anywhere near the fight. I ducked into a shop when things got heated. Not my style."

Ammar thought, No, not your style to be out among the men when things get tough, but held himself back from saying it.

Ammar couldn't look away from him, he needed to keep him there but he also needed to get Tein to get to the mosque. He took Adam by the elbow, "Let's walk over there and sit down," indicating where Tein was sitting, his shoulders slumped now, legs pulled up. His gaze shifted to the ground. Ammar thought, looking at Tein, This better not be a problem.

Adam saw the direction they were headed and pulled back, saying, "I can't."

"You can't talk? I thought you wanted to help the Imam?"

"No, they sell *nabidh* and wine there, everyone knows it. I won't sit in such a place."

"Appearances are everything. Well, let's just walk by there so I can speak to my colleague who is sitting there and then we'll find another place to talk."

Adam pulled at him slightly, becoming afraid.

Ammar said, "Come along, nothing to worry about."

Adam let himself be led, but looked around him to see who was watching and wondering if he could break from Ammar and run.

They reached Tein and he looked up, shaking his head as if waking himself out of something. Ammar said, "Adam, I would like to introduce you to my colleague, Tein ibn al-Ashiqa as-Sawda."

Adam's eyes widened at the strangeness of the name, but he said, "*Assalamu alaykum.*"

Ammar turned to Tein saying, "This is Adam." Ammar looked at Adam realizing he didn't remember his full name. He turned back to Tein, finishing the introduction, "One of Imam Ibrahim's students."

Tein didn't respond.

Ammar pushed him, "Tein, if it would not be too much trouble, would you go into the mosque and see if they're still there. I need you to talk to the one you know. Get that preacher to back down."

Tein stood up, the only acknowledgement that he had heard Ammar. Stepping forward, his sheer bulk pushed the two of them back and out of his way. Tein looked down at Adam. Adam began to shake and took three more awkward steps back. Ammar stepped back with him, putting his hand on Adam's arm to make sure he didn't run away.

Tein pulled himself up from the shame he'd been sitting in, and observed the young man, Ammar's despised elite boy. Red curls stuck out from underneath his yellow and white striped turban. This one wasn't like Mustafa. This one didn't pass the cloth under his chin, with a twist. He had just a tail down the back. Silk turban. Red and gold threads were woven through the stripes. White skin, blue eyes. No one spits at this boy despite that maybe he was a slave himself. Ammar did not say that he was a slave. His mother must be a Christian slave and he took after her. "Adam" fits that. She must have been bought by a very wealthy man, an important man, who fathered this boy. Now the boy, born into freedom and Islam, gets his name and carries his reputation. He probably thought the girl, Zaynab, belonged to him, that she was meant for him.

Ammar watched Tein making a quick observation of the student and felt relief. He's back. Maybe he can do this.

Tein walked away and Adam relaxed slightly, not entirely, just enough to show he no longer thought he was in physical danger now that Tein had left.

He looked at Ammar warily, wondering what was next, and wishing they could get as far away from the tavern as possible. They moved away from where Tein had been sitting and went through the marketplace arches where they could sit and talk undisturbed. He found a shop selling fruit juices, no hard cider, and sat him down at one of the stools.

Ammar bent his head slightly toward Adam in conciliation, "Before I ask for your help, I want to apologize."

Adam tucked his head, not knowing how to react to this man, "Apologize?"

"Yes, I'm afraid in my zealousness to deal with the situation at the Imam's home, I intimated that Zaynab might have had an inappropriate relationship with the boy who had died. I saw how that upset you, and I wanted to say I was sorry."

Adam flushed, Ammar didn't know if it was from anger, confusion, or embarrassment at having been caught out, but he answered well despite it, "On the contrary, I owe you an apology. You were simply doing your job. I understand you have to ask uncomfortable questions."

Ammar tried it from another angle, "I appreciate your understanding. I'm grateful you are willing to help now, I imagine the Imam relies on you quite a bit."

Adam replied, "I am only his humble student. I do whatever I can for him. It is only what is required of me given the gift of knowledge he shares with me."

Ammar nodded, thinking, he's got the scholar-hypocrite patter down. He approached him through conceit, "I am curious what you thought of the boy, Zayd. I'm a bit surprised he was working in such a house. Everything I hear about him, well, he seems to have been a troublemaker. More suited to the canals than the home of an important man."

Adam tipped his head in agreement, "May God have mercy on his soul. While his death has been difficult for the household, it is all for the best. As God Most High said, *You may hate a thing and it is good for you.*"

"You must have tried to do something about him. I cannot imagine you not upholding your responsibility to the Imam by ignoring the problem."

Adam shifted slightly. Ammar could see he wanted to say it, wanted someone to know that he had been right all along, "I spoke to the housekeeper about him, but she ignored me. It hadn't gone far enough to warrant speaking to the Imam. I did not want to disturb him, not yet. And now I won't have to. *Alhamdulilah*, God's wisdom is beyond our ken."

"It? What hadn't got far enough?"

Adam realized then that he had gone too far and flushed again, "Trouble. Making trouble around the house...," he stammered, "He was a thief."

Ammar saw his opening, "Ah, now you look like how you did that morning when I suggested that Zaynab and Zayd had known each other, well, in a way that they should not."

Adam's back got up, "You put this young lady at risk with your accusations. Even the suggestion of such a thing, if it got out, could ruin her."

He was trying to hide it, but no doubt about it, Ammar saw there was some real fear there. He provoked him, "You don't seem the type for chivalry."

Adam flushed, becoming angry, "Zaynab deserves nothing less!"

"No doubt." He laid it out for him, "Mind you, I wouldn't think you capable of it, but would you kill the boy to protect her honour?"

Adam's face blanched, he moved back on his stool, "I, what?"

"Would you kill to protect her honour?"

Just as quickly as he had blanched, his colour returned to him. His back was up now realizing where this man was going with the questioning and seeing his only way out, "God protect me from evil things! There is no answering that! All along you've suggested I'm not man enough in your eyes and now you want me to admit I've killed someone to prove I am. Do you think I'm so slow as to see what you are up to? Worse for you, do you even know who my father is? Hamid ibn al-Abbas! He will be the next vizier to the Caliph! How dare you speak to me this way! I'll have you removed from your post!"

Ammar stopped short. His stomach sunk as he realized who Adam's father was. He hadn't put it together when Imam Ibrahim had told him before; it was a common enough name. But this father was no common man. Self-made and as rich as they come, spreading his money everywhere; known to be a buffoon, he was nevertheless working his way into influence in every level of court to make his way into the vizierate. He could not only lose his post by this man's complaint, but also his head. He held himself to account, demanding inwardly, And so what! Lose your head, if that is what justice requires! His mind came round to the tragedy at Karbala. Will you be among those who hid in their houses in Kufa rather than stand by Husayn? His hand twitched. He wanted to grab this privileged, mother's son by the throat and watch his curls shake and his turban fall from his head. It took everything he had to hold himself in place, then to steady himself, then to speak without showing his anger. Another voice within him spoke, reasoning, Would Ali or Husayn act without knowing what this boy has done? Has this boy done anything? Find out first!

He pulled himself back, imagining Ali the Lion on the battlefield, and his restraint from killing without just reason. Then Ammar imagined himself standing beside Ali. It brought him to his senses. He collected himself. He tried to say casually, as if he were surprised by Adam's response, "I must apologize again. I never meant to imply anything of the sort. We're a bit rough around the edges. I was a *ghazi* before joining the police, you see."

At the apology, Adam sucked in some air sharply as if to say, "Just so!" But at the mention of the word *ghazi*, Adam visibly corrected himself out of respect due the title given to the Frontier fighters, managing to say, even if a bit stiffly, "Your sacrifice for the Religion and the Caliphate is well-noted. May God reward you and your family in this world and the world to come." He took another breath, allowing for Ammar's concession but still afraid, hedging the situation, "I am sure what seems rough to us in the city was nothing other than nobility on the battlefield."

Ammar said, regaining his footing, "Thank you for your understanding. If you'll forgive me for asking—I do need to ask—you seem disturbed for the reputation of a girl you should not even know. Not that it is not due her. It is just that she is in seclusion. You see my confusion."

Adam sat forward, insistent, "I don't know how to make this more clear. I need to impress upon you the need to protect the girl's reputation."

"But why?"

He was forced to say it, "We are to be married."

Ammar forced a smile, "Congratulations, may you find every happiness."

Afraid again, he said, "I must appeal to you, appeal to the chivalry of your person as a *ghazi*..." then making himself say it, "*Ghazi*, Sir. She must be protected from any gossip, even amongst yourselves in the police. This line of questioning can go no further."

Ammar softly objected, "I would like to promise, but..."

"*Ghazi*, Please understand. She is not my mother's choice."

"Oh?"

"My mother, Yasmina, was a treasured slave in the harem of the caliph al-Mu'tamid and gifted by him to my father. Do you think that she considers the daughter of a hadith scholar who teaches the children of a minor dignitary in the court for his coin good enough for me? If this gossip got out, she would not permit this marriage."

"How is it going ahead at all without her approval?"

"It is only that my father likes the idea of our household having scholarly attachments. I have many elder half-brothers and I am not his favoured son among them, despite his infatuation with my mother."

"I see."

Adam grasped the edge of the table where they were sitting and nearly begged him, "Please. It is only that I truly love her. The Imam encouraged her to come out from behind the screen when the other students were not there, so I could see her. She was without her face veil. He did it so that I would want her. He has promised her to me." Thinking of his future father in law, his officious tone returned, "Such a tedious man, only doing it to raise his own reputation. If it were not for his collection, I would not even have been there to study with him in the first place. Now I am there for her alone."

Ammar prompted, "What drew you to her?"

He softened at the question unable to help himself, "She is beautiful, but there are beautiful girls everywhere. She is a brilliant student. A brilliant mind. I love her. But I loved her even before he showed me her face."

"Does she love you?"

Adam cocked his head as if he did not understand the question, then answered, "Did my mother love my father when she was given to him?"

Ammar didn't need to know the answer. There wasn't a lot of difference between slavery and marriage when it came to what women wanted and what men got. He ignored the comment, saying evenly, "What do you think happened to the boy?"

He said with confidence, "He walked off the roof while asleep, as the housekeeper said."

Ammar pushed lightly, "I have to ask, my apologies. But this will keep me from having to discuss this any further. Where were you that night?"

Adam balked at the very thought of it, "Do you think I sleep at my teacher's house!"

"No, I don't. But you see, I have to ask."

Adam stiffened, but Ammar saw him thinking. Adam relaxed slightly, asking, "Should we walk to my father's home? You can question our guards. They can be counted on for their discretion, especially if you make it sound like it is concerning a night of carousing or some such."

Ammar sighed. He considered what would happen if he asked the guards. They would only answer in a way that would please this son of his father's household. He forced himself to consider the logical possibility of this ass of a boy killing Zayd, worried about reputation or not. If Zayd were murdered, which he did not believe he was, Adam would only have to arrange to have Zayd beaten to death in a street scrap over nothing. It wouldn't cost much. His household guard hands a few *fals* to a couple of toughs who need a meal. Done. As much as he sorely wished it in this moment, he didn't see Adam hiding out overnight in his teacher's house waiting for Zayd to go up to the roof so he could push him off of it. And he didn't see how he could have had been there overnight casually for what would have been more likely a crime of emotion and opportunity. No, he thought. He didn't do it.

Ammar said, "Thank you for the offer, but there's no need to ask the guards."

Adam asked, "Can I count on your discretion for the girl's sake?"

Ammar put his hand on his heart, but did not vow on God's name, "Yes."

Relieved, Adam said, "You never asked me how you hoped I could help you with what you needed from the Imam."

"Actually, our conversation covered it. I have one more witness to question, unrelated to anything to do with the girl, so, for your concerns, you can consider the case closed."

Adam shook slightly at the suddenness of being released, not realizing fully that he'd felt so completely trapped until that moment. Ammar saw it and took pleasure in that, at least.

Ammar stood and bowed slightly, his hand over his heart again, "Thank you for your help, *Assalamu alaykum.*"

Adam placed his own hand on his chest and nodded toward him, not getting up, "*Wa alaykum assalam.*"

Ammar left Adam at the table and felt for the hilt of his sword to steady himself. He went to look for Tein, thinking, Be honest, now. If you were a true man, true to your love of the Prophet's family, true to God, then you wouldn't dance around these rich fools. You'd leave the outcome in God's hands. Would Ali, would Husayn let this go? Answer me, man! Another thought spoke through, answering his demand. You got everything you needed, for God's sake. He told himself sharply, You would have shown the boy your sword if you had to do so. You are a *ghazi*! You didn't need to threaten him to get what you wanted.

Angry with himself still, he reached the square but Tein was no longer there. He must have gotten inside the mosque. Ammar, settled down and assured himself, I'll question Yusuf, and if there's nothing there, then we're done. It was an accident, as I suspected from the start.

He made his way to the mosque door and pushed it open, enough to get inside. He saw Tein walking to him from the back of the mosque with the Imam, near what must have been the Imam's quarters.

Tein called across to him, his voice reverberating through the mosque, "Nothing here. The Imam let them out through his door."

Ammar said, "We'll have to write this up. You'll have to name the man who helped him get out. What was his name, again? Another Sufi?"

Tein said, "Just because he counts some of the Sufis as friends doesn't make him a member of that community. You have no friends outside the police or military?"

"But what he was saying. That sounds a bit like Sufi talk to me."

"That's how little you know. Is everyone who talks politics in government? Are there no regional governments acting on their own terms?"

"Point taken, Tein. Maybe we'll make you our special investigator for Sufi matters."

"It's not funny. That's why I worry about the community. Because people like you cannot tell the difference."

"No, none of this is funny. Unfortunately, we have to head back to the office to deal with this mess. More to write up. Thank God, no one died. As it is, I'm going to have to explain why I didn't just arrest al-Hallaj for fomenting a riot before it got started."

Tein changed the topic before he could ask again for Ibn Ata's name, "Did you get what you needed from Adam?"

"Yes, we're done with him. I'll explain later. But because of this mess, we'll have to put off interviewing the other servant until tomorrow. I have to get another witness statement for a different killing in al-Anbariyya, so it makes sense to go when we'll have time to do both. A drunk old *ghazi* killed a man, he's in a holding cell until I can clear this up." He eyed Tein, "Just like you in about thirty years time. He stabbed a thief who thought he could roll the old man for some coin. The thief didn't count on him being a tough old warrior of the Frontier. We need the shopkeeper's testimony who saw the whole thing. Ibn Marwan talked to the Chief of Police about it. The Chief is prepared to judge the case as self-defence once we have all the evidence ready to submit to his court. I've got to go interview the shopkeeper, then get him to come in to make a statement."

Ammar looked around the square, "As for this riot, let's see how far we get with the paperwork and then hand it off to Ibn Marwan. I'll get a scribe in. In any case, I think you can tell your sister, as far as she is concerned, the case is closed."

Tein cocked his head, "Closed?"

"I don't think the interview with the servant, Yusuf, is going to change anything. Just let Zaytuna know."

"No details for her?"

Ammar turned on him, "She doesn't need any details. Were you getting drunk over there?"

Tein laughed at him, "Two cups of *nabidh*, brother. You think cider has any effect on me? Two cups of wine wouldn't have done it, either. I am decidedly not drunk."

"Don't do it again."

"Maybe this job isn't for me, Ammar. I'd rather carry bags of grain up from the canal on my back than put my hands around another man's throat again."

Ammar scoffed, "Is that what this is about?"

Tein looked at him sideways, "What? Because I'm not enjoying brutality anymore?"

Ammar shook his head, "If that's how you want to put it. But I didn't ask you to throttle that man. You did that."

Tein looked down, "I know."

"You've been an ass all day. There's more to this than your sudden shame over your gift for violence. Let me throw this at you. I'm not sure that you accept how this job works. Your family, your friends. This comes first. Those who joined Husayn at Karbala understood the sacrifices necessary to enact justice in this world."

Tein was still staring at the ground, so Ammar did not see his eyes widen at the idea that somehow working for the Baghdadi police was akin to standing by the Prophet's family on the battlefield. Although Tein had no time for religion, he loved Ali. He'd imagined himself more than once as the

Lion himself to get up his courage to face the enemy. This, to him, was not that. Tein only said, "Again, I'd rather carry bags of grain."

"You let me know what you decide. In the meanwhile, don't drink on the job again. Not even *nabidh*."

Tein didn't object further, saying "Front me some coin. I can't wait until the treasuries get around to my pay day. I need to find a place to sleep and I need to eat. And we never did get any food."

Ammar pulled a few coins out of his sleeve pocket and looked at them, pulled out two *dirhams* and handed them to Tein, "Tell your sister it's done. And buy yourself some black cloth for a turban."

Tein didn't reply.

"Let's get back to the scribe and get that report down."

Tein looked down at the coins in his hands and tucked them into his sleeve, "I liked you better when you weren't my boss."

Chapter Twenty-Four

Zaytuna made her way off of Basra Gate High Road without seeing the streets she walked through, winding her way through this alleyway and that. She found herself at the entrance to the Shuniziyya graveyard, looking for her mother, needing her comfort and guidance. Standing before the thick walls of the cemetery and looking at the long line of burrows that some of the poor had dug for shelter, she saw a woman's cracked and callused feet sticking out from under a lean-to, a simple reed frame of woven palm leaves, protecting her burrow from the sun. The woman had not set out her cooking pot by the road like everyone else so that someone might drop a coin in, some bread, or a small sack of grain or beans. There was always something given, even by the poorest of the poor to those poorer than themselves. Zaytuna approached, crouching down until she could see her face, "*Assalamu alaykum*, Auntie."

She saw the woman shift inside, but she did not move to meet her. She called out, "*Wa alaykum assalam*. What can I do for you my daughter?"

"Nothing. I was wondering about you. I saw you don't have your pot out, do you have something to eat?"

"I've eaten plenty."

"Today?"

"Every day."

"Auntie…"

The woman sighed. Then she rolled slightly to get out of the burrow and pushed her lean-to out a bit so she could sit up and face Zaytuna. Zaytuna took the lean-to, set it aside, and sat back on her haunches before the old woman, her knees coming up nearly to her chin. She had an old Arab face, the kind you only saw on the tribal women, and she looked at Zaytuna straight on. Her brown eyes were bright, shining out from her weathered skin, burnished by the sun to the colour of toasted wheat. She was not angry

with Zaytuna for making her shift from her place, but she was not curious
either.

Zaytuna asked the old woman, "Is this enough for you?"

The woman smiled, replying in the formal Arabic of the tribes, but
Zaytuna couldn't tell which one, "Is this not plenty for someone who's
dying?"

"Oh Auntie, are you dying? There must be something I can do for you."

The old woman tipped her chin up at her, "You might work more at dying
to this world yourself. Look at how you cling to it! Every misery you hold
dear to you like a suckling baby, refusing God's love because He did not
consult you first in His just design."

Zaytuna fell back off her haunches as if the woman had pushed her.

The woman laughed as Zaytuna righted herself, then said, "I can tell that
you know better, so why are you resisting?"

Zaytuna sat before her, knees tucked underneath her, but the heat of the
day was bearing down and she did not know how long she could stand it,
nevertheless she waited silently for the woman to speak again.

The old woman saw she was ready to listen, so she repositioned herself
with her back against the wall and said to her, her hand on the lean-to,
"Come here. We can use this to cover us both. By God's grace, there's room
enough for the two of us in this shade." Zaytuna shifted and shuffled herself
forward to sit next to her. She pulled the lean-to over to cover them both.
She had to fold herself up, slumping down, her knees to her chest, her arms
holding them in, and her chin tucked down, nearly resting on her knees. The
woman saw and nudged her slightly, saying, "Lay your head in my lap, you'll
be more comfortable. The woman held the lean-to steady as Zaytuna shifted
her body on the gravelly dirt, her *qamis* grinding into it, until she was curled
up on her side, her head in the old woman's lap, her sandaled feet sticking out
in the sun. The roughness of the woman's wool garment scratched her face
and smelled like clean, warm dust and comforting wool. Zaytuna exhaled
deeply and every muscle in her body relaxed. The gravel underneath her hip
and the sharp edge of her thigh softened such that she felt as if she were
lying on layers of sheepskins, and her feet felt as if they were in shade. The

old woman put her arm over Zaytuna's shoulder, pulling her in just a bit, and said, "That's better, yes?"

Tears came to her eyes in the sheer tenderness of it, "Yes, Auntie. That's better."

"Why do you concern yourself with suffering, girl? You only tie yourself to its dungeon walls by winding your miserable thoughts around yourself like a chain, over and over and around again. You've wound yourself up so, that even when God Himself has given you the key, you stay there as if this were the nature of things and there is no escape."

"How do I escape, Auntie?"

"By trusting that there are no chains, that there is no cell, no walls, and no dungeon. First, give up the chains. Walk toward the cell door, step by step. Walk as if there were no chains holding you to the cell wall. You will feel the pull of the chains. They are heavy still and you will feel them pinch and even cut. But you step forward. Observe how, with each step some small thing, a tiny thought, an infinitesimal matter, that you believed to be true, just as true to you as you knew this ground underneath you is as hard and sharp as stone and rock should be, is in fact, false."

Zaytuna felt herself drop even more softly into the ground, it holding her in its embrace, and she paid attention to it.

"With each step, you will feel your muscles soften little by little under the weight of the chains. These kinds of chains cannot hold a soft body. They rely on tension to keep them taut. So as you soften and loosen under them, the chains will slip from you, link by link. And as each link falls, a thick humming will begin to resonate within you. Just a trace at first. But do not dismiss it. When you feel it, know that this is a bodily symptom of love. You will object, I do not feel love, because you are simply unused to it. You have turned from every love granted to you, finding each offering lacking, as they are partnered, always in this world, with suffering and loss.

"Here you have a choice. Either pick up the chains around you and pull them back over your shoulders and around your throat, turn back to the wall, and say, if there is suffering in it, then I will suffer alone, without love, in my own peace. Or you can open your heart and hold onto every shred you feel, risking what comes, for the chance to feel love's touch again. You will begin to recognize love even in unfathomable places. Choose love and you will, with time, tremble so under its caress that it will shatter every last link that binds you. But listen to me, girl, at times you will go back. It's inevitable. Simply go forward more than back. And take care, each time you go back, losing further ground can get easier and easier, and you may find yourself chained to the wall again.

"If you choose love, look down, and you will find its key in your hand and the cell door before you. Place love's key into the lock and turn it. The cell door will open, and fall away behind you. Then step through the threshold beyond it and let the cell recede into the darkness you are leaving. Then you must climb the dungeon steps, one by one. And this will not be easy, either. Each step will disappear as your foot lifts from it to take the next one, so there is no turning back at this point. If you do, you will step back into the nothingness you have left behind.

"Soon, you will see sunlight shining through the door at the very top. The sunlight will begin to shine so brightly that you will no longer see the walls of the staircase you had been climbing or the steps under your feet. There will be nothing but light. Step out into that light and turn around. The dungeon of your suffering will have disappeared. You will have arrived at the fortress of God's help. And, my sweet, if your fortress is God's help, then, just as the Prophet found when he and Abu Bakr hid in the cave to escape the bloodthirsty Meccans, even a spider can be your gate-keeper."

Zaytuna lifted herself from the old woman's lap, pushing the lean-to back as she sat up. The midday light and heat fell on them. The old woman shielded her eyes from it, squinting, and looked up at Zaytuna now sitting before her, but ready to stand. She asked Zaytuna, "So what will you do, my daughter?"

"I am afraid, Auntie, but I will step. *Insha'Allah*." Zaytuna reached down and took the woman's hand and held it to her own heart then lifted it to her lips to kiss. "I do not know a prayer to say to you, Auntie. What could I possibly say?"

The old woman prayed, "May we accept love."

Zaytuna began to weep again, lifting her hand to wipe her eyes with the sleeve of her *qamis*, and said, *"Amin, amin, amin."* She stood and took hold of the lean-to while the old woman repositioned herself as she was when Zaytuna first found her, then placed the humble shelter over her and walked back to the cemetery gate.

She walked through the gravestones set out here and there for those who could afford them, further on to her mother where it looked like no one had been buried. A cluster of date palms grew by her grave, spreading their shade. She and Tein planted them one year, long ago, without knowing. They used to come together and sit by her grave, chatting and eating dates. They would push the seeds into the ground, and spit others into the distance. A few must have sprouted and taken root. They took turns bringing water to them during the hottest months, every year, until Tein left for the Frontier. Zaytuna saw yellow dogs asleep under their shade, their dusty fur like the colour of the dry soil, one lying nearly over the spot where her mother was buried. Her mother insisted that there would be no gravestone marking her body when she died and they'd respected that. Zaytuna knew someday that someone would just dig another body in there, disturbing her bones. As she came close to the grave, the dogs looked up at her to see what she wanted. She bent over to pick up a stone, but it was too hot now for them to care about rocks being thrown at them and they laid their heads back down. Zaytuna walked slowly to the grave, so as not to threaten them, got down on her knees, putting her hands in the dust, and lowered herself to lay across the grave, the one dog beside her. She held her mother's earth to her, and for once she basked in the love that poured from her mother, like the humming of bees, the flowing of warm honey, and felt at peace.

When her tears were spent, she got up, dusted herself off and made her way back home.

Chapter Twenty-Five

She was spent when she arrived in the courtyard. Yulduz was there. She crouched in the one shady spot before a brazier made of loose bricks arranged in a semi circle working at getting the dung fire going. Her friend, Marta, sat nearby, her faded, stained yellow wrap, around her waist like an apron, was covered in bits of palm litter as she stripped the pieces down to use for fast kindling to feed the dried reeds under the dung.

Yulduz looked up as she walked in, her eyes widening at the state Zaytuna was in, "*Ya Rabb*! What happened to you? Your clothes're filthy and dirt's sticking to the sweat on you. Go change those clothes." She pointed to the basin, "There's plenty of water in there to wash up but you could really use a trip to the baths."

Zaytuna replied, her voice tired, "*Assalamu alaykum. Alhamdulilah*, I'm fine. It's a long story."

Marta said, "A long story! We need a good story. We've finished gossiping about everyone in the neighbourhood already and we're bored." She smiled at Zaytuna, "Will there be romance in it?"

Zaytuna laughed despite herself, "Longing looks from across a garden filled with jasmine vines and pomegranate trees! My eyebrow was the bow and my glance the arrow that pierced his heart!"

As Zaytuna pushed aside the curtain of her room, Yulduz called after her, "We expect you to eat with us now you've got an appetite!"

Zaytuna, tired and embarrassed to say, now she could turn her attention to it, that she was hungry, responded, "Only if you agree to add my lentils to your pot, Auntie."

Yulduz responded, "*Insha'Allah*, it'll be a delicious stew! May God bless us with every bite. Everyone is putting something in. I've got a pile of chicory that Marta's collected. And Saliha's given us onions and salt. Dates and bread too. I've got my soup bone. It's only been boiled twice. There's plenty of flavour left in it."

Zaytuna pulled the loose end of her wrap off her head and shoulders and unwound it from where it was tucked under her arms as it wrapped around her body, and pulled off her *qamis* and *sirwal*. She could see the dirt fall from them in the sunlight streaming through the crack in the curtain over her door. She unwrapped her hair and shook out her scarf. It wasn't as dirty as the rest. She piled everything but her head scarf in the corner to be washed and pulled out her spare clothes, putting them on, but first sniffing at the wrap before winding it around herself. Tein had worn it last. It hadn't picked up any of his scent, thank goodness. She wrapped her hair again and took up the bowl of cleaned lentils, untying the cloth cover, and went back into the courtyard to Yulduz.

The dung had caught fire with not too much smoke. Yulduz fanned the pile of reeds underneath it while poking more in, here and there, until the dung was burning steadily enough to begin boiling the water. Zaytuna spoke as she came over with the bowl of lentils, teasing, "Smells like animal dung today instead of human dung, we're living the life of the caliphs now!"

Qambar laughed from where he was seated inside their room, saying loudly, "The singing girls will be by later with trays of sweets carried on their heads."

Yulduz said, "Speaking of the caliph's table, Umm Farhad collected some fallen apricots from the garden by the Great Mosque. Brought it back wrapped in her kerchief. You should have seen her! Her hair blowing in the breeze, smiling. I knew she'd got something good. She prepared some *nabidh*." Winking at Zaytuna, she said, "Let's see how long she lets that ferment!"

She called out in a louder voice to one of the rooms off the courtyard, "Isn't that right Umm Farhad, we'll all be drinking the Caliph's cider before long!"

A voice called out from within, "Don't you think I'm making hard cider, woman! *Insha'Allah*, it'll be ready by tomorrow. Besides, who says I'm sharing!"

Yulduz raised an eyebrow to Zaytuna, laughing, and placed a large ceramic pot of water with her soup bone in it onto the brazier, now that the dung was burning well, and stirred the lentils into it, and in her native Turkmen, she sang,

> I've come to wake you,
>> *Gara gozum*,
>>> to wake you.
> How beautiful the Creator has made you,
>> *Gara gozum*,
>>> has made you.
> If I were a tree, I would stand on the road,
>> *Gara gozum*,
>>> the road you walk on.
> I'd spread my shade on the road you walk on,
>> *Gara gozum*,
>>> on the road you walk on.
> On the road you walk on, I would stand,
>> *Gara gozum*,
>>> I'd spread my shade.

Zaytuna sat by the basin, saying "*bismillah*," and cup by cup rinsed the dirt from her face, hands and forearms, and feet and ankles. Each cup of water washing away the exhaustion of the day, she felt herself soften inwardly under its touch. She stood, saying "*Alhamdulilah*" under her breath and asked Yulduz, "That's beautiful, what does it mean? *Qara qozum?*"

"*Gara gozum…*" Yulduz laughed, "It's a '*gim*'! You Arabs!" Zaytuna winced at being called an Arab but Yulduz didn't seem to notice. She went on, "It means 'black-eyed beauty'." She sang, this time in Arabic, "I'd spread my shade on the road you walk on, my black-eyed beauty."

Yulduz winked at her as Zaytuna walked to her room to pray, "Some man might spread the shade of his tree for you to walk under, if you'd gain some weight."

Zaytuna laughed, "But Qambar is taken by you, Auntie. There's no good men left for whom I should fatten my behind."

Yulduz and Marta laughed again.

They heard someone coming into the courtyard. It was Mustafa. Yulduz asked, eyebrows raised in Mustafa's direction, saying, "Not even that one?"

Zaytuna didn't smile in return. At the sight of Mustafa, the softness she'd felt fled her, her mind pulled back Zayd and her awful meeting with Ammar. She said, maybe too sharply, to Yulduz, "No."

Yulduz scoffed at that, saying, "As you like."

Mustafa walked across the courtyard, saying, "*Assalamu alaykum!*" He reached Zaytuna, smiling, "Reporting back as requested. I heard something you might be interested in."

She sighed, shaking her head, "My meeting this morning with the police was awful. Maybe you can offer me some hope."

Mustafa pulled back, "What happened?"

"He was an awful man. He had some decency when he was Tein's friend. Now he's part of the caliphal administration, he thinks he knows everything."

"Zaytuna! What happened?"

"He didn't take anything I said seriously."

"Oh." Mustafa took a breath, relieved. Thank God, the girl would be safe. God knows the police wouldn't be concerned with risking her life. There must have been nothing to Zaytuna's story. Then he wished he hadn't mentioned he'd heard anything about the Imam. If he'd only waited to hear from her first.

He replied, softly, "I'm sorry. But Zay, he probably has testimony he didn't share with you that helped him better judge your information. You shouldn't take it personally. You don't know what else he knows."

She sucked her teeth, just slightly, but Mustafa heard it. She asked, "What did you find?"

"Look, Zaytuna, it's nothing. It doesn't sound like you could take it to the police. Better let it go."

"I'm not speaking to that man again."

"So no need to discuss it."

"Mustafa."

"It's not important."

She looked at him and sucked her teeth again, tsking loudly this time, "Another man deciding for me."

Yulduz and Marta looked up from where they sat, not even pretending not to listen. Mustafa saw them and lowered his voice, "Zaytuna, I didn't say that."

She heard him try to be quiet and kept her voice consciously loud enough for anyone to hear, "If you are going to be dismissive of me, then go."

Mustafa gave up, "Fine, I'll tell you. You can judge for yourself."

He walked away to the other side of the courtyard to the shared water basin, "Can't we talk over here?"

He dunked the communal cup into the basin and handed it to her. She sipped from it and smiled again, "Not as good as water from the cup you made me."

He tipped his head forward, acknowledging the peace offering, and was just glad she wasn't frustrated with him anymore. He couldn't stand it when they argued. And it was so easy for them to argue. She sat down beside the basin. He slid down the wall beside her and said, "I don't know how any of this would fit in, but it seems that some people believe the Imam forged his name on the collection of hadith he claims as his own. That means he never would have heard any of the hadith himself. He's not only not in those chains of transmission, but it would also make him a liar, a plagiarist, damning him forever from being considered a reliable scholar in the field."

With every word Zaytuna became more excited, "Mustafa! Yes, this is it! It didn't have anything to do with the girl. It was the forgery! Zayd knew about the forgery and threatened to expose him!"

Mustafa said, "Hold on, Zaytuna. First, this is gossip. Second, if Zayd knew this gossip, other people knew about it. Why target Zayd specifically?"

"No, Mustafa. Zayd knew how to read and he was studying hadith. He saw, somehow he saw, that the manuscript itself had been changed. Maybe he saw him change it himself when he was doing some work around the Imam. The Imam would never think that this servant boy knew what he was looking at and didn't think to hide it from him! It wouldn't be gossip. It would be evidence."

"Zayd knew how to read?"

"Salman was teaching him, the boys, how to read and write. And they study hadith."

"*Masha'Allah*, I never would have known. God forgive me, I thought. Well, I didn't like that he had young boys at his place. Vulnerable boys. There was wine there...."

She gasped, "God protect us from evil things! That never occurred to me."

She thought about it, then said, "There's been no gossip. For God's sake you can't do a thing around here without anyone getting wind of it."

She looked at him sharply, "In any case, if you suspected something, why didn't you say anything?"

He didn't answer, realizing heavily that he himself hadn't tried to intervene despite what he suspected.

She saw him chastened and tried to put him at ease, "Don't think about it, Mustafa, he was only teaching the boys to read and write."

"There's no money in teaching boys like that. Why does he do it?

"He cares about them. I think he sees himself in them. Pushed to the edge of society for who they are, for no reason of their own making. God forgive me for saying so, but it's not all generosity. He wants his grandfather's collection of hadith to survive, through them."

"That's understandable."

They didn't speak for a few moments. Then he asked, "What will you do with this information about the Imam?"

"I don't know. *Insha'Allah*, pursue it myself. There is no point in going to the police with it. But I cannot see how.... How can I interview the Imam?"

Her eyes suddenly pricked with tears, her limbs exhausted under the weight of it, "This is impossible. I feel like I'm supposed to do something for these children. But I don't know what."

Mustafa heard her voice catch and steeled himself against it. He knew he'd give in. "Zaytuna, I cannot speak to the man. If I hear anything else, I can tell you, but that's all."

"I wasn't asking you," she looked at him sideways. She meant it.

"I wish I could help, I'm sorry."

"It's alright. I wasn't asking, really."

They sat quietly again. They were so easy together like this, as long as they didn't talk.

She broke the silence, "Mustafa?"

"Yes?"

"Are you hungry? I'm hungry."

Mustafa looked at her, wondering what she could mean, "You're hungry... for food?"

"Saliha had some fresh cheese this morning. It was delicious."

"I'm just surprised."

She smiled at him, "Don't make too much out of it. I don't know what's going on. It doesn't feel like a craving from my lower soul. I just feel like I'm waking up from a long sleep and I need nourishment. Would you buy Yulduz, well all of us, a bone with some real meat on it for her soup? She's boiled that bone more than twice, I can tell you. She keeps it in a jar and boils it over and over. She offers to feed anyone from it, God bless her. I'm grateful to her, but I'd like to get her some meat and have some myself. I'm out of coin. I spent it on rent and Tein." She laughed, "God you should have smelled him, had to send him to the bath. Can you get something for us?"

Mustafa laughed, "Wait, you want meat to eat and you are willing to let me buy something for you?"

She leaned in and pushed him with her shoulder, "It's not just for me, it's for all of us. Anyway, don't the Sufis eat when a friend offers something?"

Mustafa smiled, his eyes taking her in with warmth, "So you are a follower of Uncle Abu al-Qasim now, too? Do you want to come with me? You can pick it out."

"Do you know a butcher who is a man of good character?"

"Of course."

They stood up and met with Saliha coming through the passageway into the courtyard. Zaytuna took hold of her, "Saliha, hold on," and called back to Yulduz. "Mustafa has kindly offered. Is there room in the pot, you think, for a little meat in our stew? We're off to get some."

The woman's eyes widened and she stiffened slightly, too proud to seem eager for something she or her man hadn't tasted in a long while, "There's no need for meat, but plenty else for Mustafa to join us."

"We'll be back in a few minutes, but please, Auntie, make room in that pot for some meat."

Saliha looked at Mustafa and tipped her head toward Zaytuna, "Meat?"

Mustafa smiled and said, "I know."

Chapter Twenty-Six

The door to Junayd's home was open. It was getting quite dark, but Mustafa could still see an unkempt man in a heavily patched wool robe was stepping through the doorway. He was closely followed by another man in a simple white muslin robe and turban. A scholar. Mustafa did not recognize him from the back, but the long tail of his turban hanging between his shoulders marked him as a Maliki. He seemed old, not frail, only stooped from years of writing over a desk, years of sitting in prayer. His hand was on the shoulder of the man in front of him. It was a gesture of companionship. To have his hand on the shoulder of such a man, Mustafa felt a little guilt. As a child, he always found a way not to sit near the patched wool wearers and even avoided them now, if he could. They smelled. Their wool cloaks and robes were patched over and over as they wore away from sleeping rough. But they were welcomed, open-handed, like this man had, by most everyone else in their circle.

Mustafa hurried to reach them calling out, "Ya Uncle, hold the door!" The second man heard him and turned, the first man in old wool disappearing into the house without looking back, as Mustafa came to a stop not far from them. It was Imam Abu Abdelrahman al-Azdi and Mustafa saw that the turban the man wore was his own.

Imam Abu Abdelrahman said, "Well met, Mustafa. *Alhamdulilah*."

Mustafa reached to take his hand, bowing his head to kiss it in greeting, but he pulled it from him and kissed the top of Mustafa's turban instead, saying, "May God open our hearts tonight to the *sama*."

"*Amin*."

Imam Abu Abdelrahman put his hand on Mustafa's shoulder and gently insisted that he walk ahead, but as they reached the end of the vestibule, Mustafa slipped to his side and excused himself to keep from showing his back to this great man and fell in behind him. One of the younger Sufis bolted the door behind them. Mustafa asked the Imam, "May I walk with you to the shaykh?"

As they came into the courtyard, he saw Uncle Abu al-Qasim look over at the two of them and smile. He thought first the look was for him, but then realized Uncle Abu al-Qasim recognized the Imam. His heart sunk at that but then rose again in pride to be seen with him. He caught himself. Look at what your soul is up to, Mustafa! God guide me from its promptings, its risings and fallings.

Uncle Abu al-Qasim looked at him and nodded, not in greeting, but rather in acknowledgement of his self-correction. Junayd began to stand and Abu Muhammad rose quickly to stand next to him. They walked together to the centre of the courtyard. Junayd took the Imam's hand. They bent over to kiss the back of each other's hands, each pulling their hand away from the kiss. As they straightened they drew each other into an embrace, as old friends do. Abu Muhammad put his hand over his heart and bowed toward the Imam and reached for his hand to kiss. The Imam pulled his hand away and kissed Abu Muhammad's turban, as he had with Mustafa.

Mustafa stood back as Junayd and the Imam spoke quietly to one another until Junayd withdrew and reached for him. Mustafa inclined his head and placed his other hand over his heart in greeting as he stepped forward to take his uncle's arm. Abu Muhammad nodded to him, giving him his place walking beside the great shaykh. They all went back to where he had been seated against the far wall with sheepskins laid out on the reed mats. Junayd gestured to the Imam to sit in his place. The Imam bowed slightly, but stood beside Junayd until he was seated again in his proper place and then sat down to Junayd's right.

Junayd nodded to Mustafa and said, "My son, come sit on the other side of me." Abu Muhammad moved to stand on the other side of Mustafa, waiting for Mustafa to sit down next to Junayd. Mustafa bowed slightly and waited, like the Imam had done, until Abu Muhammad sat down, but, as the shaykh had requested, leaving space for Mustafa next to Junayd.

The long reed mats were laid out around the courtyard walls as usual but on nights of *sama*, more of them were brought out and rolled out in rows extending the seating area into the courtyard and then covered with sheepskins, leaving a circle of empty space in the centre under the stars. Lanterns were lit and hung from the archways and here and there a floor lantern stood by a pillar sending warm light flickering from its cut metal designs across the walls. Mustafa took in the smell of burning oil in the lanterns mixed with the scent of wool from so many sheepskins placed out and the fresh night air. He closed his eyes, and was feeling at peace.

Others began arriving in greater numbers. Each made their way first to greet the shaykh before taking a spot on the floor. Mustafa looked toward the kitchen and saw the drums laid out. Dawud, charged with the task of keeping the drums, took them one at a time into the kitchen to correct their tone; he used water to loosen the skin, and heat to tighten it. Mustafa could hear the sounding of each drum until its beat resonated, travelling through his heart. He longed to hear the poetry captured by ecstatics in their reveries sung to the beat of the drum until it took him over and he would sway, his heart lost in its song. He relished the repose that came afterward with the recitation of the Qur'an. He loved the opening and sealing of the ritual with prayers on his beloved Prophet, Muhammad, the Chosen One.

As Dawud came out of the kitchen with one of the drums, a long-limbed man ducked out behind him. Warmth rushed through him; it was Uncle Nuri. A little girl sitting with her mother nearby broke free of her arms and rushed to Uncle Nuri demanding to be held. He crouched down and took the girl in his arms. Mustafa had been the same as a child.

He remembered when he was six or seven he had found a thick thorn bush branch. It was oddly shaped, long-necked with four short stems on one side that looked to Mustafa very much like legs. It was an animal, certainly. But what kind? He searched out Uncle Nuri and sat in his lap to discuss it. They considered each possible creature until deciding, finally, that it was a donkey. Uncle Nuri asked him if he would like to name the donkey. Mustafa remembered it perfectly, he said, "She's such a beautiful donkey. Don't you think she is pretty? Her name is Zaytuna."

His Uncle sent him on his way laughing, saying, "Let's keep her name between us, though. It'll be our secret."

Mustafa told Zaytuna anyway, proudly showing her the donkey, and she hit him.

Junayd saw him looking over to Nuri and said to him, "Go greet your uncle."

Mustafa got up slowly, despite wanting to rush, and walked toward the kitchen.

His Uncle Nuri kissed his cheek once he got him into his arms and then pushed him away to look at him, asking, "When are you marrying Zaytuna?"

"Uncle," he looked down, "How could we marry if she doesn't love me?"

His uncle looked at him as if they had had this conversation too many times and he was nearing the end of his willingness to repeat it, "The love is there, I've seen it."

"You always say that, but I never see it."

"I think there's been a change."

Mustafa pulled back, "What do you mean?"

"It seems that your Uncle Abu al-Qasim has gotten involved and pushed her head under, forced her to taste God's love rather than wait for her to work her way through to it."

He realized then. She was eating meat. She was enjoying her food. Maybe she was leaving her ascetic life behind and might consider marriage. Maybe she was letting her pain go. This had to be for the good if this was Uncle Abu al-Qasim's doing. He said, his chest tightening and eyes filling with tears, "God willing."

He said, "Come and sit next to me, Mustafa. I have my corner here beyond the old women. I want to hear all your news."

Mustafa wanted to sit next to his Uncle, thigh to thigh, until listening to the sound of the drums and the poetry and his own breath chanting "there is no god but God" turned into nothing but atoms moving through them all. But he said instead, "Uncle Abu al-Qasim has asked me to sit next to him for the *sama*."

Uncle Nuri pulled a face, then smiled, and pushed him off, "Go then."

Mustafa embraced him again and returned to sit next to Junayd.

Junayd turned and said to Mustafa once he was seated again, "God has brought our friend Imam Abu Abdelrahman to sit with us tonight. He is a great friend to the Knowers of God. We met on my first hajj when I went to Medina to give my greetings to our beloved Prophet."

The Imam laughed, "We were younger men then, we could sit like this well into the night and not be tired the next day. I still invite the Sufi travellers to my home for *sama* when they find their way to me. But," he laughed, "I confess I fall asleep on my sheepskin if it goes too late now."

"*Masha'Allah*, you were a kind host to us. May God always fill your house with remembrance of Him."

Gesturing toward the Imam, Junayd turned to Mustafa, "I had hoped to introduce you, but he says you have already met. I have told him all about your mother, may God be well pleased with her, and how you were born among us and grew up among us."

The Imam spoke up, "I recognized him as one of yours right away." Raising one eyebrow, he added, "Very unlike some of the other young men there."

Mustafa pretended he didn't hear it, but he felt the pleasure in what the Imam said deep in his gut and he wondered immediately if Junayd was aware of it.

Junayd asked Mustafa, "Who else was there when you met?"

Mustafa's face burned, he didn't want to say. His gut pulled him, wanting to hear what the Imam thought of Burhan and the others. Maybe even Uncle Abu al-Qasim would have a criticism for them. If he said it, he'd get what he wanted.

Junayd repeated himself, "Tell me Mustafa, who was there?"

"I'm sorry. Sharafuddin, Abdelmalik, some of Imam Hamdan's students including Burhan, and three students of Imam Ibrahim."

Junayd nodded, "Trust your heart's knowledge when dealing with these people, Mustafa. Do you think that I am beyond this stage? None of us is. In fact, it gets more dangerous as one progresses. Walk away from those who cause your heart to constrict while you are in their presence. If I want something that causes my heart shame, then I pay attention to that and leave whatever it is. You do the same. Leave the doubtful desires of this world for the certainty of God's guidance. Do not indulge in their talk."

Mustafa nodded in return. He always felt like a child with Uncle Abu al-Qasim, petulant, objecting. He wanted to say that it wasn't as easy as all that, but did not.

Junayd replied anyway, as if he had heard him, "I know it can be difficult interacting with these people. You forget I studied law and I still act as a jurist when needed."

"Yes, Shaykh," He tried not to say more, but it came out anyway, "But Shaykh, what do I do when I know something bad about someone and bringing it to light may help some people but hurt others?"

Junayd spoke, "You must weigh the harm and the good that you can see coming from it and consider the avenues of resolution. Sometimes dealing with a problem privately is appropriate. Other times, you must stand and give witness publicly. The most vulnerable need the most protection and you are required to take the greatest risks for their sakes. But you must also consider the truth of all the claims being made. At times, we get swept up in righting a wrong and no longer have a grasp on the truth. You must not oppress even in the name of seeking justice."

The Imam nodded to Junayd, then asked Mustafa, "Do you mind me asking about the problem? Your shaykh and I have seen a lot in our old age. It may be that we've crossed this road before and can help."

Mustafa could hear Abu Muhammad shifting next to him. He didn't know whether or not he should answer. He didn't want to act as though Junayd's answer was not enough for him, but he also did not want to be rude to the Imam. And he did want to talk about it. Mustafa looked at Junayd who nodded his head.

Mustafa said quietly, "It's a hadith scholar. I heard that he plagiarized his collection."

The Imam sat up at that. Junayd leaned back slightly to give the Imam the space to speak. The Imam said, "A hadith scholar? If you know anything, you must say so. The reliability of the Prophet's legacy, our practice, our faith, depends on being honest about the character of the transmitters and scholars."

Mustafa stepped ahead onto uncertain ground, "There is more to it than that. He may have hurt someone to hide the fact."

The Imam replied, "Hurt someone? This is even more serious, Mustafa. Please tell us."

Mustafa turned to Junayd saying, "Zaytuna was here the other day. You mentioned the children involved. A boy died."

Junayd said, "Ah. I understand."

He turned to the Imam, "Mustafa's cousin, a daughter of our community, is heartbroken over the child's death."

The Imam asked, "Mustafa, who is the scholar involved?"

"Imam Ibrahim al-Silafi."

"Just so. No need to say anymore. I know the gossip about him. It is just that, gossip. I have first hand knowledge that he collected the hadith as he claims. There is no plagiarism. I taught him some of those hadith myself and certified him to transmit them. I know personally two of the scholars from whom he transmits and that they gave him certificates to do so. Further, there is no Ibrahim Ibn at-Tahir al-Naysaburi as people claim. The man was concocted out of thin air to persecute Imam Ibrahim."

Mustafa was hit with shock at the news, "*Subhan'Allah*! Why would people make that up about him?" Then the shame hit him. He had found it easy to believe it. Worse, he was willing to think he could have murdered a boy because of the lies.

The Imam said, "Seeing a person whom they hate destroyed is more precious to them than bearing up under the burden of truth. Those who repeat the story without trying to ascertain its veracity are not worthy of the name 'scholar.' To suspect him of harming someone, a child at that. May God forgive them."

Mustafa could not speak. He could not say, it was me who thought that, not them.

Junayd waited a moment until Mustafa had taken a breath and could hear what he had to say, "The burden of truth requires becoming familiar with your own jealousies, resentments, and assumptions, Mustafa. Examine all the good that God has bestowed on you and then examine your own weaknesses. I promise you that you will feel ashamed. These weaknesses should be the object of your criticism. Do that and you will find little time to criticize others."

Mustafa felt the sting of his uncle's correction and began to tremble, saying to himself over and over, "God forgive me and make me familiar with my own weaknesses. God forgive me…" until the trembling subsided and he could hear conversation taking place over him.

Imam Abu Abdelrahman was saying, "…Of course there is a great deal of hypocrisy in it, people who dislike Imam Ibrahim and speak ill of him have their own connections to the court. Some of these themselves have even willingly accepted positions as judges."

Abu Muhammad replied, "The Baghdadis don't forgive and forget easily. I'm afraid the inquisition is still felt here as though it happened yesterday. Anyone who accepts patronage from the court is seen as a collaborator."

The Imam replied, "In practical terms, it always makes the most sense to be independent of a caliph's interests. You never know what will be demanded of you or what will happen to you should one caliph fall and his rival take his place."

He turned to Junayd, "I defer to you, shaykh. Would you say that only a great man could resist the temptations of caliphal power, the money, the circles of influence?"

Junayd said, "One of our friends found his way into these circles and we are seeing the results. He is beyond temptation. I do not mean to suggest otherwise. But the risks go beyond what you have mentioned. God protect us from spiritual states that make us so reckless so as to expose our secrets to the uninitiated."

Mustafa gasped. He was talking about al-Hallaj.

The Imam replied, "If I know who you mean, he was in Mecca and Medina not long ago. I understand from my colleague, the judge Abu Umar, that he's returned to Baghdad and is speaking publicly here."

Abu Muhammad confirmed, "Yes," and said no more.

The Imam knew this could mean trouble for his Sufi friends. al-Hallaj's street preaching and political interests would come crashing down on them as well. He felt for Junayd having to steer this community through al-Hallaj's ecstatic shudderings. He had only spoken publicly a few times while in Mecca and Medina and it moved the people in ways that frightened him. The poor were easily stirred up against the hypocrisy and too often dissolute behaviour of the caliph's people and their hangers-on. He would have to speak to Abu Umar about it and make sure he knew the difference between an al-Hallaj and an al-Junayd. His gaze drifted across the courtyard where it fell on Nuri chatting with Ibn Ata. He hoped they would keep circumspect during this time. He shook his head, perhaps Nuri could refrain from smashing the Caliph's wine jars again until the danger passed.

"May God protect you and keep you out of sight of anyone who would bring you trouble," the Imam said, reciting, "We have put a barrier before them and behind them and covered them so that they cannot see."

They all responded to his prayer, "*Amin.*"

Mustafa hung his head. Sitting with Uncle Abu al-Qasim was exhausting, you could hide nothing from him. He looked up at Uncle Nuri and longed to sit next to him. There was no hiding anything from him, either, but he would know he'd already been corrected and let him be for a while.

Junayd turned to Mustafa, "You haven't seen your Uncle Nuri in a while, why don't you enjoy the *sama* with him for now. Perhaps you can walk Imam Abu Abdelrahman back to Sharafuddin's father's home tonight, so he won't have any trouble in the street."

Mustafa started to get up, ashamed again because he knew Uncle Abu al-Qasim had heard his complaint. Junayd put his hand on his arm and made him turn to look at him. He looked up at his uncle and felt his love, felt his embrace and calm wash through him. Uncle Abu al-Qasim said to him, "We're very proud of you, Mustafa. You must recite the Golden Chain hadiths for us when you are certified."

Mustafa blushed, his head dropping again at the thought of it. He took his uncle's hand and kissed it before Junayd could pull it back, placing it to his forehead, and said, "*Insha'Allah.*"

He got up and picked his way through the seated crowd now filling the courtyard to Uncle Nuri and took a spot near him and Uncle Ibn Ata just as one of the musicians picked up a drum and tapped a few beats. Everyone settled down and became silent. The head reciter called out, "*Bismillah ar-rahman ar-rahim, wa salat wa salam ala seyyidina Muhammad.* In the name of God, The Merciful, The Compassionate, and blessings and peace on our Master Muhammad."

The Fourth Day

Chapter Twenty-Seven

Mustafa arrived at Zaytuna's not long after he left the mosque from performing his dawn prayer. The sky was just bright enough now to see through the streets and alleys without torchlight. He needed to tell her it was done. There was nothing left to investigate. He placed his hand on the wall of the passageway leading to the courtyard. He took up his resolve, practicing, saying aloud, but quietly, "Zaytuna, you must let it go." He stepped into the courtyard only to see Saliha coming out of Zaytuna's room nearly yelling, "I've had enough of you," her hand waving back at Zaytuna, still in her room, in a gesture of dismissal as if a wasp were hovering nearby her waiting to attack.

Mustafa rushed forward. He tried to peek into Zaytuna's room but the curtain had closed and it was still too dark outside to shed any light into it. He turned to Saliha, "What was that? What's happened?"

"She can be so selfish. *Walla!*"

"What?" He looked back to see if Zaytuna was coming out, if this argument was going to spill into the courtyard.

Saliha said, exasperated, "The other day, when we were at the mosque and she was questioning the housekeeper, she also talked to one of the corpsewashers. I ended up talking to the other." She looked towards Zaytuna's room and said loudly, to her, "I was only pulling the other Washer aside so Zaytuna could question hers."

Mustafa lowered his voice to a whisper, "Zaytuna is mad at you for that?"

"No. No. She's mad because of what I said to the Washer. I asked the woman how I could learn to be a washer too. Just to keep her busy. But the one I spoke to, she gestured to the one speaking to Zaytuna saying that she needed to replace her. That she wasn't all that discreet. She invited me to train with her."

"Why would Zaytuna be mad about that? I don't understand."

"If I train to be a corpsewasher, I will no longer be a washer of clothes."

"Oh," he said. "Leaving Zaytuna to do that without you."

"Correct."

They heard Zaytuna from inside her room, yelling, at them, "*ALLAHU AKBAR!*"

Saliha rolled her eyes, "I guess she's going to pray about how I've betrayed her."

Mustafa said gently, "Maybe she's going to pray to quiet her heart."

"Mustafa, please. Do you really think that?" She walked away from him to her own room leaving him standing by her door.

Saliha was right. Zaytuna would have her back up about this. He could never understand how someone who cared so much for others, who championed the most vulnerable, could not be more generous with those closest to her. Now he had to tell Zaytuna there was nothing to her suspicions of Imam Ibrahim. It would be a betrayal to her. Just the fact of the situation. But she would feel it as a betrayal all the same. Maybe he shouldn't tell her?

He could hear the crackling sound of her fishskin mat and the rustle of her clothes, then quietly, her voice reciting Qur'an. She was in prayer now. He sat down against the wall and waited for her to finish. But she didn't finish. She kept going. She was settled in for a long prayer. Maybe he should just come back.

As he sat listening to her movements and her voice he realized she had been reciting the same verse over and over in each cycle of prayer, "*Who is it who answers the distressed when they call upon Him? Who removes their suffering? Who has made you His advocates on this earth? Is there another god beside God? Yet you remember none of that.*"

He sighed. This conversation was not going to go well with her in this state of mind. He got up to leave.

Saliha came out, asking him, "Has she stopped praying for my doom yet?"

He shook his head. "I have to tell her something, but it can wait. I'll come by later."

Mustafa saw Saliha move toward Zaytuna's doorway. Realizing what she was going to do, he tried to stop her, "No, really. I'll come back later. Don't disturb her prayer."

She gave him a look that said, "It's fine," and pulled back the curtain, saying loudly, "Zay, Mustafa's here. Cut that out and come and speak to him."

Zaytuna responded with a harsh, "*ALLAHU AKBAR!*"

Saliha laughed, "She'll be out."

Mustafa didn't like it, "God protect me. You are worse than she is."

Saliha laughed again and went back to her own room to get ready to go to work. The sky was light now. Neighbours began moving around the courtyard. Umm Farhad came out, her hair uncovered and her wrap wound around her body, her shoulders bare. Farhad followed her, tugging at his own *sirwal* and complaining to her about something. Mustafa couldn't hear what about. She looked down at him, pushing him away from her, "Run then if you have to go. You don't need me. The latrine isn't far. Just around the corner. You know where it is." Farhad rushed off, out the passageway.

Mustafa dropped his eyes to the ground. She caught it and laughed at him, "Look you silly boy! No one has cared for this old body in many years. Maybe I'll still find me a man, but he won't be you. So don't be so scared!"

Mustafa blushed deeply and called inside Zaytuna's room, "Zaytuna, I'm leaving. I'm sorry. I had news about the Imam."

At that, he heard her quickly end her prayer. He wished he'd said it earlier. The curtain pulled back, she stepped out and said without greeting him, "What did you hear?"

"It's nothing. I mean, there is nothing."

"Mustafa, what do you mean 'there is nothing'?"

"The book of hadith isn't a forgery. You know the scholar, Abu Abdelrahman al-Azdi, who is permitting me to become certified in the hadiths of the Golden Chain?"

"Yes, yes."

"He said Imam Ibrahim was his student once. He taught him many of those hadith himself. There is no Ibrahim Ibn at-Tahir al-Naysaburi who he could have stolen the collection from. It's all lies, made up to slander Imam Ibrahim."

"Oh," she said, looking down.

"So you see, there just isn't any reason for the Imam to have killed Zayd." She didn't respond. She was still looking at the ground, or her feet. What did it matter? He didn't know what she was thinking. Maybe he could guide her. He said, softly, "Isn't it possible that you've seen too much in all this. You've seen patterns where there were none? We've looked at everything."

"I don't know."

"Layla and Zayd," he pushed lightly, "Don't you see a bit of us in them? Our childhood. Everyone's childhood here. Maybe you are trying to speak out for them because, well, who speaks for any of us when the rich can do as they please?"

"You're saying all this is in my mind."

"No."

"I don't believe it, Mustafa. How could it be?"

Her voice became desperate. Her eyes searching his for confirmation, "God arranged all this. God brought them to me."

"Maybe God brought them to you, but not for the reason you think."

"What then? What is the reason? How could I have misunderstood God so completely?"

Zaytuna fell back against one edge of the doorway and sat down hard on the floor. He watched her slide down the wall. Now seated, he saw her heart beating so hard the fabric was moving. He looked away, across the courtyard, focusing on the far wall.

She listened to her heart thumping in her chest. She could hear the percussive whoosh of it as far as her ears. Then she heard the beating of her heart as if from outside her body, and saw herself as if in front of herself, watching the colour rise up into her face.

Mustafa didn't look at her. He didn't dare. She was breathing hard, nearly panting. He was waiting for an outburst. There was nothing. Then he heard footsteps from behind him in the courtyard and Tein's voice.

"Ya Zaytuna, we have to talk."

The sound of him snapped her back to herself. She turned towards him, looking past Mustafa, finding her voice, and hissed, "You too?"

Tein stopped short and held his hands up, "What did I do? I just walked into this courtyard! Calm down, sister."

She repeated his words, "Calm down, sister."

He looked at Mustafa, "What's wrong?"

Mustafa said, "I found out there is nothing to the forgery story."

Tein gestured with his hand, "What?"

"Another reason Zaytuna was considering why Imam Ibrahim might have killed Zayd. There was no forgery for Zayd to discover and for the Imam to cover up by killing him."

Tein laughed under his breath, "Another angle."

Zaytuna repeated his words, "Another angle."

Tein ignored Zaytuna and said to Mustafa, "It didn't go so well when she spoke to Ammar."

He said, "I heard. Naturally, she was upset."

Zaytuna muttered, "Naturally."

Tein turned his hand out gesturing to her, speaking to Mustafa, "I can't do what she wants."

Saliha came out of her room. She saw Zaytuna, her back against the doorway, red faced, muttering, and the two men talking over her, crowding her down, and hurried to her, "*Habibti*, you're scaring me. Look at you. You're sweating, look at your face, it's all red. That vein on your forehead is beating like a drum. Come, come."

She pulled Zaytuna away from under them, pulling her up and over to her. She ran to get a cloth to wet at the basin. Only then did Mustafa and Tein see that anything was wrong.

Saliha placed the cloth from the basin on the back of Zaytuna's neck. Zaytuna tried to push her away, but Saliha scolded her, "Stop it right now."

The men came over. Mustafa asked, worried now, "What can I do?"

Saliha looked the two of them up and down, "*Walla*, you two are useless. One of you, get her a cup of water."

Mustafa rushed to get the water. Saliha took it from him and held it to Zaytuna's lips. Zaytuna, pushed her hand away, nearly spilling the water, spitting out the words, "I'm not a child."

Saliha looked her in the eye and put her hand on her cheek, "No you are not, so stop acting like one."

Zaytuna looked back at her just as sharply, "Fine. Give me the cup." Saliha handed it to her and she drank from it, her breathing slowing as she focused on drinking the water.

Zaytuna looked up at the two men, hovering over her again, and pushed at them with her free hand, "Get away from me!"

Tein shrugged and moved over to the far wall, saying over his shoulder, "She'll be fine. She's my sister, you think I haven't seen this before?"

Mustafa walked over to him, unwilling to say aloud what Tein had, but thinking it. He turned to Tein and asked almost in a whisper, "What did you have to say? Was it about all this?"

Tein didn't bother to lower his voice, "She doesn't think she was taken seriously." He turned to speak directly at her, raising his voice slightly, "but what she doesn't know is that Ammar questioned another person because of her and we're going to question the last possible person who could know anything later today. Two people she didn't even know about. A student in the Imam's house who is in love with Zaynab and another servant, a boy named Yusuf. He was on the roof when Zayd went over. The student couldn't have done it. He wasn't there. The servant was sleeping, but, despite her complaints that she's been treated unfairly, we're going there today to question him, too. Just to make sure."

Mustafa shook his head, "It seems that every consideration is being made."

"Ammar's not happy about any of it, though. He said it's wasting a lot of his time. I got the backhand of that for her efforts."

Mustafa looked down, speaking under his breath, hoping only Tein could hear, "I asked questions I wouldn't have, too. I shamed myself in front of an important scholar by questioning him about libellous gossip for her sake."

Saliha looked at the two of them, eyes wide, shaking her head, "You know we can hear you."

Mustafa looked stricken.

Tein said, "I haven't said anything that I wasn't going to say to her directly. In fact, I've been talking directly to her."

Zaytuna said, her face hard, trying to keep tears back, "Leave then. Leave like you always do if I'm so much trouble for you! And where did you sleep last night?"

Tein said, "I've got my own coin now. I've got a room, closer to the Basra Gate."

Zaytuna said, "Of course you do. And what about me?

"It's always about you. What am I here for? You think I can protect you? I can't protect you. I can't protect anyone. Get off my back."

Zaytuna spat out at him, "Perfect for the police then. When have they ever taken care of the likes of us!"

Mustafa took a step toward Zaytuna, she pointed at him, growling, "You, BACK!"

Mustafa's heart froze. He'd never heard this from her. He stood perfectly still, tight with fear, "Zaytuna, please. Forgive me."

Tein heard him simpering and laughed out his nose, "I'm gone. You two. You two are perfect for each other. You give right in to her. You'll be happy." He tipped his chin up at Mustafa saying, "Ask her to marry you already." He turned his back on them and walked away, wondering if Salman had replaced his stock of wine. It was early in the morning, but he already wanted a drink.

Mustafa rushed to Zaytuna, kneeling before her, but taking care not to touch her, "I would give my life for yours! Please forgive me!"

She pushed at him, "Your life! Do you truly want to marry me? Mustafa, what would make you think that? I've never loved any man other than the Prophet. Look at you! Is this how he would treat a woman? Is this the kind of loyalty he showed the women he loved? Get away from me!"

He stood slowly, backing up, and tripped over Umm Farhad and Yulduz who had been sitting by Umm Farhad's room watching the whole thing, falling beside them and landing hard, his turban falling off. He scrambled up, grabbing his turban, and ran out of the courtyard, his eyes stinging from fighting back the tears that were now coming hard.

Saliha turned to the old women, "Alright, you've had your show."

Yulduz replied to Zaytuna, "I told you whose side that brother of yours would be on."

Zaytuna wanted to reach out and slap her and looked like she would.

Saliha got up and walked over to the old women and said quietly to Yulduz, "Go inside."

Yulduz flicked her chin up at Saliha and stayed right where she was while Umm Farhad crossed her arms, settling in.

Saliha nodded slowly and said, "You'll reap what you sow, old woman," and turned her back on the two of them.

Yulduz called after her, "Say what you like, girl. But I vow I'll go see Hajja Tansholpan at the market gate for a lasting curse on that man if he turns against us."

Farhad came out at all the yelling and started crying. Saliha wanted to slap him quiet, but Yulduz had scared her. She looked back at the two women, knowing one of those cows would do it, too. Qambar came out of their room and pulled at Yulduz to get inside. Yulduz slowly rolled over to her side and pushed herself up and, for her husband's sake, went inside while Umm Farhad finally took her child in hand and walked him out of the courtyard.

Saliha got to Zaytuna and crouched in front of her. Her face had changed. It was resolute. She asked Zaytuna, "What do you want to do?"

"I need to speak to the housekeeper." She looked back at where the old women were sitting, "I never considered what an old woman might do to protect her own. If what Zayd did to Zaynab was bad enough…." She looked back at Saliha, "I have to go this morning. Did you hear Tein? He said they are going over there later today. If I don't do this, I won't know what I am for in this world. I won't know who God is anymore. *Insha'Allah*, I need to finish this. Whatever that means. And I need to finish it before they get there."

"Do you know where they live?"

"I know the street. From there, I'll ask."

"Do you want me to come with you?"

"No, I'll go alone."

"You don't need to come with me to work today. It's a small family. One house. I can do it by myself."

Zaytuna reached for Saliha's hand, brought it to her lips and kissed it, then placed the back of Saliha's hand to her forehead. Saliha pulled her hand back slightly and pulled at Zaytuna's kerchief, saying, "Look at that hair. It needs a good combing. Let's take care of you before you go."

Saliha pulled her up a bit by her arm until Zaytuna followed her into her room. Saliha said, "Sit. I'll get my comb."

Zaytuna spoke as Saliha rooted around until she found it, asking, "What will I do without you?"

"I'm not going to start washing bodies tomorrow. I'm not paid to train, so I'll wash clothes until I get paid. And when I do, you'll wash clothes by yourself. You'll knock on doors for business by yourself. You did that before I met you. You'll be fine."

"You won't move out, like Tein?"

Saliha sat down behind her, and pulled Zaytuna's kerchief off, "Zaytuna, how much do you think I am going to make? Even if I do make more, why would I move? This place is clean and safe. Those old women are difficult, but they are good women all the same, and better the good and bad you know.... Maybe I'd buy us mattresses. Huh? How would that be? In any case, no matter what, if I moved, you would come with me."

Zaytuna spoke so quietly, she could barely hear her, "Alright."

Saliha unraveled the long, thick braid tied up in a bun at the nape of Zaytuna's neck and began to comb it through, placing the matted strand threaded with the stone beads over her chest so she would not catch it with the comb. Despite having been braided, her hair was still snarled here and there, when the comb caught on them, Zaytuna pulled her head back, saying, "Ouch!"

Saliha scolded her lightly, "Woman, when was the last time you combed your hair out?"

Zaytuna was able to laugh a little at least, "What good is hair to an ascetic?"

"Ascetic? I was with you when you ate meat yesterday. Don't give me that ascetic talk."

"I don't feel much like eating today. I don't know what yesterday was all about."

Saliha's face fell a little, but she kept it to herself, "Well let's solve this ascetic hair of yours. I haven't got any oil for it, but we can take care of that when we go to the baths next."

Zaytuna said, "God forgive me, Saliha, I hate my hair."

"Why? It's perfectly straight, so thick, and such a deep black! It's extraordinary."

"I hate my hair." She wanted to cry. She touched her matted loc, feeling each bead, and said, "I only ever wanted hair like my mother. Why did Tein get her face, her skin, her hair? I'm tall, I have her bones, that's it."

Saliha put her hand on her shoulder and pulled her back into a hug, "Zay."

Zaytuna said, "I used to twist my mother's locks. They were beautiful. If we had beeswax, only sometimes did we have it, she would warm bits of it in her palms, then give me a tiny ball of it. I would sit all over her, digging into her hair. I'd be in her lap. On her back. Hanging onto her. I'd take each loc, where it was growing out, and rub the wax in, twisting with my fingers....over and over."

"It must have taken a long time."

"It did. Just the two of us. I had her to myself, as long as I liked, to twist that hair."

"How did she do your hair?"

"She would braid it. Long small braids along my scalp. Sometimes in patterns, round and round my head. But the little straight ends would stick out and ruin it."

"Let me braid your hair like that." Saliha picked up a clutch of hair on the side of Zaytuna's head. Zaytuna could feel that she took too much to braid and too gently but didn't say anything. Saliha tried to pick up more and more, braiding it as best she could down one side, but it fell apart. She said, "I didn't realize it was this hard."

Zaytuna reached up and felt what little of the braid was left.

Saliha muttered, "I've got nothing to tie this bit of awful braid with."
Zaytuna said, "It'll be alright, Saliha," as the tears came down her face.

Chapter Twenty-Eight

Zaytuna hit the knocker on the gate to Imam Ibrahim's house three times before someone answered. A young man opened the smaller door within the gate, one of his students, no doubt. He was too well dressed for anything else. Not like Mustafa. She saw how out of place he must feel in these circles. The Prophet wasn't like these people. He never dressed in finery. He was our teacher. Our guide. Our beloved. Why wasn't the Prophet's example good enough for them? Why did they think they could do better?

Poor Mustafa, she thought. Then she remembered she was angry with him, pulling herself up to meet it. Wait! Poor Mustafa? The only way he differed from these people was his worn clothing. No doubt he'd find his way into their circles soon enough and be robing himself in silk and brocade and embroidered slippers, maybe even boots in the winter. She muttered, "Uff."

The young man said to her again, "*Assalamu alaykum.*"

She realized she'd been staring at him and not speaking. She blurted out, "I'm here for the housekeeper, Maryam."

"*Assalamu alaykum,*" the student repeated.

She wanted to slap him for his pious censure but she needed to get into the house. The best she could do was a sarcastic bow, hand over heart, saying with flourish, enunciating every syllable of the extended reply, "*wa alaykum assalam wa rahmatullahi wa barakatuhu.*"

"Now, what did you need?"

She repeated herself, "I'm here to see the housekeeper, Maryam."

"Wait here, I'll get her," and he shut the door on her.

Moments later it opened again. Maryam's eyes widened seeing her standing before her. She closed the door enough so that only part of her body could be seen through it, "What are you doing here?"

Zaytuna faltered. Any sweetness that she and Maryam had shown each other at the mosque was gone. Zaytuna stumbled over her words, "I've been thinking about you since we spoke at the mosque. I mean, I hope you are well. I thought, I thought I would come by to look in on you."

Maryam's face softened only a bit, but Zaytuna saw the door open slightly. She didn't respond immediately. "I've got plenty of work to do, but if you don't mind chatting while I prepare food. Well, then, welcome."

It was a clear dismissal.

If Zaytuna had cared a thing about propriety in that moment she would have turned around, ashamed. Instead she stepped forward to go through the doorway forcing Maryam to step back and open the door completely as she walked through.

She followed Maryam into the garden. The housekeeper walked her around the side under the overhang between the two attached houses, past the small well to the kitchen door. The door was open. A small fire was going in the hearth and a pot of water getting started over it. She was surprised the room was not hot, as it should be with even a small fire on a day like this, but a breeze was coming in through the door opened to the central courtyard and the small inner window and out the door where she had come in. She showed Zaytuna to a stool on the far side of the hearth by the inner door across from where she herself had been seated only halfway through peeling a pile of soaked dried fava beans. Maryam went into the pantry and tipped a gleaming copper pitcher over a glass while a thick syrup dripped down its long stem. She then tipped another pitcher, this one much larger and the liquid flowed easily. Maryam handed it to her, saying automatically, "May it bring you good health."

Zaytuna responded as she should, "May God replenish your stores." She held the delicate cup and looked at the way the light from the door and window nearby her shone through it from one angle and the small fire in the hearth, on the far side of the room, from the other, picking up the bubbles, the curve of the blown glass, the light refracting into colours alighting on her.

She looked up at Maryam who still stood over her, saying, "May God reward your kindness." She took a sip. The water was sweetened with syrup made with sugar, apples, and fresh ginger. Her tongue held it still for a moment, as long as she could, allowing herself to taste the sweetness of the flavours brought out by the sugar, not overwhelmed by it. Who knew that apple could open up itself to another so? Each flavour revealed itself to her as she focused on one over the other. Here the apple was crisp and fresh, there warmly caramel, all the while feeling the heat and sting of the grated ginger on her tongue and in her nose as she breathed in its scent.

Maryam said, "Ginger-Apple. It's a favourite in this household."

Zaytuna replied, "I'm grateful for it. It's been a long time since I tasted anything like this. A long time since I've tasted sugar."

Maryam said, "I didn't take you for one who had ever tasted sugar."

Zaytuna didn't know if the cut was meant about her poverty or her asceticism, but it didn't anger her. Zaytuna wanted to say to her, "I don't want to hurt you," but if she were right, then she probably would and Maryam suspected as much. She held the glass, looking at it again, and sipping from it.

Maryam took her own stool before the pile of soaked dried fava beans and began popping some out of their skins and peeling back others. She wasn't going to speak first. She wasn't going to have her indiscretion in the mosque brought up. How she fell into admitting anything before this woman, she didn't know. She watched Zaytuna, all long bones, folded up on the low stool, holding the glass as if she'd never held a glass before and sipping the drink like she'd never had anything but mud in her cup.

Then it hit her, Zaytuna was there for work. She was just using their conversation at the mosque as a way in the door, not realizing how it sounded. There is no worry here. Maryam sighed and thought, poor thing she looks as if she'd break in two from labour, what could she possibly do for us? She spoke now to bring her in a bit, cover the distance she had put between them. "The Imam likes his sugar. He told me about a drink he had at Muhammad al-Khaqani's cousin's house that was made from equal parts sugar and grape juice boiled down with poppy seeds and a bit of milk added at the end."

She laughed, shaking her head, "He wanted me to make it for him until I told him how much the poppy seeds alone would cost us. Then he told me how much more he prefers our ginger-apple juice."

Zaytuna laughed lightly as she should and shifted in her seat, relieved at the change in tone, watching Maryam's hands pop the bean out of their casings. They were old hands. Swollen a bit, but the joints seemed fine. She was a tough old woman. But she wondered what would happen to her when those hands could no longer prepare food and mend clothes. She said, "I haven't been able to get you out of my mind, Auntie. I've been thinking about you, and the girl, Zaynab. I thought I'd come to check on you."

Maryam's fingers paused. She said carefully, "I appreciate your kindness, but you can see how I am. The girl is fine now too. We'll always miss the boy, as one would anyone close to the household, but God's will must be accepted with gratitude. I don't feel much like talking about it. But it occurs to me that perhaps you've come looking for work. What do you…"

Zaytuna cut her off, "I was particularly worried about the girl, Zaynab."

Maryam's face stiffened, "As I just said, I don't want to talk about it."

Zaytuna stopped and looked down at the glass in her hands, "Let me be honest, then, Auntie. I'm not here for work. I'll go in a moment, but I need to say this before I do. Layla came to see me the day after Zayd died. She was afraid and told me that she thought Imam Ibrahim had killed him."

Maryam's voice was clear, low but penetrating, "Now listen here. This will be the end of it. That girl—she's a sweet child—she said as much to me and I put her straight on it. I'm going to put you straight on it. I was there. I saw him walk off the roof. There's nothing I can do that Layla is so held in grief for the boy that she cannot believe that God would take him from her that way. But I cannot see for the life of me how this is any of your business."

Zaytuna kept on, "She seemed to think that the Imam knew that Zaynab was in love with Zayd and killed him so that there wouldn't be any trouble."

Maryam stood up, hissing her words, "Lord! Stop this, woman! Coming here upsetting our home with your idle curiosity and gossip. There is nothing to any of this but Layla's sorrowful imagination. Get up and leave. Now."

Zaytuna remained seated, "She seemed afraid that the Imam would find out that she knew."

Maryam moved towards her and stood over her, "She should be afraid of the Imam. Her spreading gossip, dangerous gossip, outside this household.

I've never hit any of the young ones who've worked for me, but if she's going on with this maybe she needs a stiff hand. I can't hit you, but, *walla*, I'll curse you if you carry on with this."

Zaytuna panicked realizing she'd put Layla in jeopardy.

She spoke quickly, "She's not said anything else. I've not heard her say anything since. Auntie, I understand the harm of all this. That's why I'm here. I'm not here for gossip."

"You are here to keep a story alive that should have died with the boy."

"Maybe the Imam killed him to protect her? But, also, you, Auntie, you knew that Zaynab's love for the boy was dangerous, dangerous for all of you. You must have wanted to protect this family, this home, your life here."

Maryam's eyes widened, heat rushing up to her face and mottling her cheeks. Zaytuna noticed for the first time a cleaver on a chopping block within reach of the woman. If she were able to kill a poor boy like Zayd to protect this family, what would stop her from killing her too? She frantically sunk into herself to listen for what to do, what to say. Then she found herself asking, without being conscious of it, hearing her voice speak in a soothing tone, one she was not well familiar with, "Auntie, forgive me, you saw him walk off the roof, all on his own, in truth?"

Maryam hissed, "Woman, how is this your business?"

Zaytuna lost the balance she had found just a moment earlier and blurted out in a voice she knew as her own, "Swear that you saw him walk off the roof! Say, '*Walla*'!"

"Alright, I've had enough of this," and she reached down and took hold of Zaytuna's arm firmly as you would a child that needed clear direction and pulled her right up off her stool. Maryam's thumb and fingers dug deeply into her arm. Zaytuna lost her hold on the glass and it fell to the floor breaking into shards. Maryam jerked her toward the door, "Watch your feet on that glass. I'm not bandaging you."

Zaytuna struggled to get her balance. They got as far as the kitchen door when a burly young man came in from outside through it. Maryam pulled Zaytuna back out of his way. He was carrying thorn bush branches wrapped in old wool and tied up with straps on his back. He looked at them both and lowered his head, saying, "Excuse me, Auntie."

There was the boy as big as Tein that she had seen in her dream. The same exact boy. As clear as day. She exhaled sharply, seeing him before her, then said under her breath, "*Subhan'Allah.*"

Maryam said, "Stack it there by the fire, Yusuf. You know. I'm showing our guest out."

Zaytuna shook her arm free from Maryam's hand and called out to the boy, "Yusuf, you were there that night! How did Zayd die?"

Yusuf shot up spilling the wood around him. Maryam spoke to him through his shock, her voice firm, "Get upstairs, to the roof, now."

He stood stock still, his eyes wide, then turned and ran past them out the kitchen door. Zaytuna pushed Maryam aside and ran after him. He ran around to the front of the house, opened the bolt, and was through the gate before Zaytuna could even get past the well. She got to the gate as quickly as she could, but could hear Maryam's bare feet slapping heavily behind her, then a man's voice calling from the front door, "What is all this noise?" She didn't look to see but heard Maryam stop and speak to him, then go inside the front door, shutting it behind her.

Yusuf was there in the road. He stood at the door of the building just next door. He held the knocker and brought it down again and again, yelling, "Layla! Layla!"

Zaytuna walked toward him, slowly. She didn't want him to run. She heard Layla yell back, it sounded like from the roof. On hearing Layla's voice, he fell against the wall and began to sob, his chest heaving with every breath.

Zaytuna heard movement behind the neighbour's door, but it didn't open. None of this seemed to register with Yusuf. It finally heaved open and a servant came out, Layla's arm in his hand, she hung off him, not able to get her own balance. He threw her to the ground and shut the door behind him. Yusuf saw and scrambled to his feet to get to her. He picked her tiny body up into his arms and placed her back on the ground standing. She straightened her *qamis* and felt for her wrap and kerchief but there was nothing there, she stood bareheaded, filled with shame, in the middle of the road. Yusuf untied the sash around his short robe and unwound the dirty wrap he had tied around his waist over his *sirwal* and put it over her shoulders, covering her head. She held it tight to herself.

She looked up at him, standing before her in nothing but his short robe and short *sirwal*, "Yusuf, what happened?"

His eyes filled with tears, his nose running and smearing his lip, he gestured with his head in the direction of Zaytuna. Layla turned and saw her. She said, "Auntie, you're here!"

Layla turned back to Yusuf, "This is Auntie Zaytuna! I told you. You have to tell her what you told me yesterday. Auntie Zaytuna can set it right."

Zaytuna took a few steps toward the pair when she heard the gate open behind her. Maryam came out. The three turned as one towards the sound of the gate at the Imam's house and saw the housekeeper standing there. She, though, was looking up and down the road and into the perforated clay screens in the windows on the houses that fronted the street, imagining who was sitting in them now, watching them. She said a little too loudly, with false cheer, "The food is ready now, what're you all doing in the road disturbing good people? Come inside. My goodness!"

Layla took Zaytuna's hand and walked toward the Imam's house, she gestured to Yusuf, "Come on." Yusuf fell in behind them and they all went back inside.

Once in the garden, Maryam hissed, "Get into the kitchen and keep quiet."

Chapter Twenty-Nine

Maryam said, "Sit down, all of you. Take care not to step in that broken glass. And keep your voices down for God's sake."

She handed Yusuf a rag to wipe his face then grabbed a broom and began to sweep up the glass while they all sat quietly watching her, wondering what she would do. Zaytuna felt like a child again, afraid of what kind of trouble she was in. Maryam picked up the pieces of glass and placed them in a bucket nearby. She took the straw broom and swept carefully, but still loosening the surface of the pounded earth of the floor in the kitchen. She threw out the fragments and loosened dirt, then pounded the spot on the floor with her heel. She took a deep breath, stood up straight, and faced Zaytuna, cold and furious, "I had this in hand."

Layla broke through, "Auntie, this is Zaytuna. You can trust her. She can set this right. I promise."

Zaytuna saw Maryam flinch with anger and feared that Maryam would hit her. She moved protectively toward Layla, but Maryam took a deep breath and let it out. Then said, "Layla, my sweet. You don't know what you've done. I had set this right already. It's not your fault, I understand that. But you need to be quiet now and let me handle this."

Layla objected, "But it's not set right. Yusuf…."

Yusuf heaved himself up on his stool and spoke, his face swollen from his tears, "It's not set right, Auntie. I can't live with myself. I can't sleep. I can't breathe from what I've done. I'm going to burn in Hell. I already decided once I finish my chores today I would go to the police and turn myself in. Who cares if the police find me and execute me. I killed him."

No one spoke. His words sunk heavily into the room.

Zaytuna couldn't find her breath. This wasn't what she suspected, at all. Without thinking she reached out to him.

He pushed her hand aside, "I don't know what you can do. I don't know what anyone can do. I'm going to Hell."

Maryam looked at Zaytuna, "Are you satisfied now? Now you've got something? Help get this boy executed, will you?"

Zaytuna was terrified, beginning to understand the lies and secrets as they unraveled before her, and said, "No, Auntie. Never." She thought of Ammar, then Tein, the bitterness rising up again, then fear, knowing they'd be here today, but when she didn't know. As sure as she knew anything, this boy was about to unburden himself to Ammar.

Zaytuna, said, "I won't tell a soul. But Maryam, the police. They'll be back later today. I heard...I heard they'll be back to question him."

Maryam's face became rigid with fear, "How do you know this?" She stood up, "We have to get him out of the house now."

Layla ignored Maryam and put her hand on Yusuf's arm, "Tell her. Tell her everything."

Maryam insisted, "There's no time for this talk now."

Zaytuna said to Layla, "Sweet one, I don't know what you think I can do. I don't know why I came here." Zaytuna turned to Yusuf, insisting, "Don't tell me." Tears welled up, mixed with anger at herself, she shook her head, standing, and said to him, "You must leave before the police get here."

Maryam spoke coldly, "A lot of good those tears will do us now. Just leave this to me and get out." She stepped towards Zaytuna.

Layla stood alongside Zaytuna, pulling her little body up as much as she could, wrapped in Yusuf's dirty wrap, looking like a twig of a tree trying to stop a wind from sweeping through, wrapping her arm around Zaytuna's, "No, Auntie. Let her hear."

Maryam said, "You're a good girl Layla, but there is a lot you do not understand about the world."

"I understand that Yusuf could be executed. Zaynab could be flogged. The Imam could lose his work. You thrown out."

Maryam lost her patience, "And all that is fine by you, is it?"

She stood firm, "Auntie Zaytuna won't let it happen."

Zaytuna turned to her, "Sweet one, it won't happen. As long as Yusuf gets out before the police get here. But this has nothing to do with me. I'm leaving. I'll never say a word of any of this to anyone. By my mother's soul, I will never speak of this."

Yusuf said, "I pushed him."

Maryam spoke sharply, "Yusuf!"

He went on, "He was saying horrible things about Zaynab. I told him to stop. He wouldn't stop. So I pushed him."

Zaytuna paused, her eyes taking him in with sorrow, not wanting to have heard it, but needing to ask, "You pushed him off the roof?"

"I just as good as did! I pushed him with my two hands and he stepped back to keep from falling. But there was a pot there by the edge of the roof. He tripped over it. He turned around fast to try to catch himself. But he went over instead."

Zaytuna stared at him, "What could he have said to you that would come to this?"

He pleaded with Zaytuna, "Don't make me say it."

Layla tugged on her hand, looking up at her, "It's got to be what I told you. I told you Zayd didn't love her. He loved me. He must have said something mean about Zaynab."

Yusuf looked at Layla, "I don't know if he loved anyone, Layla."

Maryam sat down, exhausted, and looked at Zaytuna, "You'd better be good to your word woman or you'll ruin us all. When exactly are they coming since you seem to know so much?"

Zaytuna said to Maryam, "Later today, that's all I heard. We have a little time yet. But still…." Unable to stop herself, she asked, "Were you there that night?"

Maryam sighed, resigned, "No. I was in my room. It was cooler on the roof, but the boys had been quarrelling again and I was tired of listening to them going back and forth, back and forth. So I left them alone up there. I just wanted some peace and quiet. Yusuf came down to get me as soon as it happened. I knew what to do." Maryam turned to him, "Everything would have been fine, had you just listened to me."

Zaytuna pressed, "Auntie, how did you keep him from speaking to the police?"

"I got him out of the house. That puny man, he was easy enough to trick. He thinks he is so smart. Fool. I told him the truth, just enough of the truth that the rest sounded right. I told him I love these children like my own. That is true. I do. I'd do anything to protect them. He let himself believe what worked best for him and let it go. As long as we get the boy out of the house today, I can twist him around my finger again." She spat the word out, "Police."

Zaytuna sorely wished she could throw those words in Ammar's face. She turned to Yusuf, this gentle-faced boy, big enough to be a man, and said, "You must love Zaynab very much."

He began to cry again and spoke through his tears, "I do. She's so gentle. She's always been kind to me. Never bossy. Never asked me to do a thing. We talked sometimes. I like to watch the birds when they come down and settle on the Tigris to fish to feed their babies. I told her about it. I told her about whatever I'd seen when I was out. She wanted to hear about all of it. I told her about how I want to raise sheep and goats someday. My own. She didn't laugh at me. She asked me questions about it."

He stopped and took a breath, wiping his tears, "She never loved me. I can't read like Zayd can. Zayd and her read the Imam's book together. She helped him learn it. He remembers things. He remembers things the Prophet said. He can remember whatever he wants. He memorized the whole Qur'an! He always told me she'd never love someone stupid like me. But she never called me stupid. I knew, though. I know I'm too stupid for her."

Maryam got up and handed him the rag again to wipe his face. He took it and blew his nose into it, repeating, "Stupid. I'm so stupid."

Zaytuna looked at Layla and Maryam, waiting for one of them to object, to say he was good at something, not stupid, but neither of them did. She reached across to him and knocked him lightly on the knee, saying, "You know, you remind me of my brother. He was never good with books either, but he was a very brave soldier and now he's…," she was about to say, "working for the police," but stopped herself just in time. "Now he's got a good job and can afford whatever he likes."

Yusuf, not listening, looked at her, pleading, "I'm going to burn in Hell."

Zaytuna pulled herself forward to him, "No. Only God knows where you'll end up. God is The Forgiving and The Wise. Don't you think God knows how you are feeling right now? Don't you think God knows you wish you hadn't done it?"

"God would never forgive me."

"God can forgive whomever He likes. You don't get to decide."

Maryam looked at her and raised an eyebrow.

Yusuf remained focused on Zaytuna, "Really? Do you really think God could forgive me?"

Zaytuna ignored Maryam's dissenting opinion, and spoke directly to him, "Yes. I know."

Layla piped in, "See! She knows all about God. She prays all night and never eats!"

Zaytuna looked at Layla and nearly spoke, when Yusuf cut in, "But even if God forgives me, I still killed him. He was mean, but he was still a human being. I killed a human being."

Layla said, "Auntie Zaytuna. I didn't tell you, but it's true. Zayd could be mean. He wasn't very nice to Yusuf."

"Yusuf, was he teasing you that night?"

"He wasn't teasing." He looked at Layla, not sure if he should speak. He moved closer to Zaytuna, leaning into her, praying that Layla wouldn't hear him, "Zayd said that morning he'd been alone with Zaynab. He said he did 'it' to her and afterwards told her he hated her."

Zaytuna looked at Maryam, who had heard it too, "Is this true?"

"Yusuf's not ever lied to me and Zayd could be cruel, so I don't doubt he said it. But that doesn't make it true. Zayd could lie with the best of them when it suited him. She was at her cousin's the night before and much of the next day. She, in fact, wasn't here that morning."

Yusuf looked at Maryam, disagreement on his face, "She…".

Maryam finished for him, "...was at her cousin's. It's time for you to get out of this house now, boy."

Layla broke in saying with certainty, "Zayd wouldn't have touched her. She would have had him but…"

Maryam raised her hand to slap her, "Layla!"

Layla flinched but didn't stop, "Well, he wouldn't have. He hated the rich. He hated how she smells. Her fine clothes. How she thinks she's so smart."

Maryam dropped her hand, "Enough, Layla!"

She went on, defiant, "It's not right he was so mean to Yusuf, but he had been hurt lots in life. You know how his nose got broke? He didn't even tell you, Auntie Maryam. He only told me. His parents and sister got sick and died and his cousins didn't want to feed him, so they gave him to a rich family to work. But he laughed at his master. He laughed at him because he was so ridiculous. He thought he was like a god. One day he was wearing a long turban of white silk threaded with so much gold. Zayd said it glittered in the light."

She waved her arms like she was pulling out lengths and lengths of the silk herself, "So much silk with so much gold! Zayd laughed and said to him, 'Silk and gold won't turn a donkey's ass into a caliph.' His master picked up an oil lamp and swung it at him, it hit him so hard it broke his nose clear over. Then his master wouldn't let anyone in the household set his nose back. He locked him up so he couldn't run away and tied his hands behind his back so he couldn't fix it himself. His master said Zayd should think about that next time he looked down his nose at his master. He'd see what it would get him. When it finally healed, his master kicked him to the street to starve."

Maryam shook her head, "Oh the misery these children face. When he came to us, he was knocking door to door looking for work. Goodness knows how many doors he'd knocked on. But he never gave up. That was our Zayd. And the smile on him at our gate! My goodness, such a smile on that pitiful face. And his eyes could light up a room. He knew just what to say to make me laugh. He called me 'Auntie Gazelle'. I wasn't anything like a gazelle even when I was young," she slapped her thick middle, "even before this snuck up on me. Oh Zayd," and her body slumped over and shook with grief.

Layla got up and came to hold her, kissing her cheek and wiping her tears away. She looked at Layla, her face now wet with tears and Maryam kissed her cheek in return. Layla stayed next to Maryam with her arm around her.

Maryam continued, "We already had Yusuf, but I brought him in anyway. Better for me to slow down a bit with the heavy work. The Imam approved. He knows I keep a tight purse."

Layla said, "Auntie Zaytuna. People who are hurt can be mean sometimes. He always apologized to me when he was mean. He always made up for it afterwards."

Maryam added, "He didn't show many people his true self. But this girl and I saw it. He was tender with us. He was safe here. There were nights, I don't mind telling you, when I'd wake up to find him curled up next to me like a baby. I'd hold him through the night. He never got much of that. Not even sure if he did when his own parents were alive, and he took it from me like a baby from its mother. I never had any babies of my own. You can't live without love. Survive, maybe, but not live. He had a life here with us. My man died young and I never had another chance. These are my babies right here, and Zaynab too. And I'd do anything to protect them."

Zaytuna replied, "*Alhamdulilah*, I'm grateful he had you."

Thinking of her and Tein and how they fought, the things they'd said to each other over the years, what they'd done to others themselves, she said, "How many of us have done it. We've been hard because we've been shorted love in this world."

Yusuf said quietly, looking at the floor, his large shoulders slumped over, pushed down from the weight of it all, "I don't know Auntie. It doesn't make it right. Just because he hurt doesn't make it right that he hurts people. He hurt Zaynab so much. Why should she have to hurt, too? I shouldn't have pushed him to protect Zaynab. I didn't have to. I could have walked away. I could have told Auntie Maryam what he said. She could have helped. Because I couldn't stop myself, he's dead and I hurt Zaynab, too, and all of you."

Zaytuna breathed out sharply as Yusuf's words hit her like a wave and she closed her eyes. She did not try to turn from it, she tried to gather the waters around her. She tried to sink into the pool of this hard truth that this boy knew. A boy. And how old was she, how long had she been praying through the night, how long had she been careful about what she ate, never feeding the desires of her lower soul? But she, sure as the sun rises, was feeding it sorrow and letting it do as it liked. What good is prayer? What good is not eating? What good is any of it if you make a god out of your own pain and let that god push you this way and that?

She took Yusuf's face in her hands and spoke quietly to him, not knowing if anyone else could hear her, "You boy. You are more of a servant of God than I've ever been. You boy. You are walking in the Prophet's footsteps. You are one who understands what it means to serve God."

No one spoke. She heard movement by the doorway to the courtyard. Maryam turned at the sound too and started at the sight. Zaynab was standing looking at them, holding the doorway, half in the room half out. Yusuf lifted his head and on seeing her there, stood for her, hoping she'd come and sit on his stool. She didn't move. Layla held firm, knowing it was her, and did not turn.

Maryam said, "Zaynab! Sweet one, how long have you been there?"

Zaynab said, "I'm sorry, Auntie. I've been here since you came back in. I heard the commotion and excused myself from study. Baba let me go."

Maryam shook her head, "I sorely wish you hadn't heard all this."

Zaynab said slowly, "Layla."

Layla did not turn and did not answer.

She repeated, "Layla." Then, "I'm sorry, Layla. I didn't know."

Zaytuna saw the colour rise in Layla's face again and the girl wince to fight back tears. She didn't turn, keeping her back to Zaynab, and said, "You have everything. You had to have him too."

"I didn't know."

"He loved me."

Tears were streaming down Zaynab's face, "That's true, Layla. I truly loved him. But he didn't love me. He said so that last time. He loved you."

The tears Layla had been holding back came down, but she did not bend under them. She kept her back to Zaynab and said with cold clarity, "I hate you."

Zaynab jerked back as if she had been slapped. She brought her hands to her cheeks, saying, "I've….I've always been jealous of you."

At that, Layla turned to face her, angry, her voice high and tight, "How!"

Maryam tried to shush Layla and she looked down at the old woman, saying, pointing at Zaynab, "How is she jealous of me?"

Zaynab replied, "You are free. You say what you like. You come and go as you please. You decide who sees your face. You decide whether or not you want to breathe the air with a piece of cloth in front of your nose and mouth. Layla," she paused, "You are free to love who you want. I have to marry that awful man with his stupid face and silly hair. He thinks he's so beautiful. Zayd was the beautiful one. I don't get to choose."

Layla spat back at her, "I'm free? I'm free to wash your clothes. Free to be beaten in the streets by whoever feels like taking their hand to me. Free to be beaten by my master. Free for him or his sons to rape me if they like. But now I've been thrown to the streets. I've got no more work. So I'm free to be hungry and sleep in the cemetery. I'm free alright. Zayd was all I had."

Zaynab's face had turned pale, she muttered under her breath, again, "Oh."

Then she fell silent for a moment, taking in Layla's words.

Zaynab said quietly, ashamed, "I didn't know. I didn't see. I didn't ask how you live. What happens to you. God forgive me."

All Zaytuna could think, even with the girl in such sorrow here before her, is how much her ignorance is just like the rich. Not thinking, not considering, not looking. She wanted to feel for her, she knew she should care for her, but it wasn't coming. Instead, she wanted to grab Layla's hand and hold it tight and say to her, "You don't have to forgive her."

Maryam stepped in, speaking to Zaynab, "It's a hard life for the poor, sweet one, and you've been protected from that, but every life has its own tragedies. I know you've had yours. Layla knows it too."

Maryam made Layla face her and held her hand, "Do you really think beautiful clothes and plenty to eat protects a woman from a beating, from worse than that? Come now. Think. It's true, she'll never know hunger, but you haven't been hungry in a long time and, if I can help it, you'll never know hunger again. Don't I take good care of you?"

"But who's going to take care of me now!"

"Me, my love. Me. You'll come and live here. You'll work with me."

Pointing at Zaynab, "Work for her!"

"Yes. That's true. I can't change that. She can't change that. But I'm mother to you both and that makes you sisters, like it or not. Now, listen, sweet one, sisters fight. Fight worse than friends. Don't I know it. But you'll also find a way to love each other. It'll come."

Zaynab stepped forward into the room toward Layla, but Layla stepped back. Her eyes red from anger and tears.

Maryam shook Layla's hand a little to get her attention, "What do you think comes next?"

"You're going to make me try to love her."

"I'm asking you to try. Layla. God forgive me if this is the wrong thing to say. But partly why you are so angry is that you've both lost the same thing. You've both lost your mothers. You've both lost the boy you love. It feels better to be angry at her, to keep your pain lonely to yourself, than to share the pain together. But trust me, sweet one, it's better to share it in the end."

Zaytuna heard the words as if Maryam were speaking to her, not Layla. She felt the now familiar sense of oceanic waters coming up to her, but now they came gently, holding her.

Layla turned to Zaytuna, "What do you think, Auntie?"

Zaytuna took a deep breath, "I think you should try. I have to try, too, Layla. Auntie Maryam's right. She's right about more than you know. Thank you for coming to me, Layla. You don't know the good you've done me. Hear me, girl, you are loved."

She looked beyond Layla to Zaynab still standing just outside the door, not with them. "You too, my sweet. You too, may you know a right and proper love that heals your wounds, too."

Zaynab took one more step into the kitchen. Layla stood away from Maryam, her back still to Zaynab. Zaynab stepped a bit closer and said quietly to Layla, "Sister."

Layla turned around and looked at Zaynab, considering her options. A moment passed, then she reached her hand out. Zaynab moved closer and took her hand. Layla spat it out, and it was not kind, but she said it, "Sister."

The gentleness of the ocean that encompassed and flowed through Zaytuna expanded her heart to the point that she was not sure she could bear it, and through it, an idea came to her. "Maryam, we need to get the boy out of here. Instead of an errand, well, would you be willing to give him up? I think Yusuf would do well to come with me to see Shaykh Abu al-Qasim, you know the one near the Shuniziyya mosque. I think…no, I know he could live and work there for them. They'll take him if I ask."

Maryam said, "I've heard of him. That shaykh, he won't talk to the police?"

Zaytuna said quickly, not knowing, just acting on the certainty of her feeling, "No. He wouldn't do that. Not in this case."

Maryam said, "If you promise me he won't be harmed."

Zaytuna said, "At least let me take him there, now. It will get him out of the house for today."

Maryam turned to Yusuf, "What do you think?"

He said quietly to Zaytuna, still lost, "No one can help."

She replied, "Let them try."

Layla repeated to Yusuf, "Let them try. I'm sure they can help."

Then turning to Zaytuna, she said, smiling, "Auntie, I knew you'd know what to do."

Zaytuna replied, shaking her head at the wonder of it, "There was a plan already in place."

Chapter Thirty

Zaytuna tried to hurry out of al-Anbariyya, but Yusuf was in sullen tow. She kept having to turn and grab him by the arm and push him ahead of her but moment by moment he would fall behind her again. She saw him slip back again and turned around to grab him, saying, "Yusuf, come on…," and came face to face with Tein who was walking closely behind them, almost in mirror step.

He said, "Who is this, then?"

She stopped, eyes wide on Tein, now wearing a black turban, and took firmer hold of Yusuf's arm; the boy, despite shuffling behind her, nearly knocked into her at the suddenness of their stopping. For the first time in her life she was afraid of her brother, whom she realized in that moment, just as Yulduz had warned, was not her brother anymore but the police. She threw her fear back at him, demanding, "Are you following me?"

"I told you this morning that we were coming to al-Anbariyya."

He tried to get Yusuf to look at him, "You, boy. You're a big fellow. You remind me of myself at your age. What's your name?"

Zaytuna kept her hand firmly on Yusuf's arm, willing him not to speak. There was no worry there, she felt him stiff with fear under her hand. He kept his head down, refusing to look up.

She challenged Tein, "What does he have to do with you? Go back to Ammar and keep your head in your own business." She looked around, "Where is this boss of yours anyway?"

Tein gestured, "He's just over there talking to a witness in a different case. I saw you and came out to find out what was going on. Can't I stop my sister in the road?" He repeated, "Who is the boy?"

Zaytuna scanned the shops nearby looking for Ammar, saying to Tein, "I'm walking, that's what is going on."

Ammar stepped out of one of the shops. She saw him immediately. He was looking for Tein. Then she saw him see them. He visibly sighed. She nodded to him as if to say, "I'm no happier to see you." He walked over slowly, looking like he hoped the conversation between brother and sister would break up before he got to them.

Tein repeated, "Who is the boy?"

"We're late," she turned away from him and pulled at Yusuf to walk with her.

Tein took a few quick steps to her other side and put his hand on her arm to hold her back. She let her arm go slack under his hand, like he'd showed her how to do when they were children so that she could escape anyone who grabbed her, and he lost his grip on her arm. She quickly swung her arm around and pushed at him, spitting on the ground before him, "Don't you touch me!"

He stepped back and laughed, "There's my sister! Do you know this side of my sister, boy?"

She heard Ammar's voice behind her, laughing too, "What's all this, then? Am I going to have to put you in prison for assaulting the police?"

Tein answered back, "She's not in the mood for jokes today, apparently."

Ammar said, "It is good to see you again, Zaytuna, but perhaps not in this neighbourhood. You haven't been to Imam Ibrahim's house have you?"

Tein saw the boy begin to shake, and he knew exactly who stood before him and what this boy had done, but not why. He also knew his sister. He didn't know if Ammar had seen the boy shaking or not. He took a step forward toward Ammar to draw his eyes to him away from the boy, but Zaytuna had moved in his way to get in Ammar's face, putting the boy behind her and out of Ammar's line of sight. She challenged him, "I'm not allowed to get business washing clothes in neighbourhoods where you work? Do you want to give me a list of where I might go to earn my chink of coin?"

Ammar laughed, stepping back to get some distance, and asked Zaytuna, "Who's the boy?"

Tein didn't even think about it, he interrupted, reaching out to tweak the boy's ear, "This little fart is one of Shaykh Abu al-Qasim's boys. He wasn't born right. Doesn't talk."

Zaytuna's heart went out to him, leaping so suddenly in gratitude that she nearly spoke, nearly reached out to acknowledge this crucial act of loyalty, but most carefully did not. She turned and sneered at Ammar instead, "His name is Abdulghafur. He was helping me with some heavy work today. Do you want to take us in for questioning? Did we not get a spot out? Is this a new crime come down from some vizier with nothing to do but torture the poor trying to make a few *fals*?"

Ammar smiled, "Calm down, woman. I'm just making sure you aren't getting into any more trouble."

Tein raised his eyebrows and laughed, "Not today, for once!"

She turned her glare towards Tein and pretended to regard him with the same disgust as Ammar, "Don't think I'm going to forget how you're treating me, you now in that black turban."

Ammar saw this conversation turning into a family fight he wasn't interested in witnessing, so he said, "If this family reunion is over, we have work to get to, Tein. Let's go."

He turned and walked away without saying goodbye. Tein turned to follow him, saying, "I'll see you later, sister?"

She reached out to him and took his hand, holding it for one moment. She whispered, "We actually are heading to Uncle Abu al-Qasim's."

"No fooling?"

"You must have knowledge of the Unseen. No fooling."

He turned and left, catching up with Ammar who was well enough down the road ahead of him that Tein had to pull his bad leg up with his hip with a slight swing to walk faster than was comfortable. But, Zaytuna, thought, watching him and knowing he was in a bit of pain, you wouldn't know if you weren't family. He hid it well.

She pulled Yusuf to her, her arm around his back, and lifted his face to her with her other hand. There were no tears only wide-eyed desperation. She said firmly, "Everything will be alright. Come with me now and no lagging behind."

***

Tein slammed the knocker at the gate of Imam Ibrahim's house, and stood aside waiting for someone to come. They didn't hear anyone opening the main door to the house beyond the gate. Tein gave Ammar a questioning look. Ammar gestured to him to try knocking it again. They heard the bolt slide in the door and a little girl stood before them, ridiculously covered up in an old wrap so that even part of her face was covered, "*Assalamu alaykum*, what can I do for you?"

Ammar stepped toward her, "*Wa alaykum assalam.* We're here to see the housekeeper, Maryam. You are new here? What's your name?"

"Layla, Sir. I just started here today. I'll go get her for you."

Ammar looked at Tein who acknowledged the name. Here was the infamous Layla. The girl turned to shut the door on them while she got the housekeeper, but he stepped forward and held the gate, and they stepped through behind her instead.

She turned around, brows knitted, not sure how to get these men to get back on the other side to the street, "Sir, I'm sorry. I'm instructed only to let in guests of the Imam. All others have to wait outside for the housekeeper. Please."

"It's alright Layla. We're the police, just here to follow up some matters concerning the death of your friend, Zayd."

The colour drained out of her face despite being ready for them. She stood stock still. How did they know she was friends with Zayd? She recovered herself quickly, bent her knees and turned to run around to the kitchen door to get Maryam. They followed. But by the time they'd got to the door, Maryam was on her way out and gently pushed them back into the garden by simply walking calmly into them. She smiled at Ammar warmly, "*Assalamu alaykum*, it's good to see you, Sir. How can I help you?"

Ammar felt the same tug of care toward the woman that he had when he first met her. He bowed to her slightly, "I'm sorry to bother you again, we're just here to follow up with that last witness. The other servant, Yusuf. I just need to get his account of the night, then I can tie up the paperwork on this case and close it."

"I'm sorry to say, sir, that Yusuf has left us. He was so heartbroken at the loss of his friend, he found work elsewhere and has gone off to it. I was left with no help, but Layla's come to work with me. I mentioned her to you last time. She worked next door. Still need another boy, though, but she's a hard worker and we love her here already."

Ammar asked, "Where did Yusuf go?"

She said, "Far north of the City. I think as far as Qatiat Umm Jafar, beyond the Trench, but I can't be sure. I don't know the name. A wealthy estate, don't you know it! He helped out a servant from the house one day when he'd spilled his delivery on the street—he's such a selfless boy—and they offered him work right there and then. He went north with the man that day and they sent a note to let us know he'd gone."

"Do you still have the note?"

"I'm sorry, sir. I wouldn't know. One of the Imam's students kindly read it to me. I can't see why he would have kept it afterwards. But I can ask."

Ammar asked, "He never came back? Not even to say goodbye? To get his things?"

"The note explained everything. It said he'd be back in a month or so on his first free day to say goodbye properly. Left us in the lurch, he did. But I understand the boy's heartbreak well enough," and tears began to well up in her eyes.

Ammar felt the need to comfort the woman as he did when he first interviewed her, but held back. He needed to finish this. Comforting her wasn't going to close the matter. He shook his head, not knowing what to do about the missing boy. He considered whether or not the case warranted spending weeks going door to door to find a servant or waiting a month or more for the boy to come back to close it. He'd speak to the girl instead, follow up with one more question with Maryam, then he could consider himself as having done due diligence.

He said, "We'd like to speak to the girl, Layla. Clear some matters up with her and that should handle it."

Maryam looked at him as if he must have forgotten, "I told you, sir, she wasn't here that night."

"I remember. But we have another witness to whom she shared her fear that the Imam had killed Zayd."

Maryam drew her head back, "Uff, that girl! I'll go get her immediately and we'll clear all this up."

She turned and went through the kitchen door shutting it behind her, leaving them standing by the well.

Tein said, "Not very polite leaving us standing out here."

Ammar didn't like Tein's tone, and replied to him more sharply than he intended, "It's fine. The kitchen's probably full of work. She's a busy woman. We're getting what we need."

Tein raised his eyebrow and decided to let it go. Nearly a minute passed until Layla opened the door and she and Maryam came out together.

Maryam said, "Here she is, sir. Ask her whatever you need."

Tein moved back and leaned against the well, watching the scene. Ammar moved toward her and squatted, putting himself at her level, and asked gently, "What is this I hear about you thinking the Imam killed your friend, Zayd."

Layla began to cry, "I'm sorry. I was so sad and angry about Zayd. I made it all up in my head. I told Auntie Zaytuna my story. I never should have. Maryam explained it all to me. Yusuf told me Zayd walked in his sleep all the time. But I never got a chance to see Auntie Zaytuna again to apologize." Her tears turned into sobs, "I'm sorry, sir. I didn't mean to make any trouble. Do I have to go to prison? Will I be executed?"

Ammar stood, sighing, and patted her on the head, "No dear, of course not. God forbid anything like this should happen again, but should you be in a bind in the future, talk first to your elders who will know what to do."

Tein observed the old woman watching Layla talk. Her eyes were keen on the girl, she looked like she was willing Layla to cry and tell her story just so. He laughed to himself, she and the girl were a good team. They had Ammar well tied up. He thought of how bothered Ammar was by Zaytuna challenging him and made a note to himself that a man who is unwilling to consider the roles women play in these scenes would be incapable of solving crimes involving them. He'd have to watch for that in the future.

Layla nodded to Ammar, snuffling and wiping away her tears with the edge of her wrap, and said, "Yes, sir."

He stood and dug into the pocket in his sleeve for a *fals* and handed it to her, "Here. Go buy yourself some candy."

He turned toward Maryam, "This woman, Zaytuna, she said she spoke to you in the mosque at Zayd's funeral prayer. What was that about?"

She held herself upright saying, "I'm sorry. Gossip is a terrible sin, but I believe that woman is a bit mad. I can see how she got the wrong idea from our little Layla here, but she wouldn't hear a word I said to her at the mosque. Mad, sir, I think the woman is mad."

Ammar laughed and looked at Tein, "Well, maybe not mad, but she does get ideas in her head that she can't shake, it seems. That's enough then, I can close this case for good."

Tein saw Maryam push Layla back into the house before leading them toward the gate. Once there she turned to Ammar, putting her hand on his arm, "Thank you for all the care you gave to our Zayd. Your mother must be proud of the man you've become."

Ammar looked down and blushed, saying, "*Alhamdulilah*. I'm glad we could do right by the boy. May God protect you."

"And you, sir," and she shut the gate behind them.

Ammar and Tein walked away from the house, Ammar smiling, turning to him and said, "A little more paperwork and that's that."

Tein repeated, laughing to himself, "That's that."

***

Zaytuna called out her greetings to everyone within earshot as she and Yusuf entered Junayd's home. There was no one but a young woman sitting in the reception hall and the same student who had let her and Mustafa in three days ago. She asked, "Brother, would you take our friend to go wash up? I want to bring him to meet Shaykh Abu al-Qasim."

The student replied, "The Shaykh is still at his shop. But Mustafa is here. He's in the courtyard." He took Yusuf by the hand and led him across the courtyard to the kitchen area where they had water in a large basin set out for ablutions.

Zaytuna replied, "*Alhamdulilah*, I'll wait here."

Yusuf trailed behind him, his head still hung low.

She sat on the floor against the wall in the wide reception hall waiting for Yusuf to come out, hoping Mustafa would stay where he was so she wouldn't have to deal with him.

She shook her head in sorrowful anger at him. What was he thinking telling me he loves me? All these years. I thought he understood me. What would make him think I'd let him, let any man, touch me?

Zaytuna felt hot suddenly, sweating, her skin crawling so that she could not sit still and she stood up and began pacing the reception hall. She turned at the far side of the room and there was Mustafa standing closely before her. She blurted out, "What is it with you men coming up behind me!"

A young woman sitting in the corner of the reception hall looked up at her, giving her a sharp look to lower her voice. Zaytuna stared at the girl wanting to tell her that she'd been coming here since before she was born and she, Zaytuna, had more of a right to raise her voice here than that girl had to sit in that corner, but Mustafa was already speaking.

She huffed, turning to him, "What are you saying?"

"Zaytuna, please. I am saying how sorry I am for surprising you this morning. I do want to ask you, but not in that way. Not like that…."

"Mustafa…," she said clearly, her anger no longer flailing but turned sharp and held to his throat, "You should not speak to me that way again. I will never accept you in marriage. Never. Mustafa. Hear me. Never."

Mustafa reached out to take her hands, then pulled his hands back, looking at his palms, then his knees buckled underneath him and he fell to the floor.

Zaytuna couldn't help herself, she sighed sharply, "Mustafa!" She realized he wasn't getting back up, so she crouched down on the floor next to him. The colour had drained from his face. She turned back to the young woman, who had gotten up in a start at his fall, saying, "Go get him some water! Better, get something sweet to drink from the kitchen."

The young woman ran across the courtyard to the kitchen on the other end. Zaytuna turned to Mustafa, saying, not kindly, "Breathe, Mustafa."

He took in deep breaths, one after another, until the girl returned with a cup in her hand. Zaytuna held her hand out to take it, but the young woman handed it directly to him. Only then did Zaytuna see how beautiful she was; petite, she had large, wide-set dark brown eyes, round cheeks, touched by pink, and smooth skin, not a pock mark or wrinkle on her. Her deep black hair fell out in two thick braids down her back. She spoke gently to him, her softly accented Arabic making her gesture feel even more tender, "Mustafa, here, drink this. You'll be yourself again soon."

He looked at the young woman, recovering himself through the tenderness of her face, and took the cup from her, careful not to touch her fingers with his own. He took a sip, a breath, and said, "May God leave you with nothing but thirst for His love, YingYue."

As Zaytuna watched them she realized her mouth was open in shock at the exchange and shut it. She saw the girl blush deeply at his response, bow her head, and move back from them on her knees before standing and turning away to go into the courtyard. This was the girl. The girl from Taraz he'd blushed over a few days earlier.

Zaytuna was stuck, crouched there in front of him, one part of herself searching the other to see what it was feeling. She wasn't sure. Jealous, certainly. She dug around for it and there it was. She was afraid he would abandon her. She scolded herself. Woman, what had made you think this man would always be here? What made you think you could have a man to love without…. And with those words, she saw him, her Mustafa, in her mind's eye, on top of her in a sweaty black *qamis*, and she shuddered, inwardly scrambling, kicking and pushing the image out of her mind. She felt her chest tighten the way it does when tears are coming and she forced herself to breathe to stop them. She spoke, her voice cracking with the effort, "Mustafa, I do love you, but I cannot marry you."

He looked at her, seeing her near to tears and fighting it and reached out to brush the back of his fingers against her face, not caring who saw it, and said, "Shhh. I understand. I just thought maybe you were leaving your asceticism behind. You..."

She cut him off, "No, it's not that. You know what it is. Don't make me say it."

He did not speak.

She admitted it to him, "I'm afraid I will lose you forever if I don't marry you."

"Never."

"Will you always be my friend, my brother?"

He held her eyes with his own to make sure she saw the truth in it, and said, "Yes."

She said, her tears coming as she let her fear out, "And no one will ever come between us."

"No."

She asked, laughing a little, through her tears, "Not even that pink-cheeked girl?"

He blushed, looking out to the courtyard after YingYue, and leaned forward to hold her, awkwardly bringing her to him for the last time like that, still in love with her for her stupid anger, her stupid jealousy, her stupid everything, saying, "No one will ever come between us."

She held him in return for just a moment, allowing herself to feel his shoulders against her own, his head on her shoulder, then released him and pushed herself up.

He stood, wiping his eyes, and moved close to her to bump her shoulder with his own, but she had already turned away from him toward a large boy coming across the courtyard, smiling. No, Mustafa saw, he was grinning.

When he saw Zaytuna, he picked up and ran to her, "Auntie Zaytuna!"

She grasped him, smiling back, searching his face, "Tell me, Yu.. Abdelghafur!"

"I like the name, Auntie Zaytuna, Uncle asked me what name I wanted and I said Abdelghafur, Servant of The Forgiver. He said that was the right name for me."

"Who? Who told you?"

He pointed toward the kitchen and she saw a tall man duck out from its doorway, Uncle Nuri. He was here.

Mustafa said, "With everything that's happened, I forgot to say."

"Oh it doesn't matter," she was about to call out to her Uncle, then remembered YingYue's scolding look and hurried out to him instead. "Uncle Nuri!" She reached him and grabbed both his hands kissing them and bringing them to her face before he could pull them away and take her in his arms.

"My daughter, Zaytuna." Pulling back, he said, "Let me look at you."

"You are as beautiful as your mother. I see her light on your face!"

"Oh Uncle…"

"I spoke with your boy there, Abdelghafur. He told me everything. Hilal asked him a few questions about kitchen work and he could tell the boy is skilled. The housekeeper where he lived taught him well. He'll have a place to sleep and eat here and he'll work under Hilal."

"You told him God can forgive him?"

"Of course. The Prophet said nothing is dearer to God than a repentant child. The boy will live a life of service with us. That should put his heart at ease over time. But he knows a boy died because he allowed the animal within him to attack. I asked him if he wants to learn how to control it." Nuri laughed, "He doesn't know what he's got himself into, but he agreed to it." He smiled, opening his arms out to the sky, "Leave him with us long enough and he'll repent from everything other than God!"

She laughed, "*Insha'Allah*! Sooner than I, no doubt!"

He took her hand, "Now you, come over here with me. We have to talk."

"Am I in trouble?"

He winked at her, "Yes."

"Truly?"

"A little, but it's good trouble."

He took her to a shaded spot in the courtyard and they sat down on the reed mats laid out, leaning against the wall. She could see YingYue from there, fixing the weave on some of the mats in the corner with soft straw. He saw where she was looking, then looked for Mustafa, still in the reception hall.

"So will you accept Mustafa?"

"No Uncle, I can't."

"Your mother also had no time for men."

"Uncle, it's not like that."

"You think I don't know what it's like? I've never known one of my sisters here to be shy about what men have done to them. I wouldn't have time for men, either. But I thought, maybe Mustafa, you grew up with him. He's a kind man. He takes time to observe himself, to control his animal soul. And he loves you."

"I can't."

"I understand, little one."

She put her hand on his in thanks, saying, "Oh Uncle, only you could call me 'little', you are taller than I."

Then she looked up at him, asking, "Uncle, I feel different from how I did before. Something happened. Uncle Abu al-Qasim did something to me."

"I heard. I can see."

"I don't know how, I'm not even sure, but I think I feel like I accept what has happened. All of it. My father. My mother. What I saw. I know it happened to her, but it happened to us. I don't understand it, somehow I am grateful for everything. But my gratitude feels like a betrayal to them, to myself." She said, thinking of the old woman at the cemetery, "I know I need to just keep stepping out to this gratitude. I know I need to trust. Maybe then I could find my way to Mustafa. I do love him. I just can't see my way to him now."

He nodded.

"I've changed, but I've not changed. I'm still angry. I still miss her. If anything I miss her more. I never knew her as she was."

"You are changing, little one, but this takes time. Everyone at their own pace. You have only tasted an infinitesimal drop of the ocean. You *stand* before the gate of the Grateful. You *stand* before the gate of the Accepter. You *stand* before the gate of the Lover. It is up to you whether or not you find a way through those gates. And you will not find a way to true witnessing as long as a single vein remains standing in your body. You must step ahead towards it."

"What if I cannot do it?"

He laughed lightly, "Do you want me to send you to your Uncle Abu al-Qasim for a scolding?"

She did not laugh with him. He was not truly laughing. She saw in his eyes that she should be afraid and she was. The gravity of her situation settled in on her, closing in on her chest, making it difficult to breathe. Would she put the chains back around her neck or let them go and step forward into love? Her heart beat right up into her throat. She tried to swallow it down, but her mouth was suddenly dry. She sat perfectly still but within she was a child, flailing about, trying to push love away; until another part of herself pulled it to her, holding love out to her. It's not what you want, it's what you need. She stopped writhing and pushing and looked at it. She reached out and took love, still afraid. She held love in her hands, not knowing if she held it right. If she might drop it. Harm love somehow. Ruin everything. That other part of herself spoke. Tell God you are afraid. And thank Him. She couldn't find a way to say she was afraid, but she could at least hold her fear and the love she feared out to Him. So she held out what He was forcing her to carry, her commitment to carry love without even knowing what that meant, her fear, all of it, and took one step forward, making herself say aloud, "*Alhamdulilah.*"

Nuri saw and said, "Good. The fearful one runs from her Lord to her Lord."

Her eyes were cast down, still ashamed, "Yes, Uncle."

He lifted her chin so she looked up at him, "Now, none of that, Zaytuna. You'll correct yourself to the end of your days. Love means tearing down all the veils and revealing all the secrets. Learn to speak from that voice, one breath at a time. Speak, even if it lands you in the dung heaps." He laughed, "As God is my witness, I have!"

She laughed with him, but was still unsure. They sat in silence until a compulsion to ask a question she had always been too afraid to ask grew too strong to resist. At the same time, as her heart turned to the question, she felt certain of the answer, a warm wave wash in and settled within her and around her. There was no need to ask except that she was as unsure of certainty as she was of the love she felt right then. So the need to ask and the certainty pulled at her, one exhausting her under its weight, the other light, drawing her softly to it, until she finally gave in to the exhaustion, the warmth left her, and she asked him, her eyes filling with tears, "Did she love us, Uncle?"

He sighed, sorely disappointed that she still needed to ask that question, that she gave in to asking it rather than letting it go and trusting all that had come before. He answered anyway, "She loved you with all her heart, little one. I'll tell you this now. She was sorry you were so afraid. She couldn't stop what was happening to her. But, let's be clear, she would not have even if she could have. This path is abandoning everything other than God. She told me about a woman, in one of the villages you stopped in for a few months. The woman offered to take you and Tein, raise you two as her own, so your mother would be free and you two wouldn't have to face such hardships. Your mother said she was a good woman. She had no children of her own and you two loved her. The woman let you all stay in her house during those months, not in the animal hold and the woman even dressed you in clothes she made especially for you."

Zaytuna gasped, "I remember her. Auntie Hawwa! I did love her. She put food right in my mouth. I remember that. I sat in her lap and she put food right in my mouth. I was never hungry. And I remember the *qamis* she made for me. It was so beautiful. It was yellow, even though Muslims aren't supposed to wear that colour. I just realized now, of course, she was Christian. She made it from one of her own robes. Is that why mother didn't leave us with her, because she was Christian?"

He shook his head.

"But she would have been free if she had."

"How could she be free without you and Tein? You were what God wanted from her."

He paused, then said, modulating his voice to penetrate her heart, "Your mother's love led you to this moment, to accept that you were loved completely by her and to let her go to take hold of Love Itself. Every lover in this world dies. Divine Love crushes everything in its path. Find your nourishment and healing with The Lover Himself."

She felt the wave come again, warmly, softly, and envelop her, then turn inward to saturate her, each cell falling into its embrace, one by one, until it held her completely. Then she felt it distinctly, humming within her, her mother's love, her mother's fierceness, her hold on her. She tried to grasp it to her, clenching her hands, but it was like warm honey and flowed through her fingers. She loosened her fingers as her mother's love flowed through them, one by one. It was as if she had been born with her hands gripped tight, and they were only now, twenty-seven years later, being forced to release, each muscle being made to lengthen where it had grown short from disuse. The pain was excruciating, but she did not scream. Instead, she spoke from where she was, for now, saying to him from that voice, "You were there when she walked into the reed bed and cut her feet."

He said, "No. I found her afterwards. They say she called out to God, "*Labayk*, Here I am, God!" Then she wandered into the freshly cut bed. The reeds were as sharp as swords. People tried to stop her, but they were too far away to reach her in time. When I found her she had already lost so much blood. Someone had bound her feet with rags, but I saw that she would die. It was beautiful. She never came out of her state. She returned to her Lover awash in His love."

She felt the horror at her mother's death but believed, for the first time, she didn't know how, that it had not been cruel.

He said, "I prayed then and there that God would give me such a beautiful death."

Not wanting to lose him, but knowing that it was not up to her, Zaytuna said, "May God accept your prayer."

She felt the warmth of her tears on her cheeks, "Uncle Nuri?"

"Hmm?"

"I only want to be on the side of God's Love."

Nuri replied, "My daughter, Love has no side."

Coming in 2020

The Jealous: A Sufi Mystery

A woman's howl of pain echoed through the courtyard. "She's killed him!" Her husband's face was twisted with terror, staring at something that was not there, looking at the space just over his chest, grasping at his left arm as if to wrest some unseen force away. Saliha gasped, "A jinn! God protect us from evil things!"

When a distinguished scholar dies at the Barmakid hospital in Baghdad, nearly everyone points the finger at his slave Mu'mina, as the one who called a demon to kill him. Tein, a former frontier fighter turned investigator with the Grave Crimes Section, has no time for religion, let alone jinn, and sets out to prove her innocent. But Ammar, Tein's superior and old wartime friend, has already pushed her case before the Police Chief's court where she's sure to be executed or condemned to rot in the prisons built into the damp walls of Baghdad's Round City.

With the help of his twin sister, Zaytuna, his childhood friend, Mustafa, and Zaytuna's friend, the untamable Saliha, Tein plunges into a dangerous investigation that takes them into the world of talisman-makers and seers, houses of prostitution and gambling, and the fractious secular and religious court systems, all in an effort to turn back the tragic circumstances set in motion by Ammar's destructive fear of a girl horribly wronged.

Made in the USA
Coppell, TX
29 April 2020

23389124R00157